Stonyford Submission

Bennie Ray Murdock

Wagoner Oklahoma

Published by Word Out Books
an imprint of
AZ Entertainment Group LLC
PO BOX 854
Wagoner, OK 74477

ISBN-13: 978-1-947035-59-1

Printed in the United States of America

IN MEMORY OF

Roxanne Manuel Murdock
Radelle Renee Murdock
Vanessa Elaine Murdock

For Margaret Johnson

Table of Contents

Author's Note

It has taken me some time to complete this novel. My personal experiences with extremely evil vexatious demons, who were themselves fighting me with such a driven force to where it was while trying to put this novel into form that I then realized such demoniac spirits within me who were busily trying their best to cause me to become in complete agreement with thoughts that I wish not to, in any way, value for the sake of suggestive intent.

This originally 1,041-page manuscript is about the mysteriousness surrounding a small-town community located in the northwestern part of the state of California. This dramatic presentation is structured around an old snake hunter and his snake, and the constant sighting of a little boy named Ethan and his dog. This story is also about the cruel, violent, savage slaughter and deadly malicious encroachment upon a little girl named Margaret Johnson, who would end up finding herself witnessing the horrifying mutilation and dismemberment of her sister by the wicked evilness of the devil himself, attacking and brutally assaulting both. Margaret would survive to tell the story of how the entire Stonyford region would end up becoming itself an unexpected victim of the most horrendous atrocity ever committed in the history of this town.

An aftermath is indeed my reason for the urgency to reveal this story with each account seemingly depicting a horrible death as told to me by Margaret. She so candidly talked about how feuding residents described the situation as terrifying and mind-boggling. So eager to explain each of these chilling, undesirable tales in my presence, though somewhat reluctant while holding within her delicate hands proof and documentation bearing testimony of each event, she would first allow me an opportunity to experience a brief journey into her life as an elderly woman presently residing in the state of Kansas.

She talked about how there seemed to be intense fear and deep-seated anger and animosity caused by the intentional withholding of vital information by officials assigned to apprehend a vicious killer who they felt was roaming amongst them aimlessly. But ever how unfriendly the story, vacationers continued on a deadly course into this part of the region in their unrelenting quest to get a glimpse at whatever it was that caused an entire community to just outright submit themselves to the unknown, surrendering their lives to the dishonorable discretion of another while naming Satan as the subnormal object.

Unbeknownst to a group of well-experienced journalists believing the story to be just another incredible adventure, they too would undoubtedly find themselves in a struggle to survive. Unbearable indeed, and to the point of impossible to tolerate as each member of this team would find himself in an individual plight against the odds. Trapped and unable by any means to retreat, lowering to standards put in place by Satan meant evil for evil. The team's only option: retaliate and regain control of the region.

A fierce battle would erupt high above the region, just as Satan's fallen angels begin to emerge from the bottomless pit from deep within the huge mountains and hillside terrain that overlooked Stonyford. These angels were said to be in the likeness of the human species, having interbred in an immoral category, creating organisms of particular classifications in a specific form. The category consisted of the giant imperial monkey-riding moth and the huge, deadly Chimera creature with its lion's head and goat's body and long, ugly-looking serpent tail.

There was also the Grendel-like creature, and the human-headed wasps and hornets with their abnormally huge, deviant, invertebrate-segmented body parts. Most having the triple wing created in the form of giant killer parasites, with a quadrupled body part, reproducing themselves as identical to vacationers to the region.

Also emerging from in between these mountains appeared an elite crew of the best squadron of helicopters with a payload of deadly weaponry that could devastate the enemy from an overwhelming power of strategies. In particular was the MH-53J Pave Low, a Huey gunship, and the CH-47 Chinook Troop Carrier. Amongst these were a number of UH-60 Black Hawks, AAS-72X+, UH-72 Lakotas, AH-Apaches and also a few military Ospreys.

To this day the unfolding of these old tales of mysteries continues with the war between both good and evil raging on with Satan at the helm.

Stonyford Submission

Bennie Ray Murdock

Introduction

AN AFTERMATH OF UNFORTUNATE EVENTS and occurrences is indeed my reason for deciding to reveal the true, most accurate, devastating, conflicting accounts and elements within one's most hostile and collective motives. But it is especially the thought of those recurrent desires and elements that an individual would want to seek, keep, and maintain to enhance the continuation that would provide the carrying out of an habitual's habits that we as living beings should be ourselves most concerned about to this day.

This story has been written in my onward effort to attempt revealing the truth, and nothing but the truth, to the very best of my knowledge, and to try and provide the information needed in which to substantiate proof about the situation that took place in a small-town community in the northwestern part of the state of California, who beforehand had themselves encountered the state of becoming completely submissive to the behavior and authority of something which is yet presently residing amongst us, though still to this day is very much a mystery. Undetermined and unspecified.

An extremely lethal spectacle, so distinctive, and by all means within such evil, wicked deceptiveness, and with having the soul of a vicious, venomous snake with intense uncalculating impulses, would viciously attack its victims with such overwhelming force, devastating the entirety of the seemingly quiet community.

This is the truth to the best of my knowledge as related to me.

Willing to reveal the history of Stonyford voluntarily and without reluctance, Margaret Johnson began describing her horrifying experience with this deadly and most extremely poisonous thing, or rather should I preferably be saying, this monstrous individual, or spectrum, that could only be described by surviving victims as being like a form of a radiant source, but without any graphics.

"If by chance you can, at least, remember anything," I began questioning her, "it would be very much appreciated, Margaret."

(Prolonged silence.)

"Well, let me see," she began in a very low tone. "Let me just see if I can still remember that far back. I mean, it's been so long ago, and I just don't think I'm able to remember that far back, young man."

"Anything that you can tell me," I asked her, while not wanting to sound like I was pushing her too hard to remember. "It'll be a good starter."

"Mmm," she begins mumbling to herself. "Let me see now."

"I mean—" and just when I was about say something—

"Oh, yeah," Margaret said. "I do have a few things that I can, I guess, tell you about, that I'm more than sure you'll be able to find of some interest. Oh, my, that old good-for-nothin' town. I'm surprised that it's still there. Is it really?"

"Oh, yes, ma'am," I quickly answered. "It's still there, and I believe that it just might possibly be the same way it was when you left."

"Mmm," Margaret mumbled. "You don't say."

"I really do believe it's the same," I told her.

"Well, now, just how do I suppose I can begin tellin' you about this?"

She began describing Stonyford. "I think it'll be best that I first start out by telling you about the old man and his ugly-looking snake. Yeah, I do think that'll be the best thing to do cause it's the story that was always told to all the young'uns like myself. But it's the one story that we all liked hearing about for some odd reason."

"But wait a minute, Margaret," I suddenly found myself questioning. "I mean, 'old man and his snake'? What's that about?"

"Just hold on, young man," she told me, smiling. "Just hold your horses and let me get there. So now, just where was I? Oh, yeah. Well, the actual history about the old man and his snake is still to this day very much unknown, and as much a mystery than ever before in that neck of the woods. And when it comes to describing the many horrifying events that had taken place throughout the Stonyford region, to this day, there can be very little doubt about all the things that had taken place in that town, as well as the many horrifying, agonizing tragedies the town's residents had endured. But you can surely believe that each of these events did indeed occur in that small community.

"This is also the place where not only did its residents end up becoming themselves victims to some of the most horrifying tragedies imaginable to man, but this is also that part of the region where the old snake hunter happened across an auctioneer who was about ready to shear the skin from a Naji Hanna or a Hamadryad, which is better known throughout the hemisphere as a King Cobra. To his amazement, the old snake hunter found himself making his most unusual bid in his effort to purchase the snake.

"Now, are you still listening to me?"

"Yes, ma'am," I responded. "You know I gotta hear about this."

"Okay, then," she said. "I'm just making sure, 'cause don't want you missing anything."

Margaret smiled and stared directly into my eyes.

"Now, just where was I?" she again said. "Oh, yeah. Now you see, that huge, very venomous reptile just stood there with those strange-looking designs all over it as it spread its hood wide as a warning to anyone who dared to come near it. Its size was considered as extremely massive and far much larger and different than the average size cobra of that in Asia or even in Africa.

"As the snake stood very tall above the auctioneer at nearly six feet or more, it began to sway from side to side, back and forth, influenced by the many spectators who had traveled for miles just to get an opportunity to see such a reptile. While swaying, and without the spectators realizing what was happening, it spat very large amounts of a highly toxic venom into the crowds of vacationing spectators. The venom spat was a highly effective contagious bacterial disease where, upon contact, there would begin an immediate breakdown of the immune system, causing severe deformity to an unborn child.

"Once contact is made, an immediate growth of deformity and abnormality begins a violent attack in the rebuilding of its own nucleic acid, replicating cells and proteins through its hostile, malicious corruption as it begins to attach itself to every living organ replicating itself."

"Damn, Margaret," I found myself abruptly interrupting her. "But, are you really serious about all this replicating stuff? I mean, is this really what took place in Stonyford?"

"Well," she said, "if you don't mind doing a little homework in your spare time, you can read the literary report on this subject which will give you a much broader understanding about this particular microscopic pathogen. It's also explained in a documented report that's in the medical journal by Edward Emordnys, Ph.D., D.O., R. Pojahi, and Edmiold J. Joseph via Alexander of the *Sunflower Times*, who reported that the integrated body system of organs, tissues, cells, and/or cell products such as those in antibodies that tend to at times differentiate themselves from oneself, and in some form help neutralize potentially pathogenic organisms' substance from its own attempt to destroy the immune system.

"I would say that we, as living human beings, are definitely in a losing battle once the venom from such a reptile is passed from the snake's inner cavity, or rather the thin, hollow hole from its fang which poisonous snakes use when injecting their venom, or in the present case, spat its venom. The people as reported in the report by the appropriate authorities in charge have issued a statement saying that the residents of Stonyford, as well as those who were just simply vacationing viewers to the area or who were just traveling through the town in question, are all themselves in a very serious battle once the venom has made contact with their skin as well as during regular inhalation.

"Now, what it's saying is that there will undoubtedly be an immediate breakdown of the immune system. This will most likely be from the inside outward, reaching just about every living organ in its wake. Tissue and cells, leaving each of its victims having that physical appearance of an intense, long period of painful suffering and a terrible agonizing death. During this suffering, there will be some form of an intense malformation that will cause every unborn child to be born with a series of deformities at birth.

"As in the present case, in the town of Stonyford, it's my honest opinion that in relation to those people, including the elderly, doctors have made notes and reports available for you to view from the *Willows Times*. There are even very personal explanations about this subject and also about the vast majority of deformities being so described in particular as Seed Sowing due to the town's residents being themselves involved in incestuous relationships."

"Now, this is really something to hear about, Margaret," I told her. "I mean, it's like all of this stuff has happened because of a snake spitting its venom into a crowd of people."

"That's just part of the story, young man," she said, smiling. "That was just a few bits and pieces of what you're going to be experiencing."

"But tell me something," I questioned. "Whatever happened to the old man and his snake? I mean, did he ever end up buying the snake?"

"Well, as the snake stood there standing tall with its hood spread widely apart as a warning to the viewing audience, this type of display wasn't at all any threat to the old snake hunter."

"And why was that?" I asked.

"Well, that's because he had for many years lived in what was described as the snake pit mountains of this region that surrounded him deep within his own secluded habitat. His living condition was described by residents and explorers as the private nesting place for a very large generation of venomous snakes."

"And did he end up with the snake?" I again asked.

"He did," she told me. "And although he found himself having to pay a very hefty price for this strange particular reptile, he couldn't help but to feel that the bid was definitely worth it."

"So, in other words, it really made him happy?"

"Oh, heavens, yes," she said. "He believed that he could somehow tame the snake and become its best friend. He now owned the snake."

"And did they ever really end up becoming the best of friends?"

"Well, word is that they did," she told me. "But you see, that's the mystery behind this story. Word is that they ended up dying together, and at the same time of day. Their spirits, for reasons unknown, became angry at the world because they ended up in hell. Hell is in Stonyford. That's why people die so tragically in that town."

"So, you mean to tell me that the old snake hunter and his snake actually did end up dying together, and at the same time?"

"At approximately the same time of that day and date," she told me.

"I mean, uh, did somebody actually see this happening?" I asked her.

"Well, from my understanding, there were enough rumors floating around about the old man and his snake supposing to have been seen. I guess from what those folks were saying is, they were seen traveling, swiftly, through the air like visible spirits, but in a ghostly figure, appearing to haunt the living."

"And where was this supposed to have taken place?"

"From my understanding," she began describing, "these sightings were made somewhere around a few of the campgrounds and fishing streams that ran throughout the lower elevations of the many mountains and steep hillsides. But it's as I was saying, these rumors were said to have come from people camping in this area, and from sometime hikers who spent quality time scaling the mountains as a sport."

"And these people, all of 'em, describe the same thing?" I questioned.

"Well, let me see now." Margaret began looking around the room while thinking and trying to remember what the campers were saying.

"I think it was at the time of their death, there was an appearance of what was described as these very large shadows that resembled spirits or something. These shadows were said to be immense in size, and could at times be seen from within a long distance as they traveled throughout the region."

"And what about the people who lived in this area?" I asked her. "Did any of them ever see any of this taking place?"

"Those who live in the area could only describe what they had witnessed by saying it was as if the shadow, or spirits, or whatever it was, had somehow become, I think they called it, resurrected from the dead. But not only were these sightings coming from the people who resided in Stonyford, but it was sometimes coming from the many prospectors who spent the vast majority of their time exploring the region with all their gold digging and mining excavations. It was said that they'd on many occasions found themselves terribly frightened and horrified from what they could only describe as the beginning of the apocalypse."

"Are you serious, Margaret?" I just had to ask. "The apocalypse?"

"Uh huh," she mumbled. "And some of the people were even saying that a figure which they could only describe as being like that of the image of the devil, or Satan himself, could be seen. This figure had, after many years of being bound in the bottomless pit of hell, somehow escaped.

"It was said that the huge chains that bound Satan could be seen as they swayed back and forth around his neck and shoulders, and on down to his waist and ankles. Some of the people were also saying very large, vicious dragons could be seen sitting on each side of him, as if they were in some manner awaiting their turn to be released from the huge chains that bound them together."

"And what about the old man and his snake? What was happening with them while all of this stuff was going on? You know, Satan and his chains and dragons?"

"Well, and from my understanding, as the old man and his snake continued their resurrection, it was said that horns could be heard as they blew loudly, and that the wind could also be heard as it whistled in between the thick brush that covered the entire region. During this entire ordeal, I was told, the sky had darkened and huge flashes of lightning could be seen as they bolted across the dark sky. In some areas of the region, it was said that the ground shook violently, while at the same time, in other areas, huge clouds of dry dust particles, smoke and steam could be seen being released heavily into the dark sky.

"As the resurrection continued, it was said that the conversion was as if the two spirits had now somehow joined together and become one. I was told that there could be seen what appeared to be a large, bright, shiny, yellowish umbilical cord, having five glossy attachments to it, and that these attachments were connected to each of the five figures that stood upright in sequence. Satan, the dragons, and the old snake hunter and his snake. Satan stood very tall above the two dragons with what was described as him having very distorted, grotesque wings that spread widely apart in behind him, while at the same time, positioning himself, and pointing one of his badly deformed, long, unearthly, mystical fingers in the direction of each bolt of lightning that he hurled across the dark sky.

"It was said that his fingers looked like they had been drenched within some type of a thick liquid substance that was a troubling reddish color, and dripping heavily and very laboriously around him.

"He just stood there looming above the two dragons as if on a pedestal, with those huge vicious beasts on each side of him, kneeling at the basin."

"And what about the old man and his snake?" I asked curiously. "What was happening with them at this point?"

"It was said that by this time they'd begun to encircle the area around Satan and the dragons. It was said that the umbilical cords could be seen as if they were somehow being structured in the form of a spiral dimension, as if preparing for the rebirth of Satan's army.

"This is where, I guess you can say, I closed my eyes and began to think about what was happening, and how it reminded me so much of a passage I remember reading in my Bible, where it speaks about a time when Satan and his army were apparently cast out of heaven. It talks about how he was cast out with all who had chosen to follow him during their unsuccessful rampage in an attempt to try to overthrow the kingdom of heaven."

"And that's what the Bible was talking about?" I asked.

"Haven't you ever read it? Did your parents ever read it to you?"

"Uh huh, yes, ma'am," I answered. "But, for some reason, the story seems to sound better coming from you."

Margaret smiled.

"Anyway, young man, these were those same vicious demons who had for many years been bound in the bottomless pit for their part in the crime they'd committed against heaven.

"During the conversation as described to me, there seemed to be a constant changing of what had resembled some form of a spiritual communion dance, and that this communion did indeed involve some type of a medium which could be seen as it circled around those who had themselves come to be released from the bottomless pit. As the communion continued, it was said that the old man and his snake could be clearly seen, and that the two had indeed now become one, joined together, complete, and in one single spirit.

"Are you still listening, young man?"

"Yes, ma'am," I responded. "But tell me something. After everything that's taken place, you know, all those people being attacked and everything, just why would those people wanna hang around that town?"

"Well, for one thing," Margaret told me, "throughout the years, there wasn't any gold-digging or mining, or even camping, hiking, or even exploring the Stonyford region allowed. Well, not until a whole new generation of young, stupid, and very careless families began moving into this community, only to have unknowingly awakened the evil spirit of the old snake hunter and his snake."

"And what about that huge mountain?" I questioned. "You know, the one big mountain that could be seen from miles away."

"Oh, my," she said, while looking in the direction of one of the walls where there hung a few pictures. "Boy, do I remember that mountain. I know just about everything about it, and all its little secrets. That's a picture of it right over there."

"What can you tell me about it, Margaret?" I asked her. "What is it that a person should know about this particular mountain?"

"Well, for one thing, Snow Mountain could be seen from quite a distance as it shadowed over the entire region. This particular mountain had gained its name and reputation because of its height and width for which it stood and its wide angle it projected. Some called it the spitting image of

Mt. Everest, while others called it The Devil's Playground. Nonetheless, this is where those who ventured the mountain were claiming to have witnessed seeing the evil shadow moving amongst the heavily dense brush alongside the unpaved, winding gravelly roads that lead up to the mountain and its many camp sites.

"This is also the location of the remainder of what was left of the partially demolished cabin that was once the home of the old man and his snake. Those who ventured to this particular area were said to have found themselves being subjected to the painful encounters and deadly attacks bestowed upon them by the hostile aggressiveness of the old man.

"It was said that he could at times be seen stalking and attacking unwanted snakes, and that the snake could at times be seen viciously attacking unwanted human explorers visiting the area. They'd find themselves becoming victims of these deadly attacks without warning.

"It was said that on certain occasions long before the shadows had become one, the old snake hunter could at times be seen with his long, dingy-looking gray beard and shaggy clothing, walking around in circles in the thick brush that covered the entire surroundings of his habitat. Throughout the years, campers often made claims of finding the remains of unreported missing prospectors on the many steep, rugged slopes that crossed in between these mountains."

"How would you say these events affected this town?" I asked her. "Did the people really continue to live there?"

"Well, by this time," she explained, "the course of this entire area had really begun to make some drastic changes. Stonyford's residents and their families residing in this particular area, I believe, were either forced, or ordered, to move out of the area immediately and relocate elsewhere, out of fear of themselves becoming victims of something that had for reasons unknown lashed out its vengeance in an extreme manner, as if with an intent to violate and punish not only anyone who dared to venture this region, but its vengeance was said to have been lashed out on the entire community of Stonyford. There wasn't any longer what was considered to be an ordinary day for this community, or what the town's people could actually consider as a regular typical day, or even what would be considered as a customary day for this small town.

"There were often times when hikers would return from trips claiming to have been stalked and sometimes attacked by fellow hikers. But there was never any factual identity of their attackers. Inasmuch as the town's residents would have relished the opportunity to be able to point fingers at a suspect, there was never any actual fact with which to do so."

"So, being that the people residing in Stonyford could never find the right person to consider a suspect, is this what caused the submission?"

"Well, I think it could have probably played a major part," she told me. "You see, by now, this once quiet community had now drawn a rather unique interest form very inquisitive travelers who could be seen driving rather slowly through town. At times, spontaneous flashes of light were seen, as if coming from cameras that were busy snapping photographs as if these people were trying to capture a glimpse of something that was mysteriously unseen. And at the town's supermarket, people would stand around on its wooden porch inquiring about the old man and his snake. Others could be seen pointing in the direction of Snow Mountain.

"People often gathered on the porch of the town's supermarket with an eager ear to listen to an old, gray-headed Indian known as Chief as he told them the story and history about Stonyford. He was considered by the town's residents as the great storyteller of all times. Everyone had always found his stories so fascinating to where some of the people would bring chairs and ice coolers just so that they could sit for long hours listening to him talk about the old snake hunter and his snake, and how evil they were when feeling threatened by those who tried exploring this region.

"He always made it a point to make known to his listener the many horrifying events that took place throughout this area, and that those who were themselves thinking about venturing the mountains, how they especially should take extra precaution because the evil snake hunter and his snake were always waiting for the right opportunity to attack the unwanted visitors.

"Chief would tell those who were willing to listen about how the evil shadow had often crept up on its victims in what he'd described as a vicious and aggressive manner, and how it would seize the opportunity to deprive its victims of any means possible to escape its powerful grip."

"What were the people who were listening to him doing while he was busy telling them all this stuff?" I asked her. "I mean, were they believing him?"

"Some of the people were listening intensely and in much amazement, while others might be trembling and shivering, while not hesitating to show their emotional reactions by nervously jumping with jerky movements from the slightest touch of those who stood too close. And some of the parents could be seen escorting their children both to and from the nearby restrooms."

"You mean to tell me, all of this was happening because they felt that the things the old Indian man was talking about could really happen? I mean, damn, Margaret, just what were they thinking?"

"Just remember," she told me, "their reactions were really from them thinking about the possibility of being attacked by the evil spirit. And as the old Indian continued to warn those who would listen, some of the little children who were engaged in horseplay could be heard in the distance, screaming and shouting out loudly, claiming to have seen sighting of the shadow moving about around the supermarket, and saying it was trying to attack them.

"Each claim of sightings caused a tremendous immediate response from the many listeners who were already themselves in a rather tense state of paranoia. Some of the people were even expressing a rather irrational sense of suspiciousness.

"Just as the history about the old man and his snake is unknown, the same has been said about the old Indian. When questioning the town's residents about him, the only thing they always seem to say is that he's been around the town of Stonyford for as long as anyone can remember. And when talking to him and questioning his past, he'd always point in the direction toward the many, many mountains and steep hillsides, and the slopes where there is an ancient burial ground.

"The direction in which he would always point was said to be the birthplace and resting place of his family and for those who had gone forward.

"It was also said that he had never feared or felt in any way threatened by the evilness of the old snake hunter and his snake, and that he'd always felt that the region and all its strange wilderness was a part of him."

"Well, what about the people who explored this area?" I questioned. "I was wondering if any of them ever came into contact with the old Indian while out exploring?"

"On many occasions, there were hikers exploring the area who'd return to town claiming they'd seen him."

"They'd seen Chief? The old Indian?"

"Oh, heavens, yes," she said. "They'd always see that Indian somewhere up there on those mountains. There were many times when hikers exploring the area would find themselves in so much bewilderment from the surprising appearance of Chief up there somewhere. They'd say he seem to always appear practically out of nowhere. Each of these occurrences would always happen while in some of the most extreme remote area of the region. Some of the the explorers could sometimes be within their most desperate attempts to scale the rugged slopes, when out of nowhere, the old Indian would appear from within some of the most dangerous areas of the region."

I had indeed become fascinated listening to this story about evil spirits. And what was even more amazing is that, while during the old Indian telling his story, Margaret talked about how he'd even mention her name throughout his story.

"Well, as he continued to amaze his listeners, he spoke to them about a young girl named Margaret, which is me. He told them how I was viciously attacked by the evil spirit. He talked about how the spirit had lived inside of me throughout my childhood life in Stonyford, and how it was responsible for the brutal torment of my sister."

"Margaret, are you actually telling me that you had an opportunity to hear him yourself talking to his listeners about you?"

"That's right, young man," she told me. "I was right there, up front in the best seat the whole time, just listening to him."

"And was he telling the truth about you?" I asked her.

"The whole truth and nothing but the truth," she said.

"Meaning, all of this talk about evil spirits and shadows is real?" I questioned her insistently.

Margaret knew how important it was for me to find out the reason for the submission in Stonyford. She knew she had the complete fullness of my attention. The thought of what had taken place in this small-town community was something that even the midwesterners and easterners were themselves talking about during midday discussions in restaurants, small coffee shops, city parks and major corporate offices across the country. The news about the Stonyford tragedy had made front page headlines in just about every newspaper.

Being that I really didn't have reasons to use my GPS to navigate from one point to another, though, I still found myself at times getting lost. I had on many occasions visited Stonyford years long ago, but nowadays, everything had changed. Not only had kids grown up to become themselves adults, but grandkids were now teenagers with seemingly violent, disruptive, disrespectful behavioral problems.

"While you were there," Margaret asked me, "did you have a chance to visit any of the places you remembered?"

"A few," I answered. "Just a few, but so much had changed."

"Well, did you recognize anyone? Like some of the old-timers? Or some of the old antiquated things from the past?"

"To be truthful, Margaret, just about everything I saw in the town looked old, and of ancient times. I mean, I have to admit, it felt like I'd stepped into a time-warp or something. It's like, everything had somehow become distorted."

She knew exactly what I was trying to describe. That's why she just sat there, very still, staring and listening to me recount what I had experienced while visiting Stonyford.

Yes, she knew exactly what I was trying to describe.

Prologue

RESEARCHING THE MYSTERIOUSNESS of Margaret's childhood life in the small town of Stonyford has been far beyond the scope of my imagination. It has also been beyond the term we use when describing something considered complicated.

It was on this particular day while she attended her elementary grade class that Margaret found herself within a deep trance. She was in a rather relaxed state while within the recreation of her imaginary world. She was fully aware of the noises and shouting that were going on around her, shouts that were also coming from the classroom teacher who was busy requesting her undivided attention. But it was because of her relaxed state of mind that made it impossible for her to respond. It would also have meant for her to just outright neglect what seemed to be so real to her. Margaret was later told that because of her noncooperative behavior that she would have to stand in a corner and face the classroom wall. This is where she would find herself spending the next hour as a disciplinary requirement for ill-mannered behavior.

Facing the wall with only her nose touching while struggling in an effort to balance herself, she'd become slightly incoherent from her already lengthy stand, though quickly gained control of herself in an effort to withstand the few remaining minutes.

She thought about what would happen if she were to fail her punishment, and how she would only again find herself having to repeat the punishment the following day, which she felt was out of the question.

Before she was allowed to leave the room, she was once again reminded about her behavior. She was told that she would soon find herself being expelled from school, but that was unless she did something immediately, like to start trying to correct her behavioral problem.

Margaret gave very little response, if any at all, by the nodding of her head and shrugging of her shoulders in a rather brief motion. This was her indication that she would start showing more of an interest to try and participate.

The point she wanted more than anything was to make someone aware of what was presently happening to her. She wanted to try to make known how her imaginary world had seemed to be in complete control of her. She couldn't quite understand what was happening, just as she at times couldn't understand how her imaginary world could control her in the manner it was doing. But she knew it was was the right thing to do by finding someone that she felt she could trust enough to talk to, but that person to her had to be someone she felt close to, and someone who would take the time to really try understanding what she was going through.

As she thought about the people involved in her life, it was at this instant that she found herself with the desire to attempt to talk to her teacher. He seemed to show more concern for her, and far more so than that of her own parents. His authority and influence over her had become even more than that of the young boy she knew who lived within a short distance from the family's farm, and who at one time had been considered her long-time childhood sweetheart. But even he wasn't any longer of an interest to her.

He wasn't any longer appealing to her inner appetite. She no longer desired him as she once did. He no longer meant anything to her. When thinking about him, she could think nothing except tormenting thoughts about him. No longer did she find herself desiring to stand firm beside him as she had once vowed to do by one day becoming the wife and mother to their future family.

It was on this particular evening that Margaret, while on her walk home from school, during her walk with all the other pupils, as they laughed loudly, while having typical child play, chasing each other across street after street in their games of tag, that she, once again, found herself within the recreation of her imaginary world.

It was while playing and laughing loudly with her friends that her wild journey home began once again to take control over her, except this time, whatever it was that was happening, had now become extremely aggressive. She'd begun to feel and experience the presence of not only herself, but that of also someone else deep inside her body.

She found herself acting in a manner that she had never before acted. She could feel something inside of her that was causing her to repeat certain words that were spoken in a language that she had never before spoken.

The other children could plainly hear her verbal utterance, but they thought maybe it was just her particular way of being silly while having fun. But without them being aware of what she was going through, she found herself becoming upsettingly tense from the eager thirst in her mouth which was for that of not only milk or water, but for an aggressive need.

All the children who played closely to Margaret began to notice from the expression on her face that something was wrong with her, causing them to scatter quickly. Some of the kids ran to nearby residences, screaming, shouting, and crying out loud for help. Some were said to have claimed having been attacked and injured by Margaret's violent grip as she attempted to cling onto them.

Later that evening, parents were notified by local authorities that Margaret had just been playing a game with them, and that their game playing had somehow gotten a bit too rough and out of hand. They were also told that there wasn't any reason for them to worry.

This statement was just what Margaret needed to hear. She couldn't afford to lose any friends.

For this reason, this story is being told in an effort to reveal the truth to the best of my knowledge and to attempt to comprehend the information put forth to me in my present by Margaret, who had herself been the first person to encounter the evil spirit of the old snake hunter and his snake. A deadly, vicious spectacle residing in the concealment of our everyday life, in the form of an extremely venomous snake, would up its deadliest impulsive desire, and at any given moment, would viciously attack its victims with such force and intense aggression to where it would cause an immediate devastating disfigurement that was far beyond our humanly comprehension.

This is the truth to the best of my knowledge as I sat there staring at Margaret, our eyes fixated, as I sat motionless.

I couldn't help but find myself just sitting there directly in front of her as if unable to move from the presence of Margaret's agonizing cries of anguished deception in my most unbearable condition of our so-called human understanding. This deadly, vicious spectacle residing deep inside of

Margaret was itself willing to reveal itself to me, voluntarily, and without any thought of being reluctant.

This story seemed to be its only desire. It was hoping that maybe somehow Margaret's experience, as it so openly revealed through her, could possibly one day be told and hopefully believed, and that if not by me, then maybe by means of other familiar methods of interest which it knew that I, as well as Margaret, knew would continue occurring from this present personal encounter.

Words to describe its powerful displaying demonstration from within Margaret were far beyond my intellect as I sat there witnessing the most horrifying aspects brought about through a human being as this yearning monstrous spectrum continued to display itself. These are the only means and elements that I could find in which to describe what was taking place in my presence.

As Margaret's head bent slightly downward, it was then that I began to hear low-pitched murmuring sounds coming from her mouth. These sounds were so abnormal and as if prolonged from intense pain or possibly even grief. That's when I suddenly found myself wondering just how such a sound and prolonged irritation could actually come from within the human cavity.

As I sat there, staring intently, and listening to these awful, annoying, muttering sounds which had now turned into a rather rough gurgling, a thick mass of yellow foam began to form and start bubbling around the surface of Margaret's mouth.

She then raised her head in a rather slow, sly manner. I built up the nerve to ask her if she was all right.

"Do you believe in me?" she asked me. "Do you believe in the things not seen?

"Do you believe in me?" she again asked me.

"Mmm," I mumbled. And then I said, "I don't really quite know just what you're referring to. I mean, I really don't know."

I have to be honest by admitting the fact that I couldn't help but find myself somewhat confused by her questioning. It was like being in a movie I remember viewing years ago. I believe it was called *The Exorcist*. In that movie an evil spirit or spirits were using a young girl as a means or channel to enact its ritual.

"Perhaps you would prefer to see my authority at work?" the voice yelled out loudly from within Margaret. "I am the one and only one who can make all the earth shiver. Are you not, yourself, trembling? Be my personal servant, submit your humbled gratitude unto me. I am your only God of the earth."

Listening to these words come from within Margaret, I began to think about my Bible, and how in the book of Genesis it was the serpent who was using such exact cunning words on Eve. I thought how the serpent had caused her to take of the forbidden tree of knowledge. She, in turn, using those same cunning words, did just about everything in her power to persuade Adam to himself partake the same knowledge. God had already warned them to not take of this particular knowledge by saying "But of the knowledge of this which is in the midst of the garden, you shall not take, nor shall you touch it, lest you die!"

This monstrous thing that was presently residing inside of Margaret was indeed right about what I was experiencing. I most certainly did find myself deeply disturbed emotionally and trembling from fear as never before in my life. I thought to myself how could anyone be comfortable while in the presence of such troubling display.

I could see her staring at me as if I were on my death bed. I could feel myself now trembling even more as I continued to listen to this awful thing inside of Margaret tell me about myself. Its words were as if they were being spoken from within some type of diary of personal events about the observation of my life. It had even addressed me by my first and middle name, and in the same manner that my now deceased mother had always used when calling me.

Hearing the sound of her voice made my every nerve quiver.

But I again thought to myself, "How could this be possible?"

"Do you believe in me? Do you believe in the things not seen? Do you believe in me?" it again asked me, except this time, the voice had now become rough and harsh, and as if in demand.

I replied by saying, "Again, I really don't quite know just what to believe."

"Behold, you shall become like one of us," it said strangely. "For the dust of the earth you came from, and the dust of the earth you shall return."

I then for some mysterious reason yelled, "Just who in the hell are you? Are you someone that I met before?"

"Go fuck yourself, you filthy, disgraceful, retarded bastard!" it yelled back at me from within Margaret. "Better yet, come closer to me you good-for-nothin' freakin' illegitimate fucker and let me slap that freakin' shit off your face for disrespecting me. Just who the fuck do you think I am? Mother Teresa or something, you rotten piece of filthy shit!

"Tell me who's yo' daddy, BITCH?"

I have to admit being somewhat bothered by such insults and degrading profane language. but it was the thought of my mother speaking to me through this very frail, delicate woman that became somewhat of a struggle for me to deal with. I found myself having to try hard in an effort to gain control of myself so that I wouldn't become overwhelmed from the thought of hearing what sounded like my mother's voice.

All that I could think about was how just yesterday, everything had seemed so pleasant. Today should have been an extraordinary day.

The fascination of my being a journalist from the city of Vallejo had now begun to feel as though I were somehow digging my own grave.

My few hours spent with Margaret began to feel like days into weeks, and weeks into months, with having so much yet to do ahead of me. All that I could think about in my attempts to describe this monstrous thing and all of its persuasiveness were all the enemies of our humanly nature.

I could only describe it as Evil, Vicious, Demon, Serpent, the Devil himself, Perverted Spirit, Demonic Possessor, Denunciator, and the true and only Master of deceiving deception.

These are the only means by which I could attempt to describe my most arduous state of comprehension and experience with this deadly, inhumane, vicious spectacle.

Chapter One

HEADLINE NEWS: In small towns all across the state of California, people do tend to do good deeds by keeping track of their family members and friends, and also their neighbors, without being too nosy or inquisitively probing. At no time will you ever find them snooping around in what is considered an unfriendly, subversive manner.

But in the small town of Stonyford, where the population has become far outnumbered by so many vacationers, residents have now found themselves fearing the possibility that an unknown killer or killers could be roaming their quiet roads or lurking amongst them.

KQTV's reporting shows that unsolved homicides of local citizens have become mind-boggling to the investigators. An unknown assailant, or possibly assailants, are now added to the California Bureau of Investigations Most Wanted List. Evidence at crime scenes is indicating that the alleged assailant seems to be appearing and then disappearing without ever a trace. Speculation is that the killer or killers could be using the surrounding wooded area and mountains as a means to come into these communities, and then returning to their hiding place the same way, unnoticed.

We here at KQTV understand that feuding residents are becoming extremely bitter, angry, and confused. Some have even formed unsupported opinions that are astounding. Most question that if someone local is indeed responsible, or even if it's a transient, just how is it that this person is committing these crimes without ever leaving any traces of evidence?

One of the questions most bothering these communities that has yet to be answered is how, in such a small town, where you would think there would be far more clues which point at a suspect in either direction, we can find none! This huge gap is allowing the assailant to escape and have an overwhelming advantage over us in his effort to elude being captured.

In the matter of the many horrifying mutilating homicides that continue to occur, starting in the town of Stonyford where, at present, there still isn't anyone being held accountable or anyone answerable who can at least explain to us just what is happening, we here at KQTV feel compelled to try our best to keep you, our viewers, informed.

As you know, in most cases, the CBI's list of suspects is usually a list of identifiable suspects. In very few cases are there ever profiles where there isn't anyone to point to as a possible suspect.

Again, this is KQTV News reporting to you, our viewers, on yet another strange evening about the events that have been gripping us all throughout northern California. We thank all of you, our viewers and listening audience, for tuning in to KQTV on yet another awful, unforgiving evening throughout the Stonyford region, as well as all the other nearby communities that surround this town in question, who have yourselves become deeply affected by all the many horrifying events and tragedies that continue to occur.

It seems to have all started with the death of a young girl we have come to know is Wanda Johnson. There are reports that there might have been others before her, but at present, these reports haven't yet been confirmed or corroborated. But, you can surely believe that once KQTV receives confirmation on any other homicides in the wake of these events surrounding the Stonyford region, we will not hesitate updating you, our viewers and devoted listening audience.

Here with us this evening in the news room at KQTV is a student journalist from Vallejo. We welcome Mr. Murdock to the studio this evening to assist us, for we understand that he had an opportunity to be one of the first journalists on hand during the beginning of this investigation and also the tragic situation there in the town of Stonyford.

Now, if you will, Mr. Murdock, please kind of help us out here at KQTV to have a much better understanding about what's been happening. Just how did this all begin, if you will?

Murdock: Well, first of all, I would really like to thank KQTV for this opportunity to be here in your studio. Being a student journalist from as far away as Vallejo, any time there's an opportunity to travel from one location to another, it's always a pleasure. Except in this case, this isn't really anything that a journalist would want to jump up and down and be excited about. But in the aftermath of the tragic killings that for reasons unknown have taken place in that small, quiet community, officers are very busy at work conducting what is called door-to-door canvassing of residents and this is including those who are residing in the nearby rural areas.

Additionally, officers are also conducting road checks for possible information that they could possibly gather from motorists traveling to and from these areas in question.

So often, there are innocent citizens who might have seen something, but not often, they think that what they've seen just isn't that important. So what they'll do is, they'll…they just won't report it or even tell anyone about it. But it's not that these people are in any way withholding any type of information or anything like evidence, but what's happening is that they just don't feel that what they've seen is all that important. As in most cases, people just don't want to be bothering anyone.

KQTV News: Mr. Murdock, bringing your attention to our report, there has never been any actual sign of any evidence left at any of the crime scenes—well, not anything left that'll in any way help for there to be any fingers pointing at a suspect. And again, this is from our KQTV report, that the only evidence, or should I say, the only ransack of any residence, in any in particular location which was thought to be the point of attack, the only noticeable evidence left at any of the crime scenes in question has been from that of the victims, or should I be saying the victims' bodies being thrown and scattered about, as if something or someone was in a fit of rage while during dismemberment.

Now, if you will, Mr. Murdock, could you please, to help our KQTV viewers understand, elaborate on the numerous findings of those very complex components that have most directly affected and influenced the depths of our emotions to where it's shocking for us to hear how so many of the residents of these communities are beginning to arm themselves during the wake of these tragedies with loaded weapons.

Now, in the small town of Stonyford, the residents were by this time all hoping that they could just consider and view each of these incidents as that of transients who were just passing through these towns, but, and as we are now fully aware, each of these ongoing occurrences keep continuing to happen, sometimes daily. Could you please elaborate, Mr. Murdock?

Murdock: And deadly! It's really sad to think that even in non-neighboring communities, people are indeed worried! And they should, by all means, be worried! Someone has definitely slipped onto the Johnsons' estate, tragically harming the youngest child and just outright flashed the little life out of the other.

Yes, indeed, there are many reasons to be worried! It was seemingly just yesterday when everything was like an ordinary day, and now, here we are today, making a plea to any and everyone, all across the nation, for some kind of assistance. Any assistance to try and help solve these crimes.

It's indeed mind-boggling when really thinking about the subject. All of those poor people have even put up a reward in hope that maybe somehow anyone will come forward with the right information. It's rather disappointing, when these people are busy at work pursuing this person or persons as serial killers preying on their victims.

The Sacramento Bee has reported that in the town of Colusa multiple suicide packs of local students are forming in most of their schools. This is also the report in neighboring Maxwell, Orlando, Corning, Williams, Woodland, Upland, and even Davis, and as far away as the town of Chico. Some are even reporting an inclination trend in these suicides.

KQTV News: Deadly indeed, Mr. Murdock. Deadly indeed.

And for you, our listening audience, KQTV wants you to know that in each of these neighboring towns, lights are fully burning in just about every house. It's now starting to rain outside on yet another very warm, mild evening throughout the region. Mr. Murdock, do you at all think this might end up hampering the investigation?

Murdock: Well, and as we all should know, while during any investigation and especially like the one in question, anytime it rains, there will always be the possibility that evidence could be lost under such circumstances. But, I am more than sure that everything is presently being done to try and prevent anything like this from happening.

KQTV News: And we have yet another report just in from our nearby affiliates about a curfew being put in place up around the Stonyford area. We also understand that this could end up having what some of the folks are calling a domino effect, resulting in an influence across this entire region in question. Do you think this is at all possible, Mr. Murdock?

Murdock: Well, and to be completely truthful, the magnitude of what has taken place thought out this region, and I do wish to place emphasis on region, I'm very surprised the curfew has taken this long, and in such an amount of time when knowing a killer or possibly killers are presently at large, busy lurking, tracking, and also stalking people in some of these cases. Victims of this monster are said to be chased down and brutally brutalized in such horrifying measures.

So yes, I think it's going to have a domino effect indeed at the present time. It's very important that citizens do take extra precautions in advance to safeguard themselves against being in harm's way.

KQTV News: In the case of Margaret Johnson, the youngest daughter of Paul and Sarah Johnson, at her age, is it really typical for young girls to be rebellious as she was? You know, meaning toward her parents?

Murdock: Well, it all depends.

KQTV News: At her age, wouldn't you agree that most girls are busy chasing boys and staying out past a certain time allowed for teenagers?

Murdock: Possibly.

KQTV News: This young girl who most described as your typical tomboy who, quote, "seemed to really enjoy wearing her peacoat, printed see-through blouse and bra. Tightly fitted blue jeans, and occasionally bright pink ankle socks and penny loafers." And, from our reporting, she really did enjoy going to school and quite often she could be found hanging out at the nearby supermarket which is located in the midst of town. Meaning, Stonyford.

Our reporting is that folks are saying that she was very rebellious, and mainly against her parents.

We here at press time, we're just having a hard time focusing in on this situation with Margaret as the only possible suspect in the death of her sister. And what about all the other murders? We here at KQTV can really find no relation. And, although they all tend to show some form of similarity, being in relation to each other, there at present just isn't an indication that these killings having been committed by the same person. And you would think, especially not by a child.

So come on, Mr. Murdock, do you really find it at all feasible for this young girl to actually be responsible for these gruesome crimes that have taken place in the town in question? Granted, we're talking about a child. This isn't by any means child's play, and surely, as we both know, this little girl hasn't been portraying herself as the female Chucky character, or Chucky's bride. Please!

Murdock: Well, again, from what information I have gathered, on certain evenings neighbors at times drew together to just wind down from a hard day's work and relax, while some having time and desires to just sit and listen to each other tell stories about the town and its history. It's just the kind of thing those people tended to do at times to show some form of closeness toward each other. Most of the folks in the town would find themselves laughing loudly, while some, they'd just be busy talking and listening with eager ears, trying to hear the gossip. And during most occasions, some of the town's folks just simply joked around while posing for pictures by vacationers.

Whenever there was a newborn into a family, just about everyone would come together with friendly welcoming arms, hoping they could somehow become an adoptable relative.

Now, the death of this young girl seemed to have marked a serious turning point in the lives of these people. And the murder rate is starting to really soar, becoming the deadliest time ever for homicides ever recorded in the history of the northern region of the state of California.

Someone is definitely busy at work ambushing the Stonyford residents without any sympathy whatsoever.

The death of Wanda is what seem to be bringing everything together, and from the investigative report, it can be said with a certainty that Margaret, on many occasions, attempted to tell her parents everything she could about what she could only describe as something like a monster. She told them this monster was doing things, or that something was trying to do very bad things to her. But the report isn't saying anything about whether she meant it was doing bad things to her sister or what. But that there was definitely something bad happening to one or both of them.

But whether or not we'll ever know, it'll all depend on Margaret.

KQTV News: Hm. And what was the parents' response to all of this?

Murdock: For reasons unknown, they're still believing it was Margaret.

KQTV News: But, why Margaret?

Murdock: They've always accused her of being a liar, and when it came to the situation concerning Wanda, it just added the icing to the cake.

KQTV News: This is so amazing, Mr. Murdock. But, as you can see, we have found ourselves nearing the end of this very important segment. So, tell us, what are your plans?

Murdock: Well, it was a part of my plan, after this interview, I was hoping that if at all possible, I could take a quick flight back to Vallejo.

KQTV News: Is there an airport in Vallejo?

Murdock: Ah, no, there's not. But what I was going to do is, at present I am flying one of the company's privately owned, uh, Beechcrafts. It's a nice E55, which is based in Napa.

KQTV News: So is it fair to say that you are a pilot?

Murdock: And that would be a proud "yes."

KQTV News: And do you always fly the E55? Or something else?

Murdock: Well, I have to admit that my preference is really my own, which is a 114TC Commander. It is also there at the Napa airport.

KQTV News: Hm, very interesting. Is that what you intend to use when you return to the Stonyford area?

Murdock: Well, being that this part of California is in such a rough, mountainous part of the region, and with there being so many locations to yet investigate, it's my intention to return in, I would think, a helicopter. That would, I think, be much more suitable for smooth acceleration throughout this area. Once I return I will then start the investigation assigned to me by my supervisor.

KQTV News: So very interesting, Mr. Murdock, and indeed amazing. But I have to say we're out of time. So, thank you, Mr. Murdock, and good luck to you from KQTV New on your journey.

Murdock: Thank you!

KQTV News: And please do try to keep us updated on your findings.

Murdock: Once again, thank you. You'll be the first to know.

KQTV News: Expanding on this story, KQTV has just received information we are waiting for confirming details about the possibility of another massive finding in close proximity to the Stonyford area.

Now, this remains unconfirmed at this time. However, KQTV News has once again received a message from one of our associated affiliates here in the nearby town of Maxwell that the remains of possibly yet another victim or victims from the Stonyford area have, from what we've been told, been found within the last hour.

Also, we here at KQTV NEWS are now also reporting that an individual has come forward and is claiming to have vital information in this matter concerning these events. This person or persons was supposedly caught in the process of allegedly attempting to vandalize the town's cemetery.

I can only say that the town in this report is said to be neighboring Colusa, which is right there on Highway 5. And this is near to the town of Williams.

Chapter Two

SPEAKING FROM WITHIN her small, dimly-lit apartment, a private community where the elderly citizens tended to migrate after withdrawing from the hard-working class of society upon retirement, I could visibly see and also sense Margaret being somewhat sympathetic when talking about one's involvement in personal family conflicts, and all the many agonizing tragedies that seemed to somehow always follow a person throughout their life.

As she spoke, her voice had the sound of softness, as if it were coming from a small child. As I sat there very carefully listening to her describe events that she knew were of no importance to me, I found myself in a rather awkward situation. I was trying to find a way to reason with myself to affirm the direction I felt as a means far more necessary for me to gather the information needed for the publication of this story as directed by my supervisor.

Being a reporter from the city of Vallejo, it was a dream come true to have my supervisor ask me if I would mind taking on a project consisting of a few cold-blooded, murderous tragedies and attacks that were said to have been so brutal as to cause an entire town to dwindle at an extreme rate.

As I plunged my thoughts in abruptness, an in-depth conversation with Margaret appeared to be the only direction that I found myself determined to pursue in which I could probably find the key principles for the circumstances that caused the submission in Stonyford.

Under such circumstances, and with having to use the testimony from so many opposing victims and citizens, Margaret's relation to each of these events presented would allow me to attain the information needed for the ongoing affirmation of personal examination. But, this is assuming that the direction in which to honestly define the old ancient prosody about Stonyford and all its many horrifying storytellings of each violent tragedy to be indeed accurate.

Each of these events has been described in harrowing, shocking details as intensely dramatic in nature. Some of the residents described it as Dark and Fatal!

As I sat there motionless listening carefully to Margaret, I could barely see what was now this very frail, elderly human being. She must have stood at most five-foot-two, and with what appeared to be a badly decaying physical frame. A condition that seemed to have become extremely weakened during the aging of her life.

Seated closely in front of her, I began to notice how she sat at times in a rather hunched position, as if she could only raise her head to a certain angle and degree. I could also see that her posture was slightly slumped, and far much different from the description I'd anticipated seeing when taking on this assignment. She had a very large hump on her back, a hump that was enormously abnormal for her size.

During our conversation I again found myself staring at her, trying my best to see any visible signs of scarring that she might have received during the suffering she endured from the terrible ordeal throughout her childhood life in Stonyford.

As I continued to very carefully listen to this delicate person, who would every so often pause for a brief second or two, and then would very slowly wipe her mouth with the handkerchief she kept clutched tightly in one of her hands after spitting something in the form of a thick, glossy mass of liquid substance into a small silver fruit can that she kept underneath her chair, I found myself thinking about my own parents, and mainly the grandparents I never knew. This frail, elderly woman presently in front of me reminded me so much of the grandmother I had yearned for throughout my life. To this day, I can only vaguely remember my mother showing me and my siblings photos of both Grandpa and Grandma in years long ago. Photos that are still, to this day, very much embedded in my memory.

As I sat there trying my best to observe her every move, it was then that

I began to notice how she would quite frequently lean forward, and then very slowly stretch one of her delicate, frail arms outward, in a rather downward motion, in the direction of the fruit can that she kept underneath the old antique wooden chair she sat in for comfort.

It was as if she were trying to reach for something.

Her movement at times enabled me to vaguely see certain areas of her hair which reflected a white, silky woolliness from the dense, impenetrable light reflecting throughout the room.

It was as if her hair was made from some type of a weaving fabric that was in the form of a wet, silky cotton. The reflection matched the pale, diminishing condition of her face.

The dimness in the room seemed to dilute most of my clarity and perception of Margaret.

Or, so I thought!

When really thinking about this strange dimness that surrounded me, what perception I had of her, and from also its very strange reflection, revealed an astonishing amount of wrinkles on her face and hands. Hands that would at times shake, as if unable to be controlled.

Trying to get the information she knew I was so desperately seeking, I could visually sense from her behavior that it wasn't going to be an easy task.

Whenever the subject would consist of certain events in her past, she would at times just outright sit there staring at me, pausing momentarily. She would intentionally again avoid answering any of the questions she knew were most important to me. She would instead start talking about how she had ended up in the state of Kansas, and how she was once a school teacher, starting with pre-school; and later, how she had taught elementary, and then junior high school for the Sedgwick County School District in Wichita, Kansas.

As I continued to feel mesmerized by the gentle sound of her soft-spoken voice, I couldn't help but wonder the reason for her persistence in evading my every question.

As she continued describing her past, it was during her compelling description of a particular event that she was describing in detail that I then started to understand the reasons for her elusive behavior during my questioning.

It was after her ordeal in Stonyford, after she had been finally released from the Willow's Hospital, that she was then informed about her family having moved from the state of California and relocated somewhere east of the midwest without ever notifying her of their whereabouts.

She talked about how it was after her tragic ordeal that she was removed from the custody of her parents and placed into the custody of the state. She explained how she would eventually end up being placed into an institution for the criminally insane and underprivileged people of society for an indefinite period of her childhood life.

Throughout the years, she later was once again shuffled around from one institution to another after which time during her maturity, she was finally released back into society as a highly educated faculty member of a well-respected rank.

As a lady characterized and respected by the degree of her abilities and profound intellectual integrity through her professionalism, her reputation became in great demand by scores of universities across the nation.

Teaching to educate had become her profession.

She very seldom talked about her family, and from what information I could gather, they never made any attempt to keep in touch with her. There has always been the speculation that her parents felt she was responsible for the family tragedies. There seemed to be an ongoing resentment towards her.

During her childhood in the small community of Stonyford, so many unexplained disastrous events had taken place and claimed the lives of the town's residents, after which time, Margaret, herself a victim, was placed into an asylum for the criminally insane. It wasn't until years later that it was told that she had somehow escaped the submission and had faded away without ever a trace. Her whereabouts were unknown to the remaining residents who are still to this day residing in this small community.

This is the town where so many of its residents would be deprived of life.

She couldn't quite understand the many things that were taking place, but she knew that something was terribly wrong and that whatever it was, it was very frightening to her. Her fearful reactions had begun to expose the awful marks that were manifesting its infectious vengeance on the vast majority of her young adolescent body with such intensity to where it had caused the town's people to gossip and spread rumors, accusing her of being involved in immoral activities.

Wishing not to remember the horrifying events that sent her young life into turmoil and disarray, she did make known the fact about not being molested, as once thought throughout this community. But she did describe in detail how she was very brutally and viciously attacked by something not belonging to the human race.

Something having no sympathy had viciously encroached itself upon her and had invaded her innermost guarded maidenhood without ever causing any type of structural damage.

She could only describe it as a monstrous thing inside of her, and that it was making her do strange things, and that whenever she'd refuse, it would make very bad discolored marks on her body.

"I'd just lay there in bed and cry myself to sleep at night," she told me. "Oh, it was so awful. I always felt so vulnerable and violated by this thing. It was so horrifying having this happening to me. Damn thing, it was just doing whatever it wanted to me. And it always felt like it was in there, you know, somewhere deep inside of me, just gripping and grabbing onto me deep inside. Sometimes it felt like it was wrapping itself tightly around me. Sometime when I'd be in school, I'd feel it sliding in and out of my vaginal area. I could just be sitting there at my desk doing my work and all of a sudden, I'd feel it moving around in the area of my uterus, and then, I'd feel it moving around all over my entire body.

"And then it would vanish."

"Did any of the other kids in your classroom ever notice any of these things that were happening to you?" I asked her.

"Not until it started happening to them," she told me. "That's when, I guess, they all thought it was me who was making it happen."

She talked about how when trying to get her unbelieving parents to believe in her terrifying stories and frightening experiences, they'd always end up disciplining her. Each plea for their help seemed to have always fallen on deaf ears. They would instead do just like the town folks, continue accusing Margaret of being involved in certain immoral activities in order for her to have such awful discolored marks on her body.

"And after not being able to get their attention, you know, to believe in you, what did you do after that?" I asked her.

"Well, without any success with my folks for their help, I guess you can say that I just gave in and accepted this unwanted thing that was busy at work inside of me, doing whatever it wanted to do. It was just busy trying its best to destroy my life."

"How did it feel, Margaret? Wasn't it painful?"

"Its aggression was so intense, Mr. Murdock. This monstrous thing was busy destroying me."

I observed the expression on her pale face on which, through the reflection of the dense light, I could barely see the deep wrinkles. The dense light revealed the rough surface having deep, long furrows, so irregular to where it became somewhat difficult to not stare in complete dismay from the thought of the troubled life she endured.

"And what about your sister? I'm talking about Wanda. Being that you were the one your parents held responsible for her death, I'm not only inquiring your opinion, but Margaret, the information in the report is that you were the only witness. I mean, is it true? And if so, would you care to shed some light on this particular subject?"

Margaret again began looking downward, and then on both sides of her chair as if searching for something. She began describing to me how she had become horrified while witnessing the brutal, violent slaying and horrendous torment of her sister.

"Let's see," she began to describe, "it was an unusually warm evening, which I have to say was somewhat uncommon for the Stonyford area. I mean, we'd get our share of the weather when we wanted it, but for some weird reason, was so much different than we'd had throughout the season. There was a strange feeling of humidity and moisture in the air that evening, and it felt just like we were going to get a heavy pour down of some hard, showering rain, but it didn't happen.

"Not even a darn sprinkle.

"I was just busy trying my best to hurry up and finish what work I had left to do in our family garden. I remember the sun had just begun to fade away from sight, disappearing way out there, far behind one of those huge, rugged hills, and some of the nearby towering mountaintops and steep, curved, shady slopes that surrounded the entire area. But there was still enough light that seem to encircle Stonyford, and this was even after the sun had just about completely vanished from sight. I could still see what I was doing.

"Are you listening, young man?" she asked me, smiling.

"Yes, ma'am," I answered, "I'm listening to everything you're talking about."

"Well, this old lady is just checkin' on ya. Don't want you to miss anything. So, where was I? Oh, yeah, you see, thin lines of narrow rays from the northern light could be seen as they reflected visible beams of bright, richly colorful light across the gray, dusky sky.

"I could feel the summer warmth as the soft, abnormally hot current of breezy air floated very gently, yet swiftly, throughout the region. In the distance, birds sailed smoothly through the air as if there wasn't any need for wing motion during their flight. You could also hear in the quiet distance of pure tranquility the gentle sounds of tree branches, squeaking and crackling sharply, as woodpeckers clawed the trees during their drilling through all the many thick layers of bark.

"After checking the house, that was when I thought about the cornfield which is where I remember watching our father spend countless hours out there in the fields, plowing and planting crops."

Margaret began describing her family's estate and talked about how it was purchased years and years ago, and how it must have sat on roughly fifteen-plus acres. She talked about how it was passed down from generation to generation, with her parents being its present owners.

"The population in Stonyford, at the time when I was so much younger, I'd say, something like eighty people at best. And this was including those residing at the nearby Forestry Station. Oh, and let me dare not forget to mention the fact that just about everybody who lived in that goddamn town were all very well acquainted with each other, and I do mean acquainted so well together with each other to where, some of them folks had to be at times very harshly reprimanded in a serious effort to try to discourage the social mixing of family members becoming involved in acts of incestuous relationships.

"After searching the field, I then decided to check the barn, which sat diagonal from the house. I remember how those huge doors just stood there, rusted as if unpainted, and sometimes swinging by themselves from the wind, as the air current passed through to the other side. A reddish, oxidized color formed a grimy coating on the weird-looking hinges that caused them to squeak loudly as the hot summer warmth pressed its way through the barn.

"As soon as I entered that barn, that's when I started calling out to Wanda. I had forgot all about the terrible fight that had taken place between us earlier that evening. I thought that maybe I could somehow trust Wanda enough to where, you know, we could try talking to each other about whatever it was that was causing us to always have such heated conflicts between us.

"I had tried so many times to talk to her and explain to her the many changes I had been going through, while also trying to deal with whatever it was that I was presently experiencing.

"But it was as usual whenever I tried to trust her. Her reactions just never seemed to change no matter what. She'd laugh and accuse me of being a disgrace to the family. That's why for quite a number of years I just kept quiet about my past. I had tried for so long, you know, to convince my parents to believe me, but my attempts were always to no avail. And all I was left to think about was the fact that something was terribly wrong in my young life, and that whatever it was, it had once again started its occurrences, except this time, it was with a violating vengeance as if for some type of a retaliation."

She began talking about how it would cause her to act in a manner that she had never before behaved and that whenever she would attempt to reject it, or even try to fight its aggression, it would cause terrible throbbing and agonizing pain deep inside of her with such intensity to where an astonishing amount of discoloration would form on certain areas of her skin and bruises would immediately develop.

Bruises that were inflicted by this unwanted, monstrous thing residing inside of her.

"My parents just outright ignored me. And whatever it was that was inside of me, it just continued to torture me in its most hidden, obscured manner.

"But it was Wanda who I could sense from her reactions toward me, that I just knew despised me in the worst way. She would at times intentionally do her best to instigate an already very complicated situation by trying to influence our parents to continue neglecting me. They'd always agree with whatever Wanda insinuated."

"And this is when everything began to happen to Wanda?" I asked her.

"Uh huh," she agreed. " 'Cause, it just happened to be on this particular evening while searching the barn that I begin to think about the conflicts between us. I found myself for some strange reason thinking about how Wanda had violently, and for unknown reasons, dragged me around in our bedroom by my hair like I was a rag doll. She was just outright physically abusing me in a manner that she had never before done. During all of this abusiveness done to me, she used very harsh insulting words and language toward me that was so profane to where the hurt inside of me just felt like it wasn't ever going to go away.

"Everything was happening so fast. Her abusiveness had become extremely violent. I couldn't understand how Wanda's attitude toward me could have become so violently furious with such rage."

As I sat there carefully listening to her every word, I couldn't help but begin to feel emotionally tense from the sad, unpleasant thought of what Margaret must have had to endure throughout her childhood.

I thought about her family, but I guess you can sense that it was mainly her parents. I thought about how they just outright refused to do anything to assist in comforting her, mainly during those moments in life when most parents wouldn't waste any time walking across burning, blistering rocks in their effort to aid their child.

Times when they had themselves witnessed the violent acts and behavior of abusiveness bestowed upon her, for reasons unknown, they never made any attempt to do anything to restrain Wanda or did anything to discipline her.

On this particular evening it seemed that the arguments and hostility and antagonizing conflicts and dispute between them had escalated, and become irritably heated.

The course of the morning had begun perfectly normal; well, until Margaret was abruptly interrupted during breakfast. Everything had been perfectly prepared, and the first meal of the day was ready to be served when for reasons unknown, Wanda unexpectedly pulled Margaret backward by grabbing onto her hair, causing her to lose her balance and fall onto the hard wooden floor. Their mother, Sarah, who at the time was standing in front of the stove, quickly glanced in the direction of the commotion, while at the same time, most likely forgetting about the location of each cooking utensil when reaching for the frying pan, instead, ended up placing her fingers into the hot, boiling grease that was bubbling in the skillet.

"Oh! My! God!" she screamed out in a painful fury of rage, directing her attention at Margaret. "Now look what you made me do to myself. I'm really starting to hate you, Margaret!"

Unaware of what had happened, and after trying her best to regain control of herself, Margaret was about to raise herself upward from the floor, when all of a sudden she was again struck by Wanda. This time it was across the face, sending her once again slamming forcefully down onto the hard floor.

"I just kept struggling to try and gain control of myself," she explained. "But you know, it really wasn't until when Wanda had moved to the opposite side of the kitchen table, that I began to notice our mother holding one of her hands under the water faucet. I could plainly see from the expression on her face that she was in a great deal of pain. So it was at this point that I decided to move even closer to see just what it was that had happened. When I moved close to Mother, I then noticed the area of her hand and fingers where the hot grease had splattered all over 'em. I could even see the blisters forming."

While Margaret stood trembling from the result of Wanda's abusiveness, she was battling the thought of what had happened as she nervously struggled to continue standing upright.

Moving even closer, and very slowly, toward her mother, while uttering in a low whisper, "Mother, Mother, are you all right?"

Sarah immediately rejected her, and angrily pushed her away, which prompted Wanda to once again shove Margaret around.

Margaret talked about how, during the conflict, she felt something strangely familiar with strong similarities interacting between them.

"Whatever it was that had happened," she began telling me, "it had those same familiarities just like the monstrous demon I can remember constantly complaining about when no one seemed to care about believing in me. I remember feeling this very powerful dramatic force in the walls of my stomach that seemed to violently explode, and suddenly they, I guess you can say, they burst very fast outward, causing Wanda to become airborne, and forcefully hurling her across the kitchen as if she were being slung from a slingshot. That's when my mother immediately rushed to her aid, while at the same time, she was yelling and screaming at me, outright disregarding all the abusiveness I had just suffered."

While listening to her describe what had happened, I couldn't help but think about the captivating image and haunting figure she had described as the monster living inside her. But it was during the hurling of her sister that she recalled the ghostlike figure which had emerged from within her and thrust directly in the direction where Wanda now lay motionless on the floor.

As Margaret continued to express her mild-mannered behavior and reluctancy, and also her opposition concerning her childhood life in the town of Stonyford, she finally began describing how, when searching the barn for Wanda, she called out her name repeatedly, without ever any response.

"Well, after there wasn't any response, I'd just begun thinking that maybe she wasn't in there and thought maybe she was elsewhere. Though, I knew for sure that I hadn't seen her out there in the pasture because I had just been out there picking vegetables. And I also knew she wasn't in the house because I'd not long ago left from there, too. Therefore, it wasn't until I was just about ready to leave the barn and look somewhere else that all of a sudden, I began to hear some of the most awful, confusing sounds I ever heard coming from behind me. I mean, these were some eerie, you know, *creepy* noises that sounded uncanny and scary."

"And what did you do?" I asked her.

"That was when I just froze in my tracks," she said, as if trying to tell me to be quiet. It was as if she were presently there, in this moment in time today. "I suddenly stopped, and then, I slowly turned around, hoping I could see just where all of those noises were coming from."

"And could you figure it out?" I asked.

"Oh, yes," she said. "I could hear them coming from the direction of one of the horse stables. And when I really think about it, I can remember those noises sounding like someone was sick or something. I mean, it was sounding like whoever it was, or whatever it was, they'd begun throwing up or something. And I remember just standing there very still and quiet. But I kept hearing those awful sounds."

"Were they loud?" I asked her. "Or low?"

"They were low, persistent regurgitation sounds. But what was really strange was that the sound kept changing from a low regurgitation sound to a sound like someone was moaning. And then, it was as if someone had begun crying. That's because of the way it was sounding."

Margaret began describing how she began moving in a slow motion in the direction of the stable where she heard the noises coming from. She again called out to Wanda in a low voice, and again it was without any response.

"I again called out to her, but I didn't say it too loud. But she didn't answer me. And that's when I remember saying something like, 'is anyone in there?' Meaning in the horse stable."

"How many stables were there? In the barn?"

"Well, at that time, I think there was around six."

"What, three on each side? Or six all on one side?"

"Uh, they...they were all on that one side of the barn."

"And nothing on the other side?"

"Nothing except the side door that we used whenever the main ones were being used to move junk around the place sometimes."

"So it was the first stable that you were hearing all the noises coming from?"

"Oh, no," she exclaimed. "I believe it was coming from inside the, I believe, the fourth one."

"The fourth one?"

"Uh huh, 'cause I remember thinking the noises were coming from the first one, or the second one. But it ended up being the fourth."

"Okay, then. And what happened next?"

"Well, as I was saying. After asking if or not anyone were there, and still not getting an answer, that's when I just decided to start moving slowly in the direction where I had heard those noises coming from. I was really thinking that maybe she was just playing some kind of game with me, because she just knew that I was gonna ask her if she'd help me pick all of those different kinds of vegetables from the garden. Having to pick vegetables always have been something she just really hated doing.

"But when really thinking about it, I honestly do believe that she came to dread doing anything that consisted of her having to do anything that involved being around me."

Margaret again started describing how she had moved very slowly, and even closer to one side of the stable, then decided to sneak around to the opposite side to try to prevent Wanda any means of escaping.

"Oh, heavens, yes," she said. "I was really trying my best to move as slow as I possibly could. I moved very slowly so that whoever it was that was in there couldn't hear me. And then, after I'd gotten so far, I began to raise myself upward so that I could get a much better view of just what it was that was going on, plus, if it were really Wanda, then I wanted to surprise her and make sure she couldn't get away. But that was when to my surprise, I noticed this little tiny peephole in one of the layers of wood that surrounded the stable. So, I very carefully started gliding myself alongside the sides of the stable. With only a few minor adjustments which I had to use to reach the location of the hole, I remember having to try and get a much firmer grip on the thick layers of wood paneling that enclosed nearly the entire stall.

"And after finally reaching that darn hole, I began peering through it. I stared, doing everything I could to look through it so that I could see what it was that was happening in there."

"And what was happening?" I asked her. "Could you see anything?"

"Oh, yes indeed," she told me, smiling. "I could make out a partial view of what was happening in that darn thing."

Margaret began to once again describe how she could still hear the sounds of moaning and regurgitation as she again began to shift her position in an effort to get a better view.

"Well, as I found myself peering intently into this really tiny hole, that was when to my surprise, I could plainly see that it was really Wanda that all the time I was hearing making those strange noises."

"You could actually see her?" I asked.

"Oh, yeah," she exclaimed. "And I could see one side of her face."

"What was she doing?"

"Well, from what I could see, the expression on her face seemed to reveal her as though as she were in a lot of pain. She was, you know, acting like she was desperately gaspin' for air. It was like she was impulsively breathing in and out and very quickly inhaling with her mouth wide open."

"And what were your reactions when seeing this? I mean, how did it make you feel, seeing this?"

"I just kept trying to adjust my position so that I could get a better view of what was happening. I just kept pulling myself upward very slowly in an effort to look over the top layers of wood."

"I know you were moving slowly, but were you also in a hurry?"

"Well, by then, I guess you can say that my eager curiosity had really led me to start believing that maybe it was Wanda, instead of the town's people thinking it was me, who was really involved in all that immorality crap!"

"So what happened after you made it to the top of the stable?"

"Well, finally! And I do tell you, after I finally did reach the top layer, I tell you, I was quite flabbergasted from the amazing sight that was also very troubling after finally seeing what was happening. And I do tell you, that no-good-for-nothing, and please do excuse my language, but that no good, rotten heifer was, well, I tell you no lie, she's the one who was acting in the most degrading manner instead of everyone thinking it were me."

"I mean, what was happening?" I asked, eager to know.

"From what I was seeing with my very own eyes, that no-good-for-nothing BITCH, she's the one who was just outright degrading to our family. I mean, she was just laying there expressing her erratic behavior. But I have to admit that her behavior had me then wondering if maybe she too was herself presently experiencing that same unwanted monstrous thing invading her body in the same manner that it invaded mine.

"Watching what was happening to my sister made me think about the many times I had complained to my parents, and even to Wanda.

"But it was always to no avail."

As I watched Margaret as though she were in so much bewilderment, she had again found herself thinking about the many times Wanda had done just about everything she could in her onward effort to influence their parents to disbelieve in her.

"And then what happened?" I again asked.

"It felt like I had been watching her for hours, but it was just only seconds into minutes. I was just hanging there, gripping tightly onto those planks of wood, staring and watching how this monstrous thing was by now brutally destroying her body from the inside out, with having some of the most vicious intentions, continuing its violent destruction over Wanda's now partially mutilated body.

"I remember that while during the beginning of the dismemberment, that was when I found myself extremely horrified when Wanda's body begin to very violently vibrate.

"It began to vibrate as though it were being shaken by a very powerful mixing machine. I mean the force was so powerful to where the entire barn began to shake and everything began vibrating and rattling. Even my teeth were chattering. It felt just like one of those huge, powerful locomotives, you know, like a huge long freight train was about to come speeding right through the barn. It was sounding just like the darn thing was about to come crashing through that barn at full speed. I tell you, I could hear wood crackling and snapping all around me."

"And how long did you remain there? You know, listening to all those noises that sounded like a freight train?" I asked her.

"Well, after I finally built up the nerves to, you know, finally look around that place, that's when I could see all the dust and stuff that was still falling from the ceiling. It was like everything was coming down all over the place. And the upper portion of the barn looked as if it were still moving, but now descending downward toward me. But that's the strange part about the entire ordeal, it never did come down. But I could hear all those nails that, I guess, fastened the barn together, loudly squeakin' and makin' shivering, scratchy sounds, popping and shooting in every direction all across the ground. They were everywhere. All over the place.

"Certain sections of the stables had by now begun to shake so hard and fast to where it wasn't any longer possible for me to continue to grip onto the wooden planks. I mean, I was by now just almost hanging there. But I also found it somewhat impossible for me to move."

"And why was that?" I asked stupidly. "I mean, it's really dumb of me to be asking such a question, I know, though."

"I guess you could say that I'd become afraid of just about everything around me. I was so frightened to where I really didn't quite know what to do."

Everything that was happening around her, she began describing how she was still able to see slight views of Wanda as the wooden boards would every so often protrude in an upward motion, and then shoot straight upward, very fast into the air in the direction of the ceiling, disappearing.

"Oh, I tell you, those things would disappear just as soon as they hit the ceiling. I really think they were all somehow just going through the top of that barn. You know, the roof. Because I didn't ever hear them come down and land anywhere. But with all the noises and turbulent commotion going on, it was really hard for me to pay that much attention to the sound of any one thing."

"And what was, you know, at that time, what was happening with Wanda?"

"Well, by that time, when I did look in her direction, her body, or what was left of her body, it for some very strange reasons that I just couldn't quite understand, had begun to thrust upward while still heavily vibrating on the ground. Each upward force would then slam her back onto the ground. Each impact onto the ground would send a considerable amount of dust and debris and ruins spiraling upward and into the air. And this was while her limp body continued to thrust without showing any signs of life."

As I sat there close to Margaret carefully listening to how she described the swelling in Wanda's lifeless body, I thought how I couldn't have found myself in such a situation. I couldn't imagine it even if I'd had to. I couldn't. But it was very important that I listened to her describe the events that had taken place in such a small community. Events which from my understanding had caused an entire town to submit to something that's still to this day…unknown.

"It was awful!" Margaret continued describing the death of Wanda. "As I hung there, gripping onto those weakening layers of wood that enclosed the stables, I could see her body had somehow swelled in such a horrifying way. I mean, it was so terrible. And then, all of a sudden, I begin to once again hear those moaning sounds. They were coming from her. Except, I guess that you can say that, this time, the sounds had become, become more of a sound like muttering or something. But you could tell they were from intense pain because I could hear her moaning and breathing in a gasping manner. Each thrust onto the ground, I could also hear the air inside of her being forced out. She would thrust very fast upward, then downward, onto the ground while still heavily vibrating.

"I found myself wondering if or not life was really ever meant for us to live, and if so, then how is it that such an awful tragedy could ever be taking place?

"That was also when I found myself wondering if maybe the entire ordeal was just another horrible nightmare, and that I would soon find myself awakening from this dream.

"But that never happened. And I wasn't asleep.

"I was really there, gripping onto that stable, staring intently at what was happening to Wanda. I again found myself thinking about the many times, sooo many times, that I tried my best to convince my unbelieving parents to just believe in me and what was happening to me. I just wanted them to for once believe in what I was trying my best to tell them about what was happening to me. I remember how I use to just lay there in bed and cry myself to sleep after all their rejections and disbeliefs in me. I can also remember all of those times when I would come to them crying and hurt and very frightened. I was sooo full of fear. I just couldn't understand, you know, all the awful things that were happening to me.

"And then, there were finally times that I can remember, when they'd finally sit down and start acting like they were ready to finally listen to what I had to tell them. And they'd also question me. But whenever I'd even act like I was about to mention anything about being controlled by something, and that I couldn't understand what it was, that was always when all hell would break loose in that house. I could see the pieces of my story just collapsing all around me. That's why when watching what was happening to Wanda, it made me think about all the things that happened to me.

"I thought about the many times when I was just outright rejected by my parents. I thought about how they and everybody else would accuse me of lying by saying things like, I was only trying to hide my immorality, and that they'd wished I were never born.

"And I can also remember all the many times that I received those harsh punishments, punishments that didn't always come from my parents, but were aimed at me mainly from Wanda. But they'd sometime make it a point to tell me that I was being punished because I couldn't explain to them how I had gotten all of those ugly, awful looking marks that were on certain areas of my body."

Margaret talked about how it was because of her being rejected, that that was when she decided to just accept the vicious aggressiveness of whatever it was that was happening to her that was causing the unpleasant discoloration on a large portion of her body.

"Well, since there wasn't anyone to believe in me, I just went ahead and accepted it into my life. I mean, it was like, I really didn't care any longer about what it did to me. I just accepted it. So, I guess you can say that that darn thing began to have its way with me. I just didn't care what it did or what it was about to do. I just didn't care anymore.

"But to my surprise, whatever it was, I found out that it really wasn't out to hurt me or anything.

"Now that was really surprising because, here I was giving in to whatever it was that it was doing to me, and the darn thing didn't even kill me as I were hoping it would do. I mean, I'd really expected it to."

While still witnessing the very brutal torment of her sister, she once again starting talking about how it was mainly because of Wanda that she was neglected throughout her childhood life.

"As I held on tight, clinging to that stable and watching Wanda as she continued going through whatever it was that she was going through, I all of a sudden heard those very sharp, loud, eerie, popping sounds that really caught my attention. That was also when I noticed the nipples on Wanda's breast suddenly exploding, tearing and ripping through her clothing and making a loud sputtering sound that sounded like something in the form of firecrackers, shooting each of 'em in a fast upward motion, high into the air, and leaving a thick red trail of blood squirting all over the place in behind them."

"Man, Margaret," I quickly asked in an unbelieving tone. "I mean, are you serious? I mean, come on now, you can't really be serious about this, are you?"

"And I tell you no lie, Mr. Murdock," she again repeated. "They'd just shot straight upward into the air, and across the passageway through the barn. It was as if they'd somehow been shot from one of those little revolvers that I remember seeing some of the town's folks carrying around on their hips. I just seen 'em shoot upward, spraying a thick trail of a dark reddish liquid mist in behind 'em though the air. But do you wanna know just what was really strange about the whole thing? They'd sounded just like they had been shot from one of my Papa's pistols. That's right. The sound was just like one of those darn guns that I can remember many times seeing him carrying around with him that he kept in one of his pockets.

"When I looked up at all that red stuff that was, you know, just floating everywhere in the air, it looked like all I could see was that just about everything up there on the ceiling had just about turned completely red. Just about everything it touched, everything was red. And even the mist all everywhere throughout the air, it too was all red. It was as if all of that stuff had been sprayed all over that place.

"It was all over the ceiling, everywhere."

"While all of this was going on," I asked her. "What were you doing?"

"Well, this is when, I guess you can say that, this is when I found myself identifying with what was happening to her. I mean, Wanda's outburst and violent expression of severe pain that she was suffering from while being tormented, well, it was reminding me of so much that I too had experienced during my ordeal. And as I continued to watch what was happening to her, I also watched her very brutal dismemberment."

"Dismemberment?" I questioned. "Like what?"

"Well, by this time, I could again hear those moaning sounds that were followed by this somewhat loud, eerie outcry, as it was exhaling the final eruption of Wanda's once humanity, at which time, and being that I was already very much horrified, I guess this must have been when after seeing the rest of her body exploding into pieces all over the place, I must have just started screaming out really loud from the thought of what was happening because, all that I can seem to remember is waking up in the hospital."

"Just what did you see?" I asked her. "Or can you even remember anything?"

"Look, Mr. Murdock," she started trying to explain while shrugging her shoulders. "It's just like I was already telling you, all that I can remember seeing is her body exploding into pieces. Everything just popped off and blew up, exploding all over the place. It was like when she finally went ahead and expelled what bit of air that was left inside of her, I could all of a sudden hear that something was apparently obstructing her airway, and that was when I heard that very sharp sound coming from her."

"But, what was it that you saw happening to her?" I again just had to ask. "What was happening to her, Margaret? If I may ask?"

Margaret by this time just crossed her arms in an authoritative manner to command my respect.

"Well, let me put it this way," I calmly suggested. "As you know, I'm just trying my best to get what information I can in which to put everything into perspective—with respect. So please, Margaret, please forgive me if at times it might seem as though I'm pushing a little too hard for this information. All I'm trying to do is get to the bottom of things, you know, the things that took place in Stonyford that cause the submission. So, please, Margaret, will you please try understanding where I'm coming from?"

"Well, you know I don't mind helping you, Murdock," she began telling me. "But you too have to understand that I just can't be going as fast as you would like me to. What I'm trying my best to do is try remembering everything I can about that town. I mean, to be completely truthful, I really don't wanna remember a darn thing about none of it, but for your information to be trying to put everything into perspective as you say, well then, I am ready and willing to help and assist you as much as I possibly can. But you have to try and understand that I just don't move as fast as you would want me to."

"Now we're getting somewhere," I thought to myself. "Thank you so very much, Margaret," I told her respectfully. "I really do appreciate your help, and that's from the heart."

"Well, now maybe I can go back to try and start remembering things."

"And I do believe you will," I suggested softly. "I most certainly do believe you will."

"Okay, now just where was I?" said Margaret, while attempting to share her story about Wanda. "Help me remember."

"Uh, you were talking about what was happening to Wanda," I told her, hoping it would be enough to refresh her memory. "You know, the part about…her body exploding into pieces, all over the place."

"Oooh yes," she said, while once again staring directly at me. "Really strange how you seem to remember that part. But anyway, and from what I'm able to remember, everything just all of a sudden started tearing apart. I saw a leg go one way, and then, an arm go another. And her body just, you know, blew up just like an explosion. I mean, her stomach, well, it just, I guess you can say, just popped wide open, and everything, all of her organs and everything, like all of her arteries, intestines, gobs of blood, and also her heart, it all came bursting out in an explosion. It was going everywhere, all over that barn. Nothing was left from what I could see while still gripping onto that stable. Nothing was left."

"Nothing?" I quickly asked not wanting to cause her to stop talking.

"Nothing!" she said in a doubtful voice. "And if there was anything, it couldn't have been but only some skin stuck to the ground, and I do remember hearing one of those doctors at the Willows Hospital saying something to that nature."

"So Wanda had become completely dismembered?" I questioned.

"After her stomach blew open, that was the last thing I saw before I started screaming. Everything just, I guess, turned red. That's when I woke up in the hospital wondering just what I was doing there, you know, under that sheet, and in a bed that I knew wasn't mine. I mean, I could hear some people talking on the other side of the door. That's when I realized that I was in a strange room that wasn't my bedroom."

There was a sudden silence in Margaret's voice while she was describing to me the things she'd seen happening to Wanda, and how she found herself awakening in the Willows Hospital. A silence that I have to say and honestly admit startled me with such an alarming impact, as this seemingly very fragile woman, quickly shivered, nodded, slightly bent forward and to one side, and then, she very instinctively, started moving again to the opposite side of her chair, while at the same time, she begin to reach for something down underneath the chair that was, I guess, on the floor. But it was her body motion that really seemed to startle me. It was in a rather sluggish manner for a woman so fragile.

With her head bent slightly downward as if she were thinking about what it was she was searching for, it was then that I began to notice the book, or something in the form of a photo album that I could visibly see with photos hanging out each side lying close to her feet.

This is also when I noticed how her eyes had become in a rather fixed position, wide open, and as if she were once again staring directly at me, except this time, without blinking.

I began thinking that maybe there was something that she wanted me to see. Something she knew could possibly be of some importance to me. And also something that she knew would definitely be of value to me for the publication of this story.

Using both of her hands, she finally reached the book and pulled it out from underneath the chair. She then stretched out her frail arms toward me in an effort for me to view the book and its contents inside that seemed to show photos of her during past moments when she had attended, from what I could see, was her graduation commencement ceremonies at various universities across the nation.

There were also photos of her during happier moments with her family.

After I'd politely accepted the book and had evaluated its contents, it was then that I suddenly found myself experiencing something of a rather motionless feeling throughout my entire body. It was as if I were somehow able to experience everything that she had herself experienced during her ordeal in Stonyford. It was then that I had also found myself with tears beginning to form and build up in my eyes from the mere thought of the agony this lady, an elderly woman, a sweet gentle human being, and a lady who could have possibly been my own mother, or maybe even my grandmother, but now, a very sweet, gentle, elderly woman, so pleasingly delicate and fragile, and yet, with so much to share, had gone through so much throughout her life.

This elderly woman in my presence that I could undoubtedly sense had gone through so much, had endured tragedy that I'm more than sure most of us as living human beings could have never endured such pain, and lasted long enough to talk about it as Margaret.

I couldn't help but to just sit there and stare at her while myself in deep thoughts, thinking while realizing the life she herself had become subjected to.

I found myself in deep thoughts about how lonely a life she must have had to live being by herself, all alone.

Listening to her describe certain very agonizing events in her past, and how there were so many moments when she found herself feeling as though unable to move forward, I once again began thinking that if only I could somehow turn back the hands of time, how I wouldn't waste any time in my effort to try giving back to her a complete, full rich life with all of its happiness and amenities just so that she could be able to relive her life all over again.

As I sat there staring at her in much amazement, I found it somewhat complicated for me to actually understand just how she herself could just sit there, in her chair, smiling at me, as if nothing had ever happened to her.

Feeling the gentleness of her touch as she very gently patted my hands while handing me the photo album, and speaking to me in a soft, low tone, her touch seemed to send an elaborate amount of shockwaves floating throughout my entire body with such forceful intensity to where I immediately found myself speechless, and my throat, it too immediately shifted from a normal breathing pattern to a now strange gasping sound while trying to talk.

It was at this moment while in deep thoughts about her and the awful life she lived in Stonyford that the noticeable semidarkness in the room had now somehow begun to reveal so much of Margaret. As I continued staring and trying my best to observe her, there began to reveal an image of something in the form of a ghostlike figure that seemed to emerge upward from behind her chair. It then quickly faded away into the denseness of the room.

As I slightly shifted my eyes back toward Margaret, realizing my attention had shifted elsewhere, I then found myself once again staring directly into her eyes as if I were in a deep trance of hypnosis. It was then that all of a sudden, the ghostlike figure once again appeared, but this time, it came up from in behind Margaret as if she were somehow seated in its lap. What was even more bothering to me at this time was the fact that I could visibly see that it was just, I guess I can say, it was seemingly floating. It was just hovering there in behind Margaret as if suspended in the air, and staring directly at me within an intensifying and intimidating grip, as if it were somehow talking to me in my conscious mind. It was deliberately subjecting me to its existence.

As this was taking place, I began to realize how dense the atmosphere in the room was beginning to change and become extremely chilling. As I slyly began shifting my eyes in an effort to see how just about everything in the room had begun to change its appearance, I could then see a slight formation of frost beginning to form and build up on the walls and around the window ledges. I began to notice that the figure had then, after what felt like an eternity, but only a few seconds, again quickly vanished, disappearing from my sight, only to once again fade away in behind Margaret as though it were never there.

I found myself in deep thought wondering just how this could be, whereas, just within a few seconds, it had been so warm, but then, it had become so blistering cold, dry, dense, and now, it had once again become relatively normal again.

This is when, I guess you could say, I found myself really tripping. I mean, it was like I found myself wondering whether or not I was only hallucinating about everything I had seen taking place. What I'm saying is that, I began thinking about everything, and how it seemed like just about everything in this room had become so dramatic during those few seconds which to me had felt like a lifetime experience. This is also when I found myself thinking about the comfort I felt that was traveling throughout my body from the gentleness of her touch as she continued to gently caress my hand. I thought about how I had found myself more than sure that she actually knew exactly what I was experiencing as she kept her eyes wide open and staring directly into mine.

She then began speaking to me in a soft, low tone as if I were a child, the child that I'd begun to become from the thought of not being able to say anything during my seeming immobilization.

As she spoke, I began to realize that it was through her that she'd enabled me an opportunity to see for myself the figure and image of whatever it was that an entire community of people had claimed was responsible for the submission.

She had enabled me to see, with my very own eyes, that which had caused an entire town of people to scramble for their lives from fear of the unknown.

She had allowed me an important opportunity to see and experience this one special moment without the fear of myself becoming a victim.

And she was rightfully correct, my inner fears seemed to have somehow subsided and had become less agitated and intense, completely vanished, and had now turned into a form of comforting consolation and freedom.

She had given me the strength I needed to endure such an experience from deep within her inner soul and now into me. She knew that her strength would somehow enable me an opportunity to venture into the mysteriousness of the submission.

The things I wanted to know most about her had now become an essential part of my existence.

I found myself not just taking notes, but I could sense that I was now about to start my long journey into the beginning of Margaret's life. It was at this point while during our conversation that I remembered her mentioning something about a person that I would end up meeting. She named this person by using her very own name, but before she could even tell me, I'd already sensed from her that it was time for me to leave her and start this long journey for the publication of this story. She named some of the people she felt were very important for me to remember by saying they were themselves already awaiting me in Stonyford. She also mentioned the possibility that I would most likely end up becoming the cell-mate of a person she named by calling him Ethan.

At this point she knew that her statement had me very curious. I then began to ask her just what she meant. "Excuse me, Margaret, but what are you saying? That I'm going to meet this Ethan person as a visitor in the prison where he's presently incarcerated? Or is it that you're telling me that I am going to meet him as in being myself a prisoner?"

At first, she just sat there, smiling at me, and then she very calmly shrugged her shoulders, telling me to worry not. "You have so much work yet ahead of you to do, Mr. Murdock. Lots of work. Kansas will undoubtedly end up being your final destination."

She knew that I was already still very puzzled by her first statement, which was about the way that I was suppose to meet Ethan. And now here it is, she was making another statement that really bothered me. But now that I really think about this entire situation, I guess I really won't know much of anything, well not until I make it to the town of Stonyford. But I do remember her last words were that she too would be there waiting on me, and that she wanted me to know and to always remember how sorry she is for what I was about to become subject to. "I'm so very sorry about your future, and I'm also sorry and regret the fact that I am unable to do anything in which to change your course." She again knew that her statement had a profound effect on me.

As I stood up, I looked around to try and get a much better view of the room while gazing and thinking she hadn't in any way noticed me.

But to my surprise, she did!

While deeply gazing, I could visibly see that the walls reflected a dingy color as if there were stains everywhere. The stains appeared to have come from such a long period from the lack of maintenance and proper upkeep. There were pictures hanging everywhere and also more pictures of her family members and friends. I could even see pictures of deceased presidents hanging in a rather careless, awkward fashion. And there were also pictures of human rights activists and clergymen, as well as civil rights leaders hanging on the wall as if she knew them personally.

I also noticed a few spiritual pictures that reminded me so much of a picture that I'd seen not only at my parents' home but this particular drawing or document was in just about every home I visited throughout my life. It shows Jesus kneeling beside a rock with the sky reflecting and emitting a colorful ray of light about him. Another showed him knocking on a door.

The dimness in the room also seemed to reduce the light that was reflecting from the lamp that stood on an old ancient antique lamp stand which was probably made from some type of brass. The shade that covered the upper portion of the stand reflected a somewhat gloomy tan, with a yellowish ray emitting a dusty orange color. The shade itself was also a dingy, yellowish color with a facial trimming of an ancient fantastical dragon or dragons, with huge wings and a few fire-spraying monsters that were spraying fire in just about every direction during flight.

After a few turns, at which time I found myself headed west on Kellogg, which is better known as I-54, I then found myself glancing into my rearview mirror as though I were for reasons unknown expecting to see something, or possibly someone.

After listening to Margaret, I reminded myself to remember the statement she made when telling me that she would meet me there in Stonyford. I guess maybe it was her that I was expecting to see in my rearview mirror. I thought perhaps she knew just what I was thinking. I thought how the moment I had left her, the door closed, instantly, behind me as if it were she herself standing there to close it. But I knew it wasn't her.

As I continued on Interstate 54, I still at times found myself cautiously peering curiously into my rearview mirror. I couldn't help but to find myself somewhat restless from thinking about what I had not too long ago experienced, as I watched Wichita begin to fade away into the darkening of the nightfall sky in the distance behind me.

Chapter Three

SPEEDING THROUGH THE SMALL-TOWN COMMUNITY of Stonyford with every emergency signal in full operation, Sheriff John Blake was about to come into full view of human nature's most dreaded subject: The death of a child by mutilation.

The sheriff, who was better known throughout the community as simply Blake, had been a resident of this small town for quite a few years. After receiving his honorable discharge from the military, and upon the completion of his active duty and tour in Vietnam, he'd decided to move his family from the mean, congested streets of Los Angeles and relocate to the quiet, calm and restful northern part of the state of California where he would end up as a member of the local law enforcement department.

It was on this particular evening that Sheriff Blake happened to be one of the few officers on duty when the call came over the radio requesting that all available emergency personnel were to respond to the Johnsons' residence immediately. Although it should have been his day off, sitting around his house doing nothing was something he wasn't about to allow to overtake him. He enjoyed being active, plus, the position he held was very important to him.

After responding to the dispatcher and giving her his location, he then slammed his patrol car into drive as quickly as he could, and pressed down on the gas pedal as hard as he could in his effort to increase his acceleration, and then sped at a high rate of speed to the county road, feeling the strength and force of his actions.

Thinking about the position he held in the department, a swell of pride came over him. The thought of being involved in law enforcement, as he reminisced, was a dream come true from childhood. He'd always dreamed about one day becoming a policeman or possibly working with the fire department.

He found himself with feelings of an unrestrained high.

Plentiful and abundant.

Wondering just what the problem could be for there to be an urgent emergency demand for all available emergency personnel employees to respond, and being that the dispatcher had herself sounded as if it were she who was in some type of distress, the thought was puzzling to the sheriff.

As he approached the road which led from the Snow Mountain region of this area, he was about to turn on his siren when he suddenly noticed a member of the local forestry station trying to wave him down. He too had heard the call when it came over the radio requesting all emergency personnel to the Johnsons' residence.

"Come on, dammit," Blake yelled. "Hurry up and get in. It seem like we got something serious going on over there at dat there Johnsons' place."

"Yeah, I know," said the ranger. "That's why I flagged you down."

"You heard it too?" Blake asked him.

"Uh huh," the ranger nodded. "And after hearing you responding to the dispatcher acknowledging that you would be assisting and also after hearing talk about something like a terrible accident had taken place, and needed help immediately, I thought to myself that I needed to hurry up and get over there too. And that's when I all of a sudden, you know, after hearing your response on the radio, I seen you speeding in my direction. So I thought I'd hurry up and flag you down to see if I could possibly be of some help."

"Don't quite know what to think of it," said the sheriff.

"They got much farming equipment over there?" asked the ranger.

"Farming equipment?" said the sheriff curiously. "What that gotta do with anything?"

"I don't know," responded the ranger. "Just thought maybe there might of been, you know, some kind of an accident or something."

As they hastily proceeded with the patrol car's siren loudly blaring, stridently, and in function with every emergency signal in full operation, in the direction that would end up eventually taking them to the Johnsons' residence, the dispatcher again came over the radio requesting that every emergency personnel respond to the Johnsons' residence immediately and without any delay.

DISPATCHER: One-L-Stonyford, to all available units, we need you to respond to an urgent emergency at the Johnsons' residence. Immediately!

Being that the sheriff was already within a short distance from the station, he again quickly reported in to the dispatcher in hopes that maybe she'd give him some type of information as to what was happening.

"Hell, what I need is some details," he said out loud. "You know what I mean? Just give me some in-depth detail. Some thorough in-depth details about this thing so I'll know just what we're dealing with."

"Yeah, I know exactly what you mean," said the ranger. "All of this emergency crap requesting for all emergency personnel to respond, I mean, is it really that serious?"

TRANSMITTER: Jesus Christ, Molly [said the sheriff] what's all the racket about? Hell, you got my transmitter needle jumping all over the place. Damn thing just about boilin' all the way in the goddamn red.

DISPATCHER: Well, they're havin' some kinda serious problem over there, at that there, ah, Johnsons' place.

TRANSMITTER: What kinda problem?

DISPATCHER: Well, it sounded like, something really serious, you know what I mean? It just sounded really serious.

TRANSMITTER: Like what, dammit!

DISPATCHER: Like they're really havin' a bit of trouble there or something. I think supposedly, somebody's down or something like that.

TRANSMITTER: Is that what they told you?

DISPATCHER: Well, from what I could hear, in the background, it was sounding like, somebody was sayin' something about someone was dead, or that someone had just died, or something like that. That there is what I'd reckoned I heard 'em sayin'.

TRANSMITTER: And that's it?

DISPATCHER: All I can tell ya is that, is that, what the caller said, and that was that, that they really needed someone to come out there and help them because something was wrong with one of their daughters, and they needed someone to help them immediately.

TRANSMITTER: Well, it really don't sound like they really knew what it was that's happening.

DISPATCHER: All I can say is that, you just need to get over there really quick, fast, and in a hurry and see for yourself just what the heck is goin' on over there.

TRANSMITTER: I mean, could you hear anyone in the background screaming or anything?

DISPATCHER: All I could hear was something that sounded like, somebody was in the background, yellin', and sounded like they were crying, and saying something about she's dead or something like that.

Just as the sheriff was about ready to make a quick stop at the station and had had the patrol car's door partially open as did the ranger with his door, Sheriff Blake quickly slammed his door shut, while at the same time, he began pressing down on the gas pedal as hard as he possibly could, causing the ranger to become partially ejected from the car, and losing his balance, and then, he very quickly, grabbed onto the handle strap that was fastened to the car's ceiling interior for occupational safety.

As he pressed down as hard as he possibly could on the gas pedal, the acceleration caused both rear wheels to spin rapidly in the gravel, causing small rocks on the ground to suddenly shoot upward, ricocheting off the wheels and into the air.

The ranger found himself quite stunned at the sheriff's actions, but felt that it would be best to say nothing about it.

"Just what in heaven's name is goin' on around this place?" the sheriff questioned. "Hell, Molly's actin' like the whole world's coming to an end or something. Or that it's suppose to end or stop functioning or something, and that everybody is suppose to just head straight over there to the freakin' Johnsons' place without ever even knowing just what the fuck is happening. I mean, yeah, it's as if we haven't anything better to be doing round here. And I'll tell you something else, this better be good and as important as she made it sound 'cause I was takin' a good ass freakin' nap, and really didn't want to be disturbed. So all this here emergency crap, it just better be worth being interrupted from what I was doin'.

"Oh, and you can believe I mean it, too!"

This is the statement that the sheriff found himself angrily expressing from his disappointment at the dispatcher for being unable to answer the few unanswered questions he felt needed to be answered. He felt he needed answers instead of just being told to respond to a location without there being any factual knowledge about the problem. He wanted to know the reason for considering such an emergency.

"Just whatdaya think it could be, Sheriff?" asked the ranger. "Sounds really serious."

"Just don't know," he responded. "But I tell you the freakin' truth, at this point, I'm really at a loss to even attempt tryin' thinking about all this here crap of not knowing anything. It's all bullshit if you really want to know the truth about it."

"I don't know," said the ranger. "But it sounded serious."

"Well, just what isn't serious when it come to Molly?" the sheriff jokingly stated. "I mean, hell, all she does is just sit behind that Goddamn desk all the freakin' day. And ain't no tellin' who she's screwin' there in that office. I mean, it's not like I'm there all the damn day. Hell, I'm out here working hard out here patrolling this Goddamn town twenty-four-seven to make sure everybody is safe from some darn criminal."

"So, whatdaya think?" asked the ranger.

"Well, to be quite frankly," the sheriff said, "I really don't know just what to think. And all she said was something about, somebody was yelling in the background, or something like that. I mean, it was something about needing help or somethin'. But what the hell, I suppose we just better hurry up and get our asses on over there and find out for ourselves. But it's like I was sayin', it just better be good and I mean it."

As the patrol car sped past the town's supermarket, the owner could be seen standing outside on the wooden platform pointing in the direction of the Johnsons' residence. There standing next to the supermarket's gas pump was a neighboring resident who was also pointing one of his hands in the same direction. Each individual having an astounded expression of disbelief as to what it was that had happened at the Johnson estate.

As the patrol car entered the driveway, there sat one of the many pets that the Johnson family cared for at the family-owned animal shelter. The oversized, massively built Great Dane sat in a fixed position, as if it were gazing directly at something in the direction of the barn. It sat motionless and very still, as if without a worry in the world.

It sat there staring as if it hadn't even noticed the patrol car advancing slowly past it.

"You know something?" said the sheriff. "But I know this is gonna, I guess, sound really strange, but, just what in the hell is your name?"

"What?" the ranger responded, surprised. "You mean to tell me?"

"Now, I know it's been quite a long time since we've, you know, known each other, but you know, I haven't ever gotten around to knowing just what the heck your name is. I mean, hell, I've always just called you the forest ranger. And during most occasions, hell, I'd just called you the ranger."

"All these years, and you don't know, or can't seem to remember, who I am?" asked the ranger while surprisingly smiling. "I mean, it's not like I'm without knowing who you are, you know what I sayin'? I mean, everybody here in this town knew your name way before you even made it here."

"Okay, I know it's terrible on my part to have forgotten your name, but, you know, I guess it sometime come with age or something."

"Yeah, that's what they say."

"So, dammit, man," the sheriff demanded jokingly "tell me your name!"

"Alright," the ranger told him. But, you better not ever forget it again, cause next time, I ain't gonna tell you."

"Deal!" said the sheriff. "Now tell me before I'd have to lock you up for failing to identify yourself to a law enforcement officer."

"Oh, so now you're trying to threaten and intimidate me?" asked the ranger.

"Ain't nobody tryin' to threaten and intimidate nobody," the sheriff answered. "So don't even try goin' there, cause it ain't happening."

"Yeah, right!" responded the ranger. "All this just because you forgot my name?"

"Okay, then, I do apologize for the tone of my voice that I used," said the sheriff apologetically. "Now can we get back to basics?"

"It's cool," said the ranger. "It's Bob Adams."

"Dammit!" the sheriff yelled. "I knew it!"

"Sure you did," said the ranger. "Sure you did."

"Well, I did," said the sheriff. "I just, I guess you can say, had a loss of memory, that's all."

"Wow, wow, now wait a minute," Bob quickly said in amazement. "Didn't you see that?"

"Whatcha talkin' 'bout?" asked the sheriff.

"That dog!" said Bob.

"What about 'em?" he asked.

"Man, I lie to you not," Bob began saying. "But, just when I looked at him, man, his head!"

"What about his head?" the sheriff asked curiously.

"Dude, I mean, Sheriff," said Bob in disbelief as to what he'd just seen. "The head was gone, and then, it, I mean, it was there, but, it was somebody else's head."

"For heaven's sakes, Bob," the sheriff told him, thinking that he was playing around and talking crazy. "Let's cut the crap! Ain't got no time to be joking around out here."

"But I know what I saw," Bob said. "And it wasn't no dog's head on that dog."

"Well, what is it that you think you seen, then, Bob?" the sheriff demanded to know.

"I don't know," Bob replied. "But it wasn't that dog's head, and it was staring right at me, smiling with some really ugly looking teeth in its ugly looking mouth."

"You know, Bob," the sheriff begin. "You ain't really making no sense at all. It's like you're falling off your rocker or something. I mean, all this talk about that damn dog. I tell ya, after this business here at the Johnsons' place is secured, I think you need to take a long vacation to just try and get away from things for a while."

As the sheriff looked around curiously to see if he could see the dog, it was then that he noticed it staring in the direction of the barn. He also noticed that it was itself staring directly at Paul Johnson who was standing near the entrance to the barn, shaking and trembling, involuntarily, and expressing a dreaded facial expression of fear and disbelief.

He was crying and calling out loud for help, while at the same time, motioning in the direction of the barn's entrance as if wanting them to see something.

As the patrol car came to a sudden stop, they quickly got out and began moving as fast as they possibly could, while at the same time, they'd begun equipping themselves with every resource available to try and assist Paul. While doing so, they could easily sense from the expression on his face that something had indeed gone terribly wrong, and that whatever it was, the problem had surely somehow horrified him as he was trying desperately to point one of his fingers in the direction he wanted them to go.

Entering the barn, the sheriff began to perceive the odor as it began stimulating his sense of smell like never before. He found himself in disbelief from the sight of what appeared to be a badly dismembered corpse scattered about on the ground in different directions. Different parts of the remains lay surrounded by liquid masses of internal organs and slightly recognizable intestinal parts. Forcing himself to move even closer, he could then see and recognize a certain portion of what he figured bore a slight resemblance to a face that seemed to him to resemble the characteristics of one of the Johnsons' daughters.

As he continued to very carefully examine the partial remains and mainly the face, he begin to feel a horrible sickening in his stomach from the realization of such an encounter actually being the remains of the little girl he'd on many occasions remembered seeing in this small-town community.

Grabbing his nose, squeezing each nostril together in an an effort to try to prevent the odor from entering his respiratory tract, the offensive odor began within him an uncontrollable amount of revolted vomiting from within his digestive system and out his mouth as he tried desperately to run back to his patrol car.

Within minutes, an ambulance, followed by a few fire trucks and police cars, was entering the driveway and pulling up to where the sheriff could be seen, leaning over a fence that encircled the small gazebo next to the Johnsons' house. One of the ambulances had stopped in front of the Johnsons' house, and another, which came from the forestry station, proceeded in the direction of the barn, followed by the fire trucks, which is where the sheriff had directed them to go.

After regaining control of himself, he immediately started informing them about what they were facing and the horrible condition of what could be found of the body.

"It's a little girl," he shouted to them. "Or, what was left of a little girl. So please try and be careful in there. Her little body, it's, I regret having to tell you, but it's scattered just about everywhere all over the damn place. And the head of the little girl, it's, guys, it's torn all to pieces, and laying over there looking just like it had been impaled or something.

"It's everywhere, dammit! Ain't never seen nothin' like this in all my life! Ain't never seen nothin' like this, not even during my war days in that there danggone Vietnam! But I tell you, boys, there's some freakin' shit in that Goddamn barn that'll make you drop dead. It's hard to believe. But I'll tell you one Goddamn thing that's the truth, we gonna catch the rotten son-of-a-bitch responsible for this, and you'd better believe it! I tell you all, we gonna catch 'em, and give 'em what they got comin' to 'em."

The sheriff, then, after regaining control of himself, turned and headed to where Paul was still nervously standing and shaking uncontrollably, seemingly incapable of moving as he clung onto an old, rusted, circular handrail to support himself. The sheriff began questioning him in hope to get some answers.

Paramedics could be seen from within a distance standing a few feet from the barn seemingly confused as they could be seen shaking their heads in disbelief, as if not wanting to believe the sight of what they were seeing.

Observing their behavior, the sheriff then began to hear sounds that immediately caught his attention. It was someone crying which seemed to be coming from inside the house. As he turned in the direction facing the front porch, he then noticed a figure that he recognized as Sarah Johnson, who was standing in the doorway behind what appeared to be an old, wooden screen door that lacked its upkeep.

She stood there, dumbfounded, and crying with a sound as if she were softly moaning. While staring at her, he thought to himself about her being the mother of such a sweet little girl whose body was now scattered all over the place.

As he stepped up onto the porch to get a much better view, without a word coming from his mouth, though, only staring at Sarah as she just stood there in front of him, motionless, and with a very saddened expression on her face from the realization of the horrible death and mutilation of her daughter, he then opened the screen door, and then had to carefully move slightly to one side to enter the house in his effort to prevent having to touch her as she stood there, very still, and occasionally crying and moaning.

That's when he also noticed another of the Johnsons' daughters sitting on the living room couch comforting their youngest daughter who he immediately recognized as Margaret. He could sense that from the expression on her and also from her behavior that she was in a very serious state of shock as the Johnsons' eldest daughter tried desperately to get her to respond.

After a brief moment of silence, she then got up from the couch and turned toward the sheriff, telling him that Margaret was the one who was there with Wanda when something bad had happened to her.

"She was there when it happened," she told him. "She was there when it happened, and she seen everything."

The sheriff went silent and unable to mutter a word. The statement had astounded him and caught him completely off-guard. That's when he thought to himself that she could have possibly even seen the murderer. He quickly checked Margaret to see if she could have possibly been hurt being that blood was just about everywhere in the barn.

After checking her, he then quickly rushed past Sarah who was still standing in the doorway, and out the front door to his patrol car, while at the same time, motioning and calling out to a few of the officers to come and assist him. He then yelled out to Paul informing him about Margaret needing immediate medical attention. At this time, he rushed back into the house, only this time, slightly moving Sarah out of the way so that he could check Margaret's pulse, and then, he quickly rushed back outside the house and to his patrol car, advising the dispatcher to notify the Willows County Hospital and also the County Coroner's Office about the situation that had taken place in Stonyford.

He also told the dispatcher to inform them about the need to have a full-scale investigation and also the need for all available hands.

After receiving the information about the tragic situation that had taken place at the Johnsons' residence, there was a sudden click in the sheriff's transmitter just as he was about to remind Molly about the office medical cabinet. He wanted to remind her to check it for the medicine he thought could possibly help her recent respiratory problem.

She'd come down with a terrible viral infection, and with all her weight problems and everything else to add to it, she found herself having serious problems when coughing.

"I'm really surprised she ain't dead by now," the sheriff thought to himself. "All the coughing isn't getting any better."

He continued to try and make connections to her, but each attempt was to no avail. And even after his repeated attempts from the Johnsons' place, the tone just kept on ringing without ever any answer from on the other end.

"Jesus Christ, Bob," the sheriff called out. "Just what in heavens name is going on round here? Try contacting these Goddamn people around here and all I get is a bunch of freakin' static on my Goddamn radio. No fuckin' body wanna answer the Goddamn hot line anymore. We need some Goddamn help out here, quick, fast, and in a hurry! Dammit! Somebody gotta get the hell on over there to the station and see just what in Heaven's name is going on over there with Molly. Hell! She done stopped talkin'. She ain't answering a Goddamn thing out here. And we gotta get some freakin' help out here. All them folks over there in Willows need to know about our situation. Some-a y'all need to hurry up and get over there and try to find out just what the hell is going on at the station."

He then proceeded in the direction of the barn in an effort to try and assist the paramedics who could be seen as if they were themselves very much confused in their search for Wanda's missing limbs and other various body parts.

Before entering, he could hear in the distance sirens that sounded as if they were en route. As he thought about what he was hearing, he could hear the sound of more than just one, maybe even two. That's when he stopped, turned, and faced the direction the sirens were coming from. As he continued to very carefully listen, he could then tell that they were coming from the opposite direction he'd expected. "Mmm," he began mumbling to himself indistinctly. "I wonder just who they could be, and who it was that notified them about our situation?"

"What's that, Sheriff?" asked Bob. "I didn't quite hear ya."

"Just talkin' to myself again, Bob," he told him. "I was just wondering who that is I hear coming this way."

"Might not even be comin' here," said Bob. "I mean, that sound like, you know, a drill or something."

"Better not be no Goddamn drill," said the sheriff seriously. "That, I assure you. They'd better be comin' here to help us with this situation. Ain't no drill sounding like that gone pass us by. Not at a time like this."

He found himself thinking about Margaret and wondered if she herself could possibly be responsible. The thought of a young child being a murderer sent chills throughout his body. But then he said to himself, "No freakin' way could that little girl be a cold-blooded murderer of her own sister." But as he continued to think about it, he thought how in most cases, every profile of your typical killer did tend to bear the same essential traits and sometimes, the same characteristics of a kind, both classes and groups. But in relation to certain individuals within a certain specimen, not everyone tended to share those same characteristics.

Not even Margaret.

There was a very strong offensive odor inside the barn that seemed to stimulate the thickness of the air with such a displeasing smell to where, just about everywhere you looked, you could hear very loud coughing and gagging sounds. Some of the response team could also be seen, vomiting and ejecting large amounts of a thick, reddish-yellow fluid from their mouths. While others could be seen busy and quickly assembling their air tanks and heavy breathing apparatuses.

Some also carried ladders and huge round water hoses as if preparing for the possibility of a fire.

Different departments had arrived from various nearby counties after hearing the call come over their emergency transmitters requesting help, and that all available emergency personnel were being asked to respond to the Johnsons' residence immediately.

As the offensive odor began clogging his wind pipe and was now causing his breathing to become somewhat complicated, the sheriff had himself again started vomiting and had to once again rush out of the barn in an effort to get some air. As he made it to the exit, that's when he noticed another group of rescue team members coming down the driveway in a large green and white forestry truck. This is the team he had heard before entering the barn with all their loud sirens and horns blaring stridently.

Following closely in behind them, he could see an ambulance that had stopped in front of the Johnsons' house.

He then waved both of his hands, motioning the fire truck to come in his direction.

As they approached the location in which he motioned for them to go, one of the firemen could be seen as he quickly jumped off the truck's side running board and rushed toward the sheriff. He could sense that from the expression on just about everyone's face, and mainly the sheriff, that something wasn't quite right, and that whatever it was, he could tell that something terrible had apparently happened. As he continued trying his best to figure it out, he could be seen looking around in bewilderment. He could see no fire, and the only thing the sheriff was dong was motioning his hands, while at the same time, slightly bending over to one side of a fence, loudly gagging and vomiting, and still trying to point his hands in the direction of the barn.

As they proceeded in the direction that they were told by the sheriff, the firemen very slowly peered inside the entrance to the barn, searching intently for whatever it was that the sheriff was indicating for them to see.

Glancing from side to side while still remaining at the barn's entrance was when he noticed a few of the paramedics standing near to what appeared to be a very small object lying on the ground. As he finally began to move even closer, he then began to see that one of the paramedics was just standing in a fixed position, shaking and trembling. He could see that his head was shaking in a rather disbelieving manner as though he were refusing to believe what he and the others were seeing. A few of the paramedics could be seen looking in an upward manner as if not wanting to view the object.

As he moved even closer, he stooped slightly downward in his effort to get a better view of the object. That was when he noticed that the object on the ground was colored in a rather dark, glossy, reddish color and as if it had been somehow saturated or immersed from a process of a degraded liquid, with having an appearance resembling stringy seaweeds or rock weeds encircling it.

He could also see something about the object having a very familiar resemblance to that of a human mouth, except in this case, and whatever it was on the ground in front of him, he could vaguely see that the part of the object which was reflecting such a resemblance, it had now begun to slowly move and the opening had begun rotating.

The resemblance reflecting the mouth began to open and close just as a fish would do when trying to breath through its mouth and gills from the lack of oxygen.

As he looked around, he could see everyone standing very still and silent, strikingly quiet, as if afraid to move or even say anything about whatever it was they were viewing.

The sheriff once again entered the barn, and this time, he too was wearing a self-contained breathing apparatus. He found himself thinking and wondering just how the situation had seemed to have everyone so strangely stagnated and without any progress being made in their effort to try securing whatever it was that had apparently taken place.

As the fireman continued to inspect the object, he hadn't noticed the sheriff, who stood within a few feet of him. That's when he saw how the object had now begun to resemble the head of a bloated pig, or maybe even a piglet, that was still during its death gasping for air.

It wasn't until the sheriff finally approached him and pointed toward other areas of the barn that he began to realize the dark, reddish object which lay on the ground in front of him was that of a human head. He could also see that the head was possibly that of a young child. And the hair which he thought was seaweeds or rock weeds, he could now clearly see as it covered one side of the partially disfigured face being the young child's hair that showed signs as if it had been recently soaked or painted with a thick, slimy, dark red and yellowish substance.

There wasn't any doubt as to the contents of the substance. The head was soaked with the child's own blood. And the mouth had now become wide open, revealing the teeth that could be visually seen embedded deep into each other as though some had been pulled and then replanted elsewhere. As the sheriff continued to point in the direction of the mouth, they could also see that the teeth looked as if they had been painted a dingy red, and occasionally, the mouth would seemingly move and rotate, as though it were desperately trying to say something.

"Are you looking at this, Sheriff?" asked the fireman. "Ain't no way somethin' like this could be happening coming from a decapitated head. It's impossible for something like this to be happening."

But all doubts were shattered when the decapitated head began making strange, deep, guttural sounds. "Ga-ga-ga-ga-ga-ga-gaaaaa!"

Both he and the sheriff quickly found themselves standing almost completely upright at the same time. They then noticed how everyone around them was staring directly at them, wondering what was happening. Then the sheriff looked around and started telling them about the strange actions from the head, and how it was seemingly trying to say something.

"I ain't got no reason to be tryin' to lie 'bout this," the sheriff said out loud. "But that Goddamn thing just started tryin' to say somethin'. Now I don't know just how it happened, but I tell all y'all, the damn thing was tryin' to say somethin'. I'ma serious 'bout this here now, guys. It was tryin' its damnedest to say somethin', and I got my proof right here."

The fireman looking around while shrugging his shoulders.

"He's right!" he told them. "I seen it too with my own eyes."

As everyone carefully stared at the head, they could see that the eyelids were stretched downward and deep into the eye sockets resting on the inner shell. Each nostril had been stripped completely from the facial surrounding surface and were spread widely apart. What remained of the majority of the teeth seemed to have been somehow deeply embedded into the lower gum and had shattered others. And what was left of the ears lay clinging to small masses of tissue that seemed to have been somehow ripped completely from certain areas of the facial surface.

The eyes and tongue were never found.

As the sheriff continued to question his thoughts, he then began to realize just what he was inspecting, at which time, he immediately turned around and rushed back to the entrance to the barn, while at the same time, hoping and praying out loud, and also wishing that the sight he'd seen to have never existed.

Reaching the entrance with both hands on the back of his head, he was met by a few emergency personnel who were themselves about to enter the barn. After once again regaining control of himself, he was about to inform them of their findings when he was suddenly interrupted by a few of the paramedics who'd come rushing out of the barn shaking their heads in disbelief.

One was busy trying to describe what he'd seen, but he then, suddenly, collapsed of an apparent massive heart attack.

"Oh no!" the sheriff cried out. "Somebody grab him and help get this guy to that ambulance over there."

"Hang in there, buddy," another yelled. "Just hang in there, we'll get you some help. Just hang in there, buddy!"

"What's happening, Sheriff?" another asked.

"The poor guy fainted on us," the sheriff answered.

"Is he unconscious?" asked another.

"Sheriff, I think we've lost 'im," responded another.

"Get that Goddamn oxygen machine hooked up to him right now," said the sheriff. "And hurry up and load him into that there ambulance and get him the hell outta here and to the Willows Hospital."

"Anybody know his name?" a fireman asked.

"Just call him Buddy for right now," said the sheriff. "Hell, nobody knows just what department he came from."

He was immediately loaded into one of the few ambulances on hand which proceeded in the direction of the town of Willows.

One of the other paramedics who hadn't yet entered the barn began questioning everyone about what had happened, as well as the condition of the paramedic. "What in heaven's name is going on here?" he questioned. "Hey, I'm really sorry about that guy, but, he isn't gonna make it. Can somebody, anybody, tell me just what it was that that poor fellow must have seen in there?"

By this time, one of the investigators all of a sudden came rushing out of the barn and started pounding and beating one of his fists in a repeated slow motion against one of the wooden doors that was fastened to another of the few entrances to the barn. Watching his display, they could sense how emotionally disturbed he'd become as he started crying and yelling out loudly his intent to find whoever committed such a crime. As he turned toward the sheriff, he then began attempting trying to describe the situation and condition of the mutilated body and how it seemed to be scattered everywhere in small pieces.

After hearing his statement, another of the members of the emergency team who was standing and about to enter the barn slowly stepped away from the huge, dingy-looking doors and began questioning what he'd heard.

"It's okay, dammit," shouted the sheriff. "Go ahead and get in there. I ain't never in all my years seen so many freakin' cowards. Whatcha doing in the department if you ain't gonna get your hands dirty?"

Within minutes, another patrol car that had been summoned to the Johnsons' residence from a nearby county had now pulled into the driveway. Inside, there were a few more officers wearing dark blue uniforms. As the car came to a sudden stop, it slid on the gravel driveway causing a huge cloud of dust to form in the air above it. They began to get out of the car as fast as they possibly could and rushed toward the sheriff. He was once again leaning down, vomiting, while a few of the personnel stood in a short distance from him.

The officers could see that the entire crew who were presently on location at the Johnsons' residence had been undoubtedly disturbed both mentally as well as emotionally by whatever it was that had resulted in the disorderliness of their performance.

One of the firemen who hadn't yet entered the barn quickly approached the officers and requested their assistance to help inspect the area. This is when the sheriff, who was still bending slightly over to one side, began to raise himself slowly upward in an effort to once again attempt informing the team about the horrifying findings awaiting them inside the barn.

"No, hold up for a minute before any of you guys just go off rushing your asses in there," said the sheriff. "This ain't no Goddamn fire that you-all are out here dealing with. So let me help try and let you-all know whatcha facing in there. Now, it seem that the head of one of the Johnsons' little girls been somehow cut off or something."

"Oh my God," said one of the officers.

"What?" said another.

"*Jeee*-sus Christ," another said.

"Just how did something like that happen?" another asked.

"A little girl?" another questioned in disbelief. "How did it happen?"

"All I can tell you is that," the sheriff said, "the little girl's head been decapitated from her body. That's about all we've found so far. Oh, and let me not forget to remind you that, it's a lots of little small Goddamn pieces of her body all over that Goddamn place. But just where? We don't freakin' know. But they're in there, somewhere.

"One minute we're told those little girls are playing some kinda game with each other, and the next thing you know, something terrible apparently done gone terribly wrong.

"And now it's up to us to find out just what in the hell it was."

Listening to him describe the sight which seemed to have disturbed the entire crew, the officers found themselves in a rather hesitating state of comprehension as they began walking slowly toward the entrance to the barn.

The thick, sickening odor and its extremely offensive stench could be smelled within a few feet from the entrance and began to overwhelm them as it filled the air with the decaying body flesh.

As they proceeded in the direction that was instructed by the sheriff, within seconds they could clearly see the partially deteriorated, decomposing head of the little girl as it lay, soaked in blood, on the ground looking as though there were something balancing it in a fixed position.

Strangely, the mouth was still opening and closing as if it were somehow trying to say something.

"That's right," someone in the distance spoke out loud. "You're seeing what we've all been seeing. And it ain't no Goddamn illusion either. Believe me, in no damn way are you guys hallucinating! The mouth's been moving like that ever since we found it. And those sounds you're hearing, maybe you can make some sense of 'em, because none of us been able to. Hell, one of my guys swore up and down that it was trying to say something to him. He's the one who made it to the door, and then he just...dropped dead!"

"But was he sick or something?" someone asked curiously.

"Nope, don't think he was," the person answered. "Think he was in very good health."

"Damn!" one of the officers muttered.

"Y'all just better be very careful," the other said. "Something just ain't right about this here. I gotta feelin' somebody's still here, watching us. All of us. Somebody that ain't suppose to be here. And don't for one minute let yourself believe that that there young'un did something like this to her kinfolk. If you know what I mean."

"You don't think so?" one of the officers questioned.

"Ain't no way you gonna tell me that little girl's responsible for any of this."

Wondering just what could have taken place at the Johnsons' residence had indeed become a serious question of curiosity for everyone involved in the search.

The barn itself was a very uncanny sight as its huge, eerie, unpainted doors hung askew, sloppily untidy. The barn looked as if some type of an acid substance capable of dissolving wood had been splashed over the entirety of its outer surface. It was an immense structure. Its roof slanted widely in an inclined direction on both sides. At the center of the roof there stood high above the entrance below, an old rusted miniature windmill with a dingy-looking old rusted arrow that appeared to be welded to it to keep each unit jointed together. As each mild breeze of a light current of air swiftly and effortlessly encircled the area, the windmill could be heard as it began turning in circles and making very sharp scratchy sounds. As each current of air began powering the old rusted, antique blades that shook and squeaked loudly, they began to spin very rapidly, with the arrow facing the direction in which each current of air would blow.

"Who the hell are you?" an officer questioned, referring to the person whose voice they had heard speaking in reference to someone possibly responsible for the crime still being in the barn. "What makes you so sure about us being watched?"

"Who is that y'all talkin' to in here?" the sheriff asked loudly while standing at the entrance. "Hell, can hear whoever it is all the way out here in front just as loud and spooky like those little goblins be screaming and talking loud when trying to frighten each other on Halloween. Just who the hell is that?"

"It's uh…it's uh…." one of the officers uttered. "Where are you?"

"He's over there," another officer said, pointing.

"Where?" another asked.

"Right over there," the officer continued pointing in the direction of the area of the barn the voice was heard coming from.

"*Somebody*, Goddamnit," the sheriff yelled out to the officers who were busy inspecting the crime scene. "One o' y'all put some o' dat-dere crime scene tape around this Goddamn place so we can keep people who ain't suppose to be outta here."

"He's in here somewhere, Sheriff," one of the officers said. "I believe he's over there, by that window."

"That ain't him," another said. "That's just an old coat rack you're looking at. I was thinking that was him too."

"Well, where is he then?" another asked.

"Come on out from over there," another one called out. "We know you're in here."

"Somebody get some light over there," said the sheriff. "These Goddamn flashlights ain't workin' good enough."

"We know you're still in here," another officer said. "Come on out and show yourself. Let us see who you are."

"Uh, this is Sheriff Blake," said the sheriff. "Uh, you just better do as you're told before we get one of our hounds in here, and he'll find your ass, sure 'nough."

"I think you better listen to the sheriff," one of the officers said, trying to reason with the person behind the voice. "He ain't about to be in here playin' no dang-gone games with you."

"Just come on out so we can talk about this," said the sheriff. "I do believe you know we gotta very serious situation on our hands. So just come on out from wherever you are, and we'll talk about whatever it is that going on 'round here. Ain't no need in tryin' to hide from us, 'cause we gonna find you anyway. So you just might as well come on out and show us who you are."

There was a troubling silence in the barn as the sheriff and his team of officers searched the area which the person behind the voice had been heard speaking to them from.

The search lasted until just about dawn, at which time the bright morning daylight began to reveal the clear visual remains of the dismembered body parts of the young child scattered about in many directions throughout the barn.

"Anything yet?" one of the firemen asked as he was entering through a side door.

"And good morning to you, too!" said the sheriff while rubbing both of his hands across his face. "Didn't bring us anything to eat or drink?"

"Like what?" he asked.

"Like what?" questioned the sheriff. "Hell, we've been in this Goddamn place all freakin' night, and you gone stand there askin', like what? Get the Goddamn hell outta here and don't come back until you bring us something to eat and drink, you unworthy son-of-a-bitch! Just where in the hell do you guys come from 'round here?"

"I can sure use a hot cup of coffee right about now," one of the officers said.

"And me too!" another said in agreement.

"I think we all need a little something to keep us going," the sheriff said, smiling from the thought of what he'd told the fireman. "I really hope that guy didn't take me too serious about what I called him."

"Yeah, I know what you mean," one of the officers said. "I guess you won't know until he makes it back with something. You know what I mean?"

"Hey, Sheriff," one of the officers called. "We've been out here just about all night searching for whoever that was, but we ain't found nothin'. I think whoever it was, he's gotten outta here through one of these side doors or something."

"Yeah, and the rest of these guys," another officer began saying. "It wouldn't surprise me one bit if they started falling to the ground one by one. You know, passing out or something from being so worn out and exhausted. I mean, I'm sure we're all tired."

"Well, I have to admit," the sheriff added, "the situation out here is really wearing me out, too! And my energy level is off the scale. But guys, we still got a job to do that'll sometime bring you all the way down, and especially like this one here. So let's all of us get our asses back in full gear."

The sheriff began thinking about everything that had taken place during the past few hours. The thought about the situation and the crime committed against the little girl made him shiver. He thought about how Margaret looked as the paramedics were positioning her onto the metal gurney and had wheeled her to the waiting ambulance. He thought about how he could see her pale facial complexion, with its unusual stillness as she lay on the stretcher in a slightly upward position.

Her eyes were closed and she showed no signs of movement.

As he continued staring at her, he began thinking that if only he could just somehow try asking her a few questions, that maybe she could possibly answer the question that he felt could provide the information he needed as to what had happened to her sister.

He rushed to the back of the ambulance, and carefully leaned slightly inside, and very gently shook one of her arms in an effort to try to get her to respond. After finding himself unable to awaken her, and after repeating his gentle nudging and soft poking, he found himself thinking about when he had first noticed her in the living room being comforted by her older sister.

She too had found herself unable to get Margaret to respond.

After his failed attempts to awaken her, he backed away from the ambulance and watched as the paramedics stared at him, then they closed the wide emergency door and pulled away from the front of the house, and headed down the narrow driveway and onto the road heading toward the exit out of Stonyford that would eventually take them to the town of Willows.

As he stood there staring and thinking about everything that had taken place, he could hear the emergency siren from the ambulance in the distance as he watched its flashing emergency lights fading into the winding roads and in between all the farmland with all its cattle pastures that seemed to engulf this part of the region.

He then turned in the direction of Paul who was standing on the porch still nervously shaking and crying, and wiping his face with an old dingy-looking rag that he kept in his back pocket.

The sheriff began advising him about the importance of both he and Sarah being present at the hospital during the investigation. He also advised him about an officer being available for them at all times, and that the officer was already waiting to transport them to Willows.

As the sheriff was about to get into his patrol car, he informed one of the officers to take charge of securing the area. "I want you to contact me immediately should you have to," he told him. "But better yet, you should start making notes right now, and make sure to have the men bag everything they find that relates to the crime scene. Anything they find in that place, please remind them to take photos of it. Bag it, tag it, and make sure you log it and also sign it and date it correctly. Hopefully, and if we can, I'm-a check on seein' if somebody can get a few pilots out here with one of them there, you know, helicopters, as soon as I make it to the station."

"Uh, Sheriff," the officer asked, "do you want me to send whatever we find to you directly? Or should I just wait until you get back?"

"Well, damn, man," said the sheriff. "If it's that important just use the Goddamn fax machine you got there in your car. It'll make it to me."

"And what about your cellphone, Sheriff?" the officer asked. "You got that with you?"

"Look, Goddamnit," the sheriff yelled. "Just send or contact me with whatever it is that you find and feel is important. I just want you to stay out here and take charge of things and keep trying to find out just what the hell happened around here. Something just ain't quite right around here, and I can feel it."

"Whatdaya feel?" the officer asked curiously. "I mean, is there something I should know about?"

"Goddamnit, man," the sheriff yelled. "What in Heaven's name is wrong with you? Put you in charge of everything so I can go and check on Molly, and you start interrogating me, you fat son-of-a-bitch!"

"Well, as you've insisted, sir," the officer said with respect, "I'll just do whatever I can. But I can tell you something, Sheriff, I'm really at a loss with all that's been going on around here, if you really know what I'm meaning?"

The sheriff then just stared directly at him as though he were peering deep into his brain. "Just let me tell you one good Goddamn thing, young man, just how in the hell do you expect me to know anything about what is going on 'round here? Hell, I'm as lost as you, and that Goddamn dog over there who's been just sitting there ever since we got here. Now you try figure that one out instead of thinking it's your Goddamn freaking job to be out here interrogating me, you son-of-a-bitch! I placed you in charge. So you take your fat freakin' ass over there in that Goddamn barn, and start trying to figure out just what the fuck done happen and might still be happening 'round here.

"Am I making myself clear enough for ya?"

"Yes, sir, Sheriff," said the officer. "Loud and clear."

Both the officer and the sheriff started gathering up their uncertainties in which to try conquering the unknown, though, both determining to become a topnotch investigator by solving the mysteriousness of the mission.

As the sheriff again attempted to get into his patrol car, he suddenly heard a voice calling out to him in an urgent tone. As he turned to see who it was, he could see through the breaking of dawn the strangely familiar expression on one of the officer's faces revealing something awful.

He thought to himself, "this better be important," being that the officer was in a jogging motion coming toward him.

He then made a motion with one hand to the officer in an effort to signal him to a location away from the patrol car.

"Sir!" said the officer while trying to catch his breath. "I just had to hurry up and let you know before you left that we've found some important vital parts of the remains that I thought you should know about. But it's just so strange, sir, and I'm more than sure, unusual, as to how each of these body parts were found, and the position and arrangements they were in. I mean, sir, I'm talking about, it's as if, you know, somebody put each of 'em there where we found them."

"Just what in the heck'er you sayin', son?" asked the sheriff.

"Well, what I'm trying to say is that," he began explaining, "I think you better come and take a look for yourself, sir, 'cause from what I can see, I honestly think we gotta killer on our hands. I think whoever he is, he's possibly toying around with us, if you know what I mean."

"What makes you think that?" asked the sheriff.

"Well, sir," the officer began describing. "It's like whoever it is that did this is involved in some form of something like a hideous repulsive ritual or something. You know what I mean? He's playing around with us and is using different body parts to prove to us that he mean business."

"Jesus Christ, young man," exclaimed the sheriff. "This is just the kind of freakin' news we needed, Goddamnit. I didn't need to hear any of what you're trying to tell me. I ain't got the time to be hearing anything about some Goddamn weirdo bizarre killer out here killing people just because he wanna play some kinda freakin' games. Do you hear me?"

"Yes, sir, Sheriff," said the officer. "Though…"

"Well, just let me put it this way," the sheriff began. "Not until, you know, later. Wait until I can get that dead little girl's parents far away from here. You know what I mean? I gotta try and get them into a much better environment than what we presently got going on out here. You know, a much more stable environment so they can try and get themselves together."

"Yes, sir," said the officer. "I know exactly what you mean."

"And one more thing," the sheriff told him. "Until I can get a few of them helicopters out here to assist in the search, just make sure that you and the rest of the team continue gathering up everything you can. Then we'll send everything, all the evidence you come up with, to the Willow County Coroners Office."

"Roger that, sir," responded the officer. "But, are you going to come and see what we've found?"

The sheriff once again found himself in a serious daze, thinking about the many things that tended to ponder the human mind. He kept thinking about Wanda's mutilated body, and how certain body parts that he'd already seen were just as the officer stated, placed perfectly, as if for reasons unknown to the residents of Stonyford, someone was busy toying with the team of investigators.

He thought about how optimistic yesterday had begun, and by the beginning of the evening, everything began changing so drastically. The call for all available emergency personnel to respond to the Johnsons' residence immediately and without any delay ended up being something he found himself wishing he'd never heard coming from his transmitter.

And the thought of the firemen and paramedics curiously staring in so much bewilderment as they waited for his orders was something he dreaded for hours ever having to partake as a part of his responsibility.

He couldn't help but to wonder just how it is that life can even exist for us to live, only to find ourselves dying in such a horrible, brutal, and very savage manner.

"The death of any human being is indeed tragic," he said to himself as he stared at the officer. "But Goddamnit, the mutilation of a child is out of the question and so far beyond my imagination," is what he said out loud. "I can deal with this."

He was trying desperately to focus his attention on other issues instead of just on Wanda's decapitation which seemed to cause the entire team to shiver.

He'd taken the situation personally.

The image of her remains and the partial head with its blood-soaked hair covering one side of the face continued to invade his thoughts. He just couldn't seem to find a way to shake it loose.

"Did anybody find out just who the hell that was last night?" he asked, referring to whoever it was talking to them about Margaret not being responsible. "I'm talking about that Goddamn guy who was making it a point that we didn't think this was any illusion or something."

"Ain't none of us seen him, Sheriff," one of the officers said. "The guy just upped and done vanished on us. Been looking for 'em, but ain't nobody been able to find 'em."

Without a word he turned to his patrol car and robotically got in. It was a though he were in a trance being controlled by a strong magnetic force. He then sped away from the Johnsons' residence in reverse until he finally reached the two-lane road at the entrance, at which time he then quickly shifted the car into forward, and sped away as if unnoticed.

Watching the patrol car as it turned left nearby the Stonyford grocery store en route to the station, the emergency response team found themselves speechless. As the early morning began to set in, the realization of what had happened was once again a tough reality to face. Starting a conversation didn't seem to be too hard a problem for one of the officers and especially when knowing it was a part of his responsibility to see to it that the remains made it to the coroner's office.

Although he hadn't yet become fully aware of his responsibility, it was the obligation that indeed caused him to wonder just what it was that he had to secure.

As a team of officers entered the barn, one of the firemen immediately started pointing in the direction and location of dismembered limbs. He informed them about each limb being tagged and placed on canvases that could be seen lying about the ground throughout the barn.

Staring aimlessly, Bob glanced to one side and began uttering an uncontrolled sound in a cursing manner, while at the same time, shaking his head in a downward motion, slowly backing away from the location of the canvases.

Noticing his behavior, a few members of the response team immediately rushed toward him and led him out of the barn. They could see he was in a great amount of distress which caused him to react as though it were he who'd been torn apart.

"Thanks, I appreciate your help," said Bob gracefully. "You would think that, in all my many hours in the academy, that by now, I'd know just how to conduct myself during such an emergency. But as you yourself can see, I'd never anticipated actually having to experience seeing such a horrifying sight up close and personal. I mean, hell, except for what was shown in the academy theater during training. Shit! Them movies ain't nothin' but all that Hollywood makeup crap."

"I know actually what you mean," said one of the officers. "Nothin' like real life."

"Well, as so all of them newly recruits tend to always find themself thinking when they attend training," said another. "They just for some crazy odd reason never seem to honestly believe in the possibility that such a horrifying act like this can ever really happen. But, and as we all now know, in small towns like here in Stonyford, this ain't none of that crazy ass Hollywood stuff. I mean, this really got me thinking. And to be truthful, it got me scared shitless!"

Chapter Four

UNFORESEEN INDEED! This journey has been an experience far beyond anything I could have ever expected or anticipated. This trip has so far taken me from the city of Vallejo, on up to the small-town community of Stonyford, California. From there, and from the old rough rugged mountain region of Stonyford, back down to the city of Vallejo, and then and from there, that is when I so amazingly found myself traveling east, ending up in the city of Wichita, Kansas which is where I would end up finding myself becoming a part of the most unimaginable experience that any reasonable person could have ever imagined experiencing.

"What an experience," is what I keep saying to myself repeatedly.

Margaret Johnson ended up being such an extraordinary person. She was so very remarkable, and I must admit, beyond the usual. But, to be truthful, my honest description of her, I have to admit being somewhat in the form of darkness. It was just like the darkening of the nightfall sky and gloomy dusk of a strange impeded evening filled with unselfish generosity from her that I found surrounding me as I traveled west from Wichita. I thought about the dense atmosphere, which to me was quite a phenomenon. While visiting Margaret, the temperature in the room suddenly changed and had become even more so, damply moistened, and had caused her hair to stick to certain areas of her face and neck.

Yes indeed, she knew just about everything about me. She knew everything about my parents and my entire family.

She also looked every part of a sickly person.

Never married and hadn't any children.

As I found myself trying my best to comfort her, I do believe that it was she who ended up comforting me.

She had allowed me to see and experience that which had caused the vast majority of the people residing in the town of Stonyford to become victims of a monstrous virus, leaving them in an extremely inhumane condition with very shivering deformities so contagious to where, the transmission from such violating poisonous venom had the tendency to spread very quickly, and indeed, rapidly, deforming and occasionally, destroying just about everything in its wake.

As my flight began to descend, I began thinking about my trip and the experience she had allowed me to experience.

I thought from the city of Wichita, Kansas, and now I was headed back to the city of Vallejo, and then a return to Stonyford and then to Willows. And now, I've made it back to Vallejo and en route to the Napa County area which is better known for its particular flavor of rich-tasting wine.

At the Napa airport, I found myself with a choice of helicopters to choose from. My preference is either the MH-53 J-Pave Low, or my second choice could be the Sikorsky CH-53G. But it's my guess that any true loving pilot of an aircraft would easily find himself wanting the huge MH-53. This baby is one very huge bird that's good for both high midair regional flights and also for those very low land surface ground landings for immediate exit from any surface.

I'm therefore flying the MH-53 J-Pave Low.

This bitch is everything I need for that deep, smooth, regional acceleration that'll get me moving with high intensity increasing speed throughout the rugged Stonyford mountain region and down in between all of its steep valleys.

"DAMN!" I couldn't help saying to myself. "This baby is huge."

That's when I couldn't help but to find myself laughing out loud from the thought of once again flying something so huge and brilliantly and illustriously beautiful from the inside out. This baby definitely surpassed the capacity of my privately owned Commander. And the power of this baby is exceedingly excelling during flight.

The huge rotors with its massive blades rotating horizontally while giving so much support when keeping this thing afloat with its powerful circulation I found unbelievable.

Deep, smooth 60-degree bank and 900 feet per minute. My Airspeed Indicator, my Artificial Horizon, my Altimeter and Magnetic Compass, VOR Indicators, RPM Gauges, and every engine gauge working simultaneously and in conjunction are all jamming to the heavy sounds of rock and roll coming form the built-in entertainment center. "Magic Carpet Ride," "Sweet Home Alabama," "Proud Mary," and "Sex Machine," by Sly and the Family Stone are jamming loudly from the system. "Hell yeah, old school shit," I said out loud. "Even gotta dab of some of that old school shit by that crazy ass Rick James up in here Super Freakin'! Got some of everything jamming in this bitch."

Some damn good music to be listening to when flying the MH-53. I guess the best way to describe it is like imagining having the sky to yourself.

"Look out you weird ass people in the bay area," I yelled out. "Here I come with some loud, heavy rhythmical, foot-stomping all over this Goddamn place."

As my huge craft bombarded the entire Napa-Sonoma-Mendocino County and neighboring area with the forcefully throbbing, thunderous sounds coming from its engine, while in a deep, wide, smooth, 60-degree left bank, I could see the towns of Santa Rosa, Petaluma, Sausalito and San Rafael as I headed in the direction of the Golden Gate Bridge and on into San Francisco and over San Mateo, Palo Alto, Sunnyvale, Santa Clara, and then, across to San Jose. This is where I'd ended up bringing this baby to a smooth landing to pick up a few friends who'd eventually end up making the journey with me to Stonyford.

After landing on a private section at the San Jose Airport, I was then met by Tony, Karen, and Regina who were seemingly very amazed to see me just as I too was happy to see them.

"Man, what is this?" said Tony, pointing at the massive MH-53, as they stood within a safe distance.

Upon exiting my craft, it was then that I found myself staring in much amazement directly at Karen. It had been so many years since I'd last had an opportunity to see her. She'd become so elegant in her appearance and indeed tastefully rich in her presentation. I couldn't help but to just stare at her, wondering what life would have been if only I hadn't walked out on her not long after we were married.

"Come on, man," I could hear Tony saying. "Let's hurry up and get over there and get something to eat, 'cause I'm starving to death."

It was then that I also realized Karen staring directly at me, too. But I knew I couldn't embrace her in the manner I wanted, so instead, I slightly and insignificantly, and without being rude, though with courtesy, very gently hugged her, while at the same time, fighting all temptation to cling on to her.

As we embraced, I could feel our heavy breathing from the resentment of not being able to stand too closely together. Just that quick, she was breathing heavily against the side of my neck. This is the lady that I for so many years longed to see again. I yearned to be near her, and now that the moment had arrived, it's like a forbidden fruit, I'm prohibited from tasting her.

"Is everything all right?" said Regina.

"Yeah, let's go get something to eat," Tony said again.

"Uh, yeah," I said. "That's right. We got things to do after we get something to eat."

I'm more than sure Karen could sense what I was really indicating for it was she who was responsible for originally baptizing me deep in the submerging stream of her river. For it is she that I must admit being fully responsible for educating, training, and schooling me in the sexuality part of my life.

Tall, slender, and without any doubts whatsoever, fantastically superb, and wonderfully extravagant.

She's my very fantasy come true.

I'm talking about Karen.

The lady is so very beautiful.

"Man, Tony," I asked, "What have you been up to? I mean, damn, man, I haven't seen you guys in so long."

"Ah, man, it's like, what you been up to?" he asked me, smiling. "You the one been missin' in action. We ain't seen you in days, Murdock!"

"I mean, see for yourself what I been doin'," I told him.

"Yeah, flyin' that big thang," said Karen. "Everybody thought you got caught up in the crack epidemic or something."

"Now that's really messed up," I said, staring at Karen. "You know that isn't even me. I don't even get high, and never have smoked."

Everybody laughing.

"We didn't know what had happened to you," said Tony. "You know, since that situation years ago."

"Yeah," I said, remembering what he was referring to. "Man, that was an embarrassing time in my life. It's like everything was falling apart all around me."

"Well, that's what made us think maybe you'd gotten caught up in the crack epidemic," Tony said. "Whoever we didn't see or hear about anymore, we just thought they'd become crack addicts like everyone else out here in these streets."

"Man, I know what you mean," I said. "Just about everybody I knew, they were using that stuff. That shit was some crazy contagious stuff to be smoking. It's like a disease spreading from state to state. It was everywhere."

"Uh huh," Regina said. "That shit still got these crazy fools out here robbing and killing each other. Don't make no sense. No sense at all."

Tony and Karen had a really nice looking 1978 Chrysler New Yorker Brougham. It was an original. A gorgeous classic. White with tan interior. Clean as can be all the way around, and yes, a two-door hard top.

"Man, now, I really do like this car you're driving," I told Tony. "Kinda remind me of those good old times, you know, back in the seventies."

"Uh huh," Karen uttered. "I know you don't really wanna go there, do you?"

Her comment had me thinking. So I just stared at her, knowing just what she was insinuating as she very slyly and ingeniously cut those intimidating eyes at me.

"What are you mumbling about, Karen?" Regina asked, sensing something important on her mind. "What? Cat got your tongue?"

I know one thing, being so near to Karen had me in the right mood for something special. Once we entered one of San Jose's finest and busiest established restaurants recognized for its supreme quality of food, I couldn't help but start out with the seafood salad as did everyone else. The atmosphere reminded me so much of being in Santa Monica, or just simply visiting a few of the many restaurants along the Pacific Coast Highway. No kidding, San Jose has always felt so welcoming. The Korean barbecued lamb chop with a bountiful mixed plate full of tuna fillet and pot roast, alongside a dish of pistachio Israeli couscous spaghetti squash, and some tasty freshwater shrimps. King crab legs, snow crab legs, fried BBQ chicken, fresh Pacific salmon fillets (bone out), and some damn good-tasting potato salad. Oh, and let me not forget to mention the freshly-baked apple pie, and sweet danish and muffins. And by the way, the tasty baby back ribs were off the chain.

I just had to surprise Karen with some fresh flower bunches. Well, I also surprised Regina with a few so that what I was doing wouldn't look so obvious. I even asked Karen to open her mouth, pretending that I wanted to see if or not she had all her teeth. As soon as she opened wide, I then placed a juicy red strawberry between her teeth. Of course, she had her eyes closed. That's when I placed my lips next to hers and gently bit down on the other half of the strawberry.

And where and what was Tony doing? Well, Regina was keeping him busy.

Hey, what are friends for?

Regina ordered a basket or two of nectarines and plums to take on our long journey to Stonyford. Karen got some blueberries and red and green seedless grapes. Tony got a few cantaloupes.

And what did I get?

As usual, my craving was for Karen.

"Sounds like somebody's cell is bugging off the hook," said Tony, referring to the buzzing of Regina's cellphone.

"Girl, you must got that thing turned all the way up," Karen said.

"Gotta hear it in case I'm busy doin' somethin'," said Regina.

"Anyway, you guys," I began saying, "I'm just glad you're willing to make this trip with me."

"What's this all about?" Tony asked. "I mean, I heard bits and pieces. But I haven't heard the whole story."

"Uh, don't you mean we haven't heard the whole story?" said Karen.

"Oh, yeah, I mean, we haven't heard the whole story," Tony said, trying to correct himself. "None of us heard it, the whole story."

"I remember reading something about it in a report," Karen said, while drinking from a glass of Sprite soda. "And if I'm not mistaken, they're at a dead end trying to figure out who did it."

"Did what?" Tony asked.

"Been murdering all them people," Karen told him.

"What people?" asked Tony. "What people are you talking about?"

"It's the situation that took place in Stonyford," I told him. "You know, where they've been finding bodies. They're at a dead end, and been requesting assistance from all over the place."

"Man," Tony said. "That's right! Now I think I remember reading something in the recent journal about some weird spooky shit up there in a small town called Stonyford. But, damn! From what the report was sayin' was that, it was something out of a Hollywood movie script or something. It's like, the town is haunted. You know what I mean?"

"Now nobody said anything about the town being haunted," Karen said. "I know you're not thinking about what I'm thinking you're thinking about."

"Yeah, what's that?" I asked.

"Yeah, what's that?" asked Tony.

"We gettin' ready to leave?" asked Regina, smiling slyly.

"Oh, no," Karen said, as a woman would do when knowing someone is up to something. "What are you up to, Ms. Regina?"

"Why y'all staring at me like that?" Regina questioned.

"Because we know you're up to something," I told her.

"Ain't that the truth," said Karen.

"So what's happening?" I asked her, knowing it was something important on her mind.

"What's up, Regina?" asked Tony. "Spit it out!"

"Well, you know my friend, Sandra?" Regina began. "Well, she wanna know if, you know, we'll hook her up on the trip?"

"You're talking about Chinatown Sandra?" asked Karen. "Your lover?"

"Man, Sandra's cool," Tony said. "You remember her, Murdock, she's the lady we met a long time ago in Frisco over there in Chinatown."

"The one we seen laying all under Regina," said Karen. "She's the one you kept staring at, you know, before you found out she was a lesbian. When you was probably thinking about tryin' to get in them panties."

Everybody laughed.

"He ain't tried to do nothin' like that," said Tony, defending me.

"Man, thank you, Tony," I told him. "That's something I never thought about doin' with nobody. And especially not with Sandra."

"What, my baby isn't good enough for you?" asked Regina. "What?"

"Y'all trippin'," said Tony.

"It just isn't me, Regina," I told her. "And even if I could do it, I wouldn't have done you like that."

"You need to quit it, Karen," Tony told her. "Up in here trying' to get somethin' started."

"It's not me," I told Regina. "I'm not the one, you know, who'll do something like that."

"I just wanted to hear you say it," said Karen. "I know you wouldn't, and that's the truth."

"Well, on the real, I wouldn't," I told her. "I'm only keeping it one hundred with you guys. You feel me?"

"Tell her, Murdock's cool," Tony told her. "I ain't never seen him let nobody down."

"Yeah, it's all right," I said, being in agreement with Tony. "But answer something for me."

"What's that?" asked Regina, holding her cellphone in a position so that Sandra could hear what I was about to say.

"I mean, it's like," I'd begun questioning, "are we to wait here, you know for you? Or, are you expecting us to come over there to Frisco and pick you up?"

"Sweetheart," Regina said in a soft tone to Sandra. "You want us to come pick you up?"

"Yeah, right," Tony quickly said. "What we gone do, fly over there and land that big helicopter right smack dab in the front of her house or something?"

"We can't do that, can we?" asked Karen.

"Yeah, and end up killing ourselves in the process," I told them. "No way, Jose, am I going to attempt anything like that. Plus, power lines will most likely end up electrocuting us to death, and before that happen, the FAA will be all over us."

"FAA," Regina questioned, "what's that?"

"It's the Federal Aviation Agency," I explained. "They're the ones responsible for granting the authorization to operate aircrafts to an extent limited by the type of aircraft."

"Man, Murdock," said Tony. "None of us even know what that mean, and I sure know, she don't know."

"You don't know what I might know," Regina quickly responded. "I just might fly them things, without you knowing it."

"Well, if you do," said Karen, "it ain't nothin' like what we're talking about."

"And just what is that suppose to mean?" asked Regina. "What are you trying to insinuate, Ms. Karen?"

Laughing.

"Anyway, you guys," I interrupted. "We ain't landing my craft in front of nobody's house."

"Well, couldn't she just take the bus? Or even BART?" Tony suggested.

"And then what?" asked Regina. "What we gone do, land on the top of it so that she can climb up and get inside?"

"Girl, you really need to quit it," said Karen. "Now, just how stupid is that going to look?"

"They be doing it in the movies," said Regina. "I see it happening all the time, and especially on James Bond."

"Damn, Regina," said Tony. "You got no intelligence at all."

Laughing.

"And just what's on your mind, Mr. Murdock?" asked Karen. "I know it's something going on in the head of yours."

"Yeah, well," I began, "I was thinking that maybe she could just take BART all the way over to, you know, Concord. We could then pick her up at the airport just a few miles from the BART station."

"But since we're already right here in San Jose," said Regina, "then why can't she just take the BART and ride it over here to nearby Fremont?"

"I mean, she can do that, too," I told her.

"How come we can't just pick her up at the San Francisco airport?" is what Karen suggested.

"That's possible too," I told her. "Only problem is, do she have a way to make it out there? I mean, that's quite a ways from Chinatown."

"So what are you suggesting?" asked Tony.

"Yeah, what do you think she should do?" asked Regina.

"Where do you live, Sandra?" I asked her, loud enough so that she could hear me.

"In Chinatown," said Regina.

"Yeah, in Chinatown," Karen also answered.

"I know that," I told them. "I'm thinking about, what part of Chinatown?"

"She said, right off Sacramento near Pacific," said Regina. "Closer to Grant Avenue. Big Al's and the Condor is right down the street. On the other street down near the corner, on the opposite side of the street, the World Theater is always showing Chinese pictures only. Hofbrau Restaurant where you'll always find some good Chinese food."

"Okay, that's enough," I told her. "Don't need any more food—unless you guys wanna take some Chinese food with us?"

"Just get me some of them fortune cookies," Regina told her. "I can read a good fortune or two about what'll be waiting on us at that place we are going to."

"The town is Stonyford, Regina," said Karen. "And it's waiting on you to hurry up and get there."

"Girl, let me tell you about this town," Regina could be heard telling Sandra as I planned to pick her up in Concord. It was suggested that she take BART, the rapid transit transportation express train used for transporting people throughout the Bay Area who travel long distances.

Once we boarded the craft, Tony had already parked his car in the private section of the airport that was designated for pilots. It wasn't our intention to be gone too long, so therefore, security was well in place.

Listening to the building up of the power from the engine as each swinging motion of the rotor blades began moving in circles, faster and faster, I could see the expression on everyone's face revealing an anticipating excitement from the massive piece of equipment that was about to transport us from one dimensional form to another.

As the engine could be heard grinding loudly into its stimulating exhilaration, the forceful power of my craft could be felt as it began to lift from the ground, deliberately invigorating everyone on board with such cheerfulness to where both Karen and Regina were claiming to have experienced orgasms.

Once again, my RPM gauges were all working in conjunction with each other as my craft thrust forcefully forward at a high rate of speed over San Jose, Fremont and Hayward. We were in no time sailing smoothly through the air making a low 30-degree bank over Alameda and Oakland.

We were next floating as if on a cloud listening to some sweet music by Rell, Jay-Z, LL Cool J, The Dream, and Snoop Dogg. Tank and Tupac Shakur, and also E-40. Con-Funk-Shun and Maze. And let me not forget Marvin Gaye and Mary J. Blige, along with some Maxwell and Mass Production. Oh, and by the way, as I stared to my far left at San Francisco, AC/DC was jamming *Highway to Hell* and Creedence Clearwater Revival, *Bayou Country*.

As my craft jammed on up through the outskirts of Berkeley heading in the direction of Walnut Creek, I pointed out to everyone that BART was traveling underneath us at high speed to Concord. This is the train we were hoping Sandra was riding.

"Is there any way you can drop down a little bit and slow down?" Regina asked me. "I just wanna see if she can see us."

"Are you crazy?" said Tony. "Just how the hell you think she's gone see us? Let alone we see her?"

"It's possible," I told him. "But the FAA don't play that! We can't go any lower than we already are. And I know for a fact that we're already attracting the kind of attention we really don't need."

Tony, who was sitting up front with me, was wearing my pilot helmet, dark sunglasses and gloves used when piloting any aircraft.

Karen and Regina were both seated in the passenger area where there was special equipment, special military equipment and different components that were built in a fixed position in case of an emergency. This type of helicopter was amongst the largest ever built. The MH-53 is recognized as the flying luxury Brougham of the air when it came to helicopters. Its huge, massive body and extremely large rotors were a chilling sight.

It wasn't hard to tell that this baby was built for business.

As we circled the privately owned airport before landing, Regina all of a sudden yelled out, seeing BART approaching the Concord station. "There it is," she screamed. "It's right down there on its way. You see it? It's just about to pass by that flat-looking building down there."

"Oh, yeah, I see it," said Karen. "What's it doing, slowing down?"

"Where we gone land at?" Regina asked me.

"The airport is right over there," Karen told her. "You see it?"

"Now, get ready to jump out, Regina," Tony jokingly told her. "And use that ugly-looking big ass coat you're wearing like a parachute or a floating umbrella. It'll take you just where you wanna go."

"Now, that's really messed up, Tony," I told him. "What are you going to do if she really jumps?"

"I hear y'all up in there talking about me," said Regina. "I might be a little crazy at times, but I'm not that crazy."

Tony began making snickering sounds.

"You guys up there playing around, when what you need to be doing is landing this thing so we can pick up Sandra," said Regina.

"I really don't think she's on that particular train," I told her.

"How do you know that?" she asked me curiously. "I thought I'd seen her waving at us."

"All them people down there," Tony began, "I don't think so."

"He's right, Regina," I told her. "It's no way you seen her with all them people down there walking around the place."

"Now, it's possible," said Karen. "But that's if you told her to wear a certain color. You know, something that'll make her stand out."

"But what makes you think she isn't on that one, Murdock?" she asked me.

"Because it wasn't too long ago that you talked to her," I told her. "She'll most likely be on the next one, but that's if she made to the next on time, because she just might be on the one after the next."

"Regina, why don't you just call her and find out where she's at?"

After making a smooth soft landing at the Concord airport, there was a rental car available for us. We immediately went in search of Sandra who by this time was still in San Francisco getting her hair done.

"I thought you'd seen her waving, Regina?" Tony asked her. "Man, here it is, she haven't even left Chinatown. And knowing how slow women are, we'd have enough time to drive all the way over there to Frisco, and I bet we'll still end up far ahead of her before she'll ever be ready."

"Oh, quit complaining, Tony," Karen told him. "That's all you do when things don't go your way. Complain! Complain! Complain! Never satisfied!"

"Who you talking to like that?" Tony asked her, staring at another BART train as it pulled into the station. "I can't hear you answering."

"All you do is complain about everything, and you know it," she again told him. "That's why I didn't really wanna come on this trip."

"Oh, and was that because of me?" he asked her.

"Isn't that just what I said?" she told him, jiggling her head in circular motions. "What? You're now hard of hearing?"

Hearing their conversation made me wonder if maybe she and Tony were really in a rocky relationship. Quite naturally I would find myself wondering and thinking this way, and that's because, remember, Karen used to be my girl. But not only my girl, she and I were once married. And I guess you can say that, if I had the chance, I'd beg her to give me another chance and take me back.

We finally came to an agreement to drive over to Frisco, and as I'm more than sure everyone knew, Sandra still wasn't ready. But really, I didn't mind the wait. Being in Chinatown was always exciting to me, plus, Regina had an ample amount of time to purchase all the fortune cookies she needed. And oh yeah, both Karen and Tony were still occasionally arguing about the least little thing. Still, they were all very important to me. You just don't find such good people anymore. They were all wonderful people to be around. My present relationship with Karen was so done with respect. She knew I still desired her, but that's all it was—a desire fully under control with respect.

We finally made our way back to Concord, but that was after a few too many stops in Oakland and Berkeley.

We were all considered journalists in our own right, anxiously awaiting to get that once-in-a-lifetime dissemination of news material written for publication in the media.

Aboard the helicopter, and before taking off for the trip to Stonyford, everyone began the proceeding to start recording our daily events as a legislative body. We were in this venture together and it was time to keep a personal daily record of our experiences and observations. Each having their own specialized interest as an experienced worker so distinguished and a master in journalism.

A little acceleration to lift my craft off the ground and then, it was all about my sudden increase in speed. Once again, my RPM gauges were all working in complete conjunction with each other as I pressed down on my right rudder pedal to make a steep 45-degree climb into a 2000-foot altitude over Concord and then the city of Vallejo, and on up to Fairfield, Vacaville and Dixon. When reaching Davis, I added a little extra acceleration and made a steep, sharp 45-degree left past Woodland and on up to the towns of Williams and Colusa.

That's when I suddenly found myself with a desire to take my craft even higher and to a degree hoping that we could possibly somehow see Vallejo far out to our left. We could see it, and believe me, the sight was striking and indeed very spectacular.

Everything in sight looked fantastically beautiful as both Karen and Regina, as well as Sandra, claimed to have had orgasms like never before from the thrust of the massive engine powering my craft with exceeding force.

We were next cruising at a pleasurable speed, though not at maximum operating efficiency provided for the MH-53 J-Pave Low to sail. High over the small town of Maxwell an old-school song by Prince suddenly came blasting through the surround-sound entertainment center. The song titled *When Doves Cry*, played instrumentally, followed by another of Maze and Frankie Beverly, the entire collection.

With the music loudly blasting through just about every instrument panel, and everybody singing and screaming to the sounds of *Square Congo*, by Teena Marie, it was then that I begin to realize that it was time for me to get a for-real grip on myself as we sailed thousands of feet over huge mountains and steep valleys, as this baby rocked and danced back and forth, climbing and maneuvering slightly downward into steep descents, while continuing to hold good altitude.

A quick, bumpy upward jolt and another steep 45-degree right bank, and then a 60-degree bank to my left, having more power than expected.

The instrument gauges seemed to be themselves dancing and jamming to my every maneuver.

I can just imagine the amount of wildlife I'd probably chopped up as my craft plunged deep into a sharp 45-degree right bank, and then into a a killer 60-degree left bank, and then to a shallow 15-degree right bank while maintaining good altitude as we sped steadily and smoothly through their natural environment.

I remember seeing large flocks of wildlife trying their best to get the hell out the way of this MH-53, but as is well known, when it comes to this big bird there is very little doubt about the massively built rotating blades being something dreadfully awesome and indeed a horrible experience to attempt contending with if struck.

A smooth 30-degree bank to my left while losing altitude.

My instrument panel is beginning to mellow out.

I could see in the distance ahead of me a clearance just below the horizon sunset along which the earth and sky appeared to meet.

As we continued west, the sun began to very slowly drop, as if into the Pacific Ocean, disappearing into its created spectral colors of rainbows.

We were then nearing the location which I'd intended to land for the night.

That's when I told everyone that we would be bunkering down in the small town community wilderness area of Cash Creek, an unsettled and uncultivated part of the region. We'd be staying there preparing ourselves for the trip to Stonyford. I also reminded them about how important it was for the preparation and the necessity for them to be completely ready as if going to war against an unknown element.

I then began toying with my throttle controls and checking the carburetor heat lever, making sure there wasn't any ice building up anywhere from all the maneuvering.

I thought to myself how my directional gyro and rudders had had one hell of a workout.

There was still enough light without me having to use my emergency devices as a means to prevent any unnecessary contact with wildlife elements. But I did activate my specially built illumination switch as a necessary precaution, setting in motion a reactive mixture of signal lights for identification landing in which to identify my craft.

The landing was perfect and the ground was both grassy and somewhat gravelly, allowing a few loose rock fragments to spiral continuously outward in large circles caused by the swift, swinging motion of the blades.

I then reached up and shut down, ceasing all functioning operation of my engine, halting the power to this massive piece of equipment.

I had every reason to feel proud and boastful, but I just leaned back into a relaxed, inclined position, stared straight ahead, momentarily, and let the MH-53 J-Pave Low shine like never before to the soft musical tune of Luther Vandross's *A House Is Not a Home.*

I then looked to my right at Tony, then back to where Karen had been seated, but to my surprise she, just that quick, was standing within a few inches from me.

"How could you see where to land?" asked Tony.

"That's just what I was about to ask," said Karen.

"It's all about my instrument panel," I said, pointing at each gauge as it illuminated its purpose. "Everything I want to know about on the outside, my instrument panel will tell me from on the inside."

"Man, I was wondering why you wasn't paying that much attention, you know, to what was happening outside the window," said Tony, amazed from the thought of how I was operating my craft. "I mean, it was really like, I was thinking about asking you why you wasn't looking out the window that much."

"Once you've learned to trust your instrument panel during flight, that becomes a very vital part of your training. It's like an essential part of the operation. You watch your instrument panel become full of life."

"But you really can't see anything that's happening," said Tony. "You know, on the outside."

"No," I told him. "You're right about not being able to see on the outside. But man, you have the sensors to visualize in your mind a really nice mental image of what's supposed to be happening."

"Visualize?" asked Tony. "About what? It's dark, and you really can't see anything out there."

"But you can communicate with the panel," I told him. "It'll let you see any and everything once you've learned how to communicate with your instrument panel."

"Man, I don't think I could ever learn how to do anything like that in the dark," said Tony. "I'd be done crash and killed everybody."

"Now, come on, Tony," I told him. "Everybody has a visual outlook from which we can picture something.

"You see, Tony, the creator blessed everyone with the ability to think, reason, and understand everything that seems at times very complicated to us.

"It's like, let's just take Karen, for instance. Now, we both already know how so very beautiful a person she really is. I mean, man, come on, and let's be truthful. The lady is extremely beautiful. But, check this out, can you remember what it was like when first seeing her? Now remember, I'm just using her as a means to try and help you understand where I'm coming from. I need to do this by using her as an illustrative case, you know, an example. And please, Karen, please know that it's not my intention to in any way be trying cause you to be blushing or anything, and I'm in no way trying to embarrass you. But what I'm trying to do is help you guys and enable you to understand a certain point about this instrument panel.

"So now, to try and better exemplify what I'm saying, Tony, can you remember what it was like when you first set eyes on her? Do you remember? And do you remember what exactly went through your mind at the time?

"Now being truthful, Tony, I'm really trying to make a serious point to you about this instrument panel. I'm trying to, you know, help you and teach you something about why it's so important for you to rely on the strange illumination of lights—especially in the dark.

"So now, let's just use your senses as you did when you first met Karen. Can you see her? Can you really see how nice and beautiful she looked?

"Okay then, now picture her—naked! Can you see her? And what was the rate of your heart per beat? You see, you just used a suppressed image and visualized seeing Karen without ever actually seeing her in person. It's like believing in God. You yourself have never actually seen him, but it's by using your faith that you are able to believe in the things not seen.

"Well, that's also how it is when it comes to using my instrument panel. I had to activate my faith and learn to trust that it'll always bring me home safely. And that's without me ever having to see any visual sight of my unforeseen journey.

"Visualizing is sometimes all you have left in life."

"But what if I don't have an instrument panel?" asked Tony.

"That's when your built-in, photoelectric cells come to life," I told him. "Learn to be completely sensitive to responding readily to those small changes of your conditions and environment. Teach yourself how to become readily affected by not only your own feelings and emotions, but by those also of the emotions of others under any circumstance. Once you've learned how to trust your own abilities to function through illumination, you'll then leave a positive impression with meaningful significances for others to follow."

"Man, Murdock," Tony questioned. "I never knew you knew how to, you know, do all this kind of stuff. Flyin' helicopters and things. I didn't know you knew how to do anything like this. I mean, you know, all this stuff you're teachin' me about relying on lights and everything."

"Illuminating lights," said Karen. "I'm the same as you, I never knew either."

"Yeah, that's right," said Tony. "Man, it's like, just how did you learn how to do all of this stuff? Let alone, fly something like this?"

I looked at Karen first, and then Tony, and smiled, saying, "It's all about the library, man. It's all about the library. You see, all the literary material I needed to read about everything I desired to do, it's at the city library. And whenever I have the time, that's just where you'll find me."

"And what library is that?" Karen asked.

"Any library," I told her. "I'm there, busy reading about any, and just about everything. I just like reading interesting stories. I like reading, I guess you can say, books about being creative. But not only do I just enjoy an opportunity to read about being creative, but man, I'm the type of person who'll test the water.

"Just look at me, I'm living proof."

"Amen about that, Bro," Regina agreed. "And if ever I end up going back to the other side, you know, fooling around with men, just remember, you'd be my first to hook up with."

"Regina, please," said Karen. "Girl, ain't nobody thinking about nothin' like you."

"Well, ain't nobody thinkin' about yo skinny tail, either," said Regina, smiling. "Well, let me take that back. Nobody but Tony."

"Heeyy," said Sandra. "What 'bout me?"

"Oh, you want her too?" asked Regina.

"Damn!" said Tony. "What you got going on, Karen? Sounds like Sandra wanna hook up with you."

"Nope!" Regina quickly said, snapping her fingers, making sharp popping sounds. "Ain't no happening."

"Hey, *no*," Sandra quickly responded after realizing what Tony was slyly insinuating. "Me not, you know, thinkin' 'bout anything, you say, not a like that, with tall lady-her, Karen. Nothin' like that, so you no be say, aw, nothin' like-a that, because, you make-a Regina upset at me. You know?"

"Now, why you wanna get something like this started?" Karen whispered to Tony.

"They know I was just playin'," said Tony. "They know you're not that way. Or are you?"

"You wanna get knocked outta here?" Karen told him, squinting her eyes together. "Keep it up, and you will."

"Murdock ain't gone allow that to happen," he told her. "Are you?"

"He got nothing to do with this," she told him. "So just leave him out of it."

"Man, Murdock," Tony said, looking at me. "Man, you hear this fool up in here threatening me and everything? That's why I really hate taking her anywhere."

"Is that right?" Karen questioned. "You can always take me back, or you can just drop me off at the next town. I know how to make it home."

Cellphone buzzing.

"Who is that?" I asked, looking around. "Me or one of you guys?"

"It's not mine," Regina quickly answered.

"Not me," said Sandra.

"Nope, it ain't me," said Tony.

"Is that you, Karen?" I asked her, still looking around the cockpit.

"Wish it was for me," she said in an obnoxious, smirky tone. "But too bad it isn't."

After finally realizing it was my cellphone buzzing, I quickly reached down and unfastened my adjustable seat belt and shoulder straps. I then stood slightly upright within a few inches from Karen, who just happened to be herself standing close to my chair. I then in my effort to retrieve my cellphone from the package container section on the back of my chair, gently grazed against her coming into contact with her pelvic area, at which time, I felt her, intentionally, press somewhat forcefully against me, and whisper a low, moaning sound. "Ohhhhhhh."

I was surprised Tony hadn't noticed anything, but I guess he was too busy tinkering with my radio transmitting frequencies.

After retrieving my cellphone, I heard Tony mentioning something about hearing my name on the transmitter, saying someone was trying to contact me.

"Hey, Murdock," he shouted. "Man, somebody's on here trying' to contact you."

"Yeah, right," I told him. "What'd they say?"

"Man, I'm serious," said Tony.

"What'd they say?" I again asked him.

"Man, I just heard somebody sayin' somethin' like Muuurrdooock, are you out there?"

"And that's all?"

"Well, I think I heard 'em say something like, get back at me, or, come back at me, or something like that."

"Are you sure, Tony?" Karen asked him.

"Isn't that what I just said?"

"Well, if you really heard somebody trying to contact me," I began, "I need you to go back to the channel where you heard 'em callin'."

"That's if I can find it," said Tony. "Man, you must have a million stations on this thing. I can't seem to remember where I was at."

As he continued to search, and while answering my cellphone, I couldn't help but find myself thinking about what I had just previously experienced with Karen. If it wasn't for the fact that I considered myself a decent, respectable person no matter the situation, you can believe, I would have been all over her at first chance. I mean, you know, doing just about any and everything whenever the opportunity presented itself. But that's not my style of character, plus, Tony knew that I was a person who could be trusted. But as I think about it, I guess you can say it's just like the lyrics in one of Bobby Womack's songs when he speaks about trust. Well, and to be truthful, I really wish Tony wouldn't trust me so much when it comes to

Karen.

But I refuse to do anything to in any way compromise my integrity. Therefore, my disposition and moral principles were to continue battling the desires of my fleshly body and the temptation that seeks immoral gratification.

"Yeah, what's up?" I asked the voice at the other end. "Oh, yeah, so that was you trying to contact me?—"

"Karen," Regina called out. "Where's the bathroom? Or is there even one in this thing?"

"You know where it is?" Karen whispered to Tony.

"Just ask Murdock," he told her. "I think it might be one somewhere back there in the back."

"Where?" asked Regina, desperate to know.

"Back there somewhere," Tony told her. "Just go find it, or go outside in the dark where nobody'll see you."

"Man, are you crazy or somethin'," asked Regina. "I'm not goin' out there."

"Well, it's you who gotta shit," said Tony. "Not me."

"And just who said anything about somebody having to shit?" Regina questioned him rotating her head in circles.

"Well, whatever you gotta do," he told her, snickering. "Just take your scary butt outside and do it since you don't wanna get up and go see if it's back there in the back somewhere."

"Come on, I'll go with you, Regina," said Sandra.

"It should be back there," Karen told her. "Check and see if that door's unlocked."

"What door?" asked Regina. "I didn't know it was a door back there."

"Uh huh," Karen said, pointing toward a certain area in the back section of the helicopter. "That door right there."

"Damn!" I exclaimed. "How did you notice that door when I didn't even notice it?"

"You mean to tell me you been flying this thing, and didn't think to check everything out first?" Karen asked me. "You don't know what's on board this thing. Might be smuggling illegal drugs or something."

"Might be a monster back there," Tony said jokingly. "Go see, Regina."

"Oh, funny," said Regina. "Now you wanna clown. What, you're becoming a comedian? What's the name of your circus?"

"Okay, then. Well, we'll be expecting you guys," I told one of the members from the news crew out of Sacramento who were flying to our location in a military-issued, 65 Bell UH-1H Huey helicopter.

"Mmm-mmm," Karen mumbled. "Sounds like company coming."

"Yeah," I answered. "Some news reporters out of Sacramento headed our way to assist us on our journey to Stonyford."

"What, they're driving all the way out here?" asked Tony.

"How they gone drive a car way out here in this mess?" Karen asked. "I ain't seen no roads leading out here when we was about to land."

"Naw," I answered. "They're not driving a car out here. They're flying in, in a helicopter the same way we did."

"Where they gone land?" asked Tony. "And how are they going to land? I mean look how dark it is out there. Man, what if they crash into us?"

"What? They're flying a big one like this one?" asked Karen.

"No," I answered. "It's not as big as this, but it's a nice size one."

"Oh, I know what you mean," Tony said as if he knew what I was talking about. "Those news helicopters, they're kinda small."

"Nooo, I don't think so, Tony," I told him. "This is what you call a Huey. You know, the kind I'm sure you probably seen on TV, you know, when they be showing documentaries, like on PBS, about places like Vietnam and other cities, like Cu Chi. But it was mainly used in places like Vietnam. It won the National Aviation Hall of Fame People's Choice Award."

"Well how come we flying in this big-go thing, instead of one of them?" asked Regina.

"Hold on, wait a minute, let me answer this one," Karen quickly suggested, grinning.

"Go ahead," I told her, wondering what she was up to.

"Because, big things are good for you, Regina," Karen told her staring directly at me.

Everybody laughing.

"Oh, damn," said Tony. "I know you didn't."

"Y'all, so nasty," said Regina.

"And back to what I was talking about," I hinted as an indirect indication to change the subject. "Now, where was I?"

"Oh, I know," said Regina, turning her head in the direction of the back area of the helicopter. "Somebody was supposed to be telling me if or not this thing got a bathroom in it."

"No, Regina," Karen objected. "Murdock was explaining to Tony something about Huey helicopters, or something like that. I just know that had to do with something about the news people landing out here."

"Yeah, that's right," I said in agreement with Karen. "I was talking to Tony, and explaining to him the size of the Huey, and everything this particular helicopter stood for during its mission in Vietnam."

"But wasn't you also sayin' something about some news reporters from Sacramento possibly headed our way to assist us on this journey to Stonyford?" asked Karen.

"No doubt," I told her. "They should be here in about thirty minutes."

"And they're flying in what you call a Huey?" Tony asked.

"Yeah, that's right," I answered. "A Huey helicopter. I'mma open this door so that you'll hear it coming. You know, just like I'm more than sure, we could be heard loud and clear when we was headed this way."

"Was it that loud?" asked Tony.

"Man, you can hear these things coming from miles away," I told him.

"And where is the bathroom?" Regina asked seriously. "I gotta pee, and y'all playin' around."

"I told you it's probably back there somewhere," Karen told her, once again pointing to the back of the helicopter. "Go look back there, I told you."

"Everybody be quiet," Tony whispered. "I think I hear something."

"Now, why you wanna be scarin' her like that?" Karen asked Tony. "What you tryin' to do, make her pee all over herself?"

"Be quiet, Karen, damn!" said Tony. "I told you, I think I hear something."

"Murdock, close this door," said Regina. Hurry up!"

"Hurry up for what?" Tony asked her. "Why you wanna close the door?"

"Because you just said you heard something out there," Regina told him. "And I don't want nothin' coming runnin' up in here with that door wide open like that."

"Got me tryin' to figure this one out too," said Karen. "What did you hear?"

"I think he heard, monster coming," Sandra said, peeping out the window next to her seat.

"All of y'all on some bullshit," Tony told them. "I'm talking about I think I hear the Huey coming. That's what I'm talking about. Tell 'em what I'm talking about, Murdock."

"Yeah, uh," I begin. "I thought they knew."

"Y'all really crazy up in here," said Tony. "And Regina sittin' back there about to pee all in that seat. Get yo ass back up and go back there and use that bathroom, fool!"

"Hey!" Sandra yelled out to Tony. "That's not right you call her a name like that. You make everybody think monster comin' when you say, you hear something coming outside. What da you think we suppose to know what you talking 'bout, huh? You know call her name like that no more. She nice girl."

"Uh, Tony," I suggested. "Man, why don't you just, you know, apologize so we can get back to business."

"Man," Tony said, snickering, "uh, what did I say that was so wrong? I mean, here it is, she gotta use the bathroom, but too afraid to just go back there in the back and find the bathroom. All she gotta do is open that door."

"Mentioning that door," I said, staring at it. "I can't believe it. All this time I called myself knowing just about everything there is to know and here it is, I for some reason never noticed that door back there."

Sandra still staring at Tony.

"Okay, then," Tony exclaimed. "Maybe I was wrong for playing around like that. And I'm sorry for calling you a fool. So, let the record reflect or reflex the seriousness within me, and show that I am apologizing to you, Ms. Regina, for what you are. No! I mean, for what I not long ago called you. You know, a few minutes ago."

"Oh, you must don't think anybody heard what you just said, Tony," she told him. "But that's all right."

"How you like her call you 'punk bitch,' Tony," Sandra asked him. "See, you no like."

"Didn't I just apologize?" asked Tony. "I said I'm sorry. What more can I do?"

Sandra squinting her eyes at Tony.

"I think your cellphone going off again," Karen told me. "Might be one of your ladies."

"Ain't no happening," I told her. "Nothin' like that, since you."

"Yeah, right!" she exclaimed. "I know better than that to believe that story."

"Believe what you wanna believe," I responded. "I know me, and I also know what I'm talking about."

She just stood there as if hesitating about her next question. I then after not hearing her say anything answered my call. It was a person on the other end from another news crew out of the town of Lodi near Stockton. He'd wanted to know if there would be any problem with him and a few reporters out of a small town called Galt to join us on this trip. "No, don't mind at all if that what you wanna do, but just remember, there's no tellin' what we might end up finding, I mean this isn't anything like a vacation."

By this time, both Regina and Sandra had finally made their way to the back of the helicopter and had opened the door.

"Now you see, that wasn't too hard to do, was it?" Karen asked them.

After clicking off my phone and laying it down on the top of my instrument panel, I then found myself once again staring at Karen. Tony was still busy trying to hear the Huey. "And who was that, Mr. Murdock?" she asked me, while resting her elbow on my right shoulder.

"Some more reporters wanting to know if I'd mind them assisting us to Stonyford," I told her.

"Sounds like everybody wanna ride with us," said Tony.

"You mean, fly with us, don't you.?" Karen asked him.

"Uh huh," said Tony. "Thanks for correcting me. I knew it was a good reason why I married you, Karen."

Knowing I heard Tony's statement loud and clear, it was obvious that it wasn't what Karen wanted me to hear. Especially givin' all she was busy doing to get my attention. But I have to admit, I was enjoying the thought of her vigorousness toward me. I still loved her and she knew it. If only I hadn't walked out on our marriage years ago, we'd still be together to this day.

"And what kind of helicopter are those people coming in?" Tony asked me, still listening to see if he could hear the crew from Sacramento.

"Man, Tony," I began. "I really don't know. They never said, and I didn't think about asking."

"They're coming out here where we are tonight?" asked Karen.

"From my understanding, that's what they wanna do," I answered. "It's all right with me, I mean, if that's what they really wanna do."

"Hold up," Karen shouted. "That's my song right there. You guys gotta be quiet right about now."

"Oh, I know who that is," said Tony. "It's um, um?"

"Heatwave," I told him, pointing and nodding my head toward Karen, who just happen to be slow dancing with herself to *Always and Forever.*"

"Man, y'all," Regina shouted while coming out the back area. "That's my song right there. I ain't heard that song in so long, y'all. I'm in the mood for making love right about now! Uh, to my baby."

"Well, just mood yo ass back there and flush that toilet," Tony told her, laughing.

"And here we go again," she told him. "Nobody asked you to open your mouth."

"Damn!" Karen shouted. "Why can't you guys just be quiet sometime?"

"Just look at 'em, Murdock," Tony said, referring to both Regina and Karen, but mostly Karen. "Song got 'em hooked and tripping on being in love. And you better be singing about me."

"And for your information, Tony," said Karen, "I ain't singing to nobody but myself! So just be quiet and leave me alone, for right now, if you don't mind?"

"Damn," I said to myself. "Karen is Karen, and gone do what she wanna do."

Upon finishing my statement, that's when I noticed her once again slyly cutting her eyes at me with a slight smile, while slowly gliding her tongue across her bottom lip. And yeah, I repeated the same tongue motion in return, except my tongue motion was to let her know that I wanted to kiss her in a very special way. The way she knew that I knew she liked.

"Why did you stop singing?" Tony asked her. "I thought that was your favorite song?"

Karen just stood there, speechless, without an utterance. And Regina, who was now wearing a pair of light-tinted, yellowish sunglasses, could be seen peering over the top section, staring at Karen.

"Girl, I hear you," said Regina, not aware of what was happening. "I can lay back and listen to that song all night."

Upon noticing Sandra coming through the doorway, that's when I decided to question them about the bathroom area. "So, it is a bathroom back there?" I asked Sandra.

"Uh huh," Regina quickly answered. "And something covered up under a blanket or something."

"Man, Murdock," Tony began to suggest. "Man, you need to check that out and find out what she's talking about, 'cause man, knowing her, she just might be talking about a dead body or something being covered up back there."

"Ain't nobody talking about seein' no dead body, Tony," Regina hold him. "I just seen something that looked like an old, dirty blanket or something in the middle of the floor covering something up. And, Murdock, whatever it is under there, it ain't no dead body!"

"I think it's an ATV," said Sandra. "'Cause—"

"How do you know that?" questioned Tony.

"'Cause it have, ah, small little wheels on it," said Sandra. "I take close look to see. It's like, ATV cover over it."

"Yeah," I told everybody, "I better go check this out for myself."

"I'll go with you," Karen said, standing close to me."

"No, Karen," Tony told her. "Just stay here and let us check this out."

"Well, close this door before you do," Regina suggested. "Something just might come running up in here, and you guys'll be back there and won't even know what's happening up in here."

"Now you see what you've started?" Karen said, looking at Tony. "Got her tripping on monsters again."

"Tony, just push that button right there," I told him, pointing at the large, round knob next to the center control console on the floor in between our seats. "That's it right down there on my side. That's right, now push it inward, and turn it slightly to the right. That's right, toward you."

As he turned the knob in his direction, the left side door began to slowly rise upward and close, bringing the bottom section of the door upward, electronically connecting it to the fuselage, locking it shut.

"There," said Tony. "Are you satisfied?"

"Thank you, Murdock," she said, staring at Tony. "I really appreciate you closing the door for me."

"Forget you," whispered Tony. "I bet it won't happen again."

Pushing the back center door wide open, it became obvious from just the shape of whatever it was underneath the canvas it indeed had wheels on it. The over-sized canvas could really be considered a canopy being that only a small portion had been used to cover the now visible ATV.

"Man, now I know why I felt all that drag," I told Tony, forgetting he knew nothing about the term I was using when describing something to pilots in aviation terms. "What I'm talking about is that this thing had me at times thinking I'd activated my parachute switch or something. That's why I kept looking out my window during flight. It felt like I was pulling something in behind my craft. I'm just glad the thing was tied down."

"And just think if it hadn't been?" Tony mentioned.

"Yeah, out of gear and left in neutral," I added. "Man, with all the maneuvering I was doing, sucker woulda been right up here with us, front and center, at full speed."

"We'd be done crashed by now," said Tony.

"And that would have been a for-real catastrophe," I again added. "To be truthful, I don't even wanna think about it."

"How did they get this in here?" asked Tony. "What is it, a garage door in here or something?"

"Nah, man, that's not what it's called on the craft," I told him. "But it's like a carrier unit, you know, for carrying or transporting equipment, such as this ATV. It's an aircraft storage door that opens when you need to store goods inside."

"Well, it's a big one," Tony said, looking all around it as if somehow trying to measure its dimension.

"Grab that side of this canopy, and pull this thing back a little so we can get a better look," I told him. "Yeah, that's it."

"Man, Murdock," said Tony. "Somebody musta knew it was going to be four of us because, look man, this thing got four seats in it."

"What a coincidence," I thought out loud. "Seemingly a planned sequence for us."

"I wonder what's in these boxes?"

"Well, all we have to do is open 'em up and find out."

"Nah, Murdock," said Tony curiously. "I think you better do that."

"What's wrong, you afraid or something?"

"Just my luck, I'd end up pulling the pin on a grenade or something."

"Tony, you gotta stop thinking so negative," I told him. "Now reach over there and open that box."

"And what about all of these duffel bags?" he asked me. "There must be about a good maybe fifteen or more stacked up right here."

"Just open 'em up and see what's inside."

"Ah, man, Murdock!" he shouted.

"Uh huh," I quickly answered. "What's up?"

"Hey man, look at all this stuff in here," he said, pointing at the large assortments of various rainwear, Frogg Toggs Pro Action Suits, River jackets and vests, Apex jackets and pants, pocket hiker pants and shorts, Windcrest microfiber pullovers and Three Season jackets. "There's even a few hand-held Garmin Oregon 550t GPS navigation systems in here. Camp kitchen equipment. All kinds of flashlights. And check this out, Murdock, look at these huge Cot Kit Combo tents that you can hook up to the helicopter. Man, everything is in here. Look at all these, DSI Sonar systems. All sizes. Even got a few ATV Super Winches in here, and a few fire extinguishers."

"Y'all hear that?" Karen suddenly called out. "Can you guys hear what I hear?"

"Hold up," I said to Tony, motioning with one of my hands. "I'mma pull down on this switch and open this door."

The secure latches fastening the door shut immediately begin to move, rotating electronically, unlocking the movable bar that fit into the slots on both sides of the door, releasing the latches and making a loud, clanging noise. The electronic air-compressed mechanical arms began to slowly lower the door to the ground, while at the same time making an emergency beeping sound and flashing its colorful lights.

"I don't believe it," I exclaimed. "All this time and here it is, we've been flying around with a fully equipped military ATV onboard."

"Maybe we're flying in the wrong helicopter?" Tony questioned.

"Man, we better not be, I mean, DAMN! That would really be all the way fucked up."

"Yeah, like what if this thing was all geared up for a trip to, who knows, like maybe Iraq or something. Or maybe even Afghanistan or to the Mediterranean coast, like Syria?"

"Well then, we'd just have to hurry up and get this thing over there, wouldn't you agree?"

"Nah, I don't think so," Tony said, snickering under his breath. "I'm too young for that kind of action."

"Yeah, right!" I said while securing the door. "That do sound like the Huey arriving. Better turn on the navigation switches so they'll be able to see just where we are."

"What do you mean?" Tony asked me.

"The outside identification lights on this helicopter that are all recognizable from the air," I told him, pointing in the location and area of each light.

"Karen!" I called out from outside the helicopter standing close to the pilot's window. "Can you hear me? Slide this window open for a minute. I really don't even think she heard me, Tony."

"No, she's looking now," he said. "You probably just scared the shit outa her. Call her now, or just knock on the window."

"Hey in there," I yelled. "Can you hear me?"

By this time, Karen just happened to turn in my direction, noticing that somebody was trying to het her attention on the outside of the craft, which startled her, causing her to suddenly scream out loudly and profanely.

"Woman, what's wrong with you?" I quickly yelled at her. "This is me out here trying to get your attention."

By this time, Regina and Sandra were also trying to figure out who it was staring at them from on the outside of the craft.

"Tony, go back inside and open this window. Better yet, hit that knob again while you're in there and open this door.'

While he was tending to the door, I could hear the loud pounding noise within a mere five to ten mile radius. I knew it was the news reporters from Sacramento.

Finally, the side door reopened. I entered and hastened straight to the the instrument panel, which was illuminating into what seemed like millions of different colorful lights. I immediately flipped on just about every switch to organize and activate the entire emergency navigation system.

After turning on my master switch, I then begin checking the radios, making sure the transponder was in place so that my craft was sending out the proper signals with which to identify it and our location on just about any air traffic controller's radar screen.

I then checked on the outside of the craft to make sure that all of my outside lights were working properly with the rotating beacon and anti-collision lights. The flashing red and white beacon I knew could be seen from miles away with its high intensity beam. I thought how this type of beam could even be seen during daylight.

I then turned around and could see the flashing lights from the incoming Huey within a short distance. The loud throbbing sound with all its quick, forceful pounding could be felt as it vibrated heavily on the ground rhythmically. I could also hear the craft's name being transmitted from the radio.

Transmitter: Ah, O-Niner Sacro, to that there, MH-53 Scarecrow. Do you read me?

[Sacro is the term used by the Huey identifying themselves across the transmitter from Sacramento.]

O-Niner Sacro, this that, MH-53 Scarecrow, you can Roger that.

Thank you much, Scarecrow. O-Niner can see you in the distance and approaching fast.

O-Niner, the Scarecrow is in a good clearance up ahead of you, granting you welcoming pathway.

Ah, Roger that, MH-54 Scarecrow. O-Niner Sacro coming in on its belly...

As the Huey approached for landing, I could see that this craft was a Bell UH-1C Huey gunship.

"Man, what the—?" I uttered loudly, gazing at the gunship.

"What's wrong?" Tony shouted over the noise from the throbbing engine. "What's wrong, Murdock?"

"Nothing's wrong," I told him. "Just look at that thing up there. Look how smooth it's floating in. It's like it's floating on a cloud or something."

I again had to remind myself that Tony knew nothing in terms of aircrafts.

"What I'm sayin' is that," I began, "this is the type of helicopter we would use when going to war. It's a Bell UH-1C Huey gunship. I really didn't expect them to be flying out here in something like that."

And I'm more than sure that Tony still didn't quite understand what I was talking about and especially in aviation terms.

And something else that was really strange that had taken place just as the Huey was about to land, was that, out of nowhere, a fast-moving Piper

Malibu cruised over head at a very low altitude, as if it too were looking for a place to land; as did a small Learjet. I could only guess that these were pilots who probably heard us over their transmitters and wanted in on what they felt was a splendid adventure about to take place.

"Who was that, Murdock?" Tony quickly asked me.

"I don't know," I answered. "Whoever they are, they didn't care to say anything over the radio."

"Man, I thought one of 'em was about to crash into the helicopter for a minute, until I seen he was flying higher."

"No, he knew just what he was doing. And I think maybe whoever they are, was really looking for a place to land."

"What? It's no place for 'em to land out here, is it?"

"Not out here, there isn't."

By this time, the Huey had landed, and the news crew onboard were about ready to get off, when we all of a sudden noticed another very large mass group of lights high in the air coming our way.

"Hey, Scarecrow," one of the news members yelled out, "I think that's the crew out of Lodi."

"I thought you guys were supposed to be flying in a 65 Bell UH-1HC, and not some goddamn Huey gunship. Hell, we ain't going to war!" I yelled back at them.

"It's the best we could do at the time," he shouted. "Didn't think you'd mind."

All I could see was crew members jumping out of that craft, laughing and waving their hands as a goodwill gesture.

"And you are, I would guess, the Scarecrow," one of the news members asked with a huge grin on his face that could be visibly seen even in the dark, extending his hand. "Now this is the big-ass, scariest-looking, fuckin' machine I've ever seen in my whole freakin' life. The MH-53. Now I know why it's called the Scarecrow."

"And you are?" I questioned.

"Oh, I'm just a member of this team joining you on this trip to Stonyford.," he answered. "I'm Pee-Wee, but they call me Sacro. I'm the one who's piloting this baby."

"Well, my name is Murdock," I told him. "And I'm the one who's flying the Scarecrow. This is Tony, my co-pilot, and the rest of my crew members remain onboard."

"Hey, Murdock," Pee-Wee began to ask. "Tell me something, man. What is this all about? You know, the situation in Stonyford? I mean, it's so many stories already out there floating around about some crazy shit that's, I guess, still happening up there in that town. I mean, man, it's from our understanding all the way in Sacramento that, you know, somebody is really busy savagely and brutally killing all them people, and not just in the town of Stonyford, but man, it's happening in just about every community around that place. And it's happening in the most cruel, merciless, uncivilized manner imaginable."

"Yeah, I know what you mean," I told him. "That's why we're on this mission. It's going to be our job to try finding out what's happening."

"And what are the odds of something happening to one of us? You feel me?" Pee-Wee questioned. "Nothing suppose to happen to news reporters."

"That's what they say, though," I responded. "But check this out for a minute, Pee-Wee. Man, this isn't just any ordinary trip you're takin', you know, nothing like the usual you've probably taken since becoming a part of a team of journalists working collectively. And, please, please don't think this trip to Stonyford is any run-of-the-mill. Once everyone is here, what I intend to do is let everyone know just what we're up against. So, and now, do you feel me, too?"

"But isn't it the job of the police to be investigating this, whatever it is?" he asked me. "I mean, whose job is it?"

"And you're right," I told him, "no doubt about it. But there's, and I'm only assuming, maybe over a thousand police officers, sheriff officers, highway patrol officers, rangers from the surrounding forestry stations, and just about every state outside of California is now offering their help and assistance. But check this out, Pee-Wee, it's going to be our mission to do everything we can to find out just what's really happening up there."

By this time, the third helicopter had now arrived. And to my surprise from what I was seeing, it wasn't the usual news helicopter, but they'd arrived in a CH-47 Chinook carrier. Seeing this thing slowly hovering within a few feet above the ground, as if suspended in the air, I thought about the days when I was much younger and how I'd always viewed such crafts as that like a huge grasshopper because of its strange insect-like shape.

"Are you Murdock?" a rather stocky man asked me after he'd exited from the helicopter. "Navigator of this huge, scary-looking Scarecrow?"

"That is I," I answered, feeling proud of myself from the thought of his statement. "And you are?"

"Uh, you can just call me the Cat," he said with a huge grin, smiling broadly. "That's what everybody calls me."

"And why is that?" I asked.

"That's because he's known to get into very small places," one of his crew members said, extending his hand with a greeting. "He's just like a cat. That's where the name came from. Oh, I'm MacDonald. I guess you can say I'm the co-pilot of the Lodi. I'm here to assist you, from the town of Galt. That's where the Cat picked me up in his mouth, and here I am."

"Well," I said, placing both of my hands on the back of my head, looking at Tony, "all I can say is welcome onboard for this trip to Stonyford."

Everybody laughed in agreement.

All engines were completely shut down for the night. Nothing mechanical from the three crafts was in motion except for the instrument devices on each of the fully illuminated instrument panels for communication and special identification purposes.

After seeing a few small aircrafts flying around in the distance as if searching for an airfield or runway, I then got everyone's attention, asking them to gather in a circle in the middle of where each of our helicopters had landed. It was like a triangle-shaped circle with everyone pulling up a lawn chair with water coolers, small portable tables and electric barbecue grills.

As I continued to observe the casualness about everyone, I then began to notice that there happened to be quite a number of female journalists amongst the group, which made me even more proud of the fact that we were all working collectively.

I also noticed an enormously built, movable frame of a flat screen surface on which everyone would be able to view the projection of motion pictures throughout the night if they so desired.

I even noticed the readily-available preparation for the midnight buffet in between two of the helicopters whereby a dozen or more had been gathered, busily preparing and combining large amounts of food, produce and the ingredients to assure its quality.

There were pounds and pounds of cheese, eggs and pizza rolls, Italian bread, pulled pork sandwiches, fully cooked barbecue ribs, plenty of baked beans cooked in some damn good tasty-sweet barbecue sauce, smoked brats and sausages, barbecue chicken breast, and my favorite, langostino lobsters and jumbo shrimps and hushpuppies, popcorn shrimps, plenty of fries for everyone, stuffed clams, bay scallops, snow crab legs, encrusted tilapia, fresh tilapia fillets and battered fish tenders, roast beef and bacon mushroom melt and some fresh fiesta chicken chopped salad.

The fruit was off the chain. Every type of fruit you name, it was a part of the feast at the buffet.

Selected varieties of beverages were on hand, except for alcoholic beverages. This was prohibited and respected by everyone.

Chapter Five

"IT'S SO PLEASING to see so many smiling faces ready and willing to embark upon this journey," I began my statement. "This is a venture that I can assure you that you'll never forget. I wish not to impose any type of embarrassment on you should you find yourself with a desire to, as you would say, bow out, by withdrawing yourself from this mission. But it is my hope that should you feel such a desire, that you'd reconsider, and join us in the mysterious, unexplained, mystifying, symbolic chemistry and structure of this plight.

"I am more than sure that you are yourselves just as curious as I am, but as a journalist, your profession to engage in such an organized practice is a method and business of knowledge which only you can provide through the specialized expertise and abilities of your skills. For this reason, I can find no reason why you shouldn't be a part of this team.

"As you should know, the small-town community of Stonyford, California is northwest from here. It's surrounded by a rather rough geographic region of the state. The nearby residents of quiet, well-to-do subdivisions are busy pumping money into the hands of legislative assembly people in public offices in Sacramento, demanding answers. I can only describe the situation in Stonyford as toxic, and indeed extremely deadly and destructive, to the point of being detrimental to everyone.

"By the way, and while we're at it, let me introduce myself to those of you who haven't yet had an opportunity to become acquainted. Yeah, I think I'll first start with me. I'm Murdock, navigator of the Scarecrow."

"And I'm Tony, co-pilot or navigator of the Scarecrow."

"Uh, I'm Pee-Wee, better known as Sacro from Sacramento. I'm the one navigating this baby right here. It's a Huey gunship."

"And they call me Knucklehead. I'm co-pilot of Sacro."

"Hey, y'all can just call me the Cat. I'm navigator of Lodi."

"And I'm MacDonald. I'm the Cat's co-pilot."

"And everyone else can become acquainted during the feast," I told them. "Right now, it's time to get my grub on. But check this out, people, I'll be getting back with you in about an hour or two."

I never thought I'd see so many people gathering together on a mission with one thing in mind—the reporting and broadcasting of multiple homicides. It was like a graduation ceremony at an academy for scholars of a special field. Everyone was now on a mission to report the best story, accompanied by both wives and husbands, as a team of media journalists.

Sandra, Regina, and Karen remained onboard the Scarecrow attending to the specialized equipment, such as the built-in processors, 32" Class LED 720p HDTV screens with clear projector clearance for each, heavy watt 8-disc compact stereo system, 10.2 channel receiver with 3D capability, and four HDMI wireless printers and tablets, Motorola Triumphs, laptops, cameras for the built-in security system, iPods, and compact digital cameras for the journey.

And of course, everyone had enough to eat and so much more. But it was time to get back to basics, the fundamental purpose as to why we were here in the first place. This would be the starting point resulting in something far beyond our wildest imagination. To me, it was like a game of cards whose value may vary as assigned by the holder. In this case, the killer is the wildcat hidden most likely in an uncultivated part of the Stonyford region. To the officials in charge, the endless pursuit for the assassin causes complaining about their wild goose chase possibly being beyond their reach.

"Uh, ladies and gentlemen," I called out over the microphone that was hooked up to an amplifier system. "Can I get your attention, please? Uh, yeah, let's everyone gather around for a minute. And please, bring your food with you. Hey, will somebody please save me some of that ice cream? Thank you."

"What kind?" someone asked me. "Edy's, Ben and Jerry's, or Breyer's?"

"Damn," I responded. You mean to tell me I have a choice?"

"You name it, Murdock," the voice said, "and we'll get it."

"Well, just give me a scoop of whatever it is you got," I told him or her. "You know, a scoop of each one."

"What flavor, sweetie?" the voice said, recognizing it to be indeed that belonging to a female.

"Ummm, it really don't matter that much," I told her. "But what all do you have?"

"Butter pecan, strawberry, vanilla, chocolate, peach, orange, and just a variety of selected flavors," she responded.

"Butter pecan, strawberry, and vanilla will do, thank you," I told her, while thinking back on a situation when someone answered me with such a soft, sweet voice, turned out to be this huge, muscled body builder.

"All right then," I started my statement. "Once again, thank you for allowing me your undivided attention. As you know, it was my intention to inform you, or better yet, bring you up to date, information disclosing the situation there in Stonyford. But, now what I have decided to do is, is to just wait until early dawn, before our departure from here, and then inform you what to expect."

"Hey, Murdock?" the now familiar voice called, abruptly interrupting my chain of thoughts.

All I could do was stare in the direction of the voice, wondering whether or not this soft-spoken person knew she was interrupting this meeting.

"Yeah, what's that?" I answered, trying my best to be as respectful as I possibly could.

"Would you like a large slice of pecan pie, along with a few slices of coconut cake, coconut cream pie, and some lemon meringue pie with that ice cream?"

By this time, everyone was laughing loudly and playfully, from the thought of what was happening. Everyone themselves began placing orders for such a dessert which was the final course of the meal.

I then thought to myself how precious of a person this lady could be at a time when knowing we needed it.

"Jesus Christ, June, not now," a man's voice said who could possibly be this lady's husband. "Can't you see we're having a meeting?"

"Oh, I'm so sorry, she exclaimed. "I didn't know."

"No, that's quite all right," I quickly told her. "You didn't do anything wrong. Just look around you, everybody's wanting your service."

My statement seemed to have an impact on not only her, but her husband as well. I could see the pride in his expression as everyone applauded her work by an expression of approval with loud clapping. That's when I then noticed Sandra, and then Regina, and then Karen assisting her so that she wouldn't have to do everything by herself. I saw other groups of people extending their assistance.

"Anyway," I said through the microphone, "everyone just have a damn good evening throughout the night. Just enjoy yourselves as best you can and I'll see you early dawn. That's when this mission will begin, and hopefully, if God's willing, we'll all make it back safely to this very same location, and meet once again for your journey home."

"There's plenty left to go around," someone yelled out. "We have doggy bags if you need one."

I remembered upon entering the Scarecrow how I briefly found myself closely inspecting the cargo onboard, something I hadn't had time to do since departing from the Napa airport. During my careful examination of its contents, I noticed the two 10' 6" Trophy kayaks with dual gear hatches and flush mount rod holders attached to both the left and right side ceiling panels of the craft. On one side of the wall there was a camouflage gun rack with twelve matching concealed firearms and ammunition in an ornate cabinet next to the armory cabinet. There were four 870 Bone Collectors, 12 GA. HI-VIZ Sight that accepts up to 3½" shells, 4-535 with a 22" and 28" barrel that accepts up to 3½" shells, and four 5353 thugs with 20" barrels, 12 GA. With LPA trigger and red dot scopes.

In the ATV there were at least four pair of Lug or Felt hip boots, a few more tackle bags with eight camouflage hooded sweatshirts and matching socks. Next to the door leading to the crew's cabin, I noticed another small cabinet that seemed to contain a collection of C. Caius Baitcast Combo 6'10" Field & Stream rods matched with Shimano Caius Baitcast reels and an assortment of casting rods and fishing nets with lines, hooks, and lures.

"What are you doing in here all by yourself?" a voice suddenly asked me out of nowhere.

I didn't have to look up or even attempt guessing to see who it was. I knew from the sweet, natural scent of her aroma, and the pleasant aura of her scintillating fragrance, and the distinctive, magical effect with all her fascination, keeping me spellbound to her, that was no one other than Karen talking to me.

Chapter Six

"REVEILLE! REVEILLE! REVEILLE!" someone yelled out early the following morning. "Reveille! Reveille! Reveille! Up and at it, people. Let's go!"

I couldn't fully believe what I was hearing, but I knew it had to be a member of the team that was really taking this mission seriously. And that's just what we needed, serious-minded people onboard who'd be responsible and take the situation ahead of us seriously. Not in any way thinking everyone else wasn't doing the same, but motivation and its momentum was a product needed for this mission.

"Reveille! Reveille! Reveille!" the voice rang out loudly again. "I said let's go, people. Up and at it!"

Strange to say, but whoever this person was, I was ready to abide his command. I mean, the guy was giving strict orders, specific, with narrow limits, as if imposing rigorous standards.

I briefly glanced at my watch, it was still dark outside, and the exact time was 0320, meaning he'd awakened us with his reveille call at 0300 on the nose.

"I said reveille, you bunch of sissies," he shouted. "Pow! Pow! Pow!"

"You goddamn stupid son-of-a-bitch," I heard someone yelling out loud. "Just where in the hell do you think you are? You crazy bastard. This ain't no goddamn Vietnam, Afghanistan, or even Iraq or Iran, you freak."

I'm more than sure the sounds of early morning gun fire was a shock to everyone, and especially to those who slept outside during the night. Karen and Tony slept in one of the tents from aboard the Scarecrow, and Regina and Sandra were in another. I slept on a rather small collapsible bed, better known as a cot, inside the helicopter. But quite a few people bunkered down outside their craft within a certain boundary to prevent any contact with prowlers lurking about both furtively and predatorily.

For a minute or two I just lay there sprawled with my arms and legs spread out awkwardly. I guess you can say I was deeply into reminiscing about certain events in the past. Memories I wish not to ever forget. Bygone experiences that I have to admit losing because of my immaturity and lack of development into adulthood.

Here I was the team leader of an important journey with a group of the most highly classified news journalists—finding myself in deep thoughts about Karen.

I thought how it was just yesterday when I'd landed my MH-53 J-Pave Low, now known as the Scarecrow, in San Jose. I remember seeing how so very beautiful Karen looked, tall and slim, wearing a bad-ass looking chocolate outfit from the Mac Denim Collection. I mean, damn!! It matched the entirety of her complexion with matching earrings. Stretch coordinates with seasonal style. The two parts of her outfit had this front zip and snap flap pocket. It was woven cotton spandex. You know, stretch denim jacket, and the skirt, it was back yoke and back kick pleat. Contrast top stitching with zip close and belt loops.

She was also wearing a matching pair of "Bailey" wide calf cuffed boots by Step Up Comfort with adjustable buckle, inside zipper, cushioned insole, 2 ¾" heel. Chocolate.

Sandra had on this really nice looking, heather grey, striped, double-breasted pant and skirt suit, while Regina wore a nice looking marching grey striped pantsuit. Both wore different style "Madison Scrunch Booties by Comfortview.

Only a lady would know what I've described.

I could still vaguely hear the confusing uproar going on concerning the gunfire that had taken place right after the reveille call. It was quite apparent that somebody wasn't at all pleased with whomever it was yelling reveille or doing the firing. I thought to myself maybe it wasn't at all a bad idea if I were to get up and see for myself what all the racket was about, though I knew just from my inner instinct.

"Wait a minute," I said to myself. "I think I'll just push this knob right here and open this door so that I can see what this ATV can do."

It wasn't long before I found myself coasting smoothly with very little acceleration around the boundaries of our crafts. Under no obligations were we confined or enclosed marked by limits. But being that the property we'd landed on was private and owned by close relations to me, we remained within a certain proximity in which not to attract much attention. Although each of these helicopters was obviously quite alluring because of their magnetizing size being appealing to nearby inquisitive spectators, my plans were to be airborne before sunrise.

That's when I noticed MacDonald, co-navigator of the Lodi, standing firmly at attention in a military posture with both arms at his sides, and from what I could see, his heels tightly together, both eyes were to the front center of his face—expressionless, with what appeared to be an automatic military assault rifle at his side designed for use in military attacks.

"Hey, good morning, MacDonald," I said, curious as to just what the the hell was happening this early in the morning. "You're standing there as if at attention. Is everything all right?"

"Yes, sir!" he answered, as though he were answering to a high-ranking commander-in-chief.

To be truthful, I really didn't quite know what to think or even do. I just sat there in the ATV staring at MacDonald, who was seemingly having some type of a flashback about his military days or something. He just stood there as if unmovable, firm, and as stiff as a log wearing his military clothing with boots shining brightly as if glowing in the dark. I thought to myself he must have spent hours pressing his clothing. He reminded me so much of an officer, a correctional officer, who worked at the Lansing Correctional Facility matching the same exact description. These two were identically alike and could pass for twins. Dressed to a T with clothing fully starched and immaculately stain free without one intended crease by folding or pressing and stiff as a plank. The bottom of his pants were neatly tucked inside his military style boots with the hip crease of his pants stuck deep into the crack of his ass.

"Hey, MacDonald," I said in a soft voice, not wanting to sound harsh or anything out of the ordinary. "But, um, was that you firing off your rifle?"

"Yes, sir," he responded immediately. "It was my rifle you heard."

"You can relax, MacDonald," I told him. And then I for some odd reason shouted, "Fall out!"

As a result of my shouting fall out, it seemed MacDonald immediately came to himself. He was back to normal instantaneously.

"Some of the team members were worried about you," I told him. "Are you all right?"

"Oh, yeah," he answered as if nothing had ever happened. "Why's that?"

"Just checking. You were not long ago yelling out reveille for everyone to wake up. I mean, you know, it is about that time, you know, for everyone to get up."

"Okay," he said, looking around. "Then let's start waking everybody up so that they can get themselves together."

"But I thought that was what you were doing?" I asked him, making me wonder if he was even aware of what he'd done.

After a brief moment of hesitation, he then responded by saying, "Okay then, let's do this!"

But just about everyone was already awake and moving around, gathering up their gear while others were making preparation for the morning meal. Even my crew had by now gathered their equipment together and were standing about the Scarecrow after washing up. There was still plenty of time left before daybreak. We could see in the far eastern distance the early morning aurora of a brilliant display of the still visible night sky moving slowly in our direction, turning night into day.

We still had time left to be airborne. I wanted this area cleared long before sunrise.

I then headed in the direction of my craft with the ATV's headlights on full beam emitting its shiny, glossy rays on the beautiful early morning appearances of Karen, Sandra and Regina.

I thought to myself how Tony was so blessed to end up with Karen. The love of my life. If only I hadn't been so stupid, I'd still have her in the fullness of my life. Everything I ever desired and needed in my life, she was the whole, complete fullness of it all. Full and intact with true perfection.

"Hey, yo, Murdock," I heard someone calling out to me. "Over here."

I could then see it was the Cat and Pee-Wee waving their hands, motioning for me to slow down.

"Morning, morning, morning," I said to each. "Come on and get in. I'm just chillin', you know, checkin' on everything before breakfast. So tell me what do you think?"

"I'm just waiting on you to tell us a little something about the town of Stonyford," said the Cat. "When do you intend to let us know, you know what I mean?"

"In not too long," I told him. "Most likely during breakfast, 'cause by then, we'll be gathering up to fly out of here."

"That's right," said Pee-Wee. "For my log book, just how long do you think it'll take us to get there?"

"Mmm," I mumbled.

"Shouldn't take no time," said the Cat. "I mean, that's providing we head in the direction of those mountains."

"Let's talk about this with everyone present," I told them. "I think it would be best that everybody knows our intentions. But those mountains just aren't the idea I had in mind to travel. Not unless it's what we all agree on, though?"

Chapter Seven

AWAKENING FROM HER SCREAM, Margaret found herself staring directly into very bright light, which to her appeared to be a silvery, round plate with shiny reflecting mirrors surrounding it that were focused downward toward her.

As she tried desperately to move her arms, she could feel something in the form of belts or straps that were apparently tied to her arms and holding them in a tight position too strong for her to move. As she turned her head from the bright reflecting lights, she then noticed what appeared to be the blurred, fuzzy resemblances of people standing around her. Blinking her eyes in her attempt to clear her vision began to reveal to her that she was indeed surrounded by a group of strange people wearing blue and white surgical clothing with light green respiratory masks hanging closely around their necks.

Carefully observing the people in white garments that were encircling her partially nude body dressed in a light pink and blue hospital gown and covered with a thin, white sheet, Margaret immediately began attempting to inquire her whereabouts by demanding and screaming loudly to know the reason for her being strapped to the bed.

Her behavior became so outrageously threatening to the physicians assigned to assist in the assurance of her recovery that they agreed she be fully injected with a heavy dose of medication to prevent her from further outbursts.

During the injection, one of the nurses noticed the many visible marks on Margaret's body that could be easily seen and within seconds of the injection, immediately informed the head physician about her findings. As the doctors continued their examination, Margaret finally begin to relax as the sedative injected into her childlike body begin to take full effect, calming and soothing her with such tranquilizing results to where her once outlandish violent rage came to an end.

Still at times attempting to regain her strength, it was apparent that she could barely keep her eyes open as she struggled desperately to stay awake and fully aware of what the people around her were doing, but found the struggle impossible and unable to ward off the medication.

As she lay there hopeless, assigned to a certain particular room, with straps tightly binding her, quietly still without any form of movement, with unhealthy attachments to her body in a stationary position, she found herself calm and completely silent to the strange atmospheric body of a very soft light feeling of what she felt was a compelling influence now circling around her.

Feeling the medication moving slowly throughout her body, she began to wonder if her life were just a terrible dream. She thought of herself being a child of Satan without a purpose with which to structure her life. She thought of herself as a child having the devil's worst curse condemned to eternal punishment and somehow deserving damnation.

She began thinking about the many stories in the Bible and mainly one in particular in the book of Revelation, Chapter 12: 1-5, how the red dragon appeared with seven heads and ten horns, and seven crowns on his heads. She remembered reading about how the dragon stood before a very pregnant woman as she was about to give birth. Margaret began to think about herself, and the woman being her mother. She thought of the woman being pregnant, except she envisioned herself being the baby inside the woman, and the woman being her mother, very pregnant, and about to give birth to her.

As in the book of Revelation, the red dragon stood before the pregnant woman, ready to devour the child ravenously.

As Margaret lay helpless, unable to move, the thought of her childhood life and the many times she complained to her family and mainly her parents about her frightening ordeals and seemingly spiritual experiences, they'd only ignored her every plea, accusing her of immoral activities and being involved in witchcraft and sorcery.

After the rejection, it was then that she found herself accepting this unwanted member into her young, though aging, body, with all its evilness and venomous passion. She'd convinced herself to believe that while during her birth the dragon, being Satan, had indeed devoured her, and then while still within his spiritual form, digested himself from within her, in spirit leaving her to believe that she was somehow now in the complete fullness of his likeness. She came to believe that it was after the condensation that Satan, in spirit, immediately left her in his quest to fulfill his duty in his attempt to corrupt the world thoroughly and the prophecies surrounding the Bible.

Margaret felt her life had become so defiled and corrupted by that of Satan to where such profane defilement would undoubtedly reveal its evilness soon, making known to the world the one and only true daughter of the prince of evil.

She again thought of the Bible and the book of St. John, Chapter 8:44. "Ye are of your father the devil, and the lusts of your father ye will do. He was a murderer from the beginning, and does not stand in truth, because there is no truth in him. When he speaks a lie, he speaks from his own resources, for he is a liar and the father of it."

The thought of what was being said in the chapter began to frighten Margaret and even more so as the realization of Wanda's death began pondering heavily in her mind, preventing any concentration, enabling her to realize the fact that her life wasn't a dream, but a reality. She could feel the evilness within her weakening body as she continued to fight the medication administered to her. As her state of desperation began to surrender, she turned her head to one side sluggishly, feeling as though the relaxer had somehow paralyzed her. She felt so powerless as she gazed through what appeared to be an opening in the thin, light blue curtain encircling her bed. The curtain was so thin she could see the doctors moving about on the other side.

Through the opening Margaret could also see what appeared to be a very large window, revealing the dark grayish, gloomy sky as huge, thick, darkening clouds began moving in the direction of her window. She began thinking about the clouds, wondering if maybe they were signs from the devil himself about to appear before her, as she could then see huge bolts of lightning flash across the dark sky. The room vibrated from each powerful thunderbolt, responding to each flash of lightning, as did the unusual dark clouds as they violently clashed into each other.

What had now become even more frightening to Margaret was that these clouds with all their loud clashing hadn't released any rain. The outer surface of the windows were completely dry, collecting not a single drop of rain from what appeared to have been a very intense, unsparing thunderstorm over the entire town of Willows, California.

As she continued to stare intently into the strange, darkening sky, she began to notice how the clouds seemed to be demonstrating their most mind-boggling, electrifying display.

Her eyes widened as she began to see what appeared to be a huge ball of water spinning rapidly, though as if in slow motion, circling with what appeared to be lightning flashing around it. The thunder had become even more intense and the wind could be heard throughout the hospital, as sharp piercings of cold, chilling air could be felt puncturing its way through every exit.

As she continued gazing intently out the window, tears began to form in her eyes from the thought of her existence and her reason for being in the hospital. Without realizing it, she found herself unconsciously digging her fingernails into the soft, inflatable pad used to cover the mattress on her bed, which material was made of rubber. Still unable to move her body, she began to feel the cold, chilling air from the light draft that was a breath of something like a fresh ambiance so distinctive, being blown throughout her room.

The tears in her eyes immediately began to dry as the soft breeze of air encircling her head began to seep gradually through her pores and into her stomach with an awakening scent from the medication injected into her body. As Margaret continued to stare, as if under an induced form of hypnosis, deep into the rapidly spinning ball of water with lightning flashing all around it, in the distant dark gray clouds, she suddenly noticed the forming image of what appeared to be a huge mouth that seemed to be inhaling the same fresh ambiance of air which had been gradually encircling throughout her room. As the air that had been encircling Margaret began to cease, it was then that she also noticed the straps that were used to bind her in a secured position suddenly began snapping loose.

She found herself no longer restrained from moving and immediately sat upright in a slow vertical position, in search of her clothing.

Stepping onto the cold floor, she could feel the circling current of air as it began to withdraw through the doors in her room that had been left slightly ajar. Pushing the doors closed to prevent being seen, she again found herself staring out the window into the huge, dusky-looking dark cloud that had earlier revealed itself in the resemblance of a largely formed mouth. She could now see what appeared to be the watery, wavy, wrinkling image of a degraded face with eyes in an oblique position, slanted and squinted partly closed, though the eyes could be clearly seen, intently staring directly at her as the lightning continued flashing around the huge, dark cloud that now seemed to begin changing its form.

The many clouds that surrounded the huge, dark cloud began to evaporate and very quickly disappeared as did all the flashing lightning. Even the awful loud sounds of pounding thunder which had earlier violently vibrated the entire building with its terrifying clashing, it too had now ceased its pounding.

As Margaret continued staring into the dark sky, she could now see the slight twinkling of a star as it sparkled through the few remaining clouds still vaporizing, though suspended within a distance from the hospital. As she moved even closer to the window, she placed one of her hands on the warm window ledge while thinking about everything that had taken place. She stood very still, as if a silhouette, while watching her reflection in the window staring back at her. She then leaned her head against the window and closed her eyes to the ceasing storm as it finally disappeared into the dark sky.

The only sounds she could hear were those coming from the medical team of doctors and nurses as they moved about throughout the hallway.

Opening her eyes to the twinkling light, she again found herself thinking about the terrifying ordeal that had taken place minutes before. She found herself in deep thought about Wanda and the horrible, violent event that she witnessed happening to her. She thought about the many times she turned to Wanda, thinking she could trust her by confiding in her about the things she herself was going through. But Wanda would just laugh at her and accuse her of being a disgrace to the family. During their childhood in Stonyford, Margaret had always felt that Wanda despised her and was always doing just about everything she could to turn their parents against her.

Without any success to get her parents to believe in her plea for help, or even in her stories about something being inside of her, it was then that she found herself giving in to the violent aggressiveness of whatever it was that she'd witnessed destroying Wanda. She thought about how Wanda would at times intentionally, when noticing she was trying to convince them to believe in her terrifying ordeals that she was experiencing, begin falsely accusing her of immoral activities with grown men, preventing her parents from believing in her stories which she would be trying her best to describe to them in detail.

She thought about the hatred Wanda showed toward her. The jealousy had turned into the most dangerous kind of deep, distasteful hatred one would try to bestow upon another, with such deep-seated animosity to where, whenever she was within Wanda's presence, the conflict and hostility between them could always be easily seen as though the devil himself were in their presence, revealing himself through them.

As Margaret continued thinking about the terrifying, horrific tragedy of Wanda's death, she found herself thinking about a reason for such an ordeal. It was during the argument she and Wanda had had earlier that day when, for reasons unknown, Wanda very rudely shoved her, causing her to fall forcefully hard onto the floor after losing in a game of chess. She'd become so angry to where she even disobeyed their parents, who were busy trying to ease the tension between them.

"What's this all about?" asked Paul, referring to his daughters making such a fuss over a game of chess. "What's all the racket about?"

"Daddy, Margaret's always winning," Wanda exclaimed. "She won't let me win sometimes."

"That's because I'm not a cheater," Margaret shouted. "You're a cheat, and cheats never win."

"I'm not a cheater," Wanda yelled back at Margaret. "Daddy, see what I mean about her? And you heard her for yourself calling me a cheat."

"Margaret, you quit calling her names like that," said Paul. "Or I'll send you straight to your room."

"But Daddy, that's not fair," cried Margaret. "Everybody's always on her side."

"That's it, Margaret," Paul stared at her angrily. "One more word from you like that and there will be no supper for you tonight, little girl, and I mean it!"

"Daddy?" Wanda began to ask Paul with an obnoxious, conceited grin on her face so Margaret could see. "Will you make her apologize to me for what she called me, 'cause I'm not a cheat, Daddy, you can ask Mamma, that's if you don't wanna believe in your little girl."

"Oh, you know I'mma believe you, pumpkin," Paul told her while gently caressing her hair with long strokes. "Daddy will do anything for his favorite little girl."

Margaret thought about her father being the type of person who would do just about anything in the world for his family. But couldn't help feeling neglected by him. But it was her mother she found herself wondering about and her reason for always allowing Wanda to get away with murder, even when knowing she was in the wrong. Wanda was always allowed to do just about anything she wanted and whenever she would get into trouble, it was always Margaret who'd take the blame. Not that she didn't complain about being blamed, but it was Wanda who would whine to their parents about her dissatisfaction , resenting everything about Margaret.

She thought about how her parents considered Wanda the pure, perfect angel. She was the favorite perfect child; regardless of the harmful, annoying, mischievous behavior she displayed toward her, Wanda was never to blame.

Relaxing herself against the window, Margaret began to feel a longing desire for sleep as she deeply yawned inward for a breath of air with her mouth wide open.

The medication injected into her body wasn't any longer a problem. She could sense from the strange current of air which had encircled her room that something had indeed taken place, relieving her from the sedative. She wasn't any longer afraid as she was when experiencing the changes she'd gone through earlier. She thought about how her entire life seemed to have changed completely, as if she'd become a different person.

Turning toward her bed, she began dragging herself across the floor as if somehow her legs were too heavy under her body. She could still hear the doctors moving about in the hallway as she continued slowly dragging herself past the entrance to her room. She again found herself thinking about the situation and her reason for being in the Willows hospital, wondering and wishing the entire ordeal were only a horrible nightmare and that maybe she could just blink her eyes a few times and the dream would then be over.

Finally making it to the bed, which seemed forever to do, Margaret once again found herself staring out the window and into the dark sky only to notice her reflection staring back at her. Everything seemed to be happening so fast, with an enormous amount of confusing attention drawn to her, to where the thought of being the subject of public dispute and controversies was something she strongly opposed. Margaret began to believe she'd become the subject of both God and Satan, who had the power to give and take away. Her only fears were in that of her own free will which was to live without being subjected to Satan, but to that of God, whom she felt had possibly given her to Satan allowing him the authority over her due to her experience when witnessing the death of Wanda.

Feeling her body becoming fatigued from such prolonged stress and weariness, she drifted aimlessly off to sleep.

Chapter Eight

"IT'S NOW TIME FOR OUR TRIP TO STONYFORD," I began telling everyone. "I do hope you've enjoyed the early morning breakfast and allowed yourselves a very hearty meal. In no way do I wish to begin this lecture of information with any intentions to sound spooky, or even haunting or frightening, but what I am intending to do is to inform you about the venture you are about to embark upon being something terribly strange and indeed weird, without any nonsense as we make preparations to equip ourselves.

"The elements described throughout the entire region are enough to make sure of your self-assured confidence to be present under such conditions whereas, your actions under the existing occurring events will undoubtedly form a hypothetical opinion about you. I will formally introduce you to an arena of public opinion, for then you will use the appropriate choice for scrutiny and careful inspection or study from your observation and surveillance.

"What you are about to embark upon is not a drill, but you can surely use this operation as a means to exercise and develop new skills and/or familiarize yourself with old ones.

"Any questions?"

"What's this all about?" someone asked. "I mean, you know, I've heard only bits and pieces about something up there in that town, you know, like something not in the physical form of a human being, supposedly stalking and killing people."

"Yeah, I heard the same thing," a woman's voice said.

"Is this true?" another voice asked.

"I think it's just somebody's imagination running wild," someone else suggested.

"Them there hillbillies probably up there in that damn town smokin' some of that shit, ask me," another voice said.

"They ain't hillbillies," someone quickly told the person. "Nothin' but real cowboys up there in Stonyford. I been there and can tell you right off the top, them people in that town ain't no hillbillies."

"Yeah!" another voice rang out. "Where the hell you think you are, Kentucky or someplace?"

Everybody laughed.

"This is California, buddy," the voice again spoke out loud, "and we sure don't be birthing hillbillies. Not that there is anything wrong with being one, but we sure ain't one, and I can assure you of that."

Just being a part of the humor, I just had to ask the person who made the remark about Stonyford people being hillbillies what he thought they'd been smoking. "Hey, uh, what do you think them people been smoking up there?"

"Some of that crack shit," he replied.

"Man, just where in the hell are you from?" someone asked him.

"Hell, the way that guy over there yonder mentioned, Kentucky," he told everyone, "I thought you knew. I'm a Kentuckian. Born, bred, fed, and raised right there in the mighty hills."

"A goddamn hillbilly," someone shouted.

"You goddamn right, I am," he shouted back. "And proud of it. What in the heck is your excuse?"

Everybody laughed again.

"People," I yelled. "It's time you gather up all of your belongings and board your respective choppers. It'll soon be daylight and I want us airborne."

"But, Murdock?" a voice called out to question me. "You never did tell us much about what we're up against."

When hearing this statement, I then looked around and noticed everyone had come to a complete standstill. It was like all movement had ceased, and all eyes were on me. At least, that's what it felt like. And then, I had to quickly give a brief description about the situation in Stonyford. Well, we still had a good forty-five minutes left until sunrise. I guess you can sense my objectives being that we were airborne way before the sun came up. I would also say it's just a personal thing about me that I have with the sun coming up before me. What I'm saying is that I'm just like a rooster.

You know, a cock, about to crow, about to crow early in the morning. Except, I'm in no way about to do any of that strident, shrill cry stuff with a raucous call waking everybody up. MacDonald had already done that with his reveille.

I just hate the sun rising before me; therefore, I make it a point to be up and at it every morning before sunrise.

There is just something about being up early, whether you're driving or flying or even on a train or bus or sailing on the sea. Watching the sun come up is always exhilarating. I guess you can say that it's also like watching the sunset disappearing below the horizon. The sight is always so refreshing.

"Residents have become bitterly angry and confused." I began to tell them about the people not only in the town of Stonyford, but that of also the residents in nearby communities. "They've become so frustrated from not quite knowing what to do about the situation. There is speculation that a killer or possibly killers are stalking people and could possibly be using the heavily wooded areas and nearby mountains as a hiding place to prevent being noticed.

"Crimes are being committed without there ever being any trace of evidence left at the crime scene in which to point at a suspect in either direction. And the huge gap is constantly allowing the assailant or possibly assailants to escape having an overwhelming advantage over those in authority from capturing them.

"People of all ages are being stalked, killed and then mutilated. These homicides seemed to have first started in Stonyford, where at present there are frightening opinions that if someone local is responsible, or it could even be transients, people residing in these communities are wondering just how it is that the killer, or killers, are actually getting around and committing these crimes without ever leaving any traces of evidence."

"So, what you're saying is that they don't even have a clue about this mystery killer?" Pee-Wee asked me.

"Not a clue," I responded. "All I can say is that there isn't anyone being held accountable who can explain what's happening. The assailant is a mystery to everyone involved in this effort to capture him, or her, or them, or whoever it is, or whatever it is."

"Well, what about the girl?" someone asked.

"Which one?" I inquired, uncertain who he was referring to.

"From my understanding," he began explaining, "there were two little girls supposedly to have been victimized by some sick psychopath sex offender with an aggressive mental disorder."

"Yeah," someone else began saying. "I heard something similar, except thick semen was said to have been found all over the crime scene."

"Damn!" shouted Cat. "Not tryin' to be funny, but is that true?"

Everyone looked at me confused, waiting for me to answer.

"Not true," I told them. "From my report, there hasn't been anyone claiming to have been sexually assaulted. So, please try not to allow yourselves to be misinformed at this time. It's our mission to at least try being as professional as we possibly can."

"Uh, I have a question or two that's been bothering me," someone said, raising one of his hands in the air. "Looking back when you were on the KRTV News, there was the mention of how mind-boggling everything is, and how those poor people had even put up a reward in hope that someone would come forward with the right information. There was also something about the towns of Colusa, Maxwell, Orlando, and I even think you guys were saying something about Corning, Williams, and I think even as far away as the town of Chico.

"But what I'm wondering is that you were talking about multiple packs of local students were committing suicide and that these suicide packs were being formed in schools.

"What I'm wondering is, are these packs still taking place?"

"Good you asked that question," I told him. "I do believe they are."

"Yeah," one of female crew members began to question. "I think I heard something about that, too. But I was wondering, if people are that scared, then why would they be leaving lights on in their houses burning all day and night? I mean, wouldn't that be an open invitation?"

"Man," someone started. "When you're scared, you're scared. I don't give a rat's ass who you are. A freakin' killer is running loose, dammit, and if I were living up there, I'd have all kinds of guns waiting on the crazy son of a bitch!"

"But that's just what they're trying to avoid happening," I told him. "You see, the one thing they don't need is an out of control group of angry vigilantes running around, paranoid, without any training or authority, and in this whatever it is that's happening, playing out an episode from the wild, wild west. Next thing you'll have is neighbors engaged in battles against one another. It'll be like a competition on a far more intense scale than what's presently happening. That's why it's so important none of you ends up misinforming the public about your findings. We have a very serious situation here, people, and what we don't need is to be accused of misdirecting anyone."

"I'll be passing out folders to you guys detailing descriptions," Tony told everyone, holding up stacks of important documents. "And believe me, this stuff is explicitly selected and dispatched for your particular duty. My wife, Karen, and our other crew members, Regina and Sandra, spent quality time and effort to make sure all of you ended up with a copy. So please, take the time to carefully read them thoroughly and intensively to help you understand just what we're up against."

"You see, people," I began, "the situation up there in Stonyford isn't something you just hear about from watching Hollywood movies being advertised during commercial breaks on TV, and this definitely isn't something any movie director is writing, though it wouldn't be such a bad idea if so happens one of you has such an intent. But what I am saying is, something strange is happening and I just hope none of the members of this team end up becoming victims."

"And what about this replicating virus I heard about that's supposed to be spreading all over the place?" someone asked. "Now come on, Murdock, could something like this really be happening?"

"Hold up, Murdock," Pee-Wee interrupted. "Can I answer this one for you?"

"Go right ahead," I told him. "Just keep in mind the fact that we need to start getting out of here. So don't get carried away, you know. Make it brief, Pee-Wee."

"Do any of y'all remember that movie called *The Exorcist*?" he asked. "Well, that's what we're up against. The devil and all his dirty little evil spirits are up there in all them towns enacting their killer rituals with so much evilness to where, I believe it's appropriate to say, we just might end up finding ourselves encountering some of this bullshit on the way."

"Man!" someone yelled out. "Just what fuckin' planet did you come from to be talking that shit?"

"And here we go," I told Pee-Wee. "I knew this was going to happen."

"Ain't no lie, my friend," he attempted to assure the person that was questioning him. "I came from the same planet you came from: Earth."

For a minute or two, I just stood there listening to them arguing and debating whether or not the stories were true or false. But one thing was sure, the killings were deliberate, whether anyone wanted to believe it or not. I, too, find the truth being appropriate. But for some strange reason, we as living human beings, we just don't like hearing the truth. We'd rather put up all kinds of fusses and fights than to just believe in facts. I would guess that that's why we're always so surprised when reality hits us across the head. But Pee-Wee was only doing the best he could with what he had in his head at the time to work with, because the documents Tony had passed out just hadn't been read yet, well not until everyone was airborne, and then it seemed like all hell broke loose over the airwaves. I mean, my radio just kept busy all the way to the high mountain regions of Stonyford. I mean, for a moment I could have sworn I was at the office there in Vallejo. All I could hear was yap, yap, yap, people talking relentlessly. Jabber, jabber, jabber. Everyone was chattering over the airwaves at the same time.

If those documents were all it would have taken to get one's attention, then I think it would be a fair thing to say that such documents should be distributed more often.

But let me get back to where I was at before I got too far ahead of myself.

After Pee-Wee and the other fellow finally simmered down a little, a critical question just happened to come to mind. So, before anyone could actually reach the boiling point of erupting, I asked loudly, "What if we do end up encountering some strange atmospheric phenomena like some type of an electromagnetic form of radiant emitting a strong current of gravitational activity? And what if this gravity starts drawing us into something with a tremendous amount of fearful force?"

The thought of what I was trying to describe was something to think about.

But it was also time for our crafts to become airborne, and that's just what happened.

While the engines were heavily idling and about ready to take for the sky, I looked about my craft and noticed Karen undressing. She was standing in the back section of the craft, unaware of the door being slightly ajar, wearing something like a tight-fitting, bright, colorful, rainbow-type of bikini that looked more like a swimsuit.

I couldn't help but to continue staring at what used to be mine. Deep down inside my heart, I still loved her, and if I had the chance, I'd get her back into the utmost fullness of my life.

From what I could see while I was lecturing the crew members, it seemed that everyone had been changing their clothing and preparing themselves for this trip to be dressed military style, like soldiers dressed fully in their camouflage uniforms.

I never in my wildest imagination thought I'd see Karen wearing such a uniform, but damn, the lady looked so sensationally exciting, and yes, and as you should know, delightfully and heavenly delicious.

"Damn that Tony," I said to myself. "Damn him! Damn him!"

Finally taking off was, I'm more than sure, breathtaking for everyone as each helicopter's engine roared loudly with the powerful forces of each swing blade pulling and lifting us higher and higher into the early morning sky.

"Hell, yeah," I heard someone yelling over the transmitter.

"It's all good," someone else yelled out.

"Thank you for letting me be myself, motherfucker," another voice rang out loud.

"Hey, Scarecrow," someone called. "You got your ears on?"

"Roger that," I answered. "Gimme yo hookup."

"Knucklehead puttin' a chokehold on the Sacro to bust that throttle wide open. You feel me?"

"Knucklehead better calm his ass down," a voice said, laughing. "Before he get toasted by FAA up in these skies round here."

"Who dat out there crankin' me up?" questioned Knucklehead.

"Might be yo mama, punk!"

"Whoa! Whoa! Whoa!" someone said. "Man, I know you didn't just go there with the Knucklehead?"

"Ah, man, that now that was really fucked up!" another voice said.

"Man! Fuck Knucklehead, and Pee-Wee, too!" someone else said.

"Man, I'mma tell all-a y'all somethin'," a voice said. "*Fuck* all y'all."

"Sound like that goddamn Kentucky hillbilly," someone said. "I can tell them hillbilly voices from anywhere."

"Hey, Murdock," a familiar voice came over the transmitter. "This is the Cat, navigating the Lodi. Can I get a hit-me?"

"Check and see what's happening, Tony," I told him. "It's the Cat."

"Yeah," said Tony. "The Scarecrow is answering you, but you ain't yet sayin' anything."

"Hey, the Lodi just wanted to know if a little music would do?"

"What you think?" Tony asked me.

"No problem with me," I told him. "Ask him the name of the music."

"No problem, Lodi. What's the name of the music?"

"Oh, you'll remember it once you hear it," said Lodi, laughing. "It's old school, by Cream. You know, 'White Room.' That's some damn good sounds for the perfect occasion."

"Hey, Lodi," someone called out over the transmitter.

"Yeah, what's that?"

"Can we all hear it?"

"I'm sure you can, providing you guys don't lose control of yourselves up here. I mean, you know you're at a high altitude, don't you?"

"Hey, Lodi?" another voice called.

"Yeah? What's-s-s up?"

"Who gives a fuck?"

Everybody laughed.

"Uh, this is the Scarecrow," I began to suggest. "Everybody turn your frequencies to _____."

This was done to avoid problems with the FAA.

"Thanks a lot there, Scarecrow."

"Hey, what are friends for?" Tony told them.

As I began to maneuver my throttle control to a lower altitude so that we could get a better view of the sunrise to our east; as expected, I could see Lodi and Sacro doing the same.

My reason for dropping down lower was so everyone could get a perfect view of the sun as it began to emerge from in behind towns that were far out to our east.

The sight was awesome and remarkably suited for the journey.

With the sound of Cream blasting softly throughout just about every panel, it was time for me to get a much better grip on things and keep in mind the realization that we were flying most likely thousands of feet in the air high above town after town with each craft rocking and dancing back and forth while slowly climbing higher and higher, maneuvering at times into very steep downward descents, though everyone seemed to be holding very good altitude.

Peering intently straight ahead, though at times out my side windows, I could see Lodi and Sacro hanging tight on both sides.

I then quickly made a forty-five degree right bank, quickly followed by another sharp, smooth, sixty-degree to my left while adding more power than expected just to see what this baby could do. I noticed that my instrument gauges seemed to be holding steady and firmly, while at the same time seemingly dancing and jamming to my every maneuver.

Gliding smoothly through and in between huge mountains and deep slopes, that's when we suddenly saw Lodi come pass us at full throttle with Sacro dead on his tail.

I once again found myself thinking about the amount of wildlife probably chopped up during our maneuvering through their habitat. "Okay, guys," I said over the transmitter. "I think we're having just a little too much fun this morning."

By this time, it had become somewhat quiet. The song "White Room" had ceased its blaring over the entertainment system and just most everyone was seemingly busy concentrating and directing their attention on the amount of time we had left before arriving in Stonyford.

"Look like a lots of excitement going on out there," said Tony. "Man, from up here it looks like a thousand flashing lights or something."

"Where?" asked Karen.

"You see?" he told her, pointing toward the town of Colusa, which is not too far from the town of Williams.

"That's the police cars out there, isn't it?" she asked me.

"Uh huh," I said in a mumble. "That's what it looks like."

"Must be something serious happening, said Tony. "For it to be that many."

"Hey, Scarecrow," a voice came over the transmitter. "You copy me?"

"Copy you," I answered. "But who?"

"It's the Cat, man," he said with a concerning tone.

"What's happening, Cat?" I asked.

"Looks like something serious going on not too far there to our east," he said. "Can you see it?"

"Yeah, we see it, too," someone else said over the transmitter. "Looks like a bad accident or something from up here."

"Uh, check this out, guys," I told everyone. "Lets just take it easy and drop down to a lower altitude and see what's happening."

"Roger that," a voice said.

"That's a ten-four with me, too," another responded.

A smooth forty-five degree bank to my right while losing altitude at a rapid descent, my instrument panel began to mellow out.

"Are you guys still with me?" I asked over the transmitter.

"Uh, Roger that, from Lodi," a voice said.

"Roger that, from Sacro," another voice responded.

"Okay, then," I said. "Watch your altitude, we got power lines all over the place. Watch your altitude."

I could then see all emergency signals and landing lights indicating the activation system being in motion from both Lodi and Sacro. As I reduced my acceleration in sequence to our movement to prepare for an emergency landing, Tony began mentioning something about someone on the ground attempting to guide us in to a location possibly designated for us to land.

"Hey, Murdock," he said, "I think that guy is trying to, you know, tell us to land over there somewhere."

"That's a police officer," said Regina, who was now standing closely in behind my chair, leaning farther toward me. "You see? Isn't that?"

I then leaned slightly forward in an effort to prevent coming into contact with her in an embarrassing way for the both of us. I guess she did not notice how close she'd come, especially knowing both Karen and Sandra were just feet away. Although Karen had now been married to Tony for a number of years and Regina and Sandra had themselves been in their relationship for no telling how long, I have to admit keeping distance from Karen wasn't any easy task.

After landing, it was then that I'd come to realize our reason for not having any prior contact with the situation at hand was because our frequency was on a different channel. It was only now that I reminded the crew to go back to regular frequency modulation in accordance with their input signals.

We then began to hear a mirage of people talking and questioning each other about whatever it was that had taken place in Colusa.

By now all three helicopters had landed safely and began shutting down our engines, only to find ourselves having to restart them, leaving all three loudly idling, though unproductively.

As each helicopter rested, vibrating with engines at full idle, I could see in the distance a quarter inch of the sun rising slowly with a bright, reddish, yellow reflectional beam of rays beginning to brighten up the early morning sky.

Each co-navigator was assigned to the helm in position of control while each navigator exited our crafts to assess the situation.

Not wanting to assume what had happened or just outright undertake the situation at hand with an attitude of indifference, what I could see in plain sight was that there was just something strangely weird about the accident that was proof enough to believe the deadly theory formulated by a few well-respected scientists about the phenomena beginning to take effect throughout the entire region of northern California.

It has been titled the "Stonyford Submission," being that so many people have been reported submitting to something yet undetermined and unidentified.

Assessing the accident was proof enough to believe the situation was in relation to the Stonyford theory.

"Well? Uh, what do you think?" Pee-Wee asked me. "Is there anything we can do to assist?"

"Man, I just don't know," I told him. "I mean, look at this. This is no ordinary accident. Can't you see?"

"Hey, man," said Cat. "The Cat got the jitters about this. I'm gittin' some agitation jumpin' off right about now. I'm nervous as hell. Something ain't quite right about this."

"Yeah," I told him. "I feel it, too."

"Here come two more helicopters," said Pee-Wee. "They're coming from up north. Probably Red Bluff, or maybe Redding."

"Redding?" I questioned.

"Hey, I've seen them before," Cat exclaimed. "But that was, you know, like a few months ago. I believe it was over there in Nevada at the Reno air show."

"What?" I asked Cat. "They were racing 'em or something?"

"Uh huh," he answered. "That, too. But it was the State Troopers, they were busy showing them off, you know, how fast they could fly at a certain speed, and at what altitude."

"You remember the brand name and who manufactured them?" I asked.

"Without a doubt," he said. "They're the new UH-72A Lakota light utility helicopters designed for law enforcement missions. From what I can remember the National Guard units have begun using them."

"Man, this is really somethin'," said Pee-Wee. "Just what's taking so long for the medical units to get here?"

"I was just wondering the same thing," I told him. "No ambulances and not a one medical examiner has arrived to give authorization to remove any of these people or even to ascertain the cause of death."

"Just who the hell are you guys?" one of the pilots flying the UH-72A immediately asked after exiting his craft. "Never mind, don't tell me. You guys are that crazy group of reporters that we've been getting all kinds of weird calls about flying erratically through all of them goddamn hills."

"Who? Us?" Cat said, grinning broadly, obviously feeling proud. "How dare you to even entertain such a thought about us. Surely, we don't look that devilish, do we?"

"Just who in the hell are you trying to fool, Cat?" asked the pilot. "I'd recognize that guilty face from miles away, you crazy son of a bitch. Just how you been doin', old buddy?"

Everybody laughed.

"Didn't think you'd remember me, Commander," Cat told him. "Been just fine. What about you?"

"Oh, I can't complain," said the Commander. "I'm just like y'all folks, working on this here mission round here about the situation we got goin' on up there in Stonyford."

"Excuse me for interrupting, but," I said to both Cat and his friend, the Commander, "just where in the hell is the medical response team? I mean, are we the only ones who heard about this accident, other than the officers who were already here?"

"Now, just tell me something, Sonny, or whatever your name is," asked the Commander. "Just what direction did y'all fly in from? First of all?"

"Well, first of all," I began, "the name, for your information, I am Murdock, and this is Pee-Wee. And it's quite obvious that you already know Cat. So now, the direction is from the west of here, in that direction, you see, up there from within those mountains.

"Well, nice being acquainted with you, Murdock," said the Commander, "but just how in the hell did y'all end up down here?"

"Look, Mr. Commander," said Pee-Wee.

"You can just call me Commander," he told Pee-Wee. "That'll do me far better than all the other crap, if you know what I mean?"

"Well, we was just on our way to Stonyford," Pee-Wee began to tell him, "when we noticed all these lights down here flashing. So, here we are, trying to figure out what's happening."

"Yeah, it's like he's saying," I joined the conversation. "I couldn't help wonder if there was something we could do to assist. So I had our crafts make an emergency landing."

"So, what's happening, Commander?" asked Cat. "I mean, this is a very serious accident out here and I don't see a one medical response team. Just what is that all about?"

"Well, the reason I questioned y'all about the direction you came from is because, strange to say, but every goddamn one of them ambulances crashed en route while on the way here," he said, staring at us. "Talk about some bad, serious fatalities, all up and down this highway, it's like a goddamn deadly disaster zone. It's a deplorable situation that nobody can seem to get a grip on to understand. It's like from here all the way back down to the town of Williams, and then on up to the town of Hornbrook and on into Medford, Oregon. It's been something weird going on that I'm really wondering if one of you can explain?"

"Now, wait a minute," I quickly asked. "Are you telling us there has been accidents all up and down this highway?"

"Accidents that ain't just been happening because of somebody drinking a little too much," the Commander said. "And this just ain't because of someone's negligence or careless driving, either. But something just ain't right about these accidents, and I think you guys know just what I'm getting' at."

"Hey, man," the Cat started, "we're just as confused as you. And if it hadn't been for us seeing all these flashing lights down here, we'd most likely be in Stonyford by now."

"That's right, Commander," I quickly added. "We not too long ago got airborne and it was my intention to be as the Cat said, on our way to Stonyford, until we decided to check and see what was happening with all these lights flashing. I mean, really, it was my intention to just ignore what it was that was happening down here at first, but one of the crew members just had to get a little emotional on us, and here we are."

"Emotional?" said the Commander. "Thank God that happened. Hell, all of y'all'd been long gone by now."

"Well, what is it that we can do?" I asked. "I mean, nobody has even arrived to assist. And Lord knows I hate thinking about the people hurt and all the possible fatalities."

"Has anybody thought about reporting in to one of the nearby towns around here?" asked Pee-Wee. "You know, and formally declaring this section of Interstate Five a disaster zone?"

Mumbling and shrugging shoulders.

"Yeah, right," I said, staring directly at the Commander.

"What the hell you staring at me for?" he asked me. "I-I-I think maybe that's already been done, by somebody else."

"Go ahead, Commander," suggested the Cat. "You can do it."

"Oh, hell no!" said the Commander, trying to clear his throat. "Nope, I don't think so. I'm too old to be taking on this kinda responsibility."

"What?" the Cat asked him. "Don't tell me you're afraid, as tough as you are, and feel threatened by the things you been hearing about from Stonyford?"

"Just who the fuck you think you're talking to, Cat?" the Commander shouted, before hastening in the direction of his UH-72A. "If it wasn't for the fact that I had this hernia operation, I'd knock that smirk off your face."

"Damn!" I questioned. "What's gotten into him all of a sudden?"

"Hey, Commander, man," the Cat yelled out loud. "Wait a minute, man!"

We were all stunned to witness what had just happened. A tough man who was said to withstand just about anything had just walked away from a simple conversation. I was under the impression that he could withstand any type of great strain without breaking down. The way he stood, posture physically fit and seemingly difficult to move, how unfortunate it was that he'd walked away in shame.

"Don't believe it, guys," the Cat said of the Commander. "I'd always respected him as a tough Brigade Combat Leader of a high-ranking infantry division. Seeing him walk away is like dereliction of duty. I'd bring him up for court-martial because of his actions."

"Man, what was that all about?" Pee-Wee questioned. "Y'all see that? He just upped and walked away, and now look at 'em, taking off."

"Yeah, just like he were never here," I added.

By this time, quite a few fire pumpers had arrived, as well as a number of ambulances and several police units from different police departments. In the distance, we could see the medical flight units headed in our direction.

"About time," said Pee-Wee. "Didn't think they'd ever get here."

"Man, we need to go down there and see what's happening," the Cat said, while looking around at the fatalities nearby.

"Wouldn't make any difference," I told him. "It's the same as it is right here. Bodies probably everywhere."

One of the highway patrolmen who was within distance trying to work the accident scene happened to be walking past when Pee-Wee asked, "Are you all right?" But the patrolman just kept walking, as if in a daze. "Hey, are you all right?" Pee-Wee again asked, and still, it was without any response.

"Hey, officer?" I attempted. "Are you all right? Can you hear me?"

"Man, I think that guy is really trippin' on something," the Cat said, watching the patrolman pulling something from his pocket.

"Hey, hey, watch it," we could hear another officer yelling loudly.

"What's he saying?" Pee-Wee quickly asked, wondering what he meant.

"I think he's sayin' something about, watch it, or something," answered Cat.

POW!!! was the next sound we heard as smoke could be seen above the location where the patrolman stood.

"Ah, man," Pee-Wee yelled. "That crazy motherfucker just shot himself in the freakin' head."

"Bill!" the other officer yelled out loud. "Oh no, Bill, buddy."

But it was all too late for this patrolman named Bill. For whatever reason, he'd decided to end his life right there in front of all of us, including our entire crew, who were themselves watching this horrible suicide.

"Man, Murdock," the Cat said in disbelief. "Did we just see what I am thinking we seen? Please tell me no! I'm begging you to tell me no!"

"Man, I don't believe it," said Pee-Wee. "He killed himself just as he walked past us. He really killed himself. I don't believe it."

"Somebody help me," cried the other officer. "My friend here is dead."

Without any hesitation, I found myself reaching downward to try and do whatever I could the assist the officer in distress. I could see that he was troubled greatly and needed immediate attention. His friend, I guess, had been quite distraught from the entire situation and become inattentive, and from the look on his face, when passing us, anxiety was his least worry. He'd gone insane and was suffering from a severe mental breakdown resulting from a variety of combined factors, pushing him well over the edge.

"Hey, buddy," the officer said, talking to his friend, Bill. "Can you hear me? It's me, Steven, your friend. Come on, buddy, wake up, time for us to go home."

To say that I could feel his pain would be an absolute lie. Though I most certainly did experience his grief and deep sadness. I do believe the entire crew felt the same, though it was our mission as professionals to engage in a specified activity, without allowing our emotions to become involved.

Although profanity will undoubtedly at times be expressed during our duty, it's irrelevant, regardless how vulgar at times the language.

Profane as our profession, the content of our true nature is in no way, nor by any means, blasphemous. Our actions and remarks are in no way meant to be irreverent.

The emergency response team had finally made it to assist the officer in need. And it was once again time for us to proceed to our original point intended for this trip.

Upon entering my craft, I immediately noticed how expressionless my crew had become.

"I understand what you must be going through," I told them. "But it's a part of the job, and our job is always the part that nobody really wants to see. Oh, but everybody always wanna read about, but they just don't wanna be seeing it as we do, close up and personal."

"But what was that all about?" Regina asked, sorrowful.

"Somebody that just had far too much on his plate," I told her. "He really wasn't all that ready to experience what he was goin' through."

"And that's what made him do that?" she asked curiously, staring at Sandra.

"Just another form of depression," I told her. "What he did can just about happen to anyone of us. I'm talking about when you're depressed."

"I ain't never gone be that depressed," she said. "Nothing gone ever make me so depressed to where I'll do something crazy like that! Nothing!"

"Well, let's hope not," I said. "Because, man. And if it's all right for me to say…and I tell you no lie…but my foolish move behind, Karen, I too, have to admit it had me feeling probably just like that patrolman. I wanted to literally do the exact same thing that he did. You see, she never knew it, but I sure in the hell did. I mean, I knew I'd hurt Karen, and believe me, it wasn't intentional. But in the process, it was like, you know, I had set everything in motion to kill me—and I'm not playing. What I did to her to this day is always weighing heavily on my heart."

"And how do you feel about her now?" Regina just had to ask me. "And tell the truth, Murdock!"

"I ain't gone lie," I told her. "I love her even more so today, and I wish we were together. But I can't change the past, just like I can't change what's happening today. Tony is a really good person and I'll always do my very best to respect him and his love for her."

"But?" Regina started.

"But, wait a minute," I quickly interrupted. "I must also do my very best to respect their relationship, as well as their marriage.

"So what were you about to say?"

"Never mind, I forgot."

Just as we were about to gear up for our continuous flight to Stonyford, it seemed an everlasting, relentless standstill inadvertently kept us stagnated, remaining inactive.

We were asked to remain on scene by one of the newly arrived Highway Patrolmen. He felt that we could possibly help him with the information he needed to begin his inquiry into the situation at hand.

I immediately informed both Pee-Wee and Cat to shut down their engines to save fuel, though all other power remained active, such as our emergency activation switches and power units.

"Well, as you guys know, it was my intention to be fully airborne," I told everyone over the transmitter. "But as you can see, for some weird, odd reason, we really haven't made it anywhere as of yet. But don't get me wrong about my statement, I'm sure we should all feel helpful for being a part of the first assisting team out here. From my course during navigation I would say that we're, and I'm using accurate terms, we've landed right dab in the middle of Colusa and Williams. The town of Willows is just ahead of us. And to the left of Willows is Elk Creek. It's my understanding that something terrible has happened there, too."

"Man, this is really strange," Tony said. "It's fully daylight, and just look at this, all up and down this highway all you can see is a bunch of colorful emergency lights flashing everywhere."

"And don't forget about all them bodies laying around out there," a blur of words came from Karen. "Got me trippin'."

"Can barely understand what you're sayin'," Tony told her. "You need to calm down and get yourself together. Quit taking it personal."

"Girl, what's wrong with you?" asked Regina. "Just do like what you see me and Sandra doin', write about this crazy shit."

"She got a point there, Karen," I told her, "Man, we ain't heard not a one word from Sandra. It's like she's been in here writing her butt off."

"That's what I been trying to do," said Karen. "But it just ain't comin' out the way I want it to."

"Damn!" Tony mumbled. "Just stick yo head out the window and start writing about everything you see."

"I ain't got time for your shit, Tony," Karen said seriously. "This isn't the time."

"Them people comin' this way," said Regina, pointing out one of the side windows at a few plain-clothes men, apparently investigators assigned to work the crash scene. "I think they're trying to get our attention."

"Hold on," I quickly said, peering out the window, searching for the people Regina had seen coming in our direction. "Where are they?"

"Here they are, right here, Doc," said Tony, nodding his head in the direction toward the front of our craft. "See? Right there."

"Man, let's go and find out what's happening," I suggested, motioning that he go with me.

"Who, me?" questioned Tony.

"I'll go with you," Karen said, adjusting the collar on her Burk's Bay Napa jacket.

"No, I'll go," said Tony, while gently rubbing one of his hands across the back of Karen's neck and shoulders. "I thought you wasn't feeling well, and from the looks of things, we just might be here for a while."

"I'll go," she told him. "I need the air, anyway."

"We'll both go," Tony suggested. "I can use some, too, but that's, you know, providing it's not contaminated. All them bodies laying around could be decomposing by now, polluting the air. You feel me?"

"Mmm-mmm," she mumbled. "Uh huh, I feel you."

"Whatcha think, Murdock?" he asked me. "You know, is it cool?"

"No problem with me if that's what you wanna do," I told him. "I just gotta let everybody else know what's happening."

"Hey, we'll stay onboard," said Regina, "and continue doing what we're doing. You know, what we've started from in here."

"If that's what you wanna do, it's all right with me," I told her. "But if you decide to join us, I guess then maybe Karen or Tony, or the both of you guys can come back onboard to be here. Somebody should be here at all times."

"We'll stay until you guys get back," said Regina.

"Alright with me, if that's what you wanna do," I told her.

Just as we were about to exit the craft we were met by the nearby county examiner. The investigators stood a few feet behind him, looking around aimlessly at the crash scene and at the three helicopters."

"Uh, yeah. Hi there. I am Chief Medical Examiner Nicholas Florentin, and these two gentlemen here are my assistants. Uh, well, gee, I think I could really use a little help with this situation out here, you know, trying to understand what happened to the officer. Did by chance you folks see anything?" he asked.

"Well, all I am sure I can tell you, er...?" I began.

"Uh, you can just call me Florentin," he told me. "That's what just about everybody calls me, and recognizes me by at the office."

"Alright, then, Florentin," I started. "I just think that the officer had been kinda, you know, deeply disturbed and became mentally and emotionally anxious about the situation out here. I mean, just look around you, Florentin, this can very easily drive anybody insane."

"What did you see him do?" he asked Tony.

"Man, I didn't really see him do anything," said Tony. "I just heard the sound."

"I saw it all happen," Pee-Wee told him, shaking his head in disbelief. "I seen him do it, and believe me, it wasn't a pretty sight."

"And you are...?" asked Florentin.

"I am Pee-Wee."

"Pee-Wee?" asked Florentin. "Are you with these people here?"

"Damn straight," answered Pee-Wee.

"And what's your job? If I may ask," Florentin questioned.

"It's cool," said Pee-Wee. "I fly that baby over there. It's called the Sacro, for Sacramento."

"All of you guys here from Sacramento?" Florentin asked.

"Well, hold up for a minute," I told him so I could get everyone over to my craft to be a part of the conversation. I then motioned with one of my hands to get everyone's attention. "Everybody come over here," I called out. "But leave somebody to mind your craft." Within minutes just about the entire crew was gathering around curiously.

"Oh, this is Chief Medical Examiner Nicholas Florentin and his two assistants," I began informing everyone. "As you, or some of you, saw, that one officer took his own life not too long ago, and as horrible as it was, some of us witnessed it happen. And what Medical Examiner Florentin wants to know is, those of you who actually did witness this, please do all you can to help him out by answering his questions. Thank you."

"The guy just outright shot himself in the freakin' head without ever sayin' anything," I could hear Pee-Wee telling Florentin. "And that other officer who was standing over there yelled "Bill!" really, really loud. I mean, man, it was like his friend was really trying his best to stop him. You know what I mean? But it was too late. Damn! He raised his hand up, and that was it. Pow!"

"That's what we heard, too," one of the other crew members told him. "At first, I just thought the officer was waving his hand at somebody, but then, all of a sudden, there was this bang sound, and then you could see all this smoke coming from whatever it was that he had in his hand. That is when he just dropped, you know."

"Yeah, he just dropped downward, suddenly quick," another of the crew members began describing. "But I seen the gun in his hand when he was, you know, walking past the Scarecrow. I seen Pee-Wee sayin' something to him, but he looked like he'd just kept on going about his business, ignoring whatever it was that Pee-Wee were trying to say to him. And then, "Boom! Pow! It was over. He dropped dead!"

"And that was it?" asked Florentin. "Nothing else?"

"Oh yeah, there was something else," said the crew member.

"And what was that?" Florentin asked.

"Some of his head went flying all over the place," the crew member told him. "And when he hit the ground, he was shaking like he was having some serious convulsions or something."

"But the poor guy was gone," one of the female crew members added. "I could tell he was dead before he ever even hit the ground."

Chapter Nine

THE HUGE GATHERING AT THE CARNIVAL AND RODEO was unlike anything Stonyford had ever experienced. The feasting and traveling merrymakers with so many featured exhibits and thrill-seeking rides had drawn an unusual attraction for public entertainment, alluring an appealing audience of spectators from miles away.

Hundreds, maybe even thousands, of campers, boaters, and water-skiers enjoyed themselves on houseboats, jamming the lake, while others attended the rodeo and carnival.

For entertainment, Stonyford invested in one of the largest Mega Water Slides for children's entertainment. This slide had multiple lanes for racing swiftly downhill, the racers blowing plumes of water so fast that slowing down to reduce speed was impossible. Winding curves with surprisingly sharp turns sped excited children, as well as adults, from on high down to the bottom for their immense enjoyment.

Moving swiftly and forcefully downward through water-splashing courses of twisted, gripping, wrenching colorful tunnels illuminated with very bright fluorescent lights is how most vacationers enjoyed themselves during the entertainment.

This was the first full gathering of the festive celebration for the small town of Stonyford and its surrounding communities as they struggled desperately to bring back the strength that was once shattered by tragedy after tragedy and ruins of horrible misfortunes. Though sadly, dramatic disastrous events of unseen elements would once again strike this community of festive merrymakers with such intensity and unrelenting vengeance.

Retribution for the refusal of its residents to oblige and submit to the authority and corruption of an element with degrading principles so complex to where the entire environment would become the substance characterized by a basic, fundamental component for neutralization and the constraint of the entire town of merrymakers to a high degree of extreme obligations and indebtedness.

The unrelenting vengeance of intensity so violent was about to be unleashed under circumstances unlike anything ever imagined by that of even the most distinguished mystery writer.

Stonyford was undoubtedly without the hands of mercy or compassion.

Chapter Ten

THE PEAK OF SUMMER was at its greatest ever for everyone to achieve the maximum of their enjoyment during the festive celebration. Stonyford had become like New Orleans' Mardi Gras, with thousands of people attending the feasting, carnival and parade procession and joyous ceremonial march of people dressed in a variety of bright, colorful costumes.

An ostentatious display of an elegant fashion for everyone to finally have an opportunity to place themselves on exhibit to show off their beauty so lavishly. Even the elderly could be seen leisurely walking and at times strutting in their affectedly self-important gait and manner just for the occasion.

This was day three of the celebration as merrymakers began to wind down, preparing themselves in preparation for the final evening of the event. The last episode, combining every element and its ingredients into one very huge eruption like that of the big bang theory, which would send clusters of fireworks exploding high into the atmosphere, generating tons of bright colors, smoke and loud banging noises for entertainment.

This would be the final evening for Stonyford and neighboring communities to bring forth their best display for the celebration.

The auctioneer. The panhandlers. Sophisticated prostitutes and pimps. Flamboyant people of every sexual preference and walk of life were all partakers, participating in the event, showing off their colorfully displayed fashion.

There was a display of Sodom and Gomorrah showing the town of Stony Ford being overthrown. This display was in remembrance of the fatal epidemic disease of an unknown origin that struck the town of Stonyford like a wild plague, causing severe, unsparing affliction on the entire region.

Some called the affliction the curse of the devil, while others called it a plague sent from God as a punishment to torture and agonize the residents of these small communities for their immorality, though one not subject to death.

Nonetheless, death was unleashed.

During the procession, there were Kustom "High Roller" Choppers of various form. Tom Daniel's Circus Wagon. Various Black Widow Ford T SSP, as well as a few Shelby Cobras. The Ed Roth's Outlaw, and old 1948 Ford Woody. A 1926 Mack Bulldog Tank Truck, and a number of 1949 Mercury Coupe, and convertibles. A few Mack Fire Pumpers, Yamaha Motorcycles of all styles, color, shapes and forms. There were even a few 1946 and '47 Fleetline, Chevy Sedan Deliveries. A 1901 De Dion Bouton. A 1935 Morgan SS 3-Wheeler, and a 1912 Ford Model T Delivery Truck, along with the Batman Dark Knight: Bat Pod.

There were many displays for the Star Trek lovers, with a Mr. Spock and a Star Trek USS Enterprise look-alike on hand. There was also an Elvira, Mistress of the Dark lookalike mingling with the crowd.

An eighteen-wheeler pulling a 53-foot flatbed trailer converted into a flossy, stylish flotation mantel resembling a huge pedestal was also a part of the procession. Mounted on top of the pedestal was someone dressed as Satan with the impersonator describing himself as the God of the universe. At his side knelt imaginary people who could be seen worshipping him as a huge, terrifying, mythical beast, making loud, threatening, growling sounds with deep gutturals circled them, daring anyone to attempt to escape.

Not far behind the flotation mantel was a 1926 Mack Bull Dog Log Hauler, except it carried but only one log: the cross resembling that of the crucifixion of Jesus, the Christ. The log hauler dragged behind it two more crosses, representing the two criminals who were also put to death and crucified by the nailing to the cross for their punishment.

For a joyful laugh, Curly, Larry, and Moe of the Three Stooges were also on hand for the celebration.

Deep Space Nine's Quark could be seen shaking hands with spectators.

Motor vehicles of various styles, customized to a T, were all on hand for the celebration procession, such as a 1941 two-door Plymouth coupe, (metallic purple & metallic rose), 1937 Custom Ford Roadster Top-Up (maroon), a 1939 Chevy Coupe (red), a 1940 Chevy Sedan (turquoise), the originals, 1956 Cadillac Limo Presidential Parade Car, and the 1961 Lincoln

Limo X-100 Kennedy Car.

There were also a number of old, restored, 1946 Chevy Stake Trucks with old barrels in red and different colored cabs. A number of 1946 Chevy Fire Trucks (Red/Fillmore). Hundreds of customized Harley Davidsons and Yamahas, Hummers of all types. An old 1955 Buick Century Police Unit. A few Custom VW Drag Buses, PT Cabrios, a 1931 Ford Model A Pick Up Stake Truck.

There were also eight Munster Koaches and a variety of differently colored racing cars for children to ride in for their enjoyment.

Also on hand, there were a huge collection of military vehicles and a few sweet-looking Hangman's Tow Trucks and monster trucks, Jeeps and huge dump trucks.

Beside the 1952 Nash Ambassador Airflyte-tin/Autumn Rust, there was also a 1951 Kaiser Henry J-Indian Ceramic, followed by The Spirit of America-Craig Breedlove's 2000 Jet Car, and a host of Ferraris, Porsches and Lamborghinis, and Corvettes and Vipers.

In a field across from the Stonyford grocery store, there rested a USAF C130 Hercules Gunship, a Boeing B29 Superfortress, and a few P-51 Mustangs and P-38M Lightnings. And a number of Cessnas and Piper Cherokees, and Beech Bonanzas.

There were rumors that a possible 1935 Douglas DC-3 had landed nearby in another field. Someone had also observed a person flying around on what's considered the first modern helicopter, the 1940 Sikorsky VS-300. Not far from the now-deserted Johnson's estate, which had become a project to be converted into a retirement home, there sat two 1953 Learjet-23s.

High in the sky above Stonyford, there could be seen four to six, and at times eight Vintage Wings of Canada Swordfish, flying in perfect formation to arouse the crowd as they made different types of circles and daring, dangerous loops, spraying behind them wide, colorful trails of smoke.

In the distance, you could see two fast-moving F2Gs circling as they prepared to land.

Amongst those anxiously awaiting their turn on the final evening ride of the last day of the Mega Water Slide, hundreds of people could be seen standing in line for their chance to ride the huge Monster Coiled Roller Coaster, the Double-Headed Ferris Wheel, and the jaw breaking Detonator.

There were also carousels with multi-hued lights that played soft musical sounds for the very young and the elderly to enjoy, casually, and informally.

Just about everywhere you looked, you could find a private concession stand illuminated in bright, colorful lights as a means to advertise their choice of various food products.

Hot, tasty, flavored buttered popcorn, cotton candy, candy- and caramel-coated apples, freshly-made jumbo corn dogs, a variety of flavored snow cones, and cheeseburgers and the original, hot dogs, filled the air with thick, enticing aroma meant to arouse one's desire.

In another section nearby the lake, bulldozers and other tractors had to be used to scoop up debris and remove unsettling guests, such as deadly, venomous rattlesnakes and other poisonous reptiles considered a possible hazard during the festivity.

Screaming, shouting, crying and raucous laughter were the sounds heard for miles on this section of the land used for blood-curdling rides, such as the Timber Wolf, the Mamba, the Thunder Hawk, the Zamba Zinger, the Deadly Boomerang, and the Ripcord.

Stonyford was at its best to rebound from past tragedies to triumph and jubilant victory.

This was the festivity of all festival celebrations, to say the least.

Aircrafts carrying large troops of military forces could be seen in the distance, smoothly sailing in the the direction of Stonyford, deploying its troops enabling them to engage in rich, colorful apparatus, free-fall jumps using parachutes in the perfect shape of giant umbrellas, to make huge, colorful smoke trails, glittering downward like a million falling stars.

Yes, indeed, Stonyford was definitely at its best on this particular evening.

There were even people of many disabilities and deformities attending the festivity. Most were said to have been in relationship to Stonyford during birth. Politicians in high political offices in Sacramento had seemingly found a secretly conniving way through their special interest committee to supposedly raise money and make genuine contributions to the institution selected for study by scientists and other high-ranking government structures. But during the festivity, it was apparent that those who suffered severely were found in a huge carnival tent amongst all the merrymakers on exhibit.

Occasionally, someone could be heard screaming loudly from being bitten by the unusual amount of venomous reptiles migrating to the

Stonyford region. The migration was of inconstant temperament of an unbalanced change considered relatively uncommon and extraordinary, and also outright inconceivable to actually be happening so spontaneously.

But during each scream, there were many more who yelled from laughter while enjoying themselves on the many spine-tingling rides.

Seeing so many bright smiles participating in the festivity, as well as the lengthy procession, John Blake, the head sheriff in Stonyford, held his head up high from the thought of his town's rebounding image. "Yeah, I be the man in charge of this town," he kept repeating to himself. "I be the man 'round here." But little did he know Stonyford, the town he so desperately served as chairman and used profitably in a manner requiring so much attention of the public, was about to become like that that old cunning serpent with a razor-like edge, ready to dice and slice just about every living matter in its wake.

I guess you could say that it was just like the old Proverbs in the Bible wherein it says: The Serpent come to Kill, Steal, and Destroy. Well, I think that's how it goes. But I'm more than sure you get the picture.

The man, meaning Blake, walked around with this huge cigar very neatly tucked in between those round, puffy jaws of his, with what just could have been illegal, rolled-up smoking tobacco with pot leaves as far as anyone knew, and most likely forbidden by law. But this was his town and no one dared step on his toes, that is if you didn't want to end up losing your own.

Nonetheless, Blake most certainly did "be the man." Walking around with a few of his unworthy, good-for-nothing flunkies at his side, using his reputation to rub arms with the right people in power.

But this was Stonyford, the town that suffered the most when tragedy struck, literally, and I do mean literally, almost decapitating an entire community of people in this once quiet part of the region.

No question about it, Stonyford was on a rebound, with a huge platform to stand on and deliver its message loudly and dramatically clear.

The population in this town had grown tremendously and particularly because of the rich, quiet inheritance left behind by a legacy of ancestral work. Stonyford is a place of ancestors, descendants of descendants, and predecessors of predecessors.

Sadly, the town wasn't exempt nor immune to its past, present, or the future awaiting it.

The people went right on with all their festive merrymaking, not realizing the evil, vicious spirit of the old snake hunter and his wicked, deceiving snake were calmly approaching the vicinity of Stonyford, with aggressive, malicious intent to storm this rebounding community with such forceful violence to where it would be highly unlikely and unquestionably impossible for this town to ever rebuild from such brutal devastation.

It was on this particular evening that the lines at each exhibit on display had become unusually jammed by the invigoration of so many refreshed, cheerful souls. The attraction by such an event had the attention also of a supernatural authority and philosophy relating to the existence of something yet needing to be identified.

The festivity had become like that of a ritual being enacted by evil spirits seemingly sent forth in plain sight as a responsibility to solidify Satan's military forces. The spirit of the old snake hunter and his snake was just an elaborate platform in place for the submission.

But the sheriff, after becoming fully aware of such a large number of people being seemingly, just outright attacked by various out-of-control reptiles, showed little concern, dismissing each of these attacks as simply unfortunate coincidences. "Hey, what can I say," the sheriff stated. "People get bitten all the time by something or other."

Whatever the reason for the attacks didn't concern him, but the image he wanted to project was his only concern.

"Look, we got emergency hospitals all over this goddamn place, and if anyone's life is in serious danger, we can handle it. I am the sheriff of this town, I got your back. So don't worry yourself to death over a little sting or bite every now and then. You know what I mean? I got your back."

Too proud to bend your pride is what I believe caused quite a number of people to lose out on many achievements of prosperity in life. And one would, I guess, come to believe that old Blake, well, I just think this is one of the things he felt he was completely exempted from. The thought of something going haywire and out of control in his town ever again, and especially after the Johnson incident, such an occurrence which caused so much crisis and disruption, he'd vowed would never happen again.

So he just kept right on with all his pride, not really showing much concern, if that at all, for the sake of the people visiting his town. Not realizing it was all about to catch up with him in the worst way, which would undoubtedly bring an end to his career as a well-respected sheriff.

"What's a little bite every now and then?" was his only response when questioned about the outrageous, exceeding number of people being airlifted out of Stonyford and flown to the Willows hospital for emergency medical treatment.

Not far from the forestry station on the road to Snow Mountain, many more people in the hundreds gathered together to enjoy the evening with a meal of barbecue while broiling and roasting different types of meat.

There were boundaries marked in fields and on private land as limits and borders to prevent anyone from venturing onto unsettled land and areas where wildlife live freely in their natural environment.

These boundaries were said to be where most of the people visiting Stonyford had been bitten by various venomous reptiles.

Though still, everyone just kept right on with all their joyous merrymaking like at the New Orleans Mardi Gras, with all the feasting, carnivals, and parade processions and ceremonial marches of troupes of people dressed in various colorful costumes of ostentatious display of richly elegant fashion for everyone to see and enjoy, lavishly. Well-wishes were given to those who had apparently fallen ill to the deadly poisonous venom injected into them, in hope to see them again one day, if at all.

Sadly, when truthfully thinking about it, most of those stricken would end up severely crippled and most likely lame, paralyzed, and some would be partially disabled or impaired, in one way or another, for the rest of their lives.

But the show must go on. And on it most certainly did for the town of Stonyford.

One, or a hundred and one, unfortunate mishaps just wasn't enough to slow down the organized mobilization put into motion at this celebration. I assure you of that in this town. Every exhibit was jam-packed with very large groups of people just waiting and anticipating their chance to finally experience its thrilling ride of a lifetime.

The huge Mega Water Slide was about ready to open for the hundreds of thousands of children and adults to slide down its numerous rushing waterways, speeding downward, and then upward, after what would seem like a million twists and turns, forcefully thrusting and propelling its victims onward high into the air at the ending of its projectile missile-like shunt, sending them speeding fast like bullets, splashing into the shallow waters of the Stonyford lake, where lifeguards were awaiting them on large rubber rafts, should anyone become disoriented.

Deep sea water lights used for exploring and scavenging the lake were placed in different areas of the lake to illuminate the colorful display of Stonyford's sea world exhibition. Dozens of these lights were also used at the splashing point for those preparing to be forcefully propelled into the lake.

Signs were in place, each as a warning. To "ride at your own risk."

It was like a prophecy forewarning a prediction from a divine prophet, revealing something terribly foretold.

Women were walking around like prophetesses, wearing long, shaggy, woolen clothing with long, ropy hair, dreadlocked by being twisted and then braided into a particular hairstyle.

They, too, were speaking about something terrible in Stonyford's future.

Still, it didn't stop the celebration as groups of people could be seen heading for Snow Mountain. Car loads speeding and passing each other carelessly and acting foolishly, driving along the narrow, inflexible, two-lane winding road that would take them high into the ridged mountains with barely enough space to pass an oncoming vehicle.

Drinking, screaming, yelling loudly, and being just outright highly obnoxious and definitely repugnant, with loud, profane language, stubbornly adhering to anyone's opinion, they began throwing beer cans and various beverage containers from their vehicles.

Cars, vans, trucks, Jeeps, and some were even driving fast-moving dirt bikes, darting in and out with all their sharp, rapid movement in between each vehicle, driving recklessly, heedless of any consequence.

But without them knowing, the retribution was on in full force for the town of Stonyford and the surrounding area as the vicious, evil spirits very calmly approached the festivity with devastating intent.

As each vehicle moved at an increasingly high rate of speed, illegal for such acceleration and performance throughout the region, some of the individuals were using an amphetamine drug, while others could be seen smoking from long, hollow cylindrical tubes, such as pipes and other types of illegal paraphernalia. These items, too, were being carelessly discarded and thrown amongst the thick brush, crashing into the many rocks alongside these sharp, winding roads, smashing and shattering its left-behind contents, with some loudly bursting into pieces, while other discarded items proved impervious, shatterproof.

A dangerous, hazardous obstacle to anyone who happened across such items while venturing this part of the region.

Whether or not they were aware of Stonyford's history was a question proving later that they hadn't an alternative or simply just had a stroke of sadly bad misfortune awaiting them under the conditions.

Courtesy to their demise, the road they traveled must have taken them on a journey prohibited and definitely forbidden by nature itself, from a geographical point of view.

The history of Stonyford and its origin had become a structure in a particular area of the earth where the surface had a constant geomagnetic series of sequences and numbers of forceful factors that were designed into points that were in relation to the birthplace of Satan's army. The mathematical study of the events during the celebration and configuration tended to show proof about the formulated theory of evolution, a phenomenon proving such an account to be of truth.

Stonyford is proof about the theory that evolved around the existing species (animals and plants) having developed from previous existence. A process that gradually changed, becoming what we are today.

For this reason, a sheep is another of our closest relatives, which can be proven through the geometric process. (15, 25, 125, and 625, a factor in term like an embrasure opening, whereas the door proving evolution's window of truth and sound facts can easily astound you upon studying the existing configuration.)

Stonyford itself was on a forbidden journey that was about to send an entire community crashing into piece after piece, without ever ending.

And Sheriff Blake, although he was fully aware of those who had very foolishly sped off onto the deadly rough roads of Snow Mountain, I suppose his image was all he was thinking about. He never once advised any of his flunkies to do anything about the deadly venture. Instead, he just went right on smiling and occasionally shaking hands with everyone he'd passed, puffing and smoking on that big, fat, rolled up, illegal tobacco stick that he kept squeezed tight between those nasty-looking, rotten teeth.

Teeth that were probably once belonging to a decaying corpse.

Then there were those who found themselves unable to resist listening to all the storytelling by the old storytellers about ancient times in the remote regions of Stonyford. Large groups of people sat for hours listening to the Chief, an old ancestral Native American from years long ago, tell them intense stories about the horrifying tragedies that once afflicted this community like a deadly epidemic, an extremely dreadful plague causing torturous pain and severe physical suffering, leaving its victims in the worst abnormal state to where, in most cases, death was said to be the only solution for solving the epidemic.

He spoke at great length about the Johnson family tragedy and how it was that Margaret Johnson, the youngest daughter of Paul and Sarah Johnson, had somehow escaped the devil's deadly rapturous grip, or so everyone had thought.

But not only was Chief mesmerizing the listening spectators with such ancient tales of years long ago, but there were also elderly residents of Stonyford and the surrounding communities involved in the collection of storytellings.

As they sat circling just about halfway around the town's supermarket, some could be seen standing and pointing in the direction of each event talked about.

The hills, the mountains, the thick brush and all the many deadly-steep slopes and narrow ravines that seemed to seize their victims so avidly. Everything throughout the community seemed to be so miraculously maintained and preserved, that was except for the old Johnson residence, which was being renovated and converted into the town's private retirement home.

But there sat an elderly man adjacent from the Chief, who must have stood at five-eight or -nine, and very frail with apparently badly declining health, who spoke in a soft, eerie, scratchy, gurgling sound that sounded as though he were attempting to talk just after undergoing a tracheotomy. "I seen it when it was just about over there," he said, pointing in the direction of the distant hills across from the Johnsons' residence. "It was just this big, huge, ugly, dark cloud-like thing, just up there in dem there hills, just a-hovering there, and floating around and drifting randomly all over the place. And then it did it."

"Did what?" someone asked. "It did what?"

The old man, whose eyes could barely open, also wore a dark pair of sunglasses with dark polarized lenses protecting his eyes from any form of light. He also wore something that looked like an old Humphrey Bogart hat.

"It did this," he said, removing the dark sunglasses. "This is what it did to me for refusing to look the other way. This is what he did to me."

"Who are you talking about?" asked someone else.

Removing the sunglasses revealed eyes that looked as though they were badly infected with cataracts, partially blinding him.

"Who did this to you?" another person asked. "Who are you talking about that did this to you?"

"Yeah, I mean," someone else asked. "Where is he? You know, the person responsible for doing this to you?"

"Everywhere," he told them. "It's everywhere. It was the devil himself that did this to me. He's the one in control of this town. This town belongs to him. You all belong to him now. Every last one of you, whether you want to or not. You're his now that you've come here to celebrate his day of birth."

Some of the people could be seen slightly smiling at the old man, while others could be seen laughing loudly and nodding their heads in disbelief.

"You see, you're doing the same exact thing that I did," he told them. "I, too, just laughed and thought it was just a bunch of hogwash. I said to everyone back then that it was just a bunch of ridiculous talk and that anyone using common sense wasn't going to be stupid enough to believe in the devil. But just look at me, that's right, take a real good, hard look at me, and you'll see for yourself what he did to me. And you know what? He's right here, still with us. That's right, his spirit is everywhere, and he's on his way back to finish what he started that caused the submission.

"So you can just keep right on laughing at me with all your snickering, but when he starts snatching some-a y'all, just remember to keep right on laughing, because he's gonna sneak up on all y'all, quietly, and in a creepy, stealthy way, and gonna snatch you right up."

"Hey, old man?" someone began questioning. "Aren't you the town's drunk? They say you'll do just about anything for a drink."

Everybody laughed.

"Hey, if all you want is a drink, then just ask," another told him in a joking manner.

"Yeah, after hearing that," someone else said, "I could use a drink or two myself. By the way, what's your name, old fella?"

"Uh, it's…?"

"Frank Wheeler!" a tall, slender man quickly said. "He's been living in this town from as far back as I can remember. It happened to him when he was just within distance from his farm when his truck mysteriously began to develop a rather unusual breakdown. The stalling of the engine had become very annoying to Mr. Wheeler's slobbish state of intoxication, at which time it was then that he decided he'd attempt becoming a mechanic.

"Yeah, old Frank here was definitely what you would call the town's only drunk, living in the most immoral, uncivilized manner, and not having the least bit of respect for human dignity. And I would guess you could also consider Frank a loner, 'cause for many years he lived trying his best in just about every way possible to avoid any type of confrontation with his fellow neighbors.

"Well, it was on this particular evening that while old Frank here was busy teaching himself how to become a mechanic, without knowing it, he was also about to encounter the most horrifying experience within his entire life."

Frank Wheeler, better known throughout the community as simply Frank, the young man explained, was busy trying his best to determine the problem for his truck's all-of-a-sudden breakdown, when he decided he'd position himself underneath the truck and its engine. Trying desperately to find the problem and at times trembling from exhaustion, he then found himself experiencing a rather unfamiliar vibe, something not previously known to him, very strange, causing him to become outrageously disturbed.

Without further hesitation, he immediately, while acting in fear from whatever it was that was happening, struggled desperately to get out from beneath the truck, assuring his curiosity.

A very bright light reflecting through the dark night, which was coming from the Stonyford Supermarket, seemed to give him some form of relief, though Frank still at times felt the presence of someone other than himself. He thought walking home was out of the question—well, that was until Frank, who was already heavily intoxicated, found himself nervously fumbling through his overall pockets for something to drink from his wine bottle.

Drinking profusely in large amounts while staggering unsteadily home through the dark twilight of the night sky, it was at this moment that Frank Wheeler, the town drunk, would find himself deeply shaken by an extremely strong jolt, as though he were being penetrated deep within his rectum by a thin, pointed, sharp object.

"Falling to the ground in terror, he found himself intensely frightened and terribly horrified from the pain invading him. Once again, the object began ripping through him, dragging him slowly forward on the gravel road without any sympathy, only causing more intense, unbearable pain.

"Yelling out loudly for help, while at the same time struggling to try regaining control of himself, was an unsuccessful attempt as the object once again forcefully penetrated him, twirling him rapidly in large spinning circles deep into the gravel road, sending huge amounts of dust high into the dark, clear sky from each powerful thrust.

"When Frank was finally found, he was lying spread-eagled in a state of unconsciousness just within a very short distance from his farm house, which many of you passed on the way here. This poor guy that you were laughing at must have lay in a coma for a good two to three weeks, not expecting to pull through his ordeal.

"Who is responsible? You tell us, because we sure in hell don't know!"

But old Frank Wheeler found himself awakening to the early morning chill, wondering if maybe his entire ordeal were only a horrible, drunken nightmare, scaring the living daylights out of him. He thought that maybe the alcohol had affected him so badly to where his imagination had begun to get the best of him. The thought of being attacked by the invisible man brought an embarrassing grin to his face as he shamefully knew it was impossible.

Still lying on the ground, Frank finally decided to attempt trying to position himself upright, at which time he felt a series of intense pain and uncontrollable vomiting started to occur spontaneously. He began to feel the intense pain in the lower portion of his alimentary canal, the rectum, spring to life and sending an elaborate amount of pain with a powerful, violent force shooting throughout his entire body, knocking him to the ground.

Sheriff Blake, who just happened to be out patrolling early that morning was en route to Frank's home after noticing his abandoned truck on one of the roads. Within minutes from his home, the sheriff just happened to take a brief glimpse to his side and spotted a figure which he immediately recognized as Frank Wheeler struggling to gain control of himself.

Quickly pulling his patrol car to one side and climbing out as fast as he could, he immediately started trying to help Frank get to his feet. While doing so, he began questioning him as to why his truck was in town and here he was lying out on one of the county roads, on the ground, this early in the morning, just within a short distance from home.

The sheriff then began to advise him of the possible danger he faced concerning his serious problem he was having with alcohol, suggesting the possibility of hospitalization.

It was while helping Frank regain control of himself that the sheriff noticed the expression on Frank's face and how he was acting as if he were in a great amount of pain, and as if he had been hit by a passing car. Upon questioning him, the sheriff noticed the unusually large amount of blood surrounding the crotch section of Frank's trousers, at which time he immediately told Frank to lie down flat on the ground and not to move. The Sheriff then notified the Stonyford Sheriff Department dispatcher, asking her to send an emergency medical response team to his reported location. ASAP.

The message went immediately across the transmitter to every emergency destination in the particular immediate region surrounding Stonyford.

Even Frank, himself, was now becoming frightened from the thought of wondering if maybe he were really the victim of some violent, vicious attack, depriving him of his manhood. The thought that maybe an intensive, thorough examination concerning the possibility of being gang raped would be necessary, but it was Frank's pride that made him withdraw such a thought.

Meanwhile, the sheriff had become somewhat suspicious, thinking that old Frank Wheeler wasn't at all that loner-type of person the town had, in its own way, pictured him to be. In fact, his present curiosity was leading him to believe that the old town drunk was really possibly a queer, and eccentrically odd with all his unconventional behavior. But it was a suspicious thought without any solid facts. But then he thought, 'What if he's a homosexual? Is there really anything wrong with that? I mean, Frank has always been a good friend of mine and I would never turn my back on him, no matter what."

So to not add to an open sore, he decided to just keep his opinion to himself and not question Frank's personal lifestyle, but he did indeed try his best to advise him to be more careful, and especially because of his personal appearance that should be kept concealed.

"You know something, old Frank," said the Sheriff, "Uh, that very visible stain on your trousers was, I think, enough for me or anyone to draw a reasonable conclusion about your personal lifestyle."

"What in heaven's name are you talkin' 'bout, Sheriff?" Frank quickly asked. "What private life being concealed?"

Just as he was about to question the sheriff, there was an important interruption by the sheriff informing him about his disorderly behavior and outrageous conduct, which could very easily land him in jail for sleeping on a public street while heavily intoxicated.

Against Frank's wishes, the Sheriff, upon notifying the office dispatcher to withdraw the medical response unit to his location, he then drove Frank back to the location of his abandoned pickup truck. Not really understanding Frank's reason for continuing to insist that the sheriff remain there with him until he got the truck started, which Blake thought of as very odd, and especially coming from Frank.

The Sheriff could see nothing wrong with the truck and began to view the situation as simply a matter of Frank's behavior problem. He believed that Frank was just too busy involved in his nightly activities, to where he just became too drunk to drive home and claimed to be attacked by something.

Frank again became somewhat upset after thinking about the sheriff's statement and what he had insinuated about his lifestyle being kept like a secret. "You know something, Sheriff," Frank began saying, "I really didn't appreciate what you were insinuating back there. You know what I mean? Hell, you was sounding like I was queer or something, and had been hanging out all night with the boys."

"Sorry about that, Frank," said the Sheriff. "But I think you got it all wrong. So why don't you just get on inside your pickup truck there and head on home and get yourself some sleep. You know, get yourself some rest."

"But I know what you was insinuating," Frank told the sheriff while climbing into his truck, cursing in anger, positioning his key into the ignition and gunning the engine, spinning its tires rapidly on the gravel road, spraying loose rock fragments everywhere, and sped away, while fishtailing in small circles.

After observing his reactions with his careless, reckless driving, the Sheriff was then informed by the dispatcher about an important message that was being faxed to him. It was a message from Detective Robert Miller, a special investigation officer from the Willows Homicide Division, responding to the Sheriff's request for his assistance.

The message in response to the sheriff read:

In your request for my assistance, I gladly accept, though there was no explanation to the reason or subject other than the fact that the victim's related sister is slowly on her recovery in the Willows hospital. You've also stated that the related sister, naming her as Margaret Johnson, that she could have possibly been a witness to her sister's death or murder, or could possibly be the responsible party and/or perpetrator, making her culpable of murder.

I gladly accept without any hesitation, though I must admit the fact that I am indeed very curious as to what I am agreeing to. Although it is my position as that of a homicide detective, being a detective about to become involved in the investigation and death or murder of a human being tends to violate my intelligence.

Greatly appreciated,
Det. Robert Miller

Arriving at the Willows County Morgue, Det. Miller was welcomely greeted by Sheriff Blake. Alongside him stood a tall, slender photographer named Derek Bedford. Bedford had worked on very few homicides during his short career within the small-town community of Willows and neighboring areas, but never that of the town of Stonyford, where crime and violence were really imperceptible because of its diminutive population.

The viewing of what was left of Wanda's mutilated corpse was a story of disbelief to the detectives and especially to Miller, and far beyond the imaginary state of comprehension for authors David Seltzer, Joseph Howard, or even that of Stephen King.

Wanda's remains showed definite indication of the unsparing severity of pain and visible suffering and strain she must have endured that seemed to manifest its appearance on different limbs.

It was as if an explosion had taken effect from inside her body after withholding a tremendous amount of gastroenteritis mucous chemical that had somehow combusted and ignited, exploding, shattering, and destroying Wanda from the inside out.

Miller's opinion of the remains was the possibility of her usage or trying to use dynamite for possible sexual pleasure, dismembering herself.

The head, legs, and arms, and even the nipples of what was left of her breasts, had been apparently blown completely apart from such force that each member was found quite a distance from the carcass or torso. Though still, he became somewhat optimistic as to why the body section of Wanda's remains had not been completely ripped open if it so happened dynamite was indeed the factor causing her death and mutilation.

Each organ within the structure of Wanda's body had been ripped clean from its location and resting on the ground throughout the barn. Blood was splattered everywhere, indicating something extremely powerful had taken place, leaving Det. Miller and Blake requesting Sacramento to send them an expert.

Chapter Eleven

AFTER WHAT SEEMED TO BE HOURS of unconsciousness, Margaret once again awakened to find herself surrounded by strangers, being interrogated by both Sheriff Blake and Detective Robert Miller. Alongside them, the photographer, Derek Bedford, questioning her in the death of her sister.

"Uh, excuse me, Margaret, but look, I'm really sorry for, uh, you know, having to wake you and all," said the Sheriff, "but you see, I was just busy thinking about you and have a few very important questions that I wanted to ask you about that's been weighing heavily on my mind. You do understand, don't you?

"But first, and in case you've forgotten who I am, well, just let me help you, you know, to recollect that I am the sheriff in your hometown right over there in Stonyford. And these two men here are, well, this is Detective Robert Miller, from right here in Willows. And this guy here with these cameras, well, he's also from right here in Willows. He is a photographer, and his name is Derek Bedford.

"So, I was, you know, just wondering if I could ask you a few things, a few questions. Is that all right with you, Margaret? Would that be all right with you?"

"Uh huh," Margaret said in a mumbling tone, trying her best to open her eyes wider. "I guess so."

"NOPE! I don't think so, GENTLEMEN!" a nurse quickly interrupted.

"Ah, man, Doc," Blake objected in a offended tone. "What is the problem?"

The large, heavyset nurse, with her well-developed, masculine figure, stood within a few feet of the sheriff at at six-feet-two, weighing a good two hundred and fifty pounds, with hands the size of cantaloupes, squinting her eyes hatefully, answered the sheriff in a rather deep, threatening, guttural voice by saying, "First of all, young man, the problem is that I AM NOT YOUR DOC! Doctor Aaron Smallwood isn't expected until later.

"Secondly, I am the head nurse on duty in this hospital, and you better damn well respect my position as a nurse with authority to throw your asses right out of here. You don't come barging your ass into the ICU expecting to interrogate my patients unauthorized and without first checking in with me for permission.

"And even then, you will only get my permission if you have a good enough reason and, of course, if I feel like giving it to you.

"And as for you, young man. Yeah, that's right, I am talking to you over there with that camera. I do hope you have authorization to be in the ICU photographing my patients? If not, I suggest you just put that thing away, because it doesn't belong in here.

"And now, with that said, I do hope I've made myself perfectly clear, gentlemen. Any questions?"

Margaret then told the nurse that she did remember the sheriff, at which time the sheriff again made her acquaintance with Detective Miller and photographer Bedford's position for being there.

Miller immediately began questioning Margaret, inquiring information about her present situation and reason for confinement in the Willows hospital. "Please know that I apologize for your inconvenience, you know, while hospitalized." He also explained to her that it was strictly because of her sudden outburst and uncontrollable behavior that it was definitely necessary for restraint, hoping she could understand.

During the questioning, Detective Miller found himself being interrupted by Margaret's parents, who introduced themselves as Paul and Sarah Johnson.

Paul seemed to have a considerable amount of control over himself, as well as his emotions and personal conduct, while Sarah tended to reveal her pain, emotions, bitterness, and saddened expression.

Miller then introduced himself and his position as a homicide officer from the Willows Police Department. He also explained his specification for which he was assigned to the case. He explained that Margaret could have witnessed or even herself played a major role in the dramatic events leading up to the incident in question. But he also indicated his willingness to exclude Margaret as a possible suspect, though he did make plain that the filing of murder charges could be and possibly would be withheld until further investigation. "At this time, I just don't want to be assuming anything," said Miller. "I am just trying my best to, you know, put the pieces together."

It was quite obvious that Sarah was deeply saddened and emotionally disturbed by the shocking, mutilated slaying of her daughter, for which she felt that Margaret's mysterious activities were fully responsible. "I know you did it, you little bitch!" Sarah whispered in a low, angry tone at Margaret. "I know you had something to do with killing my little girl and I hope you rot in hell, you *bitch*! She's somewhere in the ground decomposing away because of you, you rotten bastard, and you can surely believe you're gonna get what's comin' to you, I can bet you that, you fuckin' rotten cunt!"

At this, Paul quickly flung his arms around Sarah, placing his body directly in front of hers, preventing her from being able to see or even say anything to Margaret.

"Uh, why don't we just move on out here in the hallway," said Miller. "I know she's quite upset right now and don't need to be in here."

"Thank you," said Paul, embracing Sarah while guiding her outside the entrance to Margaret's room. "We've been through so much since Wanda's death. And my wife, well, you know, she's really having a hard time right now."

"I know it, Paul, said Miller. "I just wish there were something we could do to help her with this, but, you know, maybe I can make a request or something to the nurse. You know, like, see if they can give her, you know, a prescription or something to help her out."

"That'll be nice if you could, detective," said Paul.

"And, you know, something for you, too," said Miller, placing one of his hands on Paul's shoulders. "I'll see what I can do, but meantime, just the both of you stay away from this room. Will you try and do that for me?"

"I'll do my best to keep her out of there, Detective," said Paul. "There is just so much that you fellers need to know about, though."

"Well, let's just get your wife on down here to the other end of his hallway," said Miller, "and we'll find a much more comfortable and relaxing place for your wife, and then, you know, maybe you can share what you're talking about. Would that be all right with you, Paul?"

"Yeah, I guess so," said Paul, walking slowly with Sarah. "I guess it is just time for people to know what has been happening with Margaret. You know what I mean? This thing has been going on for quite some time now, and it's just time for somebody to know about it."

"Now, here we go, right here," said Miller. "Is this all right for you? I mean, I guess I could have gone to that nurse and requested a private room or something."

"No," said Paul. "I think this'll do just fine, for now."

"Well, Paul…" Miller started to question him, when the nurse he talked to earlier once again interrupted them.

"Yes, guess who?" she said, smiling at Miller. "You don't say, but it's definitely me again. But don't worry, I'm not here to chew your ass out again. But I was just wondering if maybe you'd like a place for the Mrs. to lie down. Well, being that your daughter is already here recovering. I'd thought maybe you'd like a small room where she can rest?"

"Well, that'll be really nice and considerate of you," said Paul.

"Well, then," said the nurse, again smiling broadly, "you can just consider it done. Just follow me, this way. But you, officer, whatever you said your name was?"

"It's Detective Miller."

"Oh, yeah," the nurse said, pointing downward at the hallway sofa. " I think it'd be best that you just sit your little tail back down until you've learned some manners. You know, how to respect one's authority."

Detective Miller said nothing while listening to the nurse use her power to attempt to intimidate him. Though he sat quietly until Paul returned, which had to be over an hour later.

Meanwhile, he just sat there staring in the direction of the sheriff and Bedford, the photographer, wondering just what they could possibly be thinking about the entire situation. Was Blake really ready for this part of the job? Considering the fact that he'd been in the military and all, and probably even killed a few unarmed civilians, did this make him capable or even qualified for the job?

Miller then found himself staring at the reflection that was staring back at him from an adjacent window. The reflection caused him to bring into question his own efficiency, wondering if he was performing effectively.

"I see you've finally made it back," Miller said to Paul. "I'd begun to think that maybe you decided to get yourself some much-needed rest."

"No, I don't seem to be able to get much rest since the situation, uh, with our daughter, Wanda. I guess you can say I am somewhat afraid to go to sleep from fearing that I just might not ever wake up."

"Might not ever wake up?" questioned Miller. "Ah, you really haven't anything to worry about, Paul. You just keep being strong-minded for Sarah, and I am more than sure everything will be just fine before too long."

"Well, that's easy for you to say, Detective," Paul told him. "That's easy for you to say."

Miller found himself just staring at Paul, not really wanting to know what it was like to be going through the painful events that had taken place in both his and Sarah's life. He thought how he wouldn't even want to try imagining their painful ordeal. But he knew it was time to try questioning Paul before that nurse came back, interrupting them again. "So Paul, about what you were saying, you know, about it being time that people know what has been happening with your daughter Margaret. Uh, what is it that you are referring to about her that needs to be brought to people's attention that is so important for us to know about her?"

"Well, you see," Paul began quietly, "I guess my wife, you know, for quite some time now, being, I guess, inclined to reveal just what has been happening, you know, with our daughter. Well, it was at an early age that she, for some strange reason developed a very distinctive childhood personality by, I guess you could say, claiming to have been invaded by monsters or something. You understand what I am sayin'? I mean, hell, I just thought it was her being a child with all these crazy things going on in her life. I mean, come on, she was just a child. Kids sometimes do and say some of the darnedest things to get attention.

"But anyway, there just wasn't any known significant indication directly to Margaret's physical ability to function normally, other than the fact that she could have possibly seen who it was that did that to Wanda."

"Will, that'll be enough for now," Miller told Paul. "Why don't you just go ahead and go and be there for your wife while I go and talk to a few people, you know, the sheriff, about something I need to do, okay?"

"Have you seen her yet?" Paul asked Miller, referring to Wanda's remains. "Have you seen her yet?"

"No, not yet," Miller answered.

"When are you gonna go see her?" Paul asked.

"Uh," Miller mumbled, nodding his head in a downward motion.

"It's important that you see her," Paul told Miller. "Go see her."

"I intend to, just as soon as I get a few things squared away here at the hospital," Miller responded. "And then I'll be on my way to see her."

Miller just stood there briefly, staring at Paul. He was wondering why Paul was acting like Wanda was still alive. I mean, after all, there wasn't any doubt about it, she was as dead as a doorknob, and nothing that I could think of could bring her back. Well, unless, you know, the almighty man upstairs cast down some of his miracle power. But I can assure you, until that happens, and hell freezes over, that dead girl is simply going to remain where she is—dead!

Though still, Paul just kept rambling on, talking about how it was so important Miller go and see Wanda.

"She wants you to see for yourself what it did to her," Paul kept suggesting. "She wants you to see."

By this time, Miller was really beginning to wonder about Paul. It was like he knew something and whatever it was that he knew, it had to do with the death of his daughter.

"Uh, Paul," Miller then told him. "Uh, why don't you just go on back down there to help Sarah, okay, and I will go ahead and see Wanda, as you have suggested."

"Okay, Detective," Paul agreed. "But you just hurry up and make it to see her, because she really does want you to see what it did to her—and the rest of them, you know?"

Now, this part of Paul's statement really did a number on Miller. This thing about it and them really began to touch a nerve or two. I can just imagine what was going on in the detective's mind. I mean, after all, it was a part of his job to investigate and examine the evidence of what he was assigned to investigate.

Still, it was Paul's statement that really began to bother him. And I don't mean lightly.

Chapter Twelve

DETECTIVE MILLER FOUND HIMSELF deeply saddened as he inspected the remains of what was left of Wanda's badly mutilated corpse. During his examination, he could see nothing like knife wounds that would make such clean, sharp piercing cuts in and throughout the remains. "This had to be done from a very, very sharp, specialized instrument. Possibly like that a highly skilled surgeon would use," is what he told Sheriff Blake. "Just look at these tears in her flesh; it looks as if it's been cut very neatly apart instead of ripped."

There was a strong scent throughout the room as both Blake and Miller continued to examine the remains. The scent was so overwhelming that the photographer, Bedford, had to be seated outside the room, due to his uncontrolled vomiting.

Closing the door to the hallway where Bedford had been seated, Miller, for unknown reasons, found himself skeptical and began muttering to himself, disrupting Blake. "Is everything all right?" the sheriff asked Miller.

The sight of Wanda's remains angered the detective, causing him to become an uneasy person for the sheriff to work with. But Blake knew that the anger would be temporary and continued his part of the investigation.

The scent in the examination room was unbearable and a huge part of Miller's discomfort as his nostrils became filled with the thick scent of decomposing flesh and the still somewhat moist blood resting on the surface surrounding the remains.

The relentless scent seemed to cling tightly to both Blake's and Miller's nostrils, making them extremely uncomfortable. Realizing their partnership,

Sheriff Blake began making unarticulated sounds and joking remarks in an effort to ease the tension between them. But Detective Miller thought nothing funny about the remarks while attempting to reach for what was left of Wanda's head.

Stretching one of his arms across the many bags containing Wanda's dismembered body parts, Miller found himself feeling slightly lightheaded as he stared directly into the opening of Wanda's neck. Opening the bag even wider, which contained certain sections of the body, he could then very clearly see the emptiness of her facial area appearing as though it had been somehow stripped completely of its entire mass of organ tissue.

The sheriff could visibly see the apparent curious expression on that of Miller's face as he watched his disbelieving reactions and unusually sad and angry behavior while conducting the investigation. At times coming eye to eye with the sheriff, Miller would always find himself speechless. His only expression would be a slight smile, which is what the sheriff was hoping to see.

"You know, Miller," the sheriff said. "We can't be, you know, taking this and everything that'll end up coming with it too personal. You know what I mean?"

Miller just shrugged his shoulders, and then nodded his head in a rather slow downward motion, as though he'd become somewhat puzzled from the fact that there seemed to be no clue to provide the information he needed to understand what Paul was trying to tell him. He felt that if it was actually Margaret who was responsible, as insinuated by the sheriff, any evidence leading to her being the murderer was highly unlikely and groundless. "Dammit, Blake," he shouted at the sheriff, "I can't seem to find any connection whatsoever that can be proven with what information that I have to prove to me that Margaret is the killer. Nor can I attempt trying to build anything on such a theory to begin formulating a case in my effort to prove those accounts without first questioning everybody in your town, including Margaret. Now can you just imagine the expense of that type of investigation?"

After closing one of the bags containing certain sections of remains, Detective Miller reached into his coat pocket and pull out a pack of cigarettes. He then looked downward and began to speak in a low tone, saying that the person or persons responsible for the crime that had taken place in Stonyford had to be a very sick person.

After offering a cigarette to the sheriff, he then lit one for himself and inhaled the smoke deeply into his lungs and began blowing it out slowly, as if not wanting to release it too quickly.

Sheriff Blake could see the relief on Miller's face as he watched him withdraw from what seemed to be an overabundance of uncertainties, not really knowing just where to start the investigation.

Thinking that maybe Miller would probably suggest they find a place to get something to eat, Sheriff Blake was surprised to hear Miller suggest that they again visit Margaret. Miller seemed to be more motivated than the sheriff had expected.

Quietly entering the Willows Hospital, Miller reached for the doorknob and touched it gently, and then very slowly turned it, pushing the door open to Margaret's room. As Miller, Blake and Bedford once again entered the ICU to talk to Margaret, the hallway was silent as the three stood in complete stillness, not wanting the nurse to catch them.

Each standing silently calm as a still photograph without any motion, Miller began looking throughout the room in fascination as both Blake and Bedford watched curiously.

And then, heavy footsteps could be heard coming in the direction of the room.

"For Christ sakes, Miller," said Blake, feeling stupid about once again being in the Willows Hospital. "Can't this wait until later? I thought we were going to get something to eat?"

"Quit talking so loud," said Miller. "What, you want that nurse to hear you and find us in here? I really don't think she'll let you off that easy, Sheriff."

"Whatcha mean, let me off?" said Blake in a low tone. "Hell, we're all in this mess because of you, Miller. So if anything, you're the one that fat ass pig'll be after. And I'll make sure of that."

"Well," said Bedford, "it's good those footsteps wasn't her and kept on going past this room."

"Now, wait a minute, you guys," said Miller. "Where is Margaret?"

Everyone looked around in the dark.

"Turn on the light," said Bedford.

"Hell, no!" Miller told him. "Are you crazy? Then we'll really get caught in here."

"I think we're in the wrong room," said Blake. "There's nobody in the bed, and if it is, it sure ain't Margaret."

"I think they've moved her to another room," said Miller.

"Or maybe out of the ICU," said Bedford.

"Move out of the way, Bedford," Blake told him. "I ain't staying in here like some goddamn idiot. The wrong room, a crazy nurse, and probably the wrong goddamn hospital."

Closing the door quietly behind them and heading down the hallway that would take them to the entrance to the hospital, Bedford began to apologize for becoming sick when they were at the morgue. While trying to explain his reason for the sickness, he was interrupted by Blake, who began assuring him about his sickness being understandable.

Quietly reaching the entrance, the three of them took a deep breath of air into their nostrils, refreshing their lungs from the deadly scent of Wanda's death that tended to linger deep in the cavity of the membrane, reluctant to leave.

Miller then turned to both Blake and Bedford and asked, "Do you guys appreciate this fresh air as much as I do?"

"I'm just wondering how we went from the morgue to here, and the scent stayed on us," said Bedford.

"Yeah, now that's really strange if you ask me," said Blake.

"Something has been strange about this entire evening," said Miller.

"You know," said Blake, "I was just thinking."

"Oh, yeah, about what?" asked Miller.

"You remember what you were saying about an expert?" Blake reminded Miller.

"Yeah," said Miller.

"Well, I was thinking that, you know, maybe you need to make your request known to the commissioner, you know?"

"Uh, how do I go about it?" asked Miller.

"Yep, just as I had figured," Blake told him. "Don't worry, I already did it for you."

"You mean to tell me, all this time you had already made my request to the commissioner?" Miller asked Blake.

"Hey, what are friends for?" responded Blake.

While driving away from the hospital, Sheriff Blake all of a sudden shook his head and began to gently rub and massage his neck. "Is everything all right?" Bedford asked with concern.

"This damn headache is killing me. We need to stop somewhere at one of these stores so that I can get something to ease all this aching," Blake suggested.

Before Bedford could respond, Miller began laughing at the sheriff's suggestion to stop at a store to get something for his headache.

"Tell me something, Blake," Miller began asking. "Now, just why didn't you ask that nurse while we were at the hospital for something? I'm sure she would've given you something for the pain."

As Bedford tried to pass a small container through the armrest opening between the two front seats, Miller quickly reached downward, snatching the container while still slightly snickering, tossing it out the window.

"Just what in heaven's name did you do that for?" the sheriff asked. "I tell you, you better damn well have a good goddamn reason for doing that."

Watching the expression on the sheriff's face caused Bedford to stop laughing scornfully as they proceeded toward the Willows Police Department.

Upon entering the door leading to the commissioner's office Detective Miller immediately checked in to see if the request concerning the assistance of an expert had been secured. He then reached into his private assigned mailbox, pulling out a small manila envelope containing the fax and the information he'd requested.

He could see the name appearing on the fax: Detective Goldsby, written in large, bold type. At the top of the paper there was an identification notation identifying the responding department being that of the Sacramento homicide division, Sacramento, California.

Turning toward the commissioner's office, he could see that both Blake and Bedford had already engaged themselves in conversation with the commissioner.

After explaining to the commissioner the condition of the remains, and the need for possibly more assistance, the commissioner advised them about the request being met. Bedford was then advised to start taking pictures of everything, regardless of its relevancy. "I want you to start snapping pictures of everything, Bedford," the commissioner demanded. "And I don't give a rat's ass what it is. You just start taking them pictures. Am I making myself clear?"

"Uh, yes, sir, Commissioner," responded Bedford. "Loud and clear."

"And you can surely believe that I'm depending on you," said the commissioner, staring directly at Bedford. "Those pictures will be going out all over the freakin' place."

The commissioner then made clear that having sympathy was understandable, but that being entirely too sensitive could really put a damper on their purpose.

After leaving the commissioner's office, Detective Miller then made a quick suggestion that before they headed to Stonyford, he wanted first to stop by one of his favorite restaurants for something to eat.

"Uh, hey, you guys," said Miller, while looking around the hallway. "I could really use a bite to eat right about now. Whatcha think?"

Knowing they, too, were as hungry as he was, he also knew that it would be impossible for them to say no and neglect fulfilling the craving of their appetite.

Sheriff Blake stared at Miller intently in disbelief. He began to think about the examination room and how it was then that upon leaving the coroner's office that he thought Miller would suggest they find a place for something to eat. "Why take this goddamn long?" he thought to himself. He also thought about pretending to drive to Miller's favorite restaurant, only to bypass it and continue on onto the road to Elk Creek to pay him back for tossing the aspirins out the window.

With the sheriff driving, and as they finally approached Miller's favorite restaurant, it was then that Sheriff Blake began to feel and hear the growling in his stomach. The desire for something to eat had begun to invade his mind as he found himself staring at the advertising signs that were displaying the tasty food inside.

Unable to any longer withstand trying to control the craving for food, the sheriff found himself parking the patrol car just about halfway up on the curb directly in front of the restaurant.

After both Miller and Bedford pointed out his mistake, Blake reluctantly corrected his parking with an expression of disappointment for being corrected, though he knew it was his responsibility to follow the law.

"And just what are you happy-looking gentlemen having this evening?" asked the waitress once they were seated.

"Well, first of all," Blake said, staring and smiling at the waitress, "I'd like a big, fat juicy hug from you."

"Well, I'll be," the waitress said, looking down at Blake. "If it isn't ol' Sheriff Blake from Stonyford."

"Long time, no see," said Blake, standing up to hug the waitress.

"It sure has been," the waitress said, accepting Blake's hug. "And you sure do look like you can use some attending, too, with your skinny-looking self. What's wrong, the Mrs. isn't doing her job like I can?"

"Now, Lorraine," said Blake, smiling broadly. "You need to just stop it, 'cause the Mrs. been taking care of my big, fat ass just fine."

"Well, all I want with my greedy self is a little bit of time with you every now and then—if you know what I mean?" she told him.

'But, Lorraine," said Blake, "you know I'm a happily married man, and I don't believe I'm healthy enough to deal with two wives. Hell, what do you think I'm made of? Iron or steel? Hell, just the thought of having you wrapped tight in these arms of mine is enough to kill me of a heart attack."

"Well, whenever you're ready to die of that heart attack," she told Blake, smiling, "just make sure you have it because of me being wrapped up tight in your arms, honey. But until then, look at these menus till y'all figure out what you're gonna order. I'll be back."

"After hearing that conversation," said Bedford, "I don't know if I am ready to order or head over heels in love. Isn't she the prettiest thing you ever wanna meet?"

"Just keep that goddamn tongue of yours in your mouth," Blake told Bedford jokingly. "That kinda lady is far too much outa your league, if you know what I mean. She ain't lookin' for no young 'un."

"Makes no matter what she lookin' for, said Bedford. "She give me a chance, she ain't gone never look at an old, worn-out goat like you ever again."

"Just who the hell are you callin' an old, worn-out goat?" Blake asked Bedford, while staring at his reflection in one of the many mirrors hanging on the side walls throughout the restaurant. "I'm as handsome as they come. You're just jealous because this old man still got what it takes to charm the ladies. Tell him, Miller."

"Yeah, I guess you're right about that statement," Miller said with a slight smile on his face. "Might got what it'll take, but I personally don't see nothin' charming about an old fart like you."

"Oh, is that so," said Blake. "Well, since when did you last take a good goddamn look at yourself? Since you wanna go there with your technical bullshit. Just when did you all of a sudden become a specializer?"

Both Miller and Bedford started laughing at Blake's statement.

"I'm not," Miller told him. "Though."

"If I wasn't a family man," said Blake, "I'd be in here teaching the both of you youngsters a thing or two."

"Ah, Sheriff," Bedford said, while pointing and snickering at Miller. "We know you be the man up in here."

"And just what is that supposed to mean?" asked Blake. "You're acting like you don't believe in me or something?"

"Uh, look you guys," Miller said, while motioning his head toward the waitress, who just happened to be headed in their direction. "She's coming to see what we want."

"Y'all boys ready to order?" she asked, staring at Blake. "You know what, Sheriff? I'd like to take you off somewhere far back there deep in them woods and tear you apart, just a-ripping all your clothes to pieces. Oh what, am I taunting you? A little too much this evening? Well, that's just too bad, honey bun. I'm just going to continue tantalizing you until you finally one day just give in and say those magical words."

"And what might those magical words be, darling?" asked Blake.

"Mmm-mmm," she began mumbling, "you mean to tell me you really don't know?"

"Haven't a clue," Blake told her, staring directly into her eyes. "It would be nice of you if you were to tell me just what those magical words could be, then I could probably do something about it."

"Well, if you really insist," she said, staring directly back at him and into his eyes. "I wanna hear you tell me "I do" in that there little white chapel somewhere out there in Las Vegas."

"But Lorraine," Blake said seriously. "I done already told you, I'm a happily married man, and I just don't believe I'm healthy enough to be tryin' to deal with another wife on the side. I mean, not at my age."

"Don't mean to be rude or anything by buttin' into y'all guys' conversation," a voice said from a table at a booth, saying "but why don't y'all just get hitched right here at the diner? That way, all of your, you know, friends can attend, 'cause some of us just can't afford to be trying to make that trip all the way to Vegas. We ain't got that kinda money. You know, most of us living on a rather fixed income as it is, and we would really hate having to miss out on your wedding."

"And I'd second that motion," another voice said from another booth.

"I'd sure like to get in on the action myself," another voice said. "It's been years since old Terry Brown and me been practically anywhere since he got out that prison out there in Kansas. And as long as we've been knowing you, Lorraine, we ain't about to miss you tying the knot with this here gentleman."

"Damn!" said Miller. "Whatcha think, Bedford?"

"Looks like somebody gettin' married, whether they want to or not, if you ask me," Bedford told Miller. "The bells done already started ringing, and the poor guy's best bet is to run and hide, because once his wife finds out and hears this news, I just don't think she's gonna be too happy."

"I can tell you one thing," Miller began saying. "Old charmy-boy is about to lose his charm."

"And I can tell the both of you one thing, too," Blake said, staring around at both Miller and Bedford. "I'm beginning to believe that the two of you came here because you knew this was gonna happen. You had this all arranged, didn't you? Well, it just ain't gone happen. So you can just wipe them smiles off your faces because the joke is over."

"Uh, Sheriff," said Bedford. "Seriously, this isn't any joke."

"And just who the hell do you think you're talking to, Bedford? Do I look like I was born just yesterday or something?"

"He's telling you the truth, Sheriff," Miller told him, in hope that the sheriff would believe him. "This isn't any joke. These people in here are really thinking you guys are about to get married."

"Uh, Lorraine, dear," Blake quickly called to get her attention. "Uh, see here, darlin'. I'm sure you already know or have heard about that situation that's taken place up there in Stonyford. Well, you see, we've been really busy trying our best to try and solve all the answers to that problem, and I was just, you know, wondering if we could slow things down a bit? You know, on all this talk about us hitching it up and tying the knot and things."

"What you sayin', Sheriff?" Lorraine said in a loud voice, attracting everyone's attention. "Are you getting cold feet about marrying me?"

"Uh, oh no, no, no," Blake told her, smiling guiltily. "Uh, I'm just a tad busy trying to catch our killer or killers, and I just didn't want to have, you know, everybody waiting on this marriage thing."

"Oh, no," a voice said loudly. "Y'all ain't keeping us waiting. We just don't wanna miss anything. You know what I'm sayin'?"

"Yeah, that's right," another voice said. "All of us just want to be present to show our support, 'cause who knows, next time it just might end up me and this old-timer tying the knot."

"And who is that?" a voice asked her. "Who might be the lucky fellow? What's his name?"

"All of y'all already know who I'm talking about," she told them. "It ain't like you don't know Richard Cooper or anything."

"I'd always thought you were married to, you know, what's his name? The guy down the way there?" someone asked her. "Uh, hell, what's his name?"

"I think you're thinking about Jason Dillon," a voice said.

"Yeah, that's the guy," he said.

"No, I have never been married to that creep," she told him, smiling.

"Hey?" another voice rang out loud. "Why don't you just dump Richard and give me a try?"

Everybody laughed.

"Hey, that isn't nice of you to say," she told the person. "I'm more than sure you wouldn't want somebody dumping you. Now would you?"

"She probably already did," another voice said, snickering.

"That's why I'm asking you to dump Richard and hitch the knot with a lonely guy like me," he again told her. "We can do this right here and right now, and in front of everybody. And if you still wanna, uh, you know, go on out there to Las Vegas, then I'll take you out there for our honeymoon for a week or two. Ever how long you wanna stay there, Lorraine.

"Sounds like somebody trying to move in on you, Sheriff," someone in another booth told him. "If it were me, I wouldn't let it happen. Not me. Now way, no how."

"But it ain't you, Albert Williams," a harsh, disagreeable woman's voice told him. "And you better not be trying to. Do you understand?"

The diner fell noiselessly silent, and then broke into laughter.

"Hey there, old Albert, buddy," a voice said. "You'd better stay out of this conversation before you end up getting yourself into some very serious trouble with Bertha.

"You mean, Big Bertha," another voice said seriously. "You know she ain't nothin' to be messed with."

"Well, I really do thank y'all folks in here for being so concerned," the Sheriff told everybody in the diner. "But, as some of you already know, we've got a serious situation going on up there in Stonyford and probably somewhere else, too. So, until we can somehow try and get a grip on things,

I just can't be doing any answering on the marriage subject right now."

"That's right there, Sheriff," someone said, agreeing as if they knew what he was referring to. "Just how is that Johnson family doing?"

"Hey, that's right," said Lorraine. "Isn't she right here in the hospital?"

"Well, that's just where we came from," Blake told them.

"Oh, I think I know what you're talking about," one of the patrons said. "You're talking about that little girl over there in Stonyford who got upset at her sister and slaughtered her."

"Ain't no proof she done it," a soft woman's voice said. "It's just a whole bunch of speculation going on as they always do around here."

"Well, according to the evidence, though," said a man at the counter.

"Well, I'll be," the woman's voice again started talking. "If it ain't the devil himself. Michael Kelderman. Just when in the hell did they let an old fart like you out of prison?"

"What, you sound like you really missed me or somethin'?" Kelderman questioned.

"Didn't really miss you," she told him. "Just shocked to see you made it out."

"Did anybody molest you?" someone asked.

"I hear you don't take a chance picking up your soap once you drop it in the shower, is that true?"

Snickering.

"Don't know," he told them, "never dropped mine. But maybe you should drop yours and then you'll find out."

"See what I mean," the soft woman's voice said again. "Everything ain't nothing but a bunch of speculation about everything around here. I guess you all come here just so that you can speculate on everything. Can't seem to find anything better to do, so you come in here to gossip and speculate on everything."

After they finished eating, Sheriff Blake notified the Stonyford Sheriff's Office, advising the officer on duty that he, along with Detective Robert Miller and Derek Bedford were en route and that they would be arriving shortly.

Approaching the road through Elk Creek and on into Stonyford, Miller found himself in deep thought about Wanda's death. He'd never been to the town of Stonyford, and the only person he was acquainted with from that area was Sheriff Blake. He remembered meeting him during a course while in training at the police academy, at which time they became pretty much good friends. He knew the sheriff could depend on him. Their courses while at the academy consisted of rough, rigorous teamwork, and they'd become each other's trusted partner.

Miller's thought of Bedford was that of a very quiet person who always did his job, perhaps in the most professional manner possible. A truly modest individual with good potential who could keep his attitude in check, no matter the situation. It wasn't difficult for Miller to understand Bedford's reasons for becoming sick during the examination of Wanda's remains. He thought about how glad and relieving it was that they weren't amongst the first to arrive at the Johnson's residence to see the awful sight of Wanda's mutilated corpse.

Chapter Thirteen

A FLASH OF HEADLIGHTS appearing from the dark sky began to reveal the plane as it made a sharp 45-degree left bank coming from the east, approaching the runway from 3,500 feet.

It was a Piper Chieftain, eight-to-ten-place, twin engines with retractable gear, full flaps in position. This was the plane that Detective Khaleelah F. Goldsby was arriving in from Sacramento.

Detective Robert Miller stood with a half-smirky, conceited grin on his face, though expressing the welcoming thought of an expert, one of Sacramento's finest, to assist him with the brutalized, horrible murder of a human being.

Approaching the small Willows Airport terminal with its engines in full motion and powerful propeller blades spinning rapidly, the private Piper Chieftain, owned by the state of California, began withdrawing its power before coming to a complete stop and slowly opening a side door on the pilot's side of the plane, sliding it slowly downward, though not touching the ground, exposing the fuselage and entrance to its body, which both Miller and Sheriff Blake proceeded toward.

Blake began to feel the importance of being the man in charge and responsible for solving the crime that surrounded every law-abiding citizen in this part of the region. He just stood there, occasionally rocking back and forth, as if dancing with himself to a tune that only he could hear. I reckon that pot belly of his is what really made him look as though he was in tune to a beat. And those fat, chubby-looking hands, just how in the hell he found a way to squeeze them into those tight-ass pockets is something I don't think can ever be answered.

But there he was, standing there, rocking that big, fat belly of his every which way but loose. Just puffing and huffing on that too-long-for-his-face cigar, tucked neatly in between those rotten-looking teeth.

Yes, indeed, the old sheriff was seeing his childhood dream unfolding right before him, which surely delighted his intelligence.

His dreams, they'd become a reality.

But the welcoming grin on Miller's face, well, it had now become that of an expression of disbelief, so to say. That's when it dawned on him that Goldsby was a she instead of a he. His expression began to reveal every type of shocked astonishment imaginable. The fact that he'd requested the assistance of an expert, he just knew Sacramento was sending him a male figure instead of "somebody's housewife," I suppose.

But trying his best to not act in any way prejudicially biased, under the circumstances, he watched as Detective Goldsby, who was now approaching both Miller and Blake, was smiling and expressing her appreciation for their consideration for wanting her to assist them.

She immediately started shaking their hands, most likely forgetting about the fact that she hadn't even introduced herself. It was then that Detective Miller reminded her about her identity and position, which she then proudly expressed in acknowledgement.

After arriving at the Willows headquarters, Miller stormed directly into the commissioner's office, complaining and demanding to know why his request for an expert wasn't met, but instead, he'd ended up getting some lady from who-knows-where, and most likely the mother of somebody's family. "Look, Commissioner," he started complaining, "just how is it in this goddamn place that I can come to work, and report directly to you, make my request for an expert, and end up with somebody's freakin' housewife? Do you know how this is going to make me look around her, let alone to the folks there in Stonyford?"

Miller was also complaining about her personal appearance, which to him was certainly like that of a happy hooker out for some excitement. "I mean, now come on, Commissioner," he hinted. "Really, you should have been there yourself to see her. Coming from that fancy plane that the governor and all his freakin' rich, moneymaking, greedy, guzzling, governmental criminal politicians probably spend their time using up our hard-working money to party in with every goddamn one of their secretaries."

"Must I remind you, Miller," said the Commissioner, "you're talking about the Governor. What those people do in Sacramento during their private time, that's really none of your business. They're politicians for peace sakes, let them do their job. And if it'll help you, I want you to know that it is my intention to question Ms. Goldsby, at which time I will then determine her qualification. Fairly, Miller, and that would be without prejudice."

The Commissioner immediately contacted the Sacramento Homicide Division inquiring information concerning her ability to function and perform properly. The investigating officer who had knowledge about her, and had himself worked with her personally, advised the Commissioner that judging from Sacramento's report and from his experience working directly with her, she was apparently the perfect person and one of the most highly qualified experts.

The information is what Miller was hoping not to hear. In fact, his rage became even more furious, causing him to question out loud, so that everyone in the department could hear, "I wonder if the entire Sacramento Homicide Division is really made up from a whole goddamn bunch of oddballs?"

He wanted to question his curiosity, but quickly remembered the old story about the cat, and then said to himself, in a very low tone, "Fuck it! Ain't *even* going there."

"And what about you, Bedford?" Miller asked him. "Are you feeling like we do?"

"Man," said Bedford. "To be truthful, I think I've had just about enough for today. But it's really not up to me. That decision is for you to be making and not me. I'm just the photographer here, willing to do my job."

"Okay then," said Miller, turning toward Detective Goldsby. "Why don't we just call it quits for now. Get ourselves some much needed rest. And then see how we feel from there. Is that all right with you guys?"

"Hey, anything is cool with me," Goldsby said. "But what about Sheriff Blake? I mean, what if he wants to keep at it?"

"Yeah, that's right," Bedford said. "Though."

"Man, you guys," Miller began saying. "All that's on Blake's mind is to get Stonyford back on the right track. He wants to rebuild its image."

"So, are we going to just continue staying in here, having, you know, conversation after conversation," Bedford asked both Miller and Goldsby. "I mean, it would be nice to get out of this room."

"And just look who's talking," Goldsby said, laughing at Bedford. "You just not too long ago said the decision wasn't up to you. What's wrong, all these bodies are bothering you or something?"

"No, not really," Bedford responded. "But I just thought it would be best to, you know, take our conversation elsewhere instead of continuing to be in here with her remains."

"Uh, Bedford," Miller began to question him. "You know we have been at this for quite some time now. Am I right?"

"What?" Bedford asked him.

"You know, this investigation about the little girl."

"You mean the one right here?" Bedford said, pointing at Wanda's body parts.

"That's right," said Miller. "The dead girl's remains."

"Yeah, and what's your point?" Bedford asked.

"Man, are you all right?" Miller asked him. "Is everything all right?"

"Got me wondering, too," Goldsby told Bedford.

"Okay, if you really insist," said Bedford. "Then I'll tell you what's happening. And I know it's going to sound really weird, but you see, all this time since we been standing here talking, whatever part of that little girl's body that is, it's been moving like it's alive or something."

"What?" Goldsby shouted out loud. "Man, Bedford, what are you talking about?"

"Man, you are really tripping up in here," Miller told him. "Whatcha mean, moving?"

"You see," said Bedford. "That's just what I mean. That's why I didn't say anything about it when I first seen it happening. I knew you wouldn't believe me even if it jumped up off that table and slapped you dead smack in the face."

"Smack me in the face ain't nobody gone ever have to bother with any examination on it ever again," Goldsby said. "It's gone be incinerated, and you can bet on that."

"How long is this stuff supposed to be in here?" Bedford asked.

"It can be in this place forever," Miler told him. "That's why it's called a morgue. This is where dead bodies are kept until people can figure out what to do with them."

"I already know that," said Bedford. "But what I'm talking about is I was wondering how long they're supposed to keep them? Isn't it a time period something before they start deteriorating or something?"

"You mean like, turn into dust?" Goldsby said.

"No," Miller told her. "They don't be turning into no dust."

"Well, the Bible said they be turning into ashes to ashes and dust to dust; we came from the dust, and to dust we shall return."

"Yeah, but that's the Bible, Miller told her. "It takes time for the body to fully deteriorate completely, or however you consider it."

"Well, this part of that child's body sure isn't ready to deteriorate. It's moving again," Goldsby said, while slowly backing away from the table.

"I think that's just the nerves causing it to extend like that. Most organs are capable of relaying sensory stimuli and motor impulses like this for very long periods of time. But that's only until, you know, the obvious takes place."

Miller, Goldsby, and Bedford instantly froze, holding very still without making a sound, startled by the deep voice taking to them.

"Oh, and as we know," the voice continued, "that is when the not-able-to-avoid takes place; the inevitable embalming. A sure preservative in order to prevent immediate decay, though surely destroying any chance for a return to life."

"DAMN!" shouted Bedford. "Man, who the hell are you?"

"Oh, excuse me. I'm the assistant medical examiner working alongside Chief Medical Examiner, Nicholas Florentin. He's away on important business, so I am the one in charge until he gets back."

"So!" exclaimed Goldsby. "We still don't know who you are!"

"Damn near scared the shit out of me," said Bedford. "I'm still shaking from that scare, surprising us like that."

"What's your name?" Miller asked the examiner.

"It's Christopher Trotter," he told them. "Didn't mean to scare you."

"You almost ended up on one of these tables," Goldsby told him. "You always creep up on people like that?"

"Well, frankly," Trotter began, "I feel that I was just in here doing my job. I was already informed by one of our employees that people were here in the examination room viewing this poor little girl's remains, so I thought I'd pay you a visit. It wasn't my intention to startle you. I was trying to be helpful, explaining why certain body parts tend to continue on moving seemingly yet full of life, while others, well, they seem to die very quickly."

"You definitely did do that," said Bedford. "You could have at least started out by, you know, identifying yourself first, before that long, eerie speech."

"Well, now that I've identified myself," said Trotter, "just which of you is going to be first to identify yourselves?"

"I think that'll be my job," Miller spoke up. "Now you already know our reason for being here, so therefore, we don't have to be going into that just now. So, I am Detective Miller, from right here in Willows, and this is Detective Goldsby, she come all the way over here from Sacramento, and this guy you just about scared shitless, he's our photographer from right here in Willows, his name used to be Bedford, that was until you frightened him into naming himself, well, I'd better not say it because…"

"Hey, I'm all right," said Bedford. "Just a little shaken. Nothing I can't deal with."

"Hold up," Goldsby said, raising one of her hands in the air and pointing one of her fingers in the direction of the entrance to the building.

"What?" Miller asked.

"I think she's reminding you about Blake," Bedford told him.

"Oh, that's right," said Miller. "And yeah, our boss is outside. I think he's out there waiting in his car. He got tired of being in here. His name is Blake, he's the man in charge of this investigation."

"Would that be Chief Blake, from up there in Stonyford?" Trotter asked, wondering if or not it was really the person he knew.

"That's right," Miller told him. "It's definitely him."

"I know that old fart," Trotter said, smiling. "So he's the one who's in charge of the investigation? You don't say. My old buddy from up there in Stonyford. Now that's all right."

Chapter Fourteen

STILL IN DISAGREEMENT with the idea of Sacramento sending a woman to assist him as an expert, he showed very little concert for Goldsby, if any at all. He'd deliberately, upon entering the morgue, complained about not having his folder, suggesting that Detective Goldsby go back and retrieve it from within his car.

Responding to his request, Goldsby proceeded to the car, only to find the doors locked and location of the folder completely empty of any contents. She then turned back around in the direction of the morgue, only to find that Miller wasn't any longer waiting and had quickly disappeared, along with Sheriff Blake and Bedford, without leaving the door ajar so that she could regain entry to the building.

"Now that's strange," she said to herself. "How do they expect me to get in when these doors are all locked? Guess I just have to start pounding in hope that they'll hear me. Somebody will hear me. Hopefully."

After a relentless amount of repeated pounding, Detective Goldsby had finally attracted the attention of one of the employees who just happened to be arriving for work, willingly inviting her into the building after seeing certification requirements and documents stating her position and category, specifically defining her being from the homicide division at Sacramento.

"Boy, am I glad to see you," she told him. "Guess they forgot about me being out here."

"How long you been out here?"

"Tell you the truth, it feels like forever."

"I mean, what were you doing out here? Or were you supposed to be in the building somewhere?"

"Well, I came here to examine someone. But the person who brought me here apparently thought he'd left his folder in his car, so he asked me if I'd return to the car and get it for him, but to my surprise, it wasn't there. So, there I was locked outside without a way to get in, well, that was until you came to work."

"Here to examine someone you say?"

"Uh huh."

"And may I ask who?"

"Well, being that you work here, I'd guess it's safe to say, I think it's a little girl who was found mutilated—"

"In Stonyford," the employee interrupted, breaking into what Goldsby was about to say.

"That's right. So, you already know about the case?"

"Who doesn't?"

"Is it that well known?"

"It's mysterious, if you really wanna know the truth."

"How'd you figure?"

"It's just something strange about it, that's all."

"I mean, like what? What's so strange about it?"

"Something unexplainable, that's all."

"Something unexplainable, like what? What are you talking about?"

"Just some mysterious, unaccountable things about the crime and the entire situation that you investigators are going to have to be dealing with that just seems to be hard to explain. Something just isn't adding up."

"Well, let me ask you this. Do you think whatever it was that happened had anything to do with religion?"

"That all depends on whose side you're on."

"Meaning what?"

"Meaning either God or the Devil."

"Are you serious? I mean, really serious? Come on now."

"You guys are dealing with something very powerful."

"How do you know this? And what makes you so sure?"

"I used to live up there when I was a kid, and some of the things I've seen happening just didn't make any sense to me. When I became old enough to leave, I did."

"So, you're from Stonyford, and you left because you didn't like what you were seeing?"

"That's right. Couldn't wait to leave that town."

"What, you've seen a bunch of devil worshipping going on? Or was it that you didn't like having to attend church every Sunday morning with your parents and little brothers and sisters? Or could it be that the reverence for a deity or sacred object such as a religious form scared you?"

"I'm not afraid of anything," he quickly told Goldsby. "I'm one who respects the honorable virtue of a person's position and rank. But there is just something disagreeable within me about whatever it is about Stonyford and whatever it is that killed all those people up there."

"Hold up. Wait a minute. Now just one minute. Now, what did you just say? Killed all those people up there?"

"You see, that's what I meant about unexplainable things happening. You just don't know what you're up against. What you need to be doing is talking to Margaret. She's the one who can answer your questions. She was there face-to-face with that thing. She seen everything that happened."

"That thing?" she asked him curiously. "What do you mean, that thing?"

"That thing that I'm sure came from the devil. And let's not forget to mention the evil spirit."

"Uh, okay now. Here we go again with all your hidden subliminal areas of things you keep surprising me with. So, what are you talking about now?"

"You know, the spirit. The old man and his snake."

"Just what are you talking about?"

"You never heard about it?"

"No! And to be truthful, I don't think I want to hear about it. And you know what? Nothing you're saying seems to make any sense. And one more thing, who are you? What's your name? How long have you been working here in this morgue? For Pete's sake, it's driving you crazy!"

"Well, for one thing, I'm not crazy. And my name is Gaylen Clark. You can think I'm crazy all you want to, just like everybody else. They call me weird sometimes, because when I tell them the same thing I told you about the things I've seen for myself happening in Stonyford, they laugh at me, and always be snickering behind my back. But it's like I tell 'em, I know what I seen, and one day the same thing that happened to those people will happen again. Believe me, it's going to happen again."

"Well, Gaylen, I really do have to find the people I came here with. It's been interesting talking to you. Also, thanks for letting me in, 'cause I am more than sure they've probably forgotten about me by now."

"Would you like for me to help you find your way around this place?"

"That would be very helpful of you to do that, Gaylen, but I don't want to be holding you up any longer than what I've already done. I mean, I'm sure you have work to do."

"Are you sure?" he asked Goldsby. "I know this place blindfolded, and even in the dead of night."

"Dead of night?"

"That meaning, when it's uh, you know, nighttime outside. Just me being a little sarcastic," he told her.

"Oh, okay," Goldsby responded.

"Just go that way, and then turn left, and then a quick right. Once you make it to the elevator, you'll see some stairs leading up and a flight of steps going down to the basement area. There'll be signs there pointing in the direction you want to go, plus telling you the names and locations of the rooms you're looking for, in case you get lost. Just follow the arrows."

Walking through the hallways, which were to Goldsby dim, reducing what little light there was under the circumstances, she began thinking about the fact that she'd completely disregarded the advice given to her by the employee to assist her in locating the examination room which was being used for Wanda's remains. Instead, she found herself playing a game called "Eenie, Meenie, Minie, Moe," and then pointing a finger in the direction she felt she needed to go, not realizing the examination room by this time being on the opposite side of the building.

It was Detective Miller who curiously found himself once again in deep thought, wondering about the credibility of Detective Goldsby, which prompted and aroused his curiosity to investigate her whereabouts immediately. That's when he suddenly found himself rushing to the entrance to the building, which is where he'd last seen her, wondering if she could still be on the outside trying to get someone to let her in.

Hastily moving as quickly as he possibly could without running, the eagerness to find Goldsby had caused him to move even more rapidly, as if he were hurrying impulsively.

He began to feel a deep sense of guilt within himself. The mere thought of having a female detective in such a highly qualified position was beyond his taste.

Reaching the entrance, he found himself nervously fumbling for the door handle and its knob, while thinking about how he had carelessly and clumsily mislead Goldsby. He began to feel so foolish, while thinking about what his reasons were for him to trick Goldsby, misleading her into believing he'd left his folder in his car, which he began to realize was a dirty game to be playing, especially under the circumstances and on one of the most qualified detectives.

Searching outside the premises without any luck to locate Goldsby, he then proceeded back to the location and entrance, where he then began to search the section of the building they'd entered into upon first arriving at the building.

Detective Goldsby, still very much confused and lost, was herself eagerly searching for the examination room, while still in her game of quest. Pointing her fingers was now becoming a boring task without any success, except for giving her a terrible headache, which had by now become just another of her problems.

The sound of her shoes loudly clicking and echoing throughout the hallways as she desperately searched for the examination room had now begun to sound like a group of wild horses roaming aimlessly around in circles on pavement with a craving to gallop.

The halls began to seem to draw straight outward, fuller in length, extending beyond limits, becoming darker as Detective Goldsby turned each corner breathing heavily, exhausted, slightly leaning into the walls in her effort to assure every step.

Just as she was about to turn the next corner, she suddenly came face to face with Detective Miller. "What are you doing here?" were Miller's calm words, as he pretended to have full control over his emotions. "How come you're not in the examination room? We've been in there waiting on you for the last thirty minutes."

This is when Goldsby found herself entirely too embarrassed to admit being lost, let alone how she had gotten lost, and was about to explain the reason for her absence, when suddenly Detective Miller, still pretending to project his unconcerned, tough attitude, very rudely and abruptly walked away from the conversation, gesturing with one of his hands for Goldsby to follow him.

Proceeding in a direction which Goldsby had avoided in her confusion while playing her game of finger pointing, she found that it would have been indeed her most promising result if only she hadn't neglected to listen to what she'd been told.

Chapter Fifteen

THE EXAMINATION ROOM WAS BRIGHTLY LIT by large, round lights emitting wide beams that illuminated virtually every object throughout the room.

Detective Goldsby found herself relieved after realizing that her confusion had finally been alleviated, though now she'd become completely astounded from the thought of the gruesome, mutilated body parts that were presently invading and violating her current state of comprehension.

"Well, this is what's left of that little girl," said Miller, talking to Detective Goldsby. "But just wait until you see the scene, that's really going to make all the hairs on your body stand at attention."

"What happened here?" she questioned. "What is this, a prank? Is this real?"

"Oh, it's real," he told her. "Just touch it and find out for yourself and you'll see."

"And this is…?"

"That little girl from Stonyford. Wanda Johnson."

"You mean, what's left of her."

"That's right."

"And who did you say did this?" she asked him.

"They're trying to pin it on Margaret," Blake interrupted. "But I'm just having a hard time trying to formulate that theory."

"What? You don't think so?" Goldsby questioned Blake.

"Come on now," he said, leaning against the examination table. "Nobody in their right state of mind is going to believe that that little girl is responsible for butchering and then slaughtering not only her own sister, but all those other people, too. Come on now, people, for God's sake, let's get real about this."

"This is a brutal killing, you think?" Goldsby asked Miller.

"To be truthful," said Miller, unsure of what to think, "I'm worried about this entire situation. I think somebody is doing this barbarously."

"Goddamn it, Miller," Blake quickly shouted in a whisper. "There you go, just like the rest of those quacks there in Stonyford. You're talking like this is some weird phenomenon or something."

"But that does remind me about a conversation I was having with one of the men working here—"

"And I bet you're talking about that goddamn quack named Gaylen?"

"That's right," Goldsby said. "Just how did you know?"

"Because he's another one of these weirdos with this bizarre theory about a monster or something—"

"You mean the devil," said Goldsby, interrupting Blake.

"Okay, the devil," said Blake. "But remember, it's just an assumption that we're talking about."

"Maybe the guy is onto something," said Miller. "Maybe there's really something going on that we need to investigate."

"Yeah, like a new brain for the people I'm working with," Blake told both Detective Miller and Goldsby. "And what about you, Bedford, you think you might need one too?"

"Hey, I'm just here to do my job," Bedford told Blake. "Anything to do with the devil jumping out on you guys, I'll snap a picture of it when he be taking you guys back to hell with him."

"Oh, that's just so funny of you to say," Blake told him. "If it's the devil's doing, you'll be going straight to hell with us, Bedford, and you better damn well believe it, buddy."

"I ain't going nowhere with you guys," said Bedford. "You guys're the ones whose job it is to capture him and put him in jail. And from what I understand, he's already supposed to be there anyway. Who let him out?"

"Aaall right, that's it," Blake told them. "I've had just about enough of all this mumbo jumbo crap. I'll be outside in my car if so happen you can come up with anything new."

"What's wrong, Sheriff?" Bedford asked, smiling. "Gettin' kinda hot, isn't it?"

"It is kinda hot and stuffy in here," said Miller. "Isn't there supposed to be a ventilation system in this place to keep you from becoming all congested up in here?"

"Don't know and don't care," Blake said while walking out the door and into the hallway. "I'll get all the air I need once I'm outside this place. I need to get away from all you dead folks."

"Now, Sheriff," Goldsby said, staring directly at him. "Now you know that isn't very lively of you to be saying in a place like this. I mean, now just look around you."

Snickering.

"Y'all can just kiss my big, fat ass," Blake told them, while trying to slam the door to the examination room, not realizing the door was a swinging door.

"What?" Goldsby asked Miller and Bedford. "Did I say something wrong?"

"Uh, this place is kinda, you know, a bit congested," said Miller. "I think we need to examine what we can and call it quits for the evening."

"Amen on that one," Goldsby agreed. "This has got me burned all the way out, for some reason."

Chapter Sixteen

WAITING PATIENTLY IN HIS PATROL CAR, Sheriff Blake found himself in deep thought, still investigating his curiosity concerning the possibility that maybe Margaret just might really be the innocent one here and shouldn't be regarded as the only suspect in Wanda's death.

Blake was now very seriously considering the fact that maybe Margaret became terribly horrified after stumbling upon Wanda's assailant, or even possibly assailants, who were most likely probably busy at work, mutilating what was left of her already dead corpse. "Just what in heaven's name happened out there?" Blake began questioning himself. "What did that poor little kid do to the rotten bastard to deserve being destroyed like that?"

Outrageously insulted by such heinous scandalousness, that was most likely committed by a sick, child-molesting, ignoble coward, Blake continued to find himself insulted by the fact that an uninvited intruder had somehow apparently come into his territory, unannounced, snuffing the life out of one of his most innocent citizens.

He thought about the fact that this was done by some very sick psycho, leaving no evidence or clues to trace. The only reliable information left behind was that of Margaret, who was still presently in the Willows hospital recuperating from shock.

Still within his intense concentration, Sheriff Blake's attention had now become attracted by the sounds of swiftly-revolving rotors, thick rotating blades attached to helicopters that the sheriff could see coming into view as two helicopters approached the small airport in Willows.

"Goddamn time somebody finally made it with these freaking helicopters to help us out," Blake mumbled to himself. "Wonder what took them people so goddamn long?"

By this time, Miller, along with Goldsby, Bedford and Trotter, came out of the building and approached the car. "Are those the helicopters that you had requested?" Miller asked Blake.

"It sure the hell better be," Blake responded with authority. "It sure the hell better be."

"What? We're going to fly in those things all the way up to Stonyford? And then to who knows where else?" Goldsby asked Miller.

"I do believe that's right," Miller told her. "All except for Blake. He'll be driving his car back to Stonyford on account of that he's just about had enough of flying during his tour in 'Nam."

"You mean Vietnam, don't you?" Trotter asked him.

"Vietnam, Cambodia, Ho Chi Minh City, whatever," Miller told him. "I just know the sheriff won't be flying with us to Stonyford."

"I wonder if he'll even remember me," said Trotter, walking slowly.

"Just go on around to the driver's side," Goldsby told him. "You don't know. He might be just as happy to see you as you are him. Just go ahead and go around there and see if he remembers you. Can't be scared all of your life."

"And who said anything about being scared?" Trotter exclaimed. "I can do this. Ain't no problem."

"And just who the hell are you?" Blake asked Trotter as he was getting out of the car. "Do I know you?"

"Yeah," Trotter responded nervously. "It's me, Mr. Blake, Christopher Trotter. I used to live in Stonyford a couple of years ago, before we ended up moving to Willows."

"I thought you looked kinda familiar," Blake told him. "Grown a bit, didn't you?"

"That's what everybody keeps telling me," Trotter answered, smiling.

"What are you doing here?" asked Blake. "You live around here?"

"No," said Trotter. "But this is where I work."

"Oh yeah, is that right?" Blake said. "Doing what?"

"Well, I know you're going to find this hard to believe," Trotter told him, "but I am the assistant medical examiner. I work with Chief Medical Examiner Nicholas Florentin."

"FLORENTIN?" Blake yelled. "Just where in the hell is that crazy son-of-a-bitch?"

Everybody laughed.

"He's on an important business trip," Trotter told Blake. "But he'll be back in a few days. Hopefully."

"Important business trip," said Blake. "How come nobody ever invites me on one of those important business trips, Miller? What? Ain't I pretty enough?"

"Well, look at it this way, Sheriff," said Miller. "At least you did get propositioned to by a very beautiful lady. I mean, that's more than I ever had happen to me. Just think about it, Sheriff, that pretty lady came over to you and proposed. She actually wanted to get married to you right then and there. You don't see anything like that happen too often."

"And what the heck are you smiling about, Bedford?" Blake asked. "I see you over there grinning that face of yours from ear to ear."

"Just thinking about why nothing like that has ever happened to a handsome, attractive guy like me," Bedford told him, positioning himself as a model would do for a photo shoot.

"Get the heck out of here, Bedford," Blake told him, snickering. "In case you didn't know, I'm the most gorgeous, dazzling, attractive man a lady will ever find in these parts. Tell him, Goldsby."

"Don't go putting me in this conversation," said Goldsby. "After what I've just seen in the morgue, a man is the last thing on my mind."

"Uh, coming back to reality," Miller said, "I think it's time to head on over to the airport."

"Are we really flying up to Stonyford in those things?" Goldsby asked Blake curiously.

"What, don't tell me you've never flown in a helicopter before?" he said, staring at Goldsby, wondering if she was playing. "After the flying you've been doing in that private airplane, I know you have flown in a few helicopters once or twice?"

"No, I don't think I have, Sheriff Blake," she told him. "And I really wasn't looking forward to it, either."

"Well, it's time you get over your fears when it comes to helicopters," Blake told Goldsby. "I'm the only one driving and riding in my car. And no passengers allowed."

"Are you serious?" Goldsby asked Blake.

"Tell me, Detective Goldsby," said Blake, staring directly at her. "Does it look and sound like I'm serious? It's time for you to get over your fear of flying in a helicopter, and especially while working on this case. Stonyford and its rough mountains are no joke when driving a motor vehicle. Our biggest problem is going to be those rugged, overgrown bushes and harsh shrubbery with them irritating thorns. That's the part of the terrain that can really be an annoyance."

"It's not that I'm afraid to fly in a helicopter," Goldsby told Blake, standing with one leg crossed over the other. "I just never had a reason to need one. You feel me, Sheriff Blake?"

"Oh, I feel you all right," said Blake. "You're just so used to flying around all over the goddamn country in them party jets, to where flying in a helicopter makes you feel like a lower-class citizen. But I'll tell you what them goddamn wealthy Sacramento politicians done did to you and all of the freakin' attractive women just like you, they've damaged you and spoiled you rotten. That's what they've done. They destroyed the perfection in you with all the pampering and overindulgent coddling. And now just take a good look at yourself, you're too good to fly with this team up to Stonyford in a goddamn helicopter."

"Now see what you did, Goldsby," Miller told her. "You got old Blake all wound up, and now we gotta listen to all his lecturing, like speeches that'll make you feel like you're being reprimanded."

"Don't tell me he's going to treat us like we're his audience," asked Goldsby.

"You're the one said it," Miller told her, nodding his head and shrugging his shoulders. "I didn't."

They stood patiently while Sheriff Blake mumbled on, ranting at length his dislike about the fact that Sacramento had obviously spoiled Goldsby and all the other women working in her position. "And you can just count this mission as the first one you have experienced where you have to depend on a helicopter to get the business done," Blake told Goldsby. "This is all you have, so make it your best friend. Rely on it. Trust it like it's the only friend you've got. Trust it confidently, all of you, and it'll make you feel proud to have used it on this mission."

"And what about you, Blake?" Bedford asked him, "are you going to ride with us on this mission?"

"Who in the hell are you to be talking and asking me a question like that?" said Blake, "when here it is you can't even keep the goddamn camera working right. I bet you haven't taken one picture since you been here."

"No," said Bedford. "I've taken two."

Low sounds of snickering could be heard.

"Oh, you guys think that's funny?" Blake asked everybody. "From this point on, I want them cameras working and in full operation at all times. Is that understood, Bedford?"

"Uh, YES, sir, Sheriff Blake," responded Bedford. "Everything will be just as you have said, in full operation at all times."

"No matter what!" Blake added.

"No matter what," again responded Bedford.

"And now that we've got that understood," Blake said, "why don't we all just get ourselves together and head on over to the airport. I do find a soft place in my heart to believe that them helicopters are there waiting on all of you, ladies and gentlemen. I shall help see to it that everyone board this flight safely for this trip to Stonyford, in which is where I will do my very best to meet you upon arrival. So, shall we all just, you know, get in my car? What's that? Do I hear mumbling coming from one of you? Naughty, naughty, naughty! Didn't anyone ever tell you how improper it is to be disobedient?

"*Well!*" Blake said, snickering to himself.

Chapter Seventeen

STILL WITHIN HIS INTENSE CONCENTRATION, Sheriff Blake's attention was once again attracted by the sounds of revolving rotors which were coming from the two helicopters approaching a secured location designated for them to land in a field across from the Johnsons' residence.

Emerging from the first helicopter to land was Detective Miller, followed by four investigating officers. Emerging from the second helicopter was first, the photographer, Derek Bedford, and then two more investigating officers, followed by Detective Goldsby.

As directed by Sheriff Blake, Bedford began taking pictures spontaneously, while Goldsby could be seen talking to Miller, pointing out areas of the residence that she'd intended to begin analyzing, starting first with the large barn for any possible clues leading to Wanda's assailant or assailants.

The investigation was about to shift into full gear when suddenly Goldsby hastened over to where Miller was engaged in a conversation with one of the helicopter pilots, in speculation that a chopper was going to be needed to search the higher mountain region. Miller had also enquired about the possibility that maybe during Sheriff Blake's request the nearby ranger station would be willing to assist in furnishing a few of its Jeeps.

"You know," said Miller, "with all these hills and huge mountains, from the looks of things, these hills are as high as these mountains. Been so long since I've been in this neck of the area, things have really changed or grown."

"What?" Goldsby asked. "You're not from this area?"

"No," said Miller. "I'm afraid not. And to be quite frank, I'm glad I'm not."

"Why is that?" the pilot asked curiously.

"After what I have been hearing about this place," Miller began telling him, "I just couldn't see living in fear all my life, you know, wondering and thinking that somebody is out here somewhere waiting and watching everything I do. Let alone my family."

"Ah, you really believe all that mumbo jumbo stuff about this place?" the pilot asked Miller. "I mean, hey, we've been hearing all about it, too. But I think it's just some kids getting their rocks off knowing they are scaring the living crap out of you people with their prank about monsters and the devil appearing around here."

"Hey," Goldsby quickly interrupted. "That's the same thing that guy at the morgue was in a way trying to warn me about."

"Yeah, and what was that?" the pilot asked, grinning, eager to hear.

"He was just saying something about, you know, everything up here in Stonyford being strange and mysterious," Goldsby told him, looking around as if somewhat now uncertain about her mission. "He was saying something about unexplained events, or something unexplainable. It was like it wasn't adding up or something."

"But what did he say wasn't adding up?" Miller asked her.

"And might I ask just what we're so busy debating?" Sheriff Blake asked after noticing the three talking and pointing in different directions.

"Oh, I was just talking about the need for a possible helicopter, you know, to search the higher area that I don't think a car can get to."

"And just what part would that be, Detective Miller?" Blake asked him.

"I was thinking about…somewhere up there," Miller told him, pointing. "Up there somewhere."

"What?" said Blake. "You mean way up there on Snow Mountain?"

"Yeah," Miller told him. "That's what I was thinking."

"Hell then, Miller," said Blake. "Then why don't we just fly you right over there to the Himalayas so that you can try climbing Mt. Everest? Really, what's the difference to you? A mountain is a mountain, isn't it?"

Goldsby and the pilot stared at each other, smiling and shrugging their shoulders.

"Now, who said anything like that?" Miller asked Blake, while observing the reactions of both Goldsby and the pilot. "Ain't nobody saying anything about climbing no Mt. Everest."

"Well, you might as well have," Blake told him. "That goddamn thing up there is just as high and as huge as Everest."

"I wouldn't say it like that," said Miller. "I mean, hey, Everest is nothing to play with compared to this. They might be somewhat similar in terms of being huge mountains, but man, Blake, Snow Mountain could never in this lifetime be equal to Mt. Everest, and you know it."

"Well, they could to a certain degree," said Blake.

"Yeah, right," Miller told him. "That would be if a 20.9 earthquake were to rock the shit out of the Himalayas, lowering Mt. Everest by thousands of feet, and then one hit the Stonyford area, raising Snow Mountain by the same thousands of feet."

"Well?" said Blake.

"Well, what?" said Miller.

"One day that just might very well happen," Blake told him. "And then you'll see."

"Get out of here, Blake," Miller said, laughing. "You're crazy if you really think you'll be around for something like that to happen."

"And what makes you so sure?" Blake asked Miller, looking directly at him. "You don't know, it could happen at any time."

"Not in this lifetime, it won't," Miller told him, assured he knew it wasn't going to happen. "Not in a million years."

"And now just who the hell do you think you've become?" Blake asked Miller, pointing one of his fingers at him. "One of them goddamn biology people, or something like a geologist?"

Everybody laughed.

"Maybe next you'll become a goddamn astronaut with your very own crew with a spacecraft to fly you to the moon," Blake told him. "Now wouldn't you just like to do something like that?"

"Sounds exciting," said Miller. "But I really don't think I would enjoy being on the moon, and especially if you're not there to guide me and tell me what to do with my life."

Chapter Eighteen

AWAKENING FROM WHAT SEEMED TO BE HOURS of deep sleep, Margaret suddenly became aware of the fact that she was now in a private room, at which time, she briefly evaluated, it was distinctively different, though delightful.

After carefully checking everything that she possibly could, she noticed how the room was equipped with just about every piece of necessity needed to get the attention of the nurses on duty, which she immediately took advantage of.

The room and all its amenities for pleasantness and comfort began to allow Margaret to feel as though she were the princess of a royal family. She began to think of the beauty it must be when knowing the twitch of a finger could bring her the choice of her every desire.

Looking around in search of every piece of equipment which would move the bed and anything else electronically, while within her imaginary world as the royal princess, Margaret's dream abruptly shattered when the thought of what happened to Wanda began to plunder her mind, invading it forcibly, and once again attempting to hold her captive, as if its prisoner.

It was just yesterday when her life in Stonyford was terribly shaken by the most dreadful sight imaginable, horrifying her. Looking aimlessly around the room and briefly out the window with dingy, light tan curtains drawn slightly back, allowing the evening sky to pass slowly through its opening, Margaret began to wonder if maybe God even existed as stated in her Bible.

"Why did this have to end up happening?" she questioned. "If there really is a God that we pray to, then just how come you let this happen to Wanda? Just what did she do to deserve being tormented with such infliction of torturing pain by that unwanted, vicious, monstrous thing?

This isn't the kind of God that I want to serve. This is an ungodly act belonging to only that of a God being the Devil himself."

Standing and facing the mirror, which was reflecting her now very pale image that she could see slowly maturing, she again started reminding herself about the sight she'd seen during Wanda's struggle and intense suffering. She wished the entire situation were only a bad dream. A nightmare. A nightmare that she could, at any given moment, wish away, and forget all the events from this oppressive dream.

While thinking and wishing that the entire ordeal had been only a horrible dream, she was again shaken by an intense wave of nerves that caused her to suddenly scream out in fear, as both of her parents entered the room.

"We have a code here," a nurse yelled out to get the attention of other staff duty. "We have a code here and need your help," she again called out to the nurses on her floor.

"Here I come. Here I come," another voice from a nurse yelled out. "What do we have?"

"It's over here," another nurse said, informing two more nurses where to go. "Somebody get ahold of Doctor Smallwood and tell him it's an emergency, and that it's about the girl named Margaret Johnson."

"No!" another nurse yelled out to everyone. "It's all right. It's not any emergency. It was just her parents going into her room that apparently scared her. She didn't know who they were. So please, everybody can just go on back to your work stations."

"You mean to tell me that I ran all this way for nothing?" one of the nurses asked, shaking her head in disbelief. "Y'all just might have to end up putting a respirator on me in a minute."

Everybody laughed.

"Girl, get yo butt on out of here," one of the nurses told her. "But wait a minute. Now if you're really feeling, you know, a little sick and a bit queasy, you know you can always count on the doctor to give you a little something that I've been just dying to try out on somebody."

"Uh, no thank you. That's quite all right," she responded. "Now isn't that just so amazing? I'm feeling so much better right about now. In fact, I feel so good to where I'm ready to go out and sprint a little."

"Well then," the nurse told her. "You feeling that good, then you can just sprint yourself right on back around there to your workstation. Can't you?"

"You know what?" she began telling her. "You've been reading my mind, because that is just what I was getting ready to do. Sprint myself back to my workstation."

Everybody laughed.

"See there," a voice said, still laughing in a low tone. "Miracles do be happening. Just look at you, all ready to do some sprinting."

Chapter Nineteen

THE ROOM WAS OFF LIMITS, but the sign to prevent anyone from entering and disturbing Margaret had apparently been left on the door of the other room that she had been moved from. Her present room was in a more secured section of the hospital when her parents decided they'd check on her condition.

The nurse on duty who was responsible for this section of the ICU, unaware of their presence, immediately rushed to her room, while at the same time, began calling out to any available assistant after hearing her scream.

After switching on the lights, she noticed both Paul and Sarah Johnson standing near Margaret's side. Paul began to move much closer to Margaret, and then slowly leaned forward, and, ever so gently, kissed her on the forehead, telling her in a soft voice that he and Mommy loved her.

He then held both of her hands in his and began stroking them very gently and softly in his attempt to assure her that everything was going to be all right and that she wasn't in any danger.

Margaret just stood there in complete silence, staring into the mirror at her reflection, stunned from her parents' surprising entrance into the room. Tears welled up in Paul's eyes as he lifted his head and slowly turned toward Sarah. He wanted her to try to understand what was happening. He wanted her to understand that Margaret was their daughter and that she needed for them to express their love and concern for her instead of backing away and neglecting her because of what had happened to Wanda.

He felt that her concern was just as important as his.

But Sarah just stood there, distancing herself from Margaret. Not in any way wanting to be near her and unwilling to be of any assistance.

Staring angrily and full of bitterness and revealing her hatred with an enormous amount of animosity was apparently Sarah's only desire, hoping the worst for Margaret's recovery.

Some smaller amount of interest and revulsion greeting her union with the man who once was in every way, part of and only later became the love in Margaret's eyes.

Chapter Twenty

AS MARGARET CONTINUED TO STARE into the mirror, she began thinking about her childhood life in Stonyford and the many times that she'd complained to her parents, and mainly her mother, about the mysteriousness of the unwanted thing that was busy at work invading her body.

But Sarah had never believed in Margaret's outcry for help. She felt the awful marks on her body were enough to draw her own conclusion. But it was Margaret who was trying her best to seek her mother's attention. She kept trying her best to get her family to believe that something was really happening to her. And even the residents who resided in the town of Stonyford, they too were spreading their usual gossip and unfounded rumors and speculation and opinions as to how Margaret had become the town's youngest tramp and whore slut.

All the other children who lived nearby the Johnsons' residence weren't any longer allowed to participate in any activities that Margaret would be herself involved in. Parents were punishing their children severely if ever they were caught attempting to socialize with her.

Feeling rejected by everyone involved, it was at this point in her young life that Margaret found herself giving in to the mysteriousness of whatever it was that was strangely wicked and with morally bad behavior that was very cruelly invading her body. Too young to quite understand just what was happening, Margaret found her childhood life had become indeed corrupted by the unwanted character that was busy depriving her of her virginity.

It was then that she thought maybe she could trust Wanda enough to at least try talking to her in hopes of getting her to understand what she was going through. But as expected, and yet to her surprise, Wanda turned away, just as she'd always done, influencing their mother to do the same.

Wanda would laugh and accuse Margaret of being a disgrace to their family. The only person that ever seemed to show any concern for her was her father. He was always the type of man who stood beside his family and worked hard at the sawmill in Elk Creek and would do just about anything he could to support them.

He was an honest, hard-working man trying to make the best of things.

Knowing his love and concern for her, she knew that she could turn to him without feelings of being rejected. She could never remember being turned away from him. But just like the rest of her family, she was sure that even her father had times when he must have had doubts about her. But it was Wanda that she mostly thought about and how it wasn't anything unusual being rejected by her. For quite a number of years Wanda had on numerous occasions expressed her negative attitude toward her. She would at times intentionally involve herself in conversation with Margaret only to attempt engaging in conflict to make it seem as though it was always Margaret who was the one responsible.

After what seemed to be hours of thinking about her childhood life in Stonyford, thus only minutes, Margaret found herself being embraced tightly by her father, who was also wiping his eyes from crying, while showing his love and affection, which to Margaret was very assuring.

"It's all right, honey," he whispered into her ear. "Daddy's here beside you now. You don't have to be afraid anymore. Daddy's right here beside you. I love you, Pumpkin."

"I know, Daddy," Margaret told him. "I know you do, but Daddy, I'm not a bad girl like they say I am."

"Oh, I know, baby," he told her, still embracing her tightly. "Daddy knows you're not. So just don't be worrying yourself."

"But Daddy?" I-I didn't have anything to do with it. But when, when I was getting ready to leave the barn, that's—"

Paul very gently took his arms from around Margaret and slowly, quietly, and softly, as in a whisper, started talking to Margaret in a low tone, one of his hands stroking her back in an effort to try to help her relax and get some rest. "Daddy understands you, so please try not to be worrying yourself," he told her. "I want you to try and get yourself some rest so that Daddy will be able to come get you and take you home. Okay, Pumpkin? I need you to get some rest so that the doctor will be able to let me take you home soon. You do wanna get better, don't you?"

"Yes, Daddy," Margaret told him, smiling happily to have him there.

"Well then," he told her. "Let's just try and get some rest, okay?"

"Okay," said Margaret, climbing back onto the bed.

Still gently caressing her back as she climbed in, he could feel the unsettling nerves in Margaret's body jittering as if she were being vibrated without any form of self control.

Sarah was still unwilling to share in Paul's concern for Margaret's recovery. She felt that Margaret was herself fully responsible for Wanda's death, just as she had also felt about the many other unanswered occurrences and events which to Sarah constituted Margaret's activities.

The nurse who'd entered the room after hearing Margaret's scream began informing her parents that a physician by the name of Joey Boyd had been assigned to their daughter's case. "He's a really nice fellow," she told them. "I think you'll like him." She told them that Dr. Boyd would be checking in, if not this evening, he'd surely be at the hospital first thing in the morning. "I am more than sure that he'll be looking forward to meeting you and would probably want to talk to you and discuss Margaret's condition, which is normal procedure," she told them, removing a thin, light blue blanket from the foot of the bed, only to replace it with another one, except this one was light green.

"Daddy," Margaret said, staring at her father. "Please don't leave me here by myself. I'm afraid of being here alone. Please, Daddy, please don't leave me. Please."

Margaret, who was now trembling in fear, had a tremendous affect in her voice that seemed to stimulate Sarah's emotional state of unwillingness to show concern for her, and she suddenly began to reveal the sorrow that she'd kept protected as the anger within her began to display signs of grief for not only Wanda, but also for the hospitalized Margaret.

"It's all right, honey," Paul told Sarah after noticing how her posture and mannerism toward Margaret seemed to begin to change. "She needs you just as much as she needs me. She's our daughter, for God's sake, Sarah. Can't you see how she's reaching out to us for help?"

"I don't know what to do," Sarah said, after what seemed to be hours without an utterance from her. "I'm, I'm so sorry, but I just don't know what you expect me to do."

The words came from Sarah in a whisper. She was finally showing concern for Margaret at a time when her attitude revealed so much doubt. The effect of Margaret's voice pleading to her father seemed to have finally reached Sarah.

Chapter Twenty-One

A SMILE APPEARED on Detective Goldsby's face as it did on Detective Miller's, Sheriff Blake's, the photographer, Derek Bedford's, and the rest of the crew as they found themselves experiencing a rather unusual tingling sensation throughout their bodies.

"Man, what in the hell?" Miller questioned himself.

"Don't ask," Blake told him, smiling. "I don't even wanna know."

"But did you guys feel that?" Miller asked. "I mean…?"

"Heeeyy," Bedford uttered, smiling and looking downward at his pants.

"Mmm," Goldsby mumbled. "Think I need to come here more often."

Low noises came from the rest of the crew as they claimed to have experienced feeling the same tingling sensation.

"Whatever that was about, it can just keep right on happening," one of the crew members said, walking around trying to find the exact spot where he felt the tingling.

"Hey!" Blake called out to him. "You better behave yourself. Don't wanna go fooling around with something you don't know anything about."

"I think that might've come from a broken electrical outlet somewhere underneath this road," said Bedford. "I've heard people say they felt electric currents like that before. That might be where that came from."

While standing in front of the Stonyford supermarket, Goldsby found herself feeling somewhat excited after reaching an uncontrollable orgasm. She began squeezing her legs tightly together by crossing one in front and over the other and applying pressure. After finally realizing what she was doing, she very quickly regained control of herself, turned her back to the crew, wondering if she had been noticed by anyone. She gave a sigh of relief after realizing she hadn't.

By this time, Sheriff Blake was busy questioning Damon Cox, part-owner of the supermarket. He was asking him whether he'd seen anything out of the ordinary, or anyone acting strange, or even someone like an out-of-towner, a transient that might have just happened to be passing through.

"Hey there, Damon, how you been doing, old buddy?"

"Just fine, Sheriff. Just fine. And yourself?"

"Well, you know, I really can't be too much complaining about much of anything. Although, you know, we've been, you know, meaning your family and mine. Uh, we've been here in this neck of the woods a pretty long time now, haven't we?"

"Pretty much so. I'd guess so, Sheriff. So what's the point?"

"Everything all right?" Detective Miller asked, coming through the door, followed by Detective Goldsby and Bedford.

"Yeah, I guess so," the sheriff answered. "Just here talking to one of my neighbors. Uh, Damon," the sheriff began introductions. "These are a few of my helpers, Detective Miller and Detective Goldsby. And this fellow here is a photographer named Bedford. And I'm more than sure you can see who all those other people are outside."

"Hm, looks like a bunch of police officers," said Damon.

"Yeah, that's right," Blake told him, looking around the store as if he were searching for something. "I was just wondering, though…"

After their brief conversation, Blake began to sense that Damon, being the type of person he was, would be of little help to him, which made Miller shake his head in disbelief from the thought that Blake would even spend the amount of time he did questioning him. Miller couldn't understand how a town with such a small population could even be so inconsiderate when members of this community were being slaughtered, and yet no one seemed to actually care enough to help do anything about it.

Not a single person seemed to project discomfort at having one of its citizens' lives just outright blown into separate fragments. The reactions concerning the mutilation of a little girl were unbelievable, with only a very few of the town's neighbors showing any signs of being outrageously resentful in the wake of such maliciousness.

Driving within a short distance from the supermarket, they approached the entrance to the nearby ranger station. The buildings fit the perfect description of medium-sized cabins that were made into dormitories with sleeping quarters for housing a number of people, painted in a light green color.

Approaching the main gate, Detective Goldsby, who still seemed to be in a somewhat dazzled daze from what she had earlier felt when standing in front of the supermarket, had now found herself in a rather precarious situation, somewhat confused by such an experience.

What had happened was not intentional, and the mere thought of having sex was a thought far beyond her imagination. She couldn't quite understand the meaning or even the purpose for having such an experience, especially after realizing the magnitude of its strength, being powerful enough to take full control of one's body.

But it wasn't only that the experience was unexpected, but whatever its reasons, Detective Goldsby found the tingling sensation had been the most extraordinary feeling she'd ever felt, giving true, pure satisfaction.

"Well, sure do look like we've made it here in time for a bit to eat, I think," said Sheriff Blake. "Don't you think so, Miller?"

The man behind the large wooden desk seemed to show very little emotion after hearing Blake's statement, if any at all. In fact, he even turned around and faced the opposite direction, with both of his hands still busy indulging deep into his dish.

"Uh, hellooo there, young man," Blake said, trying to get the man's attention. "You gone stop eating long enough for me to ask you a question or two?"

The man behind the desk just continued to ignore Blake.

"Uh, this is Sheriff Blake, and I'm Detective Miller. And—"

"I know who the sheriff is," the man spoke, saying in a rather rusty-sounding low tone. "I ain't that dumb, if that's what you're thinking."

"Ain't nobody sayin' anything 'bout anybody being dumb," Blake told him, standing in the middle of the floor with both hands on his belt. "Just tryin' to get your attention, that's all, young man."

"Well, now you've got it," the man said, wiping his mouth with one of his shirt sleeves. "What seems to be the problem?"

"First of all," Blake said, staring directly at the man, "is this the way you treat everybody who comes through that goddamn door trying to get your undivided attention when you be feeding your goddamn greasy face?"

"Never have anybody coming in at this time," the man told him, smiling.

Suddenly, another man, chunky in size, standing at least six-feet-four, two-hundred-sixty or more pounds, entered the room from an area in the back of the building. "Well, hello there, Sheriff Blake," the man said. "How you been doing? What can I do for you?"

"Well, I'll be damned," Blake mumbled out loud. "If it isn't my old buddy from the academy. Just how long have you been working here? It's been what? Ten, twenty years since we last attended that school?"

"Long enough," he said, "long enough.

"Hey, tell me something," Blake inquired. "Just where the hell you'd get this young man from? A non-existent company or something? Hell, he's really lacking respect and coordination to be in any way organized for this type of job."

"Oh, you mean Junior?" he said. "He's one of my young, stupid nephews just helping me out around here to keep himself out of trouble, you know. I tell you, Blake, these youngsters nowadays, well, they all seem to be so full of all that, uh, mischievous crap."

"Nephew, you say?"

"Yeah, that's right there, Blake. When my brother and his wife found themselves unable to keep an eye on that there boy, I figured I could try and do something to try saving his ass from one day ending up, you know, in the penitentiary with all the other guys he was starting to hang around with. You know what I mean? I brought him here to Stonyford to stay here with me, and later hired him here at the station to learn how to mend this here transmitter."

"I mean, is it really doing him any good?" Blake asked. "You know with all that's been going on around this town lately. But what I guess you can say I'm asking is if it's really doing him any good?"

"Well, I don't know for sure," he told Blake. "But one thing for sure, he sure haven't been into any trouble like some of the other teens his age around here and over there in Maxwell and all them other towns."

"Are you sure?" Blake asked.

"Look, Blake," he suggested. "Test him for yourself and he'll tell you just about everything that's been going on over that transmitter. Even a thing or two about that little girl, and also what's been happening with them Gilbert brothers."

"Wow!" Detective Miller interrupted. "Gilbert brothers? Could you be in any way talking about Terry Gilbert and his younger brother, Randy?"

"That's right," he said. "And just who are you?"

"Oh, excuse me," said Blake. "But this just happens to be one of the detectives working on the situation here in Stonyford. His name is

Detective Miller, and this young lady here is Detective Goldsby. She's out here from all the way over there in Sacramento. And this young man here with all these cameras, he's our photographer from over there in Willows. His name is Bedford. And I'm more than sure you can just guess who the rest of these people are. They're flying them helicopters over there."

"Oh yeah," he told them. "Now I know who was flying them things."

"And you are?" Miller asked him to identify himself.

"Oh, I'm Dan Eaton," he told Miller. "I am the one in charge of, you know, running this here ranger station. And that fellow over there mending that transmitter is my nephew. His name is Chris Van Bebber."

Dan Eaton was the man in charge of the Stonyford Ranger Station, and to Sheriff Blake, he was definitely the man he needed to talk to concerning the situation surrounding Wanda's death and other tragedies.

"Uh, you know, Dan," Blake began. "Tragic enough, meaning, you know, the situation that took place over there at the Johnson's residence. Well, what I'm getting at is that we're getting reports about misfortune or ruins happening all over the goddamn place. You know what I mean? It's like ever since the Johnson situation, they just keep on happening. Now, as you should know, them goddamn people over there in Sacramento aren't too pleased with us folks here in Stonyford not being able to solve this problem as quickly as they would like us to."

"And I understand what you're getting at, Blake," Dan told him, then turned to yell over to Chris. "Could you turn that damn transmitter down just a little bit so we can hear each other over here?"

"Uncle Dan, you really need to hear this," Chris told him.

"I can," Dan told him. "And all it is is a bunch of static, from what I'm hearing here."

"Static?" Chris yelled. "Hell, that ain't all static that you're in there hearing. That's somebody screaming out loud for help!"

"Hold on for a minute there, Blake," said Dan. "I think my idiot-acting nephew in there done just about blown one of his retardation fuses and now he thinks he's hearing somebody screaming for help over the transmitter. So, just excuse me for a few minutes so I can go check on this fool before he ends up blowing us all to hell."

"But it sounds like I heard it, too," one of the officers said, listening intently to see if he could hear it again.

"What did it sound like you heard?" asked Miller.

"From what I could hear, it sounded like somebody was yelling. I then heard what sounded like a scream for help or something," he told Miller.

"Let me take a look at this thing, if you don't mind," Blake asked as he approached the transmitter. "You don't know just what you'll hear on an old gadget like this these days. They made this type of weird contraption so you can hear just about anything. And I do mean anything. This old timer can probably doodam its way into letting you spy on your neighbors. If you know what I mean?"

"Is that what you're in here doing, Chris?" Dan asked him. "Spying on the people down the road there?"

"Not a bad idea," Chris told him, smiling while staring out the window at the neighbors' house. "What's the distance on this thing? How far of a range will it go to pick up on people talking?"

"What you mean is, how long will it be before I have your ass in some handcuffs and shackles, hauling you off to jail for possible invasion of the privacy of your neighbors' constitutional rights, don't you?" Blake asked him.

Everybody laughed.

"There, right there," Dan yelled.

"Yeah, I heard it, too," said Miller and one of the officers.

"Go back a little," Dan told Blake. "About somewhere in this area."

"Hold it right there," Miller said, pointing to a certain location on the transmitter. "You guys didn't hear that?"

"I think I heard it," said Goldsby.

"What did it sound like you heard?" Blake asked her.

"It sounded like somebody was yelling or screaming," Goldsby told him, looking around with a shocked expression on her face. "You guys didn't see how that little needle started jumping when that happened?"

"That thing been jumping around like that for the longest," Chris told her. "Ever since all this racket been going on, that needle been just about all over the place."

"Is there a way we can get a better reading on the location?" Blake asked Dan.

"I don't know," said Dan. "Might be. But that's if we can find one of them old, you know, range finders."

"And where can we get something like that from?" asked Miller.

"You should have something like that somewhere at the station," Dan told Blake.

"You remember what they look like?" Bedford asked Blake.

"Who the hell are you to be asking me that?" Blake questioned Bedford, removing his hat and then rubbing the bald spot on his head. "What you need to be doing is running them goddamn cameras you got there. We need photographs of everything."

"Is there anybody out there?" a voice came over the transmitter saying in an urgent tone. "Can anybody hear me? We need help!"

"I think we have the equipment onboard our helicopters to find them, said one of the pilots talking to Sheriff Blake. "All we have to do is pinpoint their location."

"Is anybody out there?" the voice continued to come over an emergency respondence radio, as well as the transmitter. "We need somebody to help us."

"Chris!" Dan yelled. "See if you can pick them up. Say something to see if they can hear you."

"Well, that's what I been doin', Uncle Dan," Chris told him. "But I'm thinking whoever it is, they're on a different frequency or something, 'cause this unit seems to be picking them up without any problems, but they are not hearing me when I'm trying to get them to pick me up."

"They must have one of them small hand radios or something," Dan told Blake. "We just gotta keep them talking."

"Sounds like they're somewhere in between these mountains," the pilot said. "What I can do is, I can take one of my helicopters up high enough to get a good reading on the location, and then we'll most likely zero in on our target and the location."

"You know, I think that'll be a good idea," Blake told the pilot. "Why don't you take Detective Goldsby there with you. She's been dying to learn everything she can about helicopters and quick, steep maneuvering."

Goldsby just stared at Blake, listening to his sarcastic remark.

"Hold on, I think we got something," said Dan, slowly turning the knob on the transmitter.

"Whatcha got there, Dan?" Blake asked.

"Uh, this is Uncle Dan, here at the ranger station in Stonyford" he told whoever he was talking to. "If you can read me, come back at me."

"We need help, Uncle Dan," the voice said on the other end. "We need help out here."

"Uh, where are you? Come back."

"I, I really don't know," the voice said, yelling. "I don't know! But we need somebody to help us get out of here!"

"Ask him his name," Blake told Dan. "Try finding out who he is."

"Uh, this is Uncle Dan. Could you please identify yourself? Who are you?"

Loud static sounds came from the transmitter.

"This is Uncle Dan. Do you read me? Come back. This is Uncle Dan. Do you read me? Come back."

Static and then silence.

"Chris, you keep trying to reach whoever that was," Dan told him. "We gotta find a way to figure out who that is and where they are."

"What about the helicopter?" Miller asked, turning toward the pilot. "I mean, 'cause you're the one who said you could do this."

"Well, are you ready?" the pilot asked.

"And what about the rest of us?" Blake asked. "I mean, except for me. But what about these guys? You got room for them?"

"Have you forgotten?" the pilot said, staring at Blake. "Remember, we did come here in more than just one helicopter."

"That's right," Blake said, reminding himself about the other one. "By the way, tell me something."

Blake stared back at the pilot, who was now talking to Detective Goldsby, assuring her that everything would be alright.

"But just what in the heck is your name? I mean, you know, since we left Willows, I really haven't had the opportunity to know much of anything about you and the rest of your flight crew, or just who in the hell we are talking to and traveling with. And especially since my people will be, you know, I guess, flying all around this place with you all. I'd like very much to know just who I'm doing business with."

"Well, for your information, my name is Taylor," he told Blake, with a light smile on his face from the thought of him just now questioning him about his name.

"Taylor?" Blake said loudly, as if there were something else he wanted to ask, only to forget what it was. "Taylor!"

"Yes, *sir*," responded Taylor immediately.

"Taylor?" again questioned Blake. "Taylor what? I mean, I'm already fully aware you're a pilot and everything, but wouldn't you by chance just happen to have a full name instead of just Taylor? Or at least, you know, at least a last name or something? Or better yet, what's the title for, I would guess, you know, the position you hold at your job? You know, for someone like myself, for identifying just what part you play?"

"It's as before," he again told Blake. "Except this time you've asked me my full name and position I hold, which is Flight Lieutenant Sherwin Taylor, leader of the Twenty-Ninth Squadron. Do I need to say more?"

"Hell no!" Blake said, feeling confidence. "I knew it, I knew it, goddamn it. I knew there was something special about you. I knew it from the way you carry yourself. Flying and blasting everything straight to hell is in your blood, sonny. Old Blake here sensed that you were from one of them goddamn fighter units from the first time I spotted you.

"And tell me something, aren't you that guy they were talking about on the news who'd flown that weird-looking thing called, uh, the, uh…?"

"STEALTH?" Taylor said helpfully.

"Yeah, that's it," Blake said, feeling proud of the fact that he was finally himself having the opportunity to talk to Taylor personally.

"Sir," Taylor told Blake. "You're talking about the 1981 Lockheed F-117A Nighthawk."

"That's right," said Blake. "You've described it. The Nighthawk."

"Well, sir," said Taylor. "You are definitely talking to the pilot of the Nighthawk."

"And you're really that guy that everybody was talking about who was flying that thing," he asked Taylor, excited from the thought of Taylor being in his presence. "They were saying that nobody ever really actually knew if you were out there flying that thing. And here it was, you was right there on top of them without them ever even knowing you were there."

"Ready whenever you are," Taylor told Blake.

Chapter Twenty-Two

Terry Gilbert and his younger brother, Randy, found themselves in a race to their favorite fishing spot. As they spun rapidly in circles, the two-lane, gravelly road suddenly began to wind into a sharply curved, narrow lane alongside a steep slope, and then into another narrow path where very few people traveled.

There were no accurate measures as to the precise degree of each curve as the two Jeeps sped uncontrollably fast around each bend, moving and swerving, veering swiftly past each other, with their passengers yelling, laughing, and screaming out in a drunken roar, without a care in the world, unaware of the danger awaiting them.

Avoiding what could have possibly been a disastrous collision, Terry quickly shifted gears as he desperately struggled to slow down in his strenuous effort to avoid losing control of his Jeep. He knew such a mishap would eject everyone inside and end up tossing them over the steep ravine.

Unaware of Terry's terrifying situation, Randy and his passengers were busy enjoying themselves, laughing loudly and derisively from a ridiculous joke as they sped hastily ahead of Terry, with those inside the Jeep carelessly waving their hands back at him, while swearing profanity and flashing their middle finger as a foul gesture. They were all waving and holding their arms up high into the air, with Randy showing his offensive determination to win the race at all costs.

"Slow that thing down, Randy," Terry yelled at him, noticing that his Jeep was beginning to fishtail as the tires spun rapidly in the gravel, sending a very large amount of loose rock fragments spiraling backwards and into

Terry's windshield. "What's the matter with you? Are you crazy or something?"

"FUCK YOU, fat-ass," Randy yelled back at him, laughing as one of his passengers began tossing debris from inside the Jeep, scattering it across the road.

After what could have been a dramatic tragedy in the making, Terry finally regained control of his Jeep and proceeded in the direction of a steeply inclined section of the winding curve, an area of the narrow road that was only within a few feet of something that could have been catastrophic.

Steering his Jeep steadily and firmly into each of the winding curves alongside the rough, rugged mountains and hills of the Stonyford region, Terry was then able to see his brother Randy within a short distance ahead of him, parked on the side of the road, waiting.

"What took you guys so long?" said Randy, grinning as usual.

Finally arriving at their preferred fishing spot in a narrow stream that flowed in between the rugged mountains and hills of the Stonyford region, the Gilbert brothers could sense the unusual quietude throughout this part of the surrounding mountains that brought about a slight sense of paranoia.

But it was Randy and those who had arrived with him that seemed to show less concern about the lack of activity around them. There could be heard not a single sound coming from the large groups of wildlife that usually inhabited the area. But to Randy and his group of rowdy friends, with all their noise and disorderly behavior, it was to them just an ordinary day for fun at the stream, and maybe some fishing and camping, with lots of drinking and smoking weed and wild partying.

But for Terry, he was curious, trying his best to just ignore the silence and seeming stillness in the air. He couldn't help finding himself wondering if the entire area had, for reasons unknown, been abandoned, and had somehow become contaminated by some type of dangerous chemical, and that this chemical had a mixture that caused this once-peaceful place of serenity for wildlife to outright abandon their own habitation.

Terry was sure that something very mysterious had taken place. But what really seemed to bother him the most was the fact that not a single body of an invertebrate insect could be seen or found anywhere lying still or crawling on the ground. Not even the common fly, with all of its annoyance, who could at times become such a nuisance, could be spotted with all of its what can only be described as repeated acts of preying on anyone in its sight, as a wild animal would do when hunting for food.

The fly is known to intentionally victimize its prey, while taking full advantage of the victim's weaknesses before devouring it alive.

But not even the nuisance fly could be found anywhere amongst the shrubbery and low-hanging plants and woody stems.

And once again, Terry was trying his best to ignore the silence around him. Well, that was until it occurred to him that even the fish that could usually be seen splashing and dashing around in the stream were now neglecting their favorite bait. They, too, had seemingly abandoned the area for mysterious reasons.

Something wasn't right, and it caused Terry to find himself with a desire to investigate whatever it was that was happening. And to his surprise he could see that he wasn't alone. In fact, the entire group found themselves as eager as he was, curiously wondering the reason for everything to be so silent and completely still.

"What do you think, Terry?" he was asked.

"I don't know, guys, but this is really weird," he said, looking around as if he was trying to recognize something. "It's like we're somehow on a different planet. You know what I mean?"

"Yeah, I know what you mean," said one of the females. "You guys think it's all right for us to be here? I mean, just look around. What do you hear? Not a bird in the sky flying around the place like they used to be doing. And I don't even hear any frogs making all that crazy, weird noise."

"Yeah. And what about hearing tree branches crackling in the distance?" one of the guys said, shrugging. "I don't even hear nothin' like that happening."

"Hey! Hold up. Be quiet for a minute, you guys," someone said. "I thought I heard something."

"Like what?" he was asked.

"It sounded like a scream or something."

"Quit playing around, Brian," one of the teenage girls told him.

"Yeah, Brian. We're trying to be serious—if you don't mind," one of the other teenage girls said.

"But I really do think I heard something like a scream," Brian told them.

"TERRY," another of the teenage girls said, expressing her annoyance concerning Brian. "Are you going to just let him keep on talking like that?"

"Hey, Brian," said Terry. "Uh. I think that screaming noise you heard that sounds like someone crying out for help is my stupid little kid brother over there on the other side of that hill acting crazy."

"Well, if that's who you really think it is, then why don't you guys just, you know, go on over there and see for yourselves, just to make sure," Brian suggested.

"Good idea," said Terry. "Let's all of us sneak up on him and surprise his little smart-ass."

"But, what if he's um, you know?" one of the girls said.

"What?" asked Terry.

"Like trying to make someone a proposition," she then said, giggling shyly.

"That little piece of shit ain't got a proposition idea," said Terry. "He ain't got a one idea about how to do anything like that that you're talking about. Believe me, that's my kid brother. I should know."

"Are you really sure that that's your kid brother over there?" asked of the teenage girls. "I mean, I think I just heard something. But whatever it was that I heard, it came from a different direction."

"Yeah, she's right," said Brian. "I think I heard it, too, and it sure, you know, didn't sound like something your brother would be doing to be making that kind of noise. I'd like to find out where it's coming from."

"All right, you guys, I've had just about enough of this," said Terry. "I'm really tired of you guys saying you're hearing something like screaming, when I still haven't heard none of this stuff you're talking about."

"All right, then, why don't you just call out your brother's name and see if he'll answer you," said Brian, smiling. "And if he don't, then, well, we'll go on over there and search for whatever it is that's making that noise."

"Hey, I'll go with you if they don't," one of the teen girls said.

"No, we'll all go," another of the girls said.

"Why don't you just go ahead and call out his name," said Brian.

"That's just what I intend to do, for your information," said Terry.

"Why don't we just do this together?" Brian suggested.

"No," said Terry. "You guys let me first call him by myself. That way, it won't be sounding like a bunch of crazy weirdos yelling out my brother's name, just so the whole world can hear it echoing all over the place. You know what I mean?"

"Weirdos?" one of the girls said, laughing. "Just who are you calling a bunch of crazy weirdos? Your brother is the one over there somewhere making all of that weird noise like somebody screaming and acting like he's crazy by making that noise. He's the weirdo!"

"But how do you know that's really my brother?" asked Terry. "That could, you know, be a wild animal, like a hungry bear or something. It could be anything, like a mountain goat, or a lion."

"A lion?" she questioned. "Yeah, right!"

"As you know, there are wild bears around here," said Terry.

"Bears are everywhere these days," said Brian, looking around. "That's what people around here think attacked those people down in Stonyford. But somebody just had to go and start this weird rumor about the devil and some of evil demons supposedly around Stonyford late at night stalking people."

"Yeah, I think I heard about that story, too," one of the girls said. "But word is that something was attacking people. The rumor was saying something, I remember, about an old man and a poisonous snake. Or something like that. They was saying that the snake would bite you, or supposedly attack you, and then I guess it would spread its deadly disease all over the place."

"Well, from what I heard it was a wild 'Beast' that was attacking people," the other girl said. "My mom said it was an extremely vile person that lives out here in the woods, and that it be raping people, and that it be devouring all the elderly people in a ravenous manner. My mom was telling us that some old rancher not far from here was telling everybody that one evening he was able to get a good look at the thing."

"Oh, yeah?" said Terry. "And what did your mom say the old rancher said it was, and how it looked?"

"She said he was telling 'em that it walked upright, just like a man," she told Terry. "Except it resembled a four-footed animal. But then, there were other people who claimed they'd seen it too, and that it stood on two hoofs, with feet like a pig, and that it, too, was walking upright."

"You guys know what?" said Terry. "I think you're all crazy. That thing you're talking about and trying to describe could be anything, as far as the story goes. That could be anything."

"And what makes you so sure about that?" Brian asked him.

"I never said I was really sure about it," said Terry. "I'm only saying that whatever it is that we heard that was supposed to have ripped that little girl to pieces, it sure wasn't no human being to do something like that."

"Maybe it was somebody who believes in cannibalism," said one of the girls.

"Are you really serious?" asked Terry. "It didn't eat her flesh, and from what I heard, it didn't even take any of her body parts."

"*It?*" Brian questioned. "Just what in the heck do you mean by calling the thing an It?"

"Look, man. That was just, you know, a figure of speech," Terry explained. "Since no one has ever actually seen this thing, none of us can really claim its description."

"Well, I think I just might know who 'It' is," said one of the girls, who was pointing a finger in the direction where the noise was coming from. "It just might be your kid brother. Just listen to 'em."

"Good try. But I really don't think that's him," said Brian. "I mean, that noise isn't anything a kid like Randy would be making."

"No. Just listen," another of the teen girls said. "That's gotta be him."

"You don't even know what you're listening to," said Terry. "That could be anything."

"Just listen," she said again, except this time in a whisper. "You mean to tell me you didn't hear that? Just listen, you guys."

"What?" Terry asked her. "Listen to what?"

Suddenly, they could all hear a strange crunchy and scratchy sound coming from the other side of one of the hills that surrounded them. The sound was more like that of a machine used during an underground excavation from which minerals, as metals or coal, can be extracted.

But then, there was what sounded like a violent explosion of energy coming from the ground beneath them. They could feel something like a sudden burst of warm air being released, though there were no signs of an interruption or any breakage in the ground where they stood, paralyzed and afraid to move from fear of being possibly swallowed up and consumed by the unknown.

"Hold up, don't nobody move," Terry said in a whisper.

"Ah, man, you guys," Brian then said, staring intently in the direction of a particular section of the road where a small amount of steam could be seen as it seeped very slowly through small openings throughout the surface. "Just look at how all that steam is coming up out of the ground. It sounds like someone is up there sharpening something like possibly a blade of something that's used to cut through these rocks."

"I know one thing for sure," one of the girls said. "I don't think that's a bear up there sharpening his claws."

"Or maybe their claws," another of the girls added. "You know, with those long, sharp, pointed, curved nails."

"You know something, you guys are really starting to freak me the fuck all the way out," said Terry, who was ready to start calling out his brother's name to get everyone to shut up. "It's like, just when are you guys going to quit?"

Just when Terry was about to call out to Randy, one of the girls suddenly started screaming in a low whisper, startling everyone.

"What the hell is wrong with you?" asked Terry, grabbing her the arms.

"Look, it was right there," she said, staring as if she'd seen a ghost. "It was right up there."

"Where?" Brian quickly asked, while trying to figure out what it was she saw that frightened her. "What'd you see up there?"

"What'd you see, Lori?" Christine asked. "What was it that scared you?"

"I don't know what it was," said Lori. "But something was just standing right up there by that huge rock. It was standing there looking down at us."

"Was it Terry's kid brother, Randy?" Brian asked her. "Was it him?"

"Yeah, that's probably that little weird piece of shit up there making all of that noise and trying to scare us," Christine said to Brian. "What is he, some kind of acid freak or something?"

"I tell you, man, that's not my brother up there acting like that," Terry said, sounding angry that they would even think of Randy doing anything like what they were suggesting. "I know my brother can be doing some crazy shit every now and then, but believe me, you guys, that isn't him up there playing around like that."

"Then just who is it, Terry?" Christine asked him, obviously upset. "Who is it, Terry?"

"I don't know, said Terry. "But it's not Randy."

"What was it, and who was it that you saw, Lori?" Brian again asked her.

"I don't know," Lori again answered. "I don't know, but whatever it was, it was up there just standing still and staring down at us. All of us. It didn't look like it was human or anything."

"What?" Brian questioned. "Uh, just what in the hell are you saying? It didn't look human?"

"Hey, Brian," Terry yelled. "Man, that's enough of that shit. Just lay off of her until we can figure this out."

"You guys know what I think?" said Brian. "I think she's losing it. She's seeing things that really aren't even there. Next, she'll be telling us she's seeing monsters and the freakin' Easter Bunny up there staring down here at us, with no telling who else is standing beside him with a bag of jelly beans in his hands."

"It's all right, you guys don't have to believe me," Lori cried out. "But I know what I saw, and it, whoever he was, was just standing there, like he was smiling or something, with those big teeth in his mouth, standing there, looking down here at all of us. And it wasn't Terry's brother, Randy."

"It was staring at all of us?" asked Brian.

"Yeah. It was up there staring at all of us, Brian," she told him.

"Smiling?" Brian then asked, staring directly at Lori.

"Yes, Brian. It was *smiling*," Lori again said, sniffling and trying her best to prevent nasal fluid from trickling out through her nose. "It was just standing there right up there by that huge rock, smiling, and staring down here at us. Including you, too, Brian."

"But what makes you think he, or whoever it was, was smiling, Lori?" Terry questioned her. "I mean, hey, just look at the distance between us and, you know, that rock up there where you're saying it was standing. We're all the way down here at the bottom of this hill."

"Look, I know what I saw, Terry," said Lori. "And I really don't care if you guys believe me or not. I know what I saw, and it wasn't any human being. And it surely wasn't a reindeer or a mountain goat or even a bear."

"Well, did it look like it could've been, you know, uh, that thing everybody calls Bigfoot?" asked Brian.

"RANDY!" Terry suddenly yelled. "Come on man, we know that's you up there. Quit playing around and get your ass down here. We don't have time to be out here playing around with you."

"Yeah, Randy. Get your ass down here and stop playing around. We know it's you up there," said Christine. "Game over."

"Yeah, uh. Hey, buddy," Brian then called out to Randy, while moving slowly backward from the hill. "Uh, look, man, we're all really tired of this crazy, stupid game you're playing right now. So why don't you just come on down so we can get the hell out of here."

"Uh. Hold on. Wait a minute," Terry suddenly said, pointing at something up on top of the hill. "What the heck is that thing standing up there?"

"Holy shit!" Brian shouted. "What the fuck!"

"Come on, you guys, I think we better get out of here," said Christine. "I don't think that's Randy up there."

"You see? What did I tell you?" said Lori. "Now do you guys believe me? I told you I saw something up there that didn't look like no human being. Could that thing be your kid brother, Terry? Is that really him standing up there looking like some huge gorilla with a stocky body and dark, coarse hair covering his entire body?"

"Hey!" Terry yelled up at the figure. "I just want you to know that we're not here to be trying to cause you any problems or anything. We just came here to do some camping and fishing like we always be doing. That's all."

"I really do think we better be going," said Christine, staring up at the figure standing on top of the hill. "Whoever that is up there, he really is starting to give me the creeps."

"Giving you the creeps?" said Brian, frozen in his steps. "Whatever that thing is, it *is* the creeps. Just look at it! I mean, what is that? Look at that thing. Could that be the person in the Bible called Goliath?"

"Yeah, well," said Terry, "if that's Goliath, then you better hurry up and get your sling shot ready, Brian. And get prepared to go to battle like David did."

"Well, if you still think that's your kid brother up there, then tell us just who's that coming in that Jeep?" asked Christine. "Isn't that Randy?"

"You see, you guys," said Lori. "I knew there was something strange about whatever it is that's standing up there. And you thought it was Randy."

"Just what the heck are you guys doing over here?" asked Randy, smiling. "And who is that you're looking at up there? Who is that?"

"We don't know," said Terry. "But they thought it was you."

"Me?" said Randy with a shrug. "What made you guys think that was me?"

"Everybody was down here thinking that was you up there playing games, acting really crazy, Randy," Christine told him."

"Yeah," Brian agreed. "We thought that was really you standing up there playing some kinda weird game with us."

"Me?" said Randy. "But what is it that made you guys think it was me? Do I really look that ugly? Do I? Really?"

"We…we thought…" said Terry, looking at Randy. "They thought—"

"Hey, now. Wait a minute," said Christine, looking at Terry. "It was really Lori's idea. She was the one who seen that thing first. In fact she even said it was up there smiling at her—as if you don't remember her saying that."

"Is that right, Lori?" asked Randy.

"Well, it wasn't just up there smiling at anybody in particular," said Lori, shrugging. "But when I first saw that thing, it had this, you know, bizarre expression on its face. A creepy kind of expression."

"And you actually could see it smiling from all the way down here?" Randy asked her, while looking in the direction of the figure. And you really thought that thing was me standing up there?"

"Well…" Lori said, with another shrug.

By this time, Randy's group of passengers had gotten out of the Jeep and were themselves looking up at the figure standing on top of the hill, wondering just what was going on for everyone to be staring in that direction.

"What's the problem, Randy?" his girlfriend, Melody, asked him. "Why are you guys just standing here lookin' up there at that thing? Is it dead to be, you know, just standing there like that?"

"No, it's not dead, Melody," Randy told her, while placing one of his arm around her and resting it on her shoulder. "For some odd reason, they really thought that that was me up there playing games with them."

"You?" Melody said, with herself a shrug. "Why would anybody think something like that about you? That thing don't even look nothing like you, Randy. Just look at its size. You're not that big—I mean, maybe down there, but not—"

"What is it that he's wearing?" one of Randy's passengers asked. "A fur coat or something?"

"I think that's what you call a shag. Or something like that," Brian said to a guy named Travis, who was one of Randy's passengers. "Or it just might be the fur from a fox or a beaver he's wearing like that, to cover himself with."

"You guys really wanna know what I think?" asked Lori, looking around and then back up at the figure, who could be seen staring down at them. "I really don't think that's anything that he's wearing up there—if you really know what I mean."

"Then, just what is it that you're trying to insinuate, Lori?" asked Randy.

"I think that that furry, shaggy-looking stuff is a part of him," said Lori.

"You know what, Lori?" said Travis. "I think you're right. I think we are the ones who can really say that we've found that creature they call Bigfoot all the way down here in Stonyford, California."

"Goddamn it, Travis," Randy shouted. "Man, this isn't the time to be joking with everybody. Can't you see that whatever that is up there, he's just waiting to come rushing down here, and ain't no tellin' what it'll try doin' to us for being here."

"Man, check this out, dude," said Travis. "Whoever that is up there, that fool ain't that crazy enough to be trying anything. You feel me? I mean, that punk might be crazy, but he ain't that crazy, you know, to be rushing down here like that on nobody. And if he really wanna get some shit started, it's like, hey, he better bring all of his friends for some serious backup, 'cause it's only one of him against all of us. You know what I mean? So let that punk bring it on."

"But, he's just standing there," said Melody. "That thing gotta be dead or something, Randy. He hasn't moved since we got here."

"Hey, you up there," Travis called out to the figure. "What the fuck's your problem?"

"Yeah, what's up?" Randy yelled to the figure. "You look like you got a problem or something for being here. And if you do, why don't you just bring your ugly-looking, Bigfoot ass on down and handle your business."

Indistinct laughing.

"I really don't think that was cool, Randy," said Terry. "I mean, that guy just might, you know, be on something that really got him fucked up. You know what I'm sayin'?"

"What, like some heavy medication or something?" said Melody, snickering.

"Could be up there high on crack, or some of that K-2 bullshit," Brian said, laughing.

"Or on some of this shit we been using before coming here," said Randy.

"Yeah, and that's why everybody be calling you a bunch of meth-heads as it is," said Lori.

"Well, I ain't gone stop using just because of how everybody be feeling me and what I like doin'," said Brian. "I like the way it makes me feel."

"Hey, up there. Let me see you roll on down here like a freakin' cannonball, you goddamn retarded freak," Randy yelled up to the figure. "You think you'll be able to do that, you fuckin' faggot?"

More indistinct laughing.

"I don't think he's paying any attention to you, Randy," said Christine.

"Yeah, and I think I just saw that thing flip you the bird," said Brian.

"Hey, I know you hear me up there, fat-ass," said Randy, yelling up to the figure, "Ugly piece of shit probably couldn't even make it down here if he tried."

"But seriously, Randy. You don't even know anything about whoever that is up there to be calling out, challenging him like that," said Melody. The figure on top of the hill now looked like he was busy grooming himself, stopping to stare at them now and then.

"You know something, I think she's got a point, Randy," Terry told him, while looking at the figure. "It's like, just what the fuck are you going to do if so happen that thing, whoever he is, or whatever it is, starts charging down this hill after your dumb ass? Then what?"

"Oh, I see what's happening now," said Randy, slowly moving backward as though upset at Terry. "I see what's really happening with you and my girl, Melody. Y'all really think I'm afraid of that thing up there and can't handle him if it came to that. Well, let me tell you something. I ain't afraid of nothin'."

"Man, Randy," said Terry. "You my brother, and I love your crazy ass, even with all that weird stuff you sometime be doin'. I still love you from way deep down inside my soul."

"Well, I just want you motherfuckers to know that I ain't scared of that thing up there," said Randy, while ripping off his outer shirt and undershirt. "Hey, you up there, you goddamn freak. You want some of this with your jeepers creepers-looking ass? Do you really want some of this, motherfucker?"

Randy was once again calling out to the figure atop the hill, while holding both of his arms high in the air, dancing around in a circle, as if he were shadowboxing with an imaginary opponent.

"Did you hear me?" he again shouted up to the figure. "I said, do you want some of this—YOU PUNK-ASS BITCH!"

"Holy shit, you guys," Brian said with a jittery voice, getting everyone's attention. "Did you just see that?"

"Yeah, I think I did," Ashley said softly, her voice jittery and nervous.

"Now what?" Terry asked Brian. "What'd you guys see?"

"Yeah, what did you see?" Christine also asked Brian, looking around.

"Whatever that is up there, it was, like, you know, when Randy called out to it and started challenging it to a brawl, I could see that that thing was just standing there, and then it started, you know, like, rocking back and forth. And then it glanced down here and showed its teeth," Brian said, still looking up at the figure on top of the hill. "I think that thing is planning something."

"You see? Now what did I tell you guys earlier?" said Lori, reminding them that she'd proven her point. "I told you that thing smiled at us with those ugly-looking teeth in its mouth. But, no. You guys didn't want to believe me."

"Uh, guys," Travis said to get everyone's attention. "It looks like our secret admirer is about to take Randy up on his challenge."

"What the heck you talking about, Travis?" Terry asked him.

"I think that thing's getting ready to come down the hill and take your brother up on his offer," said Travis.

"I think he's right, Terry," said Melody. "He's staring down here at us like he's getting ready to come charging."

"You guys are really tripping on that thing," said Terry with a chuckle.

They were all watching and observed the huge figure as it began to move slowly to one side, as though it were in slow motion, with huge steps downward, sliding, as if the figure were somehow gliding on thin air, and was now making its way down the hill in their direction.

"I don't know about you guys," Brian suddenly yelled, "but I'm getting the fuck out of here."

"Uh, hold up, Brian," Travis shouted. "I'm with you, bro! Fuck this shit."

"What's it doing, coming down here?" screamed Christine, while watching the huge figure as it floated sluggishly in slow motion, moving down the hill.

"Yeah, Randy," Lori cried. "You're the one who should know what it's doing. You're the one who started this by challenging that thing, when you should've kept your mouth shut. And now it's coming after you. You're the one who challenged it to a fight."

"Quick, you guys," Terry yelled. "Everybody in the Jeeps."

"Come on, Melody, and you too, Travis," said Randy, scrambling hastily to his Jeep. "Come on, hurry up, you guys, before that thing makes it down the hill."

"Oh, yeah. That's right, tough guy," said Christine, yelling at Randy while he was rushing to his Jeep. "What's the matter, tough guy? Scared the monster gonna get your dumb ass and tear you apart?"

"Man! Fuck you, Christine!" Randy shouted at her. "This isn't the time for that bullshit you're talking."

"He's right, Christine," said Terry, starting the Jeep's engine. "This isn't the time for that stuff about him."

"Oh. Well, that isn't what you was saying when your stupid-ass brother was calling him, challenging Mr. Bigfoot up there. That's why he is the one that thing is after. Not us."

"What makes you think it's after any of us?" Brian asked Christine. "It could just be coming down the hill to, you know, talk to us or something. I mean—"

"Yeah. Right, Brian," said Christine. "If that's what you're thinking, why don't you just stay here and wait for that thing to get down here, then you can, you know, have a nice conversation with it. And who knows, it just might greet you with a really nice bear hug."

"Wait a minute. Hold up, Terry," Brian quickly yelled. "Man. Wait just one minute. Look at that thing."

"What about it?" asked Terry.

"Look at it," Brian said, pointing in the direction of the figure seemingly floating down the hill in slow motion.

"Hey, Terry," Randy called out from his Jeep, following closely in behind him. "What the fuck, bro! Why are you guys stopping?"

"Look!" Brian yelled to Randy, while pointing at the figure. "What the fuck is that thing doing?"

"Looks like it's falling apart or separating into pieces," said Christine. "Or disappearing or something."

"What?!" Terry shouted. "Disappearing?"

"Maaannn," said Travis in disbelief, while climbing out the back of the Jeep. "Shit look like it's happening in slow motion."

"What in the heck you think you're doing, Travis?" Lori yelled at him. "I know you're not that crazy, trying to be, like, stupid, Randy."

"Are you guys seeing this?" said Melody, wondering if they were even noticing how quickly the figure disappeared.

"Where'd it go?" Terry yelled out to Randy. "What happened to it?"

"Drive, Terry. Drive!" Randy suddenly shouted. "DRIVE!"

"GO! GO! GO!" Brian yelled, telling Terry searching everywhere to see where the figure went. "Go, Terry. Hurry up! Let's get out of here before that thing comes back."

Both Jeeps sped quickly forward on the gravel road, speeding down its two-lane, narrow path, leading alongside each of the winding curves, which would take them in the direction of the nearby boys' ranch for juvenile offenders, run by the government.

Shifting through each gear at such a high speed required Terry, at times, to suddenly slam on his brakes, causing the Jeep to fishtail around just about every curve in his attempt to avoid oncoming vehicles.

Both Jeeps could be seen by the few vacationers and residents of Stonyford who were hanging out at the nearby campground, sliding and fishtailing across the road that was within a mile or two of the boys' ranch, speeding at a high rate of speed uncommon for the area, driving in an extremely reckless manner, careless and heedless of any consequences.

Upon passing the boys ranch, Terry finally decided to slow down, after realizing the distance they'd traveled, bringing his Jeep to a dead stop near the stream where this group of irresponsible teenagers had intended to camp in the beginning of their trip.

"All right, you guys," said Terry, after turning around and staring into the bewildered faces of those who were with him. "Somebody please explain to me just what the fuck it was that we just went through."

"Where's my cell phone?" asked Christine, looking around the Jeep for her bag and carrying case. "I need to call my mom, like, right NOW!"

"Hey," said Lori. "Uh, why don't you call my mom, too, while you're at it. I think I wet my pants."

"You think that's something?" said Brian. "I think I crapped in mine."

"That is so gross, Brian," Christine told him, frowning. "If you really did do something like that in this Jeep, you are so foul."

"Hey, you guys," said Randy, pulling up in his Jeep and parking next to what looked like a giant claw print embedded in the dirt. "Now, that was really something, wasn't it?"

"Yeah, that definitely was, Randy," said Terry. "Where the heck is Travis?"

It was quite obvious that Randy and Melody were completely unaware of Travis's disappearance. You would think that no matter the situation, you couldn't actually lose one of your passengers without noticing it. But as the story goes, that is exactly what ended up happening throughout all the confusion and reckless driving, trying to avoid capture by the figure.

As the monstrous creature glided slowly down the steep hill, floating in slow motion, it suddenly disappeared right in front of the group of teens. And now the disappearance of Travis gave them something far more to worry about instead of that important phone call home to mom. Nonetheless, the problem they faced at hand was only the beginning of their worries.

"Randy!" Melody screamed, frantically looking around, confused. "What happened to Travis? Where is he?"

"How in the hell do I know, Melody?" Randy screamed back at her, shrugging. "You was the last one talking to him."

"That's not true, Randy," said Melody, starting to shake uncontrollably. "I wasn't the last one to talk to him. It was Lori. She was yelling and telling him to get back inside the Jeep."

"No. That isn't true!" shouted Lori. "It was Brian. He was the last one to talk to him."

"And just how do you figure that, Lori?" he asked her in a harsh, disagreeable tone of voice. "What makes you think I was the last one?"

"Because it was you who was telling him that this wasn't the time to be trying to play hero," she told Brian. "And then you said—Tell 'em, Randy."

"Yeah, I think she's right, Brian," said Terry, watching Melody as she was climbing out of the Jeep.

"What's happening?" Christine asked Terry curiously. "What's wrong?"

"Ah, it's Melody," said Terry. "I really think she's having what looks to me like a nervous breakdown or something."

"Then why don't we do something to help her?" said Christine, teary-eyed.

"But what about Travis?" said Lori, climbing out of the Jeep to see what was happening with Melody.

"Christine, did you find your carrying bag and case yet?" asked Randy.

"No. But I know it's here somewhere," she told him, while reaching down and checking underneath the seat. "I know it's here somewhere."

"Hey, Randy?" Terry called out to him. "Man. Ask Melody if she by chance brought her carrying bag with her? Or if she has her cellphone?"

"It should be in my coat pocket," said Melody. "And I'm right here, Terry. You really could've asked me yourself."

"Well, I really didn't know if—" Terry questioned his thought. "It was just that, you know, the way you were just a few seconds ago shaking. I was thinking that maybe you was having a nervous breakdown or something. And that is the reason why I asked Randy, since he was right there with you."

"Well, there isn't anything wrong with me," said Melody, reaching inside of her coat pocket for the cellphone. You see, it's right here. But I really think we're out of range."

"Check and make sure, Melody," said Randy, while checking his now-shredded shirt pocket for his pack of cigarettes, that he'd earlier ripped off when challenging the figure just before it came charging down the hill.

"Hold on," said Terry. "I think Christine just found hers."

"Let me check it out, Christine," said Terry. "I do believe we just might be in business."

"Hey. I think Melody's is working, too," shouted Randy.

"And if we can't reach anybody," Brian said to Terry, "then one of us just might have to climb up one of these hills to get some reception."

"Not me," said Christine. "No way."

"No, me either," said Melody. "No way."

"Hey, don't be looking at me," said Ashley, after being quiet most of the time. "That monster could be up there waiting to get one of us."

"What about you, Randy?" said Lori. "It's your fault we're in this mess in the first place. I think you should be the one to go up there."

"I know you would just love to see that thing get me—wouldn't you?" said Randy. "But I ain't gone make your day, Lori. Not now, not ever."

"Well, I guess that only leaves you and me, Terry," said Brian.

"Looks like you're right, Brian," said Terry, smiling. "Me being such a damn good leader, I think it'll be best for me to be an alternative. That way I won't be depriving you of your venture to the top of one of these hills. You know what I mean?"

"Hey, you guys," said Christine. "What about the people that were standing around not far from that campground? I could see that they was, like, watching us coming around those curves."

"What about 'em?" said Brian.

"I don't know," said Christine. "But maybe they can help us."

"Where did you see 'em?" asked Terry. "How far from where we are?"

"Hey. You know what? I think that's a good idea," said Randy. "They might be willing to help us out as far as Travis."

"Oh, yeah?" said Terry, disagreeing with Randy.

"What?" said Randy. "What's so wrong with seeing if they will be willing to help us find Travis? They just might be able to explain what that thing is that came after us."

"Yeah. They'll help us out, alright," said Terry. "Turn us over to that freakin' Sheriff Blake. And then we'll be up on a goddamn first degree murder charge, accused of killing Travis. And then all the newspapers will be saying we probably tried to hide his body by dumping it out in the woods somewhere so that nobody could find it."

"Why would they be saying something like that about us?" Melody asked. "We didn't do anything like that to Travis."

"Oh, yeah. I can just imagine what we'd look like on the news," said Randy, trying to make a mean-looking facial expression. "They'll show all of us standing in front of a picture of the electric chair in San Quentin with the name 'Old Sparky' in big letters above our heads."

"Yeah. And all of you guys will be crying and sobbing, scared as hell. And be pointing the finger at each other," said Ashley with a chuckle.

"All because of you, Randy," said Lori. "You're the one that drove off and left Travis to be stalked and probably killed by that Bigfoot-looking monster, who could really be the Crooked Man or another Frankenstein creature."

"I hope you end up in San Quentin, and burn in hell, Randy," Melody yelled at him. "You left Travis out there so Freddy Krueger and Jason could get him. I hate you!"

Everyone stared at Melody.

"All right, you guys," said Terry, while observing Melody's behavior. "It's time to get a grip on ourselves before we end up losing control of what we're supposed to be doing. We don't know what happened to Travis. We don't even know at what point it was that he disappeared. All we know is that he's missing."

"But what if he's somewhere up there, hurt and waiting for us to come back and get him?" Melody said, sobbing. "I'd hate to think that ugly-looking hunchback thing's got 'em up there eating him."

"You guys know what I think?" said Brian. "I think we're the ones who're supposed to be responsible enough to contact the sheriff and, like, hey, let him know just exactly what happened to Travis. It'll be the truth—won't it?"

"Look, why don't we just head on over to where Christine said there were a few people stand around," said Ashley with a shrug. "I mean, didn't you say something about them watching us as we was coming around those curves?"

"That's what I seen them doing," said Christine, looking around at everyone. "They was watching us the whole time."

"Then maybe they just might be willing to help us find Travis," said Ashley, with her arms folded and staring at the ground. "And they just might be able to help us contact somebody in town to get us some help up here."

"You guys know something, I really do think she's right," said Christine.

"All right," said Terry. "I mean, you know. If that's what you guys want to do then let's do this thing before it starts getting dark out here."

"Hey, you guys? What about the boys' ranch?" said Brian. "Think maybe, like, we could check with the people who run that place and see if they can help us? I mean, what do we have to lose?"

"But what if they don't want to get involved?" said Terry. "Then what?"

"Mmm," Brian shrugged, mumbling to himself. "Didn't think about that."

"I really don't think that'll be a good idea," said Terry. "What's a place like that doing up in these mountains, anyway? What's so important about it?"

"I was just thinking that, since they help young kids stay out of trouble, maybe they wouldn't mind, you know, helping us," said Brian.

"Let's just get the heck out of here," Randy suggested, climbing back inside of his Jeep. "Man, I really got a bad feeling about this place."

"Oh, no. And here we go again," said Lori, frowning with distaste toward Randy. "Just what are we about to experience now?"

"Just what is your problem, Lori?" Terry asked her, while climbing into his Jeep. "Every time I turn around you're talking trash on Randy. What is it, that Bigfoot creature got you thinking he's coming after you or something?"

"I bet that's what it is," said Randy, grinning.

"Fuck you, Randy," Lori shouted. "Your brother is the problem, Terry. He's really enjoying whatever it is that we are going through. Even that creature."

"You should have learned a little something about him by now, Lori," Terry told her. "My kid brother is just like a little kid pretending to be an adult, instead of the teenager he is. Nothing is ever really that serious when it comes to him, except when he's trying to prove that he can beat me at my own game. Or, like wanting to race me around these mountains. Any other time, dude is really useless. And I do mean, useless."

"Hey! How long are we going to just sit here while you guys are talking to each other, and you listening to her sobbing about me?" Randy asked Terry.

"I think you meant 'snobbing,' didn't you, Randy?" Lori said, laughing. You are more of a snob than I'll ever be, and all of us put together. But I really don't mind being snobbish at times."

"I think I have to disagree with you on that one, Lori," said Christine. "I think Randy's been a bit too snobbish ever since we got here."

"That's bull, Christine," said Randy. "I think you're the one wearing that hat."

"No way!" said Christine, laughing out loud. "I don't know where you've got that from, Randy."

"Umm. Hey, you guys," said Terry. "Uh, I do believe we are supposed to be on our way to where those people was standing around at the campground, if I'm not mistaken. Travis is still missing. Have you forgot?"

"Yeah. He's right. Let's get the hell out of here," said Randy, starting up his Jeep's engine. "Hope those old ranchers are kind enough to help us out."

Terry started his engine and began moving slowly toward the road leading to the campground. "Now, do you see what I mean?" asked Terry.

"Randy just has to race me just about everywhere I go."

"What's wrong with him?" Ashley asked Terry. "He's acting just like he is high on something."

"I think your kid brother was born on something, ask me," said Brian with a chuckle.

"Just wait until he really gets excited," said Terry. "Just wait. You guys haven't seen anything yet."

Suddenly, just as they were about to enter the road that would take them in the direction of the campground, they could hear a massive outburst of noise like an explosion. It shook the entire area violently. The explosion was so intense that huge clouds of dust and large rock and trees and other chunks of debris went spiraling hundreds of feet into the air with increasing speed.

The impact of the explosion caused the region to shake and tremble as with an earthquake, as a series of waves from the explosion caused the disintegration and collapse of various structures.

"What in the hell was that?" Melody cried out, looking in the direction of the fishing spot they'd found before Travis went missing.

"Man, what the fuck was that?" shouted Terry, noticing all the debris that was billowing high into the air.

"Jesus Christ, Christine," Brian yelled out loud, seeing what looked like a swell of smoke rolling along the ground, moving rapidly in their direction. "Where'd that come from?"

"How am I supposed to know, Brian?" said Christine, in a state of panic. "I'm in here with you."

"Hurry up, Terry!" Randy yelled. "Move that thing out of the way so I can get past. That fuckin' shit is coming this way."

"Is this another one of your games you're playing, Randy?" Lori shouted at him asking.

"Man, Lori. Fuck you, bitch," shouted Randy, speeding past them in his Jeep. "I hope that shit catches up with you. That's that monster's coming to get you and that bitch, Ashley."

"Hold on, everybody!" Terry suddenly yelled. "I don't think Randy's going make that curve up there..."

Don't miss the exciting next installment of the *Stonyford Submission* story coming soon from Word Out Books!

Self-Taught

While in deep thoughts reminiscing on the very first beginning of this journey to fulfill my dream to become an author of literary work, I could not help being energized when thinking about family and loved ones, and their sincere love and concern for me. This type of concern prompted me to find myself thinking about one of my favorite, but now posthumously deceased, authors, Donald Goines, and how he was said to have just sat there in his assigned cell for countless hours, in deep thoughts, thinking about how so very much he loved and missed Shirley, and the life he so desperately desired to share with her.

I, too, have found myself on many occasions thinking about Vanessa, just as I often think about Karen. My sincere love, loyalty, and deep compassionate commitment and devotion for both, and the life that I honestly looked forward to sharing with them.

I think about how it was possible for me to become just as Donald, a well respected writer, and could for once in my life discard each of the ugly, offensive-looking, heavy iron shackles that had somehow kept me in bondage for many years throughout my life.

Considering myself a political prisoner, crime to me was believed to be at the time where the money and action was. But just as Donald, I, too, had become far wiser than expected—and genuinely talented. I knew for a fact that there just had to be another way in which for me to actually become the successful person I'd envisioned for myself.

While incarcerated, I became just as Donald. I began to view my life and everything involving me in a much different light and on a different scale. Just about everything became so much clearer. I began to recognize various shapes and patterns, negative patterns, that in one way or another plagued me deeply like that of a deadly parasite, paralyzing and afflicting me with retribution and vengeance for reasons that are to this day unknown.

The responsibility of this vision did indeed seize me. It enabled me an opportunity to come to terms with my problems. It caused me to finally realize that it was time for me to, for once in my life, take full control of myself and learn—and also relearn—just how important it was for me to start communicating my thoughts and actions on paper, for then, and only then, would the world be able to have a much better understanding about me, and a much broader, in-depth description of the essences and elements of my plight.

I have become a self-taught writer of literary work.

I am more than just some deplorable degenerate number.

I am, HE!

I am a genuinely talented author.

I am a creator in my own right.

I am of Integrity and Incorruptibility.

I am Complete and Undivided.

I am that I am.

I am, HE!

I am the one you know and the one you see.

I am in the same exact likeness of the one within me.

I am that I am.

I am, HE!

I am,

YOU!

Bennie Ray Murdock

AUTHOR'S STATEMENT

Wrongfully Convicted

To support Bennie Ray Murdock's defense fund, contributions can be sent to:

Bennie Ray Murdock
c/o Clarence Murdock 607050309
Bank of the West
3400 Lakeshore Avenue
Oakland CA 94610

ORDER ADDITIONAL COPIES

To order additional copies of *Stonyford Submission* directly from the publisher, please send your request with $10.99 per book plus $6.00 shipping and handling per address, payable to **AZ Entertainment Group LLC,** to the following address:

AZ Entertainment Group LLC
PO BOX 854
Wagoner, OK 74477

~~~~

www.ingramcontent.com/pod-product-compliance
Lightning Source LLC
Chambersburg PA
CBHW011518170626
46810CB00010B/3405

* 9 7 8 1 9 4 7 0 3 5 5 9 1 *